The Blood of Father Time, Book 1

THE BLOOD OF FATHER TIME
DUOLOGY #1

THE BLOOD OF FATHER TIME, BOOK 1

THE NEW CUT

ALAN M. CLARK, STEPHEN C. MERRITT, & LORELEI SHANNON

FIVE STAR
An imprint of Thomson Gale, a part of The Thomson Corporation

Detroit • New York • San Francisco • New Haven, Conn. • Waterville, Maine • London

The Blood of Father Time Duology #1.
Thomson Gale is part of The Thomson Corporation.
Thomson and Star Logo and Five Star are trademarks and Gale is a registered trademark used herein under license.

Set in 11 pt. Plantin.

LIBRARY OF CONGRESS CATALOGING-IN-PUBLICATION DATA

Clark, Alan (Alan M.)
The Blood of Father Time: Book 1: The new cut / Alan M. Clark, Stephen C. Merritt & Lorelei Shannon. — 1st ed.
p. cm. — (Blood of father time duology ; bk. 1)
ISBN-13: 978-1-59414-595-7 (alk. paper)
ISBN-10: 1-59414-595-4 (alk. paper)
1. Time travel—Fiction. 2. Tennessee—Fiction. I. Merritt, Stephen C. II. Shannon, Lorelei. III. Title.
PS3603.L3554N49 2007
813'.54—dc22 2007000526

First Edition. First Printing: May 2007.

Published in 2005 in conjunction with Tekno Books and Ed Gorman.

Printed in the United States of America on permanent paper
10 9 8 7 6 5 4 3 2 1

Inspired by the dastardly deeds of Big and Little Harpe, the true-life adventures of our great American hero, Virgil A. Stewart, and the notorious land pirate, John A. Murrell.

ACKNOWLEDGMENTS

Many thanks to Beth Massie, Susan Stockell, Jack Daves, Diana Rodgers, Dan Carver, Jeff Oliver, Ken Bryant, Claire Peper, Martha Bayless and Bovine Smoke Society.

1

Joel took a stiff drink from his pint of rye and stared at the package. His belly slowly filled with ice, and he didn't know why. The package was brutally stuffed into his mailbox, the brown wrapping paper shredded and torn. The book inside the paper was partly exposed, its spine skinned and damaged. The book was obviously very old. Joel touched it, nearly sick with dread. Abruptly irritated with himself, he ripped the return address from a loose flap of the brown wrapper and squinted, trying to focus. *Billy.* He squeezed his eyes shut as pain thudded in his chest.

Joel knew the title of the book. Billy had sworn to find Joel a copy of it, and when Billy said he'd do something, it always got done. *Now I'll never get to thank him.* He crumpled the address in his sweaty palm and dropped it into the mud.

Goddam, I miss you Billy, he thought. *And screw you for leaving me when I needed you most.* He took another deep pull on his pint of rye, thinking childishly of how much Billy would disapprove.

Billy Howard was the only person Joel Biggs had ever really trusted. They held a truth between them about their past that they could not reveal to anyone else. The truth was unbelievable, Joel knew—he had a hard time believing it himself—but having asked Billy to confirm that truth so many times over the years, he had only to look at his friend with the question in his eyes for Billy to nod his head in affirmation.

It hadn't always been that way. Joel had spent most of his high-school years trying to pretend Billy didn't exist. If Billy didn't exist, what had happened to them couldn't exist. That was what he told himself, anyway, as he spent his teen years stealing his father's liquor and chasing tail.

Joel was a drunk by the time he entered college. Nobody knew it. He functioned well, he attended his classes, studied, even got decent grades. But every night he dropped into a dreamless, alcohol-soaked sleep, where the world was what you saw, and there were no nasty surprises waiting for you just down the creek. A world where a boy named Mark still lived, where Mark had not vanished into a place that just shouldn't exist.

Joel was a young professor when Billy showed up on his doorstep one night. Joel had stared into Billy's face, unable to react. But when Billy grabbed him in a fierce hug, it all came roaring back, everything that had happened that summer, twenty years ago. They'd stayed up all night talking, assuring one another that they weren't crazy.

Billy had used the respect and powerful trust they had in each other, their connection to life-altering events—any emotional tool he could lay his hands on—to convince Joel to stop drinking and start attending meetings of Alcoholics Anonymous. It had taken years and much discussion. During this time Joel's life had consistently spiraled downward: Two DUIs, a broken arm from falling down a flight of stairs, most of his family and friends disowning him, and the university threatening to terminate him if he didn't stop teaching his classes while drunk or hung over.

Billy stayed in constant contact with him, even when his job had taken him to Memphis. Billy's efforts had finally paid off, and Joel had become sober a little over a year ago.

That's all gone to shit now. Thanks to Miss Nina "Hot-crotch" Bryant, I'll be lucky to find anyone who'll hire me to teach. That's what you get for sticking your neck out and trying to help folks. . . .

Joel bowed his head in shame, looking at the package stuck in his mailbox.

"Hey, Billy," he said out loud. "I know you didn't plan it that way. Fucking car wreck wasn't your idea. I just really—" His voice caught in his throat.

His rye-fogged mind drifted to the bogus sexual-harassment charge at the university. Joel had known he'd be able to get through it with Billy's help. Suddenly that was not going to be possible. He'd held it together after the complaint was filed, with Billy jollying him along. His friend had even promised to come to Dexter to visit. Then he was dead. The pain of that was too much to bear. For the past three weeks, Joel had plunged into alcohol with a vengeance. With every drink, he half-hoped he'd die.

Joel carefully worked the package free, his movements made blunt and clumsy by the rye. When the book came loose, the rest of his mail tumbled out onto the ground. He gathered it all up and stumbled across the street to the bridge over Brown's Creek, dropping a trail of junk mail along the way.

He went down to the mailbox at about the same time every afternoon. But it wasn't the mail that drew him. It was only an excuse. Once he had walked to his mailbox, it was only a few more steps to cross the intersection and stand on the bridge over the creek at the property where Billy grew up. There he would sit on the raised concrete edge of the bridge and look at The New Cut, as he and his boyhood friends used to call that stretch of slow-moving stream. Joel would look into the water and wonder how he could have made things turn out differently. After all these years, he still looked for Mark.

He sat, his feet dangling over the side of the bridge, and stripped away the ragged paper from the old book. A card fell from its pages and landed on his electric bill, now two months overdue. Hand trembling, he picked it up.

For my best friend, the card read, *thanks for all the good times in the tree house.*

A sudden cry caught in Joel's throat, and his pulse pounded in his neck. Washing the pain away with the last of the whiskey, he dropped the book and staggered clumsily to his feet. Looking up, he gazed out over the creek and saw his boyhood friends, Billy Howard and Mark Ryder, splashing in the water. The smile was on his face before he could stop it, and he reached out, starting to call to them, but it wasn't Mark and Billy. It was two boys he didn't know.

"You kids get outta there!" he shouted, suddenly filled with panic.

The boys ignored him. They were just kids wanting a cool place to play on a hot day. They didn't understand that they were playing at the mouth of hell.

When Billy had still owned the property, he and Joel had come up with many plans over the years to wall off, reroute, or somehow destroy this stretch of Brown's Creek, but since this was a flood zone, the city would not allow anything that would constrict the flow of the creek. They had once erected a high fence and posted "no trespassing" signs, but kids had just crawled under the bridge from the other side. Occasionally another child would go missing here.

"You kids don't belong here!" Joel shouted again. "This is private property." Joel stumbled off the bridge and onto the grassy verge and lost his footing. He fell forward, landing hard on his forearms and skinning his elbows as he slid down toward the creek. A rush of sour stomach acid and cheap liquor seared his throat, filling his mouth, and he spat it out. He was just getting his feet under him, clawing his way back upright, when he heard their laughter.

"Look out," one of the boys shouted, laughing, "he's gonna

barf on us!"

Joel roared and threw his empty bottle, hoping to scare them into running. It broke against rocks jutting up out of the creek.

The boys retreated upstream, into The New Cut. Horrified, Joel looked at the steep eight-foot banks of The New Cut, then down, through the water to the shattered remnants of some twenty years of drinking. He'd thrown a lot of broken glass in there. It was meant to be a sharp obstacle against the kids who wanted to play here. But he didn't really want to hurt them.

Joel stumbled along the bank until he was directly above the boys. "You kids know where you're headed, don'tcha? You're gonna disappear down that creek just like all the others. You've heard the stories about it, haven't you?"

"Yeah, everyone has, but we ain't scared," said the dark-haired one, sticking his chin out defiantly.

"Aw, shut the hell up, you fuckin' drunk!" This from the smaller boy, dirty blond hair, skinny arms like spider legs. He was looking at Joel the way he might have looked at a smear of dog shit on a new sneaker.

"Get outta the water, now!" Joel yelled. "It's fulla broken glass!"

"My ass!" yelled the older boy. "C'mon, Jeffy." He started leading the younger boy upstream.

Now Joel was angry and desperate. He ran ahead of them along the bank, unzipped his torn and ratty chinos and began pissing into the water, just upstream of the boys. Shouting insults, the boys turned back and ran, high-stepping through the water.

"Look out!" Joel bellowed, but they hit his booby trap of glass. The boys yelled in pain and danced toward the opposite bank, scrambling up, their torn feet leaving bloody prints in the mud.

"Serves you right!" Joel hollered. "Don't you ever come back!"

"I'm gonna tell!" the bigger boy yelled, standing in the red-streaked grass. The smaller one sat in the mud and sobbed.

Joel shook his fist and bellowed as they staggered away, arms around each other. He suddenly felt sick, and it wasn't the whiskey this time. *Kids, they're just poor stupid kids. . . .* But cut-up feet were nothing, nothing at all, compared to what could have happened.

When they had gone, Joel noticed he'd misplaced the book. Backtracking to the bridge, he found where it had fallen, its pages fluttering in the breeze.

He read the title and winced at the stab of associated memories—*The History of Matthew Crenshaw and His Adventure Exposing the Great Land Pirate, Jarrett Cotten and the Mystic Clan.* Joel ran his hand over the tan cover, touched the gouges and scrapes his friendly neighborhood postman had inflicted on it. *Goddam, how I wanted this book.* The copy he'd had as a child was somehow lost; or, he suspected, stolen. As an adult he'd searched for another copy over the years, in every dusty bookshop, with one rare book service after another. Where the hell had Billy found it?

After all the crap I gave him . . . all the shit he put up with from my drinking, he still did this for me. Guilt stabbed Joel through the chest, and his mouth filled with bitter sorrow. Now that he had the book, he didn't even want to look at it.

Tucking it under one arm, Joel headed across the street for home.

And more whiskey.

The idea hung accusingly in the air before him, but he couldn't argue with it. He knew he would be passed out by sundown. And this time, when he awoke at midnight, hungover and hurting, wanting another drink to kill the pain, Billy wouldn't be around to stop him.

His shoulders sagged as he entered the run-down house his father had left him. And, as always, when he looked into the mirror just inside the front door, he was greeted by the cruel ghost of his drunkard father. Same dead black eyes, same bruised purple bags beneath them. Same wet, slack mouth and sunken cheeks. Joel closed his eyes and turned away.

If I could start over and be a kid again, I wouldn't come home. I would stay and find some way to survive. Anything would be better than this.

He snagged another fifth from the near-empty pantry and sank down into his stained and sunken pit of a recliner. As he took a deep, burning pull, Joel remembered. He remembered when the future was something other than a stinking abyss, when the days were turning from warm to summer-hot, and he was about to embark on the greatest adventure—the only adventure—of his wasted life.

2

Joel Biggs thought of summer break as the longest weekend imaginable—and no homework, either!

He had made it through the torturously slow weeks of May by making plans for the coming months. He and his friend, Mark Ryder, devoted all their spare time and energy to expanding and repairing their tree house, stockpiling candy, sodas, and comic books, preparing for this Friday, the last day of the school year, the first night of summer.

Joel's anticipation simmered silently in the last few minutes of class and, with the ringing of the final bell, his excitement boiled over and he ran screaming with the others for freedom.

Now, surrounded by the dusk, Joel and Mark prepared to surrender themselves to the night. They had hauled Mark's dog up into the tree house on a rope and rigged a trouble light on a chain of extension cords that ran all the way back to Joel's house.

The humidity weighted down their clothing and left them feeling sticky and irritable. As Joel was hunched over the radio, trying to fix it, trickles of sweat were drooling out of his blond crew cut, burning his dark eyes and tickling his dimpled chin. Just glancing at his friend made him even hotter. Mark's dark, curly hair was matted with sweat, plastered to his head; his white T-shirt darkened by perspiration. A drop of sweat rolled down the bridge of his broad nose and hung from the tip.

The screeching of the horde of cicadas filling the trees

periodically became a flying-saucer whirring sound. Joel didn't mind them, but he knew Mark didn't like bugs.

"If the radio worked, maybe it would drown out the insects," Mark said. He looked really nervous. Joel was glad to see him wipe the drop of sweat from his nose, anyway.

"Shit." Joel slapped the side of the radio a few times, which, of course, did no good.

"Hey, Joel, try turning the batteries around."

"No way—they're dead. Whadya bring a radio with dead batteries for, you dumbass?"

"Well, how about some cards?"

"I forgot 'em." Joel threw the transistor radio at his friend.

Mark ducked, caught the radio before it could shatter on the floor.

"Hey, Mark, you think you could get that bony sister of yours to let me feel her tits?"

"God, Joel, you're so gross."

"Watch what you call me, moron," he said, kicking Mark.

"Whaddaya say we go back to your house and find out what's on TV?"

"No," Joel said flatly. "It's time for the reading of the Crenshaw book. We begin at the beginning again tonight."

"We've read the whole book, what . . . like five times now?"

"It's a tradition, a ritual. What did we build the shrine for if it wasn't important? We come to the tree house, we read about the great deeds of a great man from the past—from this part of the country—and we learn to have courage ourselves. One day we will do great things." The words felt grand in his mouth, meaningful, like the words in the Crenshaw book.

"Joel, it's just a book. I know you stole it from the stupid school library."

"Did not."

"I seen the library card in the back."

"Was Moss, sent it to me. He stole it from the high-school library."

"Stuff in that book probably never happened."

Joel pushed down a hot flare of anger. "No, it's history. It's *our* local history. Crenshaw was a man from *this* part of the country. Since he came from here and he did such a great thing, it means we ain't living in the middle of nowhere. Or it means it doesn't matter where you come from, everybody's got a chance to be important."

"Yeah, but in the end, he had to go into hiding and he was broke."

"So we learn from his mistakes. Are you gonna go along with this, or am I gonna have to hurt you again?" Joel smiled, to let his friend know he didn't really mean it.

Mark smiled uncertainly. "Okay. It *is* a really *cool* story."

Joel opened the book and began to read.

Matthew Crenshaw is the name history records for the man who brought down Jarrett Cotten and the criminal organization known as the Mystic Clan. His real name is unknown, however, and in all of his dealings with the outlaws, Crenshaw is the name he assumed for his own protection.

He was a man of modest beginnings, being born of good stock in March of 1800 in Blount County, Tennessee. Having received a liberal education in Nashville in spite of his father's meager income, he was engaged as a writer by the *Nashville Sentinel,* but soon became restless.

Determined to settle in the frontier territories of west Tennessee, he removed with his properties in the fall of 1833 to Madison County, where he took up tutoring.

In the fall of that same year, Crenshaw was employed by

an elderly farmer, Hume Stogdon, and his son, Stephen. He moved to their farm where he was boarded while he taught the two gentlemen to read and write.

When the Stogdons came to Crenshaw one afternoon complaining that an outlaw, named Jarrett Cotten, had stolen two of his negro slaves, Crenshaw determined to do what he could to remedy the situation. . . .

3

Joel plopped down in the old bile-yellow easy chair, which was patched many times over with threadbare duct tape. It coughed out a cloud of his father's stink and he shrank from the swarm of stinging memories—the rotting breath that surrounded his father's curses, his violent mood swings, the crack of his fist, and cruel bite of his belt. As always, Joel forced the memories aside and idly fingered the remote control. The television came to life, filling the dingy room with an actinic glow. He stared at the images on the screen without focusing on them, their hypnotic movements an effective distraction.

Grabbing the nearly empty fifth off the coffee table, he opened it and swirled the contents, wondering if there was enough left. He wanted to pass out, wanted to let the day go. He took a swig and leaned back, his breath breaking from between his lips in a ragged raspberry. It struck him as pathetic that each time he drank, he did it in the same room where his father had always gotten drunk—the room in which his father had died of his alcoholism, vomiting up his esophagus and bleeding to death.

Joel had seen alcoholism at its worst, and he had promised himself that the same fate that his father had suffered would not claim him. He would drink socially, casually. He would not use it to anesthetize. Yeah, right. . . . It was in his blood. He was raised by a drunk to be a drunk.

Getting sober had been difficult for Joel, to be sure, but staying sober was the hard part. Until recently, he'd had Billy's continued help. If need be, Billy was willing to spend long nights sitting up with Joel, and they'd talk their way around the desire for drink.

After a couple of months of meetings with other sober alcoholics in A.A., Joel had become hopeful. Along with his sobriety came a strange, glowing feeling that he'd been wrong to think so poorly of human beings and of himself. He was floating on a pink cloud as he watched the young men and women bare their souls in the A.A. meetings, gain understanding of themselves and win sobriety. He tried to do the same, and for the first time in many years he was free of the childhood memories that had plagued him. For a while, he was able to live in the present.

Joel decided it was time to start trusting people more, to take some risks. He'd felt like he had something to offer the world and that he could potentially help to better the lives of others. He'd begun to feel that perhaps he too deserved some of the good things in life and that if he extended himself to help others that perhaps his life would become a rich, meaningful experience. One day he might even meet someone and fall in love.

That was fucking clear thinking. Stuck my neck out and almost got my head lopped off.

Joel had spent nearly all his time since in this room, drinking when not sleeping, abusing himself with memories and liquor.

Aside from the television and the chair, the room contained nothing but shelves full of books. The shelves extended to the ceiling and were so overburdened they looked as if they might collapse at any moment. The books piled onto them were mostly histories, a subject he had taught at the university for many years.

Thinking about losing his position at the university, it surprised him to realize he didn't really care.

Now, the only thing Joel did care about were his books. His childhood memories were back and they were demanding a lot of attention. In his collection of local histories, some exceedingly rare, he looked for himself—evidence that Billy, Mark, and he had spent part of their childhoods in the year 1811.

Was it real? Or just something we pretended so hard I started to believe it? The question arose in his mind where in times past there was no question at all, corrupting everything that he had once believed and making him fear for his sanity. When Billy was alive, he'd always been there to confirm the truth of it. But now, Joel wondered if his friend had only been humoring him.

In the month since Billy died, Joel had spent many hours poring over his books in an alcoholic haze. When the puzzle got the better of him or when he was too intoxicated to read the words on the page, he drank until he passed out, carrying his ever-mounting frustration to the next day.

Between the books and his drinking, he was damn near dead broke. He would be better off, he supposed, if he had any friends, but he'd driven everyone away—not even his family would have anything to do with him.

He considered his books, thought about going through his volume of *The Mississippi Runs Backwards,* by J. Hunter Daves, but knew he didn't have the energy to get up. Joel finished off the whiskey and tossed the bottle aside.

I wish I hadn't come back. I wish I'd stayed with Mark.

And as he'd known he would, he awoke around midnight with a bad hangover. His skull pounded, his mouth was filled with a rancid sweetness, and his nostrils were stuffed with the bouquet of cheap whiskey.

Forcing himself to his feet, he stumbled into the kitchen and took a six-pack of beer out of the refrigerator. It would take three cans to take the edge off his hangover and make him painless, the rest of the six-pack to put him under again. He popped one open and drank it down before carrying the beer to the dining room. He sat at the table, opened another beer and drank half of it all at once. Absently, he reached for one of the many history books strewn across the table—*Spawn of Evil,* by Paul I. Wellman—picked it up, and thumbed through it without focusing on the words. He drained his beer and opened another, tossed the book aside, and picked up another—*The Outlaw Years,* by Robert M. Coates.

I know everything that's in this book, he thought, seeing its contents all in one flash. *It isn't in the words!*

"Goddammit," he said, pushing the book away, "we weren't part of this! I'm fuckin' nuts, is all."

But it's gotta be here somewhere, underneath it all. Something very small, trivial, that I've overlooked many times already.

But he'd gone over this time and time again, and like a dog chasing its tail, Joel went in circles. He resented having been left out of history—hell, he had been a friend of the infamous outlaw, Wesley Pike!

Sitting back, he crushed his beer can and threw it across the room, then opened another. At least his head wasn't pounding any longer—that was something. A pleasant numbness was spreading out from a warm spot in his gut.

He took a sip and noticed the present Billy had sent him. *The History of Matthew Crenshaw and His Adventure in Exposing the Great Land Pirate, Jarrett Cotten and the Mystic Clan.*

Joel reached for it, opened the cover, and scanning a page at random, smiled. He turned to the title page and looked at the author's name: Anonymous.

Largely unknown to all but the most serious of local historians, the book had long been at the center of controversy in that rarified field. Despite the prevailing belief of those living in the time it was written, it was not fiction—Jarrett Cotten and his Clan had indeed existed and much of the story was history. That it was written in the early 1800s was undisputed, but it could be argued that it was a fictionalized account. Just how much of it was fiction was unknown. Some of the controversy revolved around the identity of the author. One school of thought believed that it was written by a playwright of the time; a dandy and gadfly who kept his name from the book in order for it to be taken seriously. This was the most popular belief since the book read more like a novel than a factual account. A few believed that it was written by Matthew Crenshaw himself. They argued that the unusually rich descriptions and intimate dialogue lent believability to their theory. Joel had always liked the idea that Crenshaw had written it.

Jarrett Cotten and the story of his fraternity was one of his childhood favorites. The copy of the book he and Mark used to read when they were children was missing when they returned from the 1800s—probably stolen out of its shrine in the tree house by some other kids. As he turned the pages and began to read, he had the feeling he was visiting an old friend.

> Having learned from a neighbor that Jarrett Cotten would be headed for Memphis the morning of November twenty-fifth, Crenshaw and Stephen Stogdon planned to pursue him in the hope of recovering the stolen negroes. With this in mind, Crenshaw awoke early on the twenty-fifth to find Stephen in the depths of a fever. The young man tried to rise, but yielded when Crenshaw put him at ease, saying, "I'll pursue your father's negroes as if they were my own."
>
> Old Hume bade him farewell, and Crenshaw set out into bone-chilling weather after his quarry. He hoped to catch up with Cotten at the ferry across the Vess River, or at least hear word of his passing.

Approaching the river, he found the ferryman struggling to free his barge from the ice along the bank.

"Good sir," Crenshaw said to him, dismounting, "have any other travelers passed this way thus far today?"

"Not a one," the ferryman said.

"I'm after a man named Jarrett Cotten. Do you know him?"

"Only from a distance."

Even as they spoke, Crenshaw heard someone approaching on the road behind him. He turned to see a well-dressed rider on as fine a piece of horseflesh as he had ever seen. The gentleman was wearing heavy furs to keep out the cold, and a superb beaver hat. There was an air of affluence about him, and Crenshaw, because of his lowly station, was at first reluctant to approach. The urgency of his mission, however, forced him to action, and, as they waited together for the ferryman to finish his preparations, they fell into conversation.

"The weather is foul, sir," Crenshaw offered. "Is it not?"

"Yes it is," the gentleman said in a cultured voice. "Yet beautiful in its way. The light catches on each ice-sheathed twig, lending mystery to the world."

Once the barge was freed from the ice, the gentleman dismounted, led his horse onboard, and paid his fare, followed by Crenshaw. The ferryman gave Crenshaw a knowing wink as he approached.

Did he mean by this that he knew the gentleman to be Cotten? Crenshaw decided that he did.

"If I might be so bold, sir," said Crenshaw, as the ferryman began to haul the craft across the river, "would it not be advantageous for us to share our road, at least as long as we travel in the same direction?"

The gentleman looked at him suspiciously and then lowered his gaze. "It would be more agreeable to pass the time in pleasant conversation. . . ."

As Joel dozed, cheek pressed to the open book pages, he could see Mark's young face, eyes bright, while Joel read to him from the Crenshaw book. Joel smiled in his sleep.

4

The full darkness of night had settled outside the tree house as Joel read. He could tell that Mark was into the story once again in spite of himself.

Crenshaw and his companion left the ferry and rode in silence for several miles. With the rosy morning light dancing off the veil of ice, Crenshaw imagined they traveled within a cut-glass goblet, and was beginning to understand the gentleman's appreciation for this deadly landscape. Occasional crashes in the forest on either side punctuated their passage, as limbs overburdened with ice gave way and fell with a sound of breaking glass.

Crenshaw struggled to find the words that might entice his reticent companion to speak, and perhaps divulge some useful information of himself, yet it was the gentleman who spoke first.

"If you don't mind me asking, sir, what business takes you abroad in such weather?"

"I am trying to find a horse that wandered away," Crenshaw said, "or was stolen from my property, not a week hence."

"If it wandered off in this bitter weather, it has surely perished."

The wind shifted, cutting through the gaps in Crenshaw's clothing. He bundled the collar of his coat up around his ears and pulled his hat down over his brow.

"Yes," he said, then had an idea for drawing the man out. "I would rather think that some resourceful fellow has taken the poor beast." He gave the man a conspiratorial glance.

The gentleman nodded with a slight smile. "I am from Denmark, thirty miles west of here. Do you live nearby? Are you acquainted with the country hereabouts, the people and goings on?"

"No sir, not at all. I am from Adams."

The gentleman cocked an eyebrow. He shifted uncomfortably in his saddle, dropped the reins, and rubbed his gloved hands together. "You must love this horse very much to so stubbornly pursue it."

"He's practically all I've got. The horse I ride now is borrowed." Crenshaw gave the gentleman a knowing wink as he patted the animal affectionately on the neck.

"You say you're from Adams," the man said, with a troubled expression. "Then you must know something of the dreaded Bell Spirit there. . . ."

"I've heard some really creepy new stuff about the Bell Witch," Mark interrupted. "You know even though she's been around for a long, long time, she's not too proud to use modern stuff. She rides the telephone lines these days so she can get into anyone's home anytime she wants to."

"She wasn't really a witch, flicto. She was just this weird spirit that haunted the Bell family, like a poltergeist or something. No one knows what she was really doing there, but she was mischievous, and really cruel sometimes. She could foretell the future and stuff like that. She played practical jokes on people she didn't like. She did a couple of nice things for Lucy, John Bell's wife, 'cause she liked Lucy for some reason. In the end she killed John Bell with poison 'cause she hated his ass."

"But I thought she was still around."

"Well yeah . . . and no, not really," Joel said. "Kids have always just told stories about her like she still haunts parts of Tennessee, but there hasn't been anything well documented since the early 1800s."

"Well that's good anyway. I wouldn't want her comin' through the phone line and going in my ear or somethin'." Mark looked deeply relieved.

Joel huffed in disgust. "Just shut up, doofus, I'm reading here."

> "I've had an encounter or two," Crenshaw said, noting the man's strange reaction to the subject of the Bell Spirit and storing it away. "How far are you going on this road and what is your business?"
>
> "I am engaged in several errands at once," the gentleman answered, "and depending upon my people, I will get more or less done. But tell me, sir, if you would, are there many speculators in your part of the country?"
>
> "Speculators, sir? What do you mean?"
>
> "Thieves and such. You know, those clever and resourceful fellows who take advantage of the fat of others."
>
> "Ah," Crenshaw said, trying to conceal his excitement. "My name is Matthew Crenshaw, and it is a pleasure to meet a man whose mind is of a similar bent. And as to your question—not so much. There's not much to steal thereabouts, being but a frontier town. I had hoped for better, and may be moving on soon. The pickings are slim

in Adams."

His companion's gaze sharpened, and Crenshaw saw him make the slightest of nods, as if the man were pleased by what he heard.

"I am Jarrett Cotten, good sir, and likewise it is a pleasure," the outlaw said, riding closer and extending his hand. As soon as Crenshaw clasped his hand, Cotten tightened his grip and held on. "There is a rogue band determined to conquer this country," he said. "Their organization has many members in high places. They are invincible. No one can stand against them, as anyone who tries finds the world turned against him. A clever and friendly young man, such as yourself, couldn't help but prosper in their company."

Cotten gave him a slow, malevolent wink and released his hand. "I speak of the Mystic Clan, and I am their leader. Won't you join us?"

"My opportunities are currently quite lean," Crenshaw said, trying his companion's verbose manner of speech. He didn't want to sound too eager.

"Perhaps you can assist me in my current endeavor," Cotten said. "I have been dealing in stolen slaves, as the risks are slight and the rewards substantial. A couple of my clan members and I stole some slaves just recently. They've gone ahead as I was delayed. Now I am hurrying to catch up with them."

Crenshaw hoped Cotten was speaking of the Stogdons' slaves. He wanted to question the outlaw concerning the location of the theft, but thought that might tip his hand.

"If you will travel with me to the Mystic Clan's wilderness fortress," Cotten continued, "I will introduce you to my fellows and find a place for you within our company."

"I thought you were going to Memphis," Crenshaw said.

"Wherever did you get that idea?"

Crenshaw couldn't admit that he had heard it from one of Hume Stogdon's neighbors.

"It is nothing. I misremembered."

Cotten gave him a look of suspicion, but this quickly passed.

Though frightened by the prospect, it appeared to Crenshaw that Cotten might take him right to Stogdon's stolen slaves. "I am inclined to accept your offer," he said at last.

"Splendid," Cotten said. "I suggest we pause alongside the road for a spell and toast our newfound friendship and warm our bones."

"That would be very agreeable" Crenshaw said.

When they had dismounted, and were seated on a log, the outlaw offered him a flask of brandy. "To your future with the Mystic Clan. . . ."

"That's enough for tonight," Joel said.

He put down the book and pulled out a pack of cigarettes. "Hey, I stole these from my dad's girlfriend this afternoon," He took one out, acted like he was going to put it in his mouth, but quickly reached over and stuck it between Mark's lips instead. Then he fished out another and put it between his teeth.

Joel knew his friend hated smoking, but Mark didn't put up a fight when Joel whipped out his Zippo and lit the cigarette for him. He seemed to take only a small amount of smoke into his lungs, trying hard not to cough. Mark just wasn't any good at it, but Joel intended to make a smoker out of him yet.

Joel lit his own cigarette, took a long drag, then eyed his friend with satisfaction through the centers of blue smoke rings.

Ebbie, Mark's golden retriever, squatted and began to pee on the mildewed scraps of carpet on the floor. Disgusted, Joel kicked the scraps through the ladder hole and moved away from the stained boards.

"Just sit *down,* Ebbie," Mark told her, pushing down on the dog's hindquarters.

"If you can't get that dog to behave, I'm gonna throw her over the rail!"

"Oh no you *won't.* She just pissed. She never takes a dump without sniffing around a whole lot first. Besides, she's our protector, nobody can get at us without her waking us up."

"An Indian could," Joel said. He opened a candy bar and began to eat.

"How dumb can you get? There ain't no Indians around here." Mark glanced around nervously.

"Used to be. And in this part of Tennessee, there were long-hunters too, and cannibal land and river pirates that would roast ye like a pig with your dick in your mouth." Joel leered, gave Mark a chocolate seefood.

"You talk about the past like it'd be so cool to live then, but those Indians and pirates would kill you in a heartbeat. They'da squashed you like a bug."

"Like hell, Mark. I could've handled myself all right."

"Bullshit, Joel. You wouldn't have lasted a minute and you know it. Life was nothin' but tryin' not to get sick and tryin' to kill everyone else before they killed you."

"Like I said, *I'm* as tough as the worst of 'em." Joel spat on the floor next to Mark. "And that arm of yours I broke says I'm right."

Mark looked away.

It happened late last summer on the first day of school. The minute Joel met Mark, something told him that Mark was the one. Fearstink was all over Mark—the way he walked along with his hands shoved in his pockets and his head down, the way he avoided eye contact, the way he grinned nervously if you bumped into him. Joel was a transfer from another school and he needed to beat the crap out of somebody to establish himself as a tough guy. Later, even Joel admitted he'd gone too far, breaking Mark's arm in their first, and only, fight.

He hadn't meant to do it. Not really. He was sitting on Mark's back, twisting his arm, ordering him to say he was a goddam pussy. Mark was trying, between sobs. Then there was this godawful snap, and Mark had stopped crying. He stopped breathing, for just a second. Then he sucked in air and he screamed, loud and high-pitched, like a girl. Joel had thought for a moment that he would throw up. He thought that he had never regretted anything more in his life. But it had done the job, everyone was afraid of Joel.

As punishment for fighting in school, both boys were given three-day suspensions. Mark's father whipped him with his belt and then grounded him for a month.

Joel had been offered a choice: a year's stint in reform school or an apology to Mark and his family. The apology hadn't hurt his pride too much. After all, he really was pretty sorry. Afterward, Joel made every effort to win Mark over, at first just hanging out with him, then introducing him to smoking, shoplifting and skipping school. Mark was first fearful, then flattered. And although Mark was a reluctant apprentice, Joel was gradually wearing him down.

Joel knew that for the very same reasons Mark feared him, he considered Joel an invaluable ally. Joel found out that Mark had always been picked on, and he sure as hell was no good in a fight. With Joel as his friend, Mark had a bodyguard by default and gained status by association. And, the truth was, Joel liked him. Mark wasn't exactly brave, but he was loyal, and sometimes, he was pretty damn funny. And he was the only person in the school, maybe the only person in the world, who knew Joel's secret; he was smart. He loved to read, and he loved the raucous history of the river country. But he wasn't about to let anybody find out, and think he was some wimpy, geeky egghead.

"I wish we could go back and meet some of those people—the outlaws, the Indians—and see what this area was like when it was still wild," Joel said.

"My grandma always says, 'The blood of Father Time only flows one way.' "

"You're a dork and so's your grandma."

The boys fell silent. Joel looked out into the night, his imagination peopling the surrounding woods with figures from the past; the heroic men who had settled the area last century, the savage Indians, and the outlaws. Men like Matthew Crenshaw were great because of their courage in facing the threat of the land pirates. Joel had great respect for him, but what he didn't tell Mark was that he loved the criminals the best; characters like Samuel Mason, the Pike brothers, John Long and James Ford. While reading the Crenshaw book, Joel was always secretly rooting for the outlaw, Jarrett Cotten, even though he knew the land pirate got it in the end. The man had had such charisma and style!

"Those bad guys you like so much, they weren't so tough. They weren't invisible, like Superman. That guy Jamus Cooke brought 'em all down."

"Invincible, eedjit," said Joel, feeling a little unsettled. It was like Mark had just read his mind. "Yeah, Jamus Cooke broke the back of the Mystic Clan when he turned himself in and squealed on everybody. But that didn't make him a hero. Some say he was none other than Jamus Pike, Wesley and Virgil Pike's older brother. They say he never made up his mind whether to be criminal or law-abiding. I think he was a goddam traitor, that's what. He turned on his own."

Joel glared at Mark, daring him to disagree. Mark looked out the window.

" 'Course some say there never was a Jamus Pike," Joel grumbled. He went back to staring out the window.

Insects had gathered in greater and greater numbers around the yellow trouble light as night settled in around them. From beyond the patchwork walls, the monotonous song of the insect choir filled the night with a rhythmic whirring.

"If we were up at Reelfoot Lake," said Joel, "we could use these bugs for bait and go fishing. You ever been up there?"

"No, my dad don't take me anywhere. I've never even been out of Dexter."

"It's only . . . what . . . like ten, maybe twenty miles north of here. It's real weird too—got all these dead trees sticking up out of it, and in a boat you gotta go real slow 'cause there's all kinds of stuff hiding just under the water waiting to grab you and haul you down."

"Yeah, well, *you* can go fishing with 'em. They give me the creeps."

Joel grinned, delighted with Mark's fear of the thousands of cicadas around them, the insects crawling freely about the tree house, inside and out. He grabbed one from the wall and shoved it in Mark's face. "What's so bad about 'em, anyway?" Joel thought their black, ridged bodies were a little gross, but their red jeweled eyes and clear, veined, crystal wings were kind of pretty. The cicada buzzed angrily, twisting in his fingers and waving its thick, black legs.

Mark frowned and slapped the bug out of his hand. "Last week," Mark said, "when the cicadas were just coming up out of the ground, Mama told me the last big cicada invasion happened the year I was born. She said they were everywhere—so many they'd pull clothes off the line from their weight, coated the streets with slime from cars runnin' over 'em, even clog the cars' engines. I thought she was nuts—there could never be so many bugs. I thought she must've been exaggerating. She don't like bugs neither. But then the cicadas just kept coming. This invasion's much worse than what she told me."

"They're just bugs," Joel said, casually flicking a couple off the edge.

"But they're *everywhere.*"

"Jeez, Mark, relax. You sound as bad as Billy."

"Fuck you. One or two are no big deal, but this swarm. . . ."

"Hey they won't hurt you or nothing. They can't even bite."

Ebbie stood beneath a branch dripping with cicadas, enthusiastically gobbling the creatures. Caught between the dog's teeth, the insects continued to buzz wings and thrash legs. With great crunching noises, she chomped down, using her tongue to draw them in, cicada juices flowing into the foamy corners of her black, bumpy dog lips. When the chitinous mass was small enough, she swallowed it all at once.

"Oh God, that's so gross," Mark said, backing up and pressing dangerously against the flimsy wall. "That's it, I'm outta here!"

"*No way,* Mark—don't be a pussy. You're not gonna let a few damn bugs ruin our night. We're having a great time."

"Maybe you are, asshole."

"We've seen the worst of it, and Ebbie here protected us—just like you said. Look, they're dying down now. Tomorrow, before we explore The New Cut, we'll put up some screens or something. Whaddaya say?"

Mark looked doubtfully from Joel to the light. "Okay," he said, grudgingly. He slid into his sleeping bag and zipped it up all the way and peered through a tear in the fabric with one eye.

"Great! Here, you want one of these Caca Crusties or a Sugarbutt?"

"Naw," came Mark's muffled reply, "I don't think I can eat anything right now."

Ebbie found a new source for cicadas toward the back where another branch dipped in through a makeshift window. "Aw, Christ, cut it out!" Mark yelled. Ebbie looked at him reproachfully. He called her over to sit next to him.

A loud rumbling came from Ebbie's gut and she belched. Her sides heaved twice and she coughed, her eyes bugging. Mark was out of his sleeping bag and nearly took a dive off into space as she vomited on the particleboard floor. The countless insect bodies that spilled from her gullet were still alive. They formed a buzzing, flapping, chunky pool that soon began to break up and crawl apart.

Joel began to squeal with delight.

Then, the dog's head lurched forward with a chomp and crunch, forcing the insects back into her mouth. Ebbie chewed, some wings and a leg or two leaking out before she swallowed.

Mark, white-faced and shouting, started down the ladder. On the ground, he untangled his bike from Joel's and climbed on.

"What about your dog?"

"You can have her—she's full of bugs!"

Joel's laughter chased Mark all the way to the next corner and up the long drive to his house.

5

"Mama!" Mark said for the fifth time.

"Not *now,* Mark, I've got to get your sister ready for ballet class."

He had followed her all over the house, from the baby's room upstairs to the laundry room in the basement to the linen closet in the hall, and would have followed her outside to the patio garden if his sister, Kathy, had not demanded their mother's attention and stopped her dead in her tracks in the living room.

"But, *Mama,* I wanna go to the creek with Joel."

"Kathy, there's a hole in your leotards, and I just bought them!"

Mark stomped his foot, crossed his arms, and stared back at the knots in the pine paneling. They looked like taffy-stretched faces, eyes out of place, mouths wide and screaming. Today they seemed to be mocking him.

"Mama, I can't go with torn leotards!" Kathy said, her face frantic. "The girls will think we're poor."

"Kathy, you'll just have to make do." Mama turned to Mark, who was tugging at her sleeve. "I don't have time to fool with you right now."

"Well I'm gonna go ask Daddy," Mark said, turning away.

I wouldn't be bothering you, Mother, if I didn't have to ask your permission before I so much as take a whiz.

He found his father in the study working on a plastic model of a Chevy Impala.

"Daddy, I wanna go to the creek with Joel."

His father didn't seem to hear him and remained hunched over the model, applying glue to a black manifold held in a pair of tweezers.

"Well, can I go?"

"You can, if you'll take your baby sister with you."

"Daddy, I can't take her there, she'll drown!"

He's trying to pawn her off on me so he won't be bothered while he works on his damn model.

"I guess you're right," his father said without looking up, "but I don't want you hanging out with that *Biggs* boy."

Mark felt his face flush with anger and gritted his teeth. He watched impatiently as his father carefully installed the manifold.

It's like I'm not even here.

"Daddy, I'm going now. I'm not taking Kelly with me and I'll be with Joel all day!"

"That's fine, just be sure to do your chores before you leave."

Mark said nothing and stomped out the back door.

To hell with chores and to hell with Mama and Daddy. If they don't have time for me, I don't have time for them either.

But dammit, when they start looking for me later on and can't find me, they're gonna be really pissed off and I'm gonna get punished. It's not fair!

Maybe I just won't come back.

6

His father was right where Joel expected him to be, planted in front of the television with his feet propped up, his first beer of the day in hand.

"Dad, if you let me go down to the creek with Mark, I'll clean out the gutters."

"You're grounded and you know it," his father rumbled without looking up from his baseball game. "You didn't do your chores. You're grounded and don't think I've forgotten."

"But, Dad, I only wanna go to the creek. It's not like I'm going far—just across the road. I won't be gone long, and I'll come right back and clean out the gutters."

I gotta get outta here before you get really shitfaced.

"Joel, I'm not in a bargaining mood. You never live up to your end of the bargain, you little shit."

On the television someone hit a long fly ball, and his father was up and out of his worn recliner, screaming "All right!" at the top of his lungs. He plopped back down, the old cushions coughing out a stench of stale sweat and spilled beer. He drained the can and, crushing it in his hairy fist, he dropped it on the floor beside last night's leftovers.

"Get me another one, boy."

"We're all out, Dad," Joel said, hoping against hope that his father would believe him.

"You're a goddammed liar."

His father was fast. Joel didn't see the open hand coming,

but he sure felt it crack into the side of his face and knock him to the floor.

"If you're not willing to do me a little favor, I don't want you in my hair. Go to your room!"

Joel got to his feet and darted from the living room. Passing through the kitchen, he gave the loose grating on the bottom of their aged refrigerator a swift kick and then ran down the narrow and peeling hall to his cramped bedroom. Before entering, he glanced at the back door and saw that the deadbolt was locked.

Moments later he heard the refrigerator door squeak and the top of a beer can pop open.

I'm locked in with that drunken bastard again.

For the hundredth time, Joel tried to think of a way he could get the key from his father's pocket without him knowing it. But the keys were never out of his possession—he slept in his clothes and just transferred the keys when he changed his pants.

He glanced at his bookshelf, his usual escape route. Crammed into every available space, mixed in with the plastic models of tanks and planes, were his books. Amongst the Bradburys and Tolkiens were books on history—great battles and generals, Indians, archaeology—and an old and battered set of encyclopedias. But Joel wasn't in the mood to read—the thought of his father, a drunken time bomb ticking away down the hall, made him too damn jumpy. Once again, he cursed his mother for dying and leaving him with *her* drunk.

He considered his bedroom window. In an effort to cut off all escape, his father had installed storm windows and hammered in wedges from the outside so they couldn't be opened.

From the living room, his father roared.

Joel pulled out his Swiss Army Knife and went to work on the window. He broke the screwdriver tip, but finally managed to remove the pane. He breathed in the sweet summer air, wriggled through the window, and escaped.

7

The creek was a great living thing that wound snake-like through the boys' neighborhood, a pet to be played with, a wild and mysterious animal that lent its personality to an otherwise ordinary middle-class landscape of streets and houses. As far as Joel was concerned, it was his and was meant to be explored, no matter whose property he had to pass through to do it. Although "The New Cut" was just a deep, man-made gouge—the result of straightening the creek—it represented unexplored territory, an irresistible challenge.

"Backhoe's gone," Mark said, looking at the mountains of earth beside the new stretch of creek. "I guess that means they're finished."

"You think they could've made it any deeper?" Joel said. "I mean the banks are only, what, like eight feet tall?"

"Who cares?" Mark shrugged, wiping the sweat from his forehead. "We oughta just get in."

"Go ahead! Sure is muddy, though. No tellin' what all's in there."

It was a blistering, humid day and the scant breeze did them little good. Occasionally a car whooshed by on the nearby road, the wind in its wake like a blast of steam. The water would be nice and cool but they hesitated above the giggling surface.

Mark's golden retriever showed no fear whatsoever. She was already crouched down with her head half submerged, gulping water. Water bugs skated about her head, dancing in and out of the waving spray of her long red-gold fur. Her ears wiggled in the gentle current as they floated on the water. Joel wondered how many of the creek bugs she had swallowed over the years.

"So, Joel, whadya do to Ebbie? She was limping this morning."

"Well, she wouldn't have been if you'd been around to help me haul her outta the tree house. She weighs a ton. You're lucky she didn't leave a crater in the ground."

"Well, thanks for helping her down, anyway," Mark said grudgingly.

Joel kicked a clod of loose dirt into the water. "You think this creek's big enough to float a raft? We could build one from that dead sycamore," he said, pointing, "and ride it all the way to the Mississippi."

"It's big enough here only because Missus Howard had it gouged out. But you know how thin it gets at the Canals."

"We'll build it there, then. That's right where the woods start on the Maxwell farm, and you know how deep it gets after that."

"We're gonna need food for a couple of days, and water too."

"I've got a couple of canteens. But we won't need to bring any food. I'll bring my .22 so we can hunt us up some squirrels and rabbits, just like in the olden days."

"What if we got lost?"

"With me around?" said Joel, grinning. "Ha! I never been lost yet and don't aim to let that happen anytime soon."

A car horn sounded from the road behind them and they turned to see Mrs. Howard waving from her blue Nova. The boys waved dutifully as she rounded the corner and pulled into her driveway.

"Billy!" she called, stepping out of her car. "You boys seen Billy?"

"No, ma'am," Mark said.

"*Hell* no," Joel muttered under his breath to his friend. "My father says she's a stupid old bitch and just wasting her money. Says she expects to sell off half her lot now that the creek don't wind all through it. What she don't know is the codes—they say you gotta have two acres 'cause we got no sewers." Mrs. Howard bustled into the house with her groceries. Joel winced at the sight of her huge butt bulging through white stretch pants.

"All them Howards are just stupid," Mark agreed.

"Oh yeah?" came a small but defiant voice.

Where the hell did Billy come from? Joel wondered. He was always popping up like that, horning in like Joel and Mark were his friends or something. He was only seven and never any fun because he only knew how to do little kid things. They weren't baby-sitters, goddammit.

But there he was, standing on the shoulder of the road. He was wearing short blue pants, the stupid little boy kind with the key clip on one loop, and a bright yellow T-shirt. He had girlish red hair that was almost blond in places and gleamed in the sun. Across his cheeks and nose was a goofy spray of freckles that had been darkened by the sun. And what pissed Joel off the most was that stupid smirk he always seemed to be wearing.

"Well, my mom would get her boyfriend to beat your daddy up if I told her what you said." Billy's chin jutted, little fists planted on his hips.

"Teddy?" Mark said. "Teddy against *my* father? You've got to be kidding—my daddy who was head of the boxing team in college?"

Joel walked up to the small boy. "My daddy said your mama spent a fortune straightening this creek for no good reason, and I'll whip your ass if you don't agree with me." He pushed him and Billy spilled painfully onto the chewed-up, rocky ground. He began to cry.

"Mark, I'm gettin' tired of standing around," Joel growled.

"If you're so scared, you can stay here and cry with Billy."

He took off his shoes, tied the laces together, and hung them around his neck.

"You're gonna step on glass and cut up your feet," Mark said.

"There's no glass down there. It's fresh dug. Besides, I ain't gonna walk around with mud and rocks in my shoes like a dumbass."

"You know glass is always rolling down from upstream and if it's clear, you can't see it."

Joel gave Mark a defiant look and hopped recklessly off the edge, sliding on his butt down the nearly vertical bank, a small avalanche of raw dirt cascading after him.

"Crybaby," Mark tossed over his shoulder at the still-sniffling Billy, as he scrambled after his friend. "Follow if you want. But remember, the snapping turtles are waiting to get you."

The older boys moved along The New Cut, turning over rocks, chasing salamanders and harassing crayfish. They passed through a short stretch where the light bouncing off the surface of the water filled the air with too much light, as if there were reflections coming from more than one sun.

Ebbie stopped dead in her tracks, then began leaping about and barking as the boys moved on.

"Stop that, Ebbie," Mark said, "we're busy and we're not gonna play with you right now." He sat in the water and removed his shoes. "Damn periwinkles hurt my feet."

Joel looked over at him and gave him a look that said, "dumbass," and then went back to working on the creek bed. He had discovered a fossilized mollusk shell frozen in the bedrock and was down on his knees trying to break it free with a loose stone.

"Damn," Joel said, throwing the stone away, "I busted up this neat—"

His voice trailed off as he caught sight of a shiny black shape coiled on a sunny rock next to his head. He hadn't noticed it until it began to move. It was rearing its head to strike and hissing loudly.

Water moccasin! his mind screamed. *Get up and run!*

Instead he tried to become perfectly still, wondering if, like he'd read, the snake couldn't see him if he didn't move. As the soft mud beneath his knees gave way, he began to fall forward and slowly put out his hands for support.

Out of the corner of his eye, Joel saw Mark had put on a beard and mustache of the long, stringy algae that drifted down from upstream.

"Hey, Joel," his friend said, laughing, "look at me!"

Joel couldn't take his eyes off the snake and he was sure Mark would think he was ignoring him again—sometimes Joel did that just to piss him off.

"Look at me, dammit!" Mark said. He placed his foot on Joel's butt and gave him a hard shove.

"Water moccasin!" Joel yelped, toppling into the water.

The snake slipped into the stream and swam between Mark's legs. Mark shrieked and jumped out of the water, clung to the roots hanging out of the bank. The snake disappeared downstream.

Joel was relieved that his friend was too distracted to notice how frightened he was.

"That was a cottonmouth, wasn't it? It could've *killed* us."

"Well it didn't," Joel said, feigning disgust. "So stop crying about it."

"We gotta get outta here!"

"God, you're such a spazmoid. Calm your little butt down—the cut ends just ahead."

No longer exploring, they moved forward in silence. Ebbie barked at them from the lip of the bank, above. When Mark called to her, she sniffed out a way down and joined them.

"Hey, it's not ending. I think we're going the wrong way."

"No way," Joel said, finally looking up. "What are you saying—we're lost? The creek only goes in two directions. Only a flicto like you could get lost walking a straight line."

But then his cockiness wavered and he looked around in bewilderment—nothing seemed familiar.

"Isn't this only supposed to be about a hundred yards long?" Mark asked. He looked a little scared. "I mean we should be at the end by now, *shouldn't* we?"

"I don't fucking recognize any of this shit!"

Joel looked back the way they had come. It all looked the same, the creek and its steep banks running straight until lost in the hazy distance.

"Hey, Joel, maybe they came back and cut some more last night while we were asleep."

"God, you're so *stupid.* It looks different 'cause it's all tore up. See, Ebbie's not worried—we'll just follow her home when we're ready."

"Yeah, I guess so."

Joel picked up a flat stone and tried to skip it across the surface of the water. It skipped once and thudded into the muddy bank.

"It's not wide enough here for skipping stones," Mark said.

Ebbie retrieved the stone and dropped it at Mark's feet.

"Oh yeah?" Joel bent and chose another. This time the rock skipped once, as if to prove him right, bounced and hit an unusual stone embedded in the bank. The stone was round and broke open when struck. Mark splashed through the water to investigate.

"Hey, Joel, lookit this!" he cried out. "It's hollow!"

As if sensing Mark's mood, Ebbie started barking and bounding about.

"Maybe it's a geode," Joel said.

The stone was slippery, hard to get a hold of, and it took both of them to free it from the mud. There was a wet sucking sound and the thick smell of clay. A thin, shell-like fragment had broken away and they could see the stone was full of earth and tiny rootlets. It slipped out of their grasp and fell with a splash. Growling, Ebbie followed it as it rolled sluggishly under the water. The boys retrieved it, and when they turned it over, they saw its features well enough through the clay that skinned it to know what it was. The white gleam of teeth, eye sockets filled with black mud.

"It's human!"

8

"Hey guys," Billy shouted for the third time. *"Come on, say something, please."*

Mark and Joel seemed to be ignoring him—not an unusual thing—as they retraced their steps, passing what looked like a muddy stone back and forth between them. Even the dog would not respond to him.

The air between Billy and the other boys had a strange quality to it, something like a heat shimmer, but with a silent-film-type flickering quality as well.

Nobody wants me around, not Joel and Mark, not Mom and her stupid boyfriend.

Billy's mom had been saying "get lost" to him in one form or another ever since she met up with her new boyfriend. But recently it had taken on new meaning. They were at his Great Aunt Ester's house for a family reunion and Mom and her Teddy had wanted to go for a walk in the garden, alone.

"Take a hike, kid," Teddy said.

"Mother's busy, dear. Why don't you go play in the pool, or something?"

"But *Mom!*" Billy said, but she hurried away.

Bored, he wandered around until he found himself at the pool. It was loud and bright and full of cousins he didn't know. They looked like they were having fun though, and since he wasn't, he thought he'd join them.

Billy took off his shirt and jumped in. Unfortunately, he was at the deep end and sank eight feet, straight to the bottom. He screamed out all his air, kicked off the bottom and scrambled upward. Breaking the surface just long enough for a single desperate, gulping breath, Billy tried to call out for help, but had no time. He sank immediately.

The drain in the bottom of the pool loomed toward him, sucking him down. His feet touched bottom and he desperately kicked off, rising through the dark, cold water to the shimmering light above.

He broke the surface with the pool's edge just out of reach. Billy sputtered and gulped air in the instant before the drain sucked him back under. Billy fought the drain, rising and sinking over and over, until he felt he had taken his last breath and would finally be sucked into the sewer.

A cousin, the only one at the reunion he knew by name, pulled him out just before the drain claimed him at last. Nathan left Billy lying by the side of the pool. And since his mother had not returned for him, he stayed there long after the other guests had gone home. He watched the drain with burning eyes. It stared up at him and winked malevolently through the ripples on the water's surface.

Ever since, the drain had dwelled within him. Left alone too long, he would feel it sucking him down and then it would wink, as if to say, "One of these days. . . ."

Billy kicked a clod of dirt into the cut and began a string of curses unlike anything he'd ever dreamed possible. He knew that if his mother could hear him, he'd get a whipping. He didn't care. He wished he was saying it right to her face. Tears slid down his hot cheeks as he used every swear word he'd ever heard, and made up a few as well.

His anger faded as his voice grew hoarse. He stood silently, watching the boys pass out of sight around a bend. The drain was beginning to tug at him when he caught sight of Mark's striped shirt in the distance through the shimmering, flickering air. He bolted in their direction, shouting, “Wait up!”

9

They were heading back to Mark's house to clean up the skull when they decided they had somehow gotten turned around. Now, nothing looked familiar to Mark in either direction.

"Hey, I've got it," Joel said, "if we watch the water, we can figure out which way it's moving."

Mark looked down at the empty cicada shells that littered the surface and wanted to kick them away, but he tried to be still. With their thick legs and oversized claws, they looked like little 1950s' movie monsters as they bumped against his legs. Despite the heat, he shuddered.

"Damn, Joel, I can't see it moving."

"Me neither."

Mark looked hopefully at his dog. She was snuffling along the rooty bank, as if she knew where she was going.

"Let's follow her," Mark said.

Ebbie dashed out into the water and splashed around before running on ahead. When she stopped and looked back, Mark realized she was just taking her cues from them.

Tired of carrying the skull, Joel placed it within a tangle of sycamore roots hanging over the edge of the bank.

"We'll come back for it."

10

With a throbbing headache, Joel awoke to the soft purr of the mail truck's engine, followed by the squeal of disk brakes as it pulled up to his mailbox. Lifting his head from the dining-room table, he pushed the Crenshaw book away, knocking some of his empties onto the floor.

It irritated the shit out of him that he responded to this same call day after day like some idiotic Pavlov's dog. It wasn't like he was expecting to get anything. He never did. But his mailbox was the last real connection he had with the outside world—the people who sent the junk mail didn't know he was a drunk.

Joel stood, walked to the front door, and opened it, squinting painfully at the early afternoon light. It was raining lightly, though the sun was out.

Devil's beating his wife.

In spite of the throbbing pain in his head, he trudged out into it. Joel pretended not to see the unopened mail from days past that littered his dewy lawn. He was embarrassed to see how fast it built up, but not nearly as much as he had been a couple of weeks ago, when two of the neighborhood women had cleaned up his yard, leaving the clumps of moisture-ruined junk mail in a neat cardboard box on his doorstep, with a little note which read "God Bless."

Joel was nearly to the street when he slipped in the wet grass. He caught himself awkwardly on one arm before landing heavily on his side. Picking himself up, trying not to puke, he found a sodden envelope plastered to his shoe. He shook his foot, but the envelope remained glued in place. Hissing, he kicked out savagely and lost his balance. He let out a yelp as he landed hard on his butt. The impact sent jagged lightning through his thundering head, and he cradled himself and moaned.

Cursing, he reached down and peeled the envelope off his shoe. He glanced at the return address and saw it was from Moss Phelps, his "cousin," whom he had not spoken to or thought about in years. How long had it been lying on his lawn? The postmark was dated a week ago.

"Sonuvabitch!" he said, ripping it open and accidentally tearing it in two. A bus ticket fell from the envelope and landed in his lap. He opened the pieces of the letter and held them together.

Dear Dunderpate,

Heard you been having a hard time lately and I thought maybe you could use a break. Why don't you come see me, Lynn and the kids? I've got a month off from work so I could work on our new house. The place is near Jackson. We may be living in the sticks, but it's gorgeous country and there's not a soul around for miles.

Here's a bus ticket. Why don't you use it? Give us a call and let us know when you're arriving and we'll pick you up at the bus depot. Use the number below.

I only ask one thing—if you come up, you gotta stay dry. We'll put you up as long as you like, but the deal is, you can't drink. Sorry if I sound like a hardass, Joel, but you know I'm really just trying to help.

All the love in the whole fucking world!
Moss

"Well fuck you too!" Joel wadded up the letter and threw it in the ditch. "Who the hell asked you to save my goddam life!

Nosey-ass motherfucker. If I wanna fuck up my life, it's my own goddam business."

He picked up the ticket, ripped it into dozens of pieces and tossed them into the air, muttering under his breath.

Someone's watching me. Joel looked up to see his next-door neighbor, old Mrs. Devereaux, standing at the corner of her yard, staring at him.

"Mind your own goddam business, you fucking busybody!"

She blanched, one hand rising to her trembling lips.

"Well I never!" she said, hurrying off down the street.

When his anger had subsided, all that was left was an all-too-familiar embarrassment. These days his actions seemed to bring him nothing but regret. He picked himself up and, wiping at the wet seat of his pants, tried to scoop up the pieces of the bus ticket.

"Fuck, I'll never be able to pick 'em all up." He dropped the scraps and kicked at them, then remembered the letter and the telephone number.

I might go a couple of days without drinking, he thought, *'sides, it'd be good to see Moss again.*

The ditch was full of water, moving rapidly.

Shit—no telling where it is!

He jogged along the ditch, each footfall sending bright flares of agony through his head. Finally, he caught sight of the wadded letter as it entered the pipe that ran beneath his next-door neighbor's driveway.

"No you don't, goddammit!" he shouted as he lunged for it.

Not twenty feet away, Mrs. Devereaux wheeled around. "Don't you come any closer!"

He missed the letter and watched it race through the pipe. As he was climbing out of the ditch to cross the driveway, Mrs. Devereaux was rapidly backing away, her high heels clicking on the pavement, hands held out for balance.

"You get back. Don't make me call the police!"

Joel ignored her and ran across the driveway. He jumped into the ditch with a great splash and snagged the letter as it sped out of the pipe. He emerged dripping wet, mud streaming off of him.

"Just look at you, Mister Biggs," said Mrs. Devereaux with a grimace.

He made as if to lunge toward her. Squealing, she wheeled around and ran back toward her house. Halfway, she broke a heel and stumbled forward. His laughter followed her the rest of the way.

"Hey, Moss, this is Joel," he said, feeling like an asshole, "you know, Dunderpate!"

"Yeah, Joel—glad you called! How long's it been?"

"Too damned long."

"So you got my letter. You comin' up to see us?"

"Yeah, well, that's why I called. I'd sure like to, but. . . ."

"Well you got the bus ticket, right?"

"Well, yeah, but. . . . When I opened your letter the ticket fell out in a puddle . . . uh . . . of . . . juice. It's all sticky and I—"

"Just dry it off. They don't care. They'll still take it."

"Well, uh, the truth is, it kinda got ripped."

"What do you mean, Joel? How did it 'kinda get ripped'?"

"Okay, I got pissed off at your letter and tore it into a million pieces and—"

"Joel—"

"It's not that you were wrong in what you said. I got pissed off 'cause you were *right.* I gotta real problem and I could really use your help."

Joel's cheeks burned as he waited for Moss to respond, hoping he would offer to buy him another ticket. *I really need this,* he realized. As the silence stretched on, Joel wondered how he was going to admit that he couldn't afford his own ticket.

"I'll send you another, no problem. You've been honest with me and I appreciate it. If you can admit you've got a problem, you've made one step—an important step—in the right direction."

I've heard it all before. You don't have to goddam preach to me.

"Thanks, Moss. It'll be great to see you again."

"No problem. What about the deal? Can you live up to your end?"

Joel didn't want to hesitate, but couldn't help it, feeling stripped of his dignity. He'd always looked up to Moss though he hadn't seen him in years. He didn't want Moss thinking poorly of him, but apparently it was too late. Who had he been talking to?

"Yeah. If I take things one day at a time."

Yeah, that's just the kind of crap Moss'll want to hear.

Jesus, I'm already trying to manipulate him—and he's the only friend I got left. Better can that shit real quick.

"Good, then that's just the way we'll take it. I'll call the Dexter bus depot as soon as we hang up, and there'll be another ticket waiting for you. When can you come?"

"This afternoon. The sooner the better."

"Yeah, I think there's a three-o'clock departure. I'll set that up for you."

"Great. I'll see you."

"Bye."

Joel stripped off his muddy clothes and took a long, hot shower, washing away days of grime and whiskey-stinking sweat. He wandered into his tiny bedroom, dressed, and stuffed clothes at random into a ratty khaki duffel bag. The shiny pants and threadbare shirts embarrassed him, but he wasn't exactly in a position to go shopping for new ones. *Moss'll understand. He's expecting a bum, and that's what he'll get.*

Joel had about thirty minutes before he should leave for the bus station. He sat at the dining-room table and picked up the Crenshaw book.

"Now, let me tell you something of the laws concerning slave theft," Cotten said. "If a negro escapes and his master puts up a reward inviting any man to catch the negro, such an advertisement constitutes a power of attorney entrusting the captor to take the negro into his possession. If the captor puts the negro to his own use, instead of returning him, no theft has been committed and the only redress for the master is to be had in civil action. The Mystic Clan holds nothing but contempt such trifling suits."

The outlaw took another drink from his flask and passed it to Crenshaw.

Crenshaw said, "No thank you. Tell me more of this fascinating and devious plan."

"The Mystic Clan makes a fortune selling the slaves over and over again. Before each sale, we arrange a meeting place with the slave so we can steal him back. We have found the promise of eventual freedom keeps the negroes loyal. After four or five sales, before the risk becomes too great, we simply kill the slaves. The fish of the Mississippi are fattened on their corpses."

Crenshaw had difficulty concealing his shock. To cover it he began to cough. "What a waste," he said. Cotten gave him a cold stare, and Crenshaw hastily added, "When the slave might still be put to work somewhere."

"The more a slave is passed around, the more people become acquainted with his face, the more we risk being found out. If I can't afford to kill a negro, I won't steal him."

Crenshaw was appalled as the villain spoke of the Mystic Clan's adventures, the manner in which they dealt out death as casually as one might pull on one's boots. He knew they must be the cruelest band of land pirates that had ever existed.

When the outlaw offered the brandy again, Crenshaw wanted the drink to steel himself against the dire images conveyed by Cotten's high-flown speech, but knew that he must keep his wits about him.

"Now let me tell you of the Mystic Clan's Grand Plot," Cotten said, turning to Crenshaw with his brows raised to excite a sense of wonder. "Our Grand Plot involves a slave uprising."

He allowed a long pause before continuing.

"As I've explained, our activities with the slaves have never been limited to financial gains alone. We are always on the lookout for just the right type of negro. Those brutish enough, yet clever enough for us to train to excite other slaves to rebellion, are recruited as officers to create armies of slaves. We win them over by telling them that most of the world has abandoned slavery and that the slaves in the West Indies won their freedom through a revolt much like the one we are proposing. We tell them that the United States has become fattened and soft on the fruit of their labors, and that, should they win their freedom, they would be on an equal footing with the whites.

"We explain that there are thousands of white men willing to die alongside them, fighting for their freedom. Then we swear them to secrecy with a long, drawn-out ritual full of magical threats. I have found the negro to be much given to superstition and have made good use of it.

"Then we sell them to planters with large holdings and instruct them to incite their fellows to rebellion."

Cotten, riding ahead of Crenshaw, gestured expansively as he spoke.

"All up and down the Mississippi our slave officers are busy fomenting discontent among the slaves and offering them freedom. On Christmas Eve of next year, we will provide the officers with liquor for their armies. I know of no surer method to bring them together. By midnight the armies will be liquored up, and they will be instructed to kill all the whites but for a few who will join them in their struggle. They will attack in the night. Dawn on December twenty-fifth will see the rich brought to their knees. While the country fights to put down the slave revolt, The Mystic Clan will loot the South."

"How will the slaves be armed for this?" Crenshaw asked. "How will you get the weapons to them?"

"The Mystic Clan has set aside a percentage of our considerable income to purchase weapons. These are cached throughout the countryside in strategic locations. They will be distributed amongst the slaves at the proper time.

"All the great cities of the South will be destroyed. In the midst of this revolt, in the confusion and rubble, the Mystic Clan will sack the burning cities. The plunder will be unimaginable.

"We will let the negroes fight for us, all the while thinking they are fighting for their freedom. This will be a glorious massacre. For the slaves, it will all be for nothing. The whites will organize and destroy them all.

"I will become known for having shed more blood than any other conqueror known to history. I'm sure this seems the most outlandish of plots to you, Crenshaw, but I pride myself on its audacity."

Crenshaw was a simple man, a man without wealth and power. All his life, however, he had felt it was his duty to better the lives of others. He had always striven to do the right thing. Even so, he felt he could do more. After all, his life had to count for something in the eyes of the Lord.

Now he had his chance—he must halt the outlaw's diabolical course.

He only hoped that Cotten wouldn't see through his act and turn on him.

He took a deep breath before speaking. "I understand and appreciate your methods, which to any other person would seem cold and merciless. But great leaders must make hard decisions, and in these there is no room for emotion. I'm sure the members of your fraternity regard you as a great leader, as a George Washington, dare I say, or a Napoleon Bonaparte, and heap upon you wealth and power."

Jarrett Cotten swelled visibly with the flattery, and Crenshaw knew this may prove to be his greatest weapon against the man, for the great outlaw was a victim of his own pride.

"Our accommodations for the evening will bear you out. We travel to the home of one of my confederates, where we will be treated like royalty."

Joel walked out into the pale-blue sunshine, allowing himself a tiny taste of hope. He squinted at the muddy water in The New Cut. *Billy. How could Billy be dead?* Joel could still see him, standing on the bank in his stupid little boy shorts. He smiled a little, trying not to cry.

11

From above, Billy followed the boys as they moved back and forth within the cut. Shouting and throwing rocks at them had failed to get their attention and now he was tired. He sat on the lip of the cut and dangled his feet over the edge.

"It's *my* creek," he muttered.

Reaching into his pocket, he pulled out the guts of a golf ball. He had removed the skin to see if there really were a million rubber bands inside.

"Even in my own yard they don't let me play with 'em. It was like that when the creek was crooked and it's the same now that it's straight. Mama won't do *nothin'* about it, and she won't get Teddy to run 'em off neither."

He used a pair of fingernail clippers to cut through several strands of rubber band. The ball squirmed in his hands as the ubber worms, once drawn tight, were suddenly set free. The lippers fell from his grasp and were lost in the creek.

"Damn!"

When they call me names, Mama tells me to ignore 'em, but when all 'em names back, she sends me to my room. If they're playin' in yard, Howard law says I get to play with 'em, dammit!

Ie looked at the hairy rubber ball for a moment and then w it into the creek.

'ut I'm gettin' hungry, though." He turned to look across ream at his house.

t wanting to walk all the way down to the corner where

the concrete bridge crossed the creek, Billy looked for an easier way across the deep cut. He clambered down a tangle of roots and stood atop a rock jutting from the bank, then made his way across by leaping from stone to stone, careful not to touch the water and arouse the attention of the deadly snapping turtles.

"They won't let go 'til it thunders," Joel had once told him.

When Billy climbed out of the cut onto the opposite bank and looked up, his house was gone. He ran from side to side, straining to see through trees that were suddenly thicker than before.

The drain winked at him.

Fighting back sudden tears, he looked for Mark and Joel. He swallowed the lump in his throat and ran along the creek bank, dodging vines and branches. A snaking root tripped him up, and he landed painfully, nearly tumbling off the lip of the bank.

The older boys looked up at his cry and Ebbie began to bark.

"Dammit, Billy!" came Mark's exasperated cry, his voice echoing along the wide banks of the stream.

Billy looked around, startled. Nothing looked familiar. This wasn't the creek he knew so well—it appeared to have become something of a river.

12

Mark knew they really were lost when Joel decided their next step should be to climb out of the cut and look around.

"It's not as steep on this side," Billy called down from above.

"Yeah, but my house is on *this* side," said Joel.

Trying to scale the steep bank, Mark lost his grip and slid back into the water. "Shit, I can't get anywhere in this mud!"

"Watch me, idiot." Joel grabbed a couple of roots sticking out of the mangled bank and lifted himself. With a sucking sound, the roots pulled free of the mud and Joel fell back into the water with a loud splash that silenced the insects and animals.

By their sudden absence, Mark was made aware of the unusual number of living voices surrounding them.

"Did you hear that?" he asked. Mark chuckled nervously, sensing with a flash of goose bumps that he was far from home.

Joel wasn't listening. He was preoccupied with the broken roots in his hands. Getting a better look, Mark saw they were actually human femur bones.

"*Cool!* Are they real, Joel?"

"Yeah, I think so. God, when they cut through here, they must've gone right through an old graveyard."

As Billy began to whistle *The Old Man and the Clock* the animals and insects resumed their conversations. Ebbie scrambled up to join him and began the long wavering howl she normally reserved for the sirens of emergency vehicles.

Joel tossed the bones aside and swiftly wiped his hands on his pants. "C'mon, Mark, let's get the hell out of here."

They climbed up to join Billy, and Ebbie greeted them by wringing out her coat, giving them all a liberal spray of river water with essence of dog.

"My house is that way," Billy said, pointing, "but it's gone. If you help me find it, you can eat lunch with me."

"No," Joel said, "we ain't going back that way again. I can see which way the water's running now. Hendersen's Garage is down near where it runs into the Mississippi. Mark, we'll call your mom from there and she'll come get us."

13

Being in unfamiliar territory was a bit creepy, but Billy was finally getting to play with the big boys.

Two hours passed as they continued to follow the stream. Billy's stomach burned with hunger as Mark and Joel argued over possible landmarks—one would swear he recognized a tree or rock that was totally unfamiliar to the other.

As the stream became wider and deeper, it branched, winding off in several directions. They stayed out of the water, to prevent being washed away in what was now a considerable current.

"Shouldn't we head north?" Mark asked.

"No, dumbass," Joel said, "if we do that, we'll end up in Reelfoot Lake. We gotta head west, toward the Mississippi."

Without another word, Joel forged ahead, leading the way. At each new branch, he followed the left-hand bank toward the setting sun.

Holding onto her collar, Mark kept Ebbie close, not allowing her to leave his side.

They had entered a forest like none Billy had ever seen. The trees, giants towering over them, wore weirdly vivid greens and browns. The underbrush was a dense tangle of vines and brambles stretching between cottonwood and oak trunks that were fifteen feet or more around. What sunlight did reach them was heavily filtered through the leafy net overhead. It weakly illuminated the emerald plaid of saplings and fallen trees that rose nearly impassable on either side. *It's like being underwater,* Billy thought. *Like being a fish in the bottom of a dark, mossy lake.*

Above the constant hum of forest sounds, there rose the endless whirring of the cicadas. The three boys did whatever they could to fill the air with their own noise, chattering, whistling, and singing to mask the unstoppable voice of the wilderness.

As he became more and more tired, Billy also became frightened. "I wanna go home," he said, tugging on Joel's sleeve.

"Is little boy gonna cry, now?" Mark asked.

"I'll give you something to cry about," said Joel, sweeping Billy's legs out from under him.

He landed against a sapling and a shower of cicadas fell buzzing into his lap. "Bugs!" he shouted, dancing to his feet and flailing his limbs. "Get 'em off!"

"Hold him down, Mark."

Mark forced Billy to the ground and pinned his shoulders against a log. Joel picked up an empty cicada husk and leaned over the helpless boy. "You know what this is?" he asked, thrusting the shell into Billy's face.

The giant-clawed monstrosity came rushing toward the younger boy. Through its translucent exoskeleton he could see its organs working, no doubt secreting poisons to spit in his face. Reflexively, he closed his mouth but kept his eyes opened because it was worse not being able to see death coming.

"It's a cicada!" Joel shouted. "Big fuckin' deal!"

Now Billy could see that the cicada was only an inch long and translucent because nobody was home. It made little difference—the thing was still a bug and he could feel the urine running down his leg.

Embarrassed for the little boy, Mark felt they were being unnecessarily cruel. He lowered his gaze and watched absently as a pupal cicada blundered from the raw earth that had been its home for many years.

"An' you know what, Billy?" Joel shouted.

The terrified boy made no response, but kept his wide, panicked eyes glued to the insect shell.

"These cicadas are worms under the ground for thirteen years."

"Unh-unh," was Billy's only response.

Mark watched the cicada claw mechanically at a stone in its path. After a moment, it stopped trying to dig through the rock and turned to go around it.

"How would you like to live under the ground for that long?"

"Nunh-uh." Billy shook his head as Joel buzzed his tightly clenched lips with the insect form.

"When their thirteen years is up, they grow legs and one of these shells and crawl outta the ground. That's when they look like this."

"Ugly little sucker," said Mark, as the insect below climbed onto the toe of his sneaker. "Like someone else I know around here."

Joel glared at Mark for interrupting. "Then they hook onto something alive, like a little shit named Billy, while their shell gets hard and cracks open."

Billy began to squeal.

"When they crawl out, they got wings so they start flying around and fucking other cicadas. That's all they can do 'cause they ain't got mouths and can't eat nothin'. What they got instead of a mouth is this real sharp blade and they come back to the little shit boy named Billy, and they start cuttin' into him and laying eggs inside."

Bored with it, Mark knocked his foot against the log, dislodging the cicada. "Then the eggs start eatin' your guts up 'til they fall out your butt," Mark said, then grinned.

"Shut the hell up, Mark!" Joel shouted. "You pencil dick, I'm tellin' this true and you don't know nothing. I read all about it in the encyclopedia."

Mark spat, relaxing his grip on Billy.

Wriggling his shoulders, Billy almost got away, but Joel shoved him back. "Lemme go. Bugs make me sick!"

Mark wondered what had set Joel off this time, and why he was helping him. But sometimes he did that—he helped Joel push some wimpy kid around, play keep-away with some dweeb's glasses, swipe some loser's lunch money. And goddam it, sometimes it felt good. Before he met Joel, Mark had always been the victim. When he was with Joel, he felt tough. He felt big. He felt important. There was a guilty, nasty pleasure to be had from making another kid crawl. But why were they picking on Billy? What did they have against him, anyway? He was just a little guy. As Mark looked at him, skinny and small and terrified, he flashed on himself, sobbing on the ground with a broken arm.

Ashamed, he looked away and ground his heel into the cicada.

"You're not going anywhere—I'm not through with you yet." Joel pinned Billy with a knee. "Nine months later, your skin explodes with thousands of cicada worms popping out all at once. After that, they dig into the ground and the whole thing starts over again, 'cept you're not here to see it 'cause you're lying on the ground, full of holes, *dead.*"

"I'm-a tell," Billy threatened, face red, mouth trembling.

Ebbie began barking, loud and urgently. The boys looked up to see a pair of dark-skinned figures crouched at the edge of the clearing. Light flashed along the edge of a knife.

Mark froze, his heart racing as he remembered stories he had heard of what happened to little boys who trespassed. Billy broke free and ran screaming for the trees while Joel grabbed Mark's sleeve and towed him into the brush. Ebbie barked twice at the figures and then chased after the boys.

They ran wildly, crashing through the underbrush, tripping over roots, branches slashing at their faces. Mark heard no sounds of pursuit, but he wasn't convinced they were not being chased.

Joel skidded to a stop at the lip of a ravine. He started to shout a warning to Mark, but it was too late—his friend, looking back, collided with him and they tumbled off the edge. In a tangle, they rolled down the slope, crashing to a stop in a canebrake. Fighting the cane, Mark released a trapped stalk that whipped up and hit him in the face.

"Ow, goddamit!" He cupped his bleeding nose.

Their struggle only tightened the interlocking bars of their cane prison.

"Sssh!" Joel hissed, lifting a warning finger to a torn lip.

Mark heard a rustling above them and crouched down beside his friend just as Ebbie exploded down the slope.

"Jesus, it's just your damn dog!"

Ebbie couldn't get to her feet in the cane. Wallowing and clawing, she whined and thrashed in a panic. But the boys, their feet painfully wedged between the stalks with every step, came to her aid.

As they labored out of the living trap, they heard Billy screaming, his voice filling the woods first to their right and then left, calling their names as he ran. Mark started to answer, but Joel stopped him, clapping a hand over his mouth.

"He'll be okay, Mark. What the hell would they want with a little shit like him, anyway? He'll probably get home before we do."

14

As the two boys trudged onward, the sun sank to the horizon and the forest gloom thickened. Joel's feet were leaden, muscles sore and armpits and thighs chafed from endless walking through the heat in the nearly impenetrable forest. He was hungry in a way he had rarely experienced. The thought of crawling into bed eclipsed his senses and, one foot after the other, he moved mechanically forward.

Mark tripped and fell into Joel's path, nearly knocking him down.

"Watch where you're going, *dumbass,*" Joel said, dancing out of the way.

"You're the dumbass! I thought you *never* got lost."

Joel threw a fist into Mark's stomach. He doubled over, gasping, and then charged Joel, trying to ram him in the gut with his head. Joel grabbed him by the shoulders and threw him into a snarl of undergrowth and then pinned him, his knee pressing painfully against Mark's neck. Ebbie barked and danced from foot to foot, perhaps wanting in on the game.

"Screw you!" Mark hissed up at Joel, thrashing out weakly.

Joel held him until they had both cooled down. They breathed each other's air for a moment, unable to do more than glare.

"You smell that?" Joel asked.

"What—did you poot?"

"No, it's smoke."

"Yeah, I smell it," Mark said, looking away.

Joel helped him to his feet.

They followed the smell and it led them to a place where the trees were all dead. Joel pointed out the thin ring cut in the bark around each one.

The crickets were coming out, and, off in the distance, bullfrogs were croaking—the sounds of an ordinary summer evening blending with those of the cicadas.

Now they could see the smoke rising into the darkening sky. Ebbie pranced out into the tilled patch of ground that lay before them. As they moved out of the trees and walked around the field, a cabin came into view.

The small building was of rough-hewn logs and chinked with hairy clay. Small and windowless, it had a roof of oak shakes. The whole thing leaned to one side, and looked as if a high wind could take it down.

The deepening blue of the sky had brought with it a slight chill. The warm smell of the fire and the orange glow coming from under the door gave them hope and they quickened their steps.

"Telephone," Mark said, hugging himself more to ward off his fear than from the chill. "Go knock on their door, Joel."

"What, are you *scared?*"

"No, it's just that you talk to people easier than I do."

Joel approached the cabin. "Look at this weird door, it ain't got no knob."

"Name ye'selves!" the door seemed to bellow in a deep male voice.

The boys started and took a step back. Ebbie began to bark.

"I'm Joel Biggs, and my friend here is Mark Ryder."

"Call off ye dog!"

"We just need your phone to call my Mom," Joel said, while Mark hushed Ebbie.

The door remained silent for a moment and then the boys

could hear a female voice scolding. Finally the door opened and they were greeted by the barrel of a rifle. Behind it was a bear of a man and a scrawny young woman with two youngsters of indeterminate sex hanging onto her skirts. Ebbie growled.

"Royce, i's jes sum childerns," the woman said. "No need ta waste shot on 'em. They ain' goin' ta hurt n'body."

Grudgingly, the man lowered his gun. "Ye childerns c'mon in quick, 'fore ye let in the night."

Joel and Mark pushed through the thin crack that was all the man seemed willing to afford them. He held Ebbie back with one scabrous boot, and shut the door in her face.

It was dark inside except for the orange firelight and a couple of yellow candle flames. It took their eyes time to adjust. The air was close and hot and filled with the smells of rancid sweat, excrement, and the pissy odor of burning elm. A thick blanket of smoke hung in the air. It burned their eyes and made them cough. A steaming pot hung over the fire and another was half-buried in glowing coals. From beneath a soiled quilt in one corner came the soft squealing of a piglet.

"Where ye boys from?" the man asked.

"Um," Joel began, nervously, "east of here, I think."

The man nodded as if this explained everything. He sat down at a puncheon table and looked squarely at the boys.

"Ye should know better than ta be runnin' 'round out there at this hour. There's things in the night as might git ye—like the Mingit Toad."

Mark and Joel looked at each other with expressions that said, "What the hell?"

"The Mingit Toad is a *giant* toad, easily as big as you, or even me, and it'll steal yer soul if'n ye look 'im in the eye. An' don' think ye kin git a looksee, an' jes look away quick-like. Nossir—even Injuns ain't that quick. He's been known to lasso small childerns wit' 'is long, black tongue, reel 'em in, an' swaller 'em down."

He made a long, drawn-out slurping sound. Joel could feel the sticky, slimy tongue wrapping around his stomach and yanking on him. The thought of it gave him a cold chill.

"Ol' wiley Toad, he'll git ye every time. Sneak up on ye an' jump out at ye when ye least 'spect, an' bang!" He slapped his hand loudly against the table, making the boys jump. "An' jes like that, yer *his!*"

The man looked to his children. "Ain't that right, Junior? An' Nettie, ye know all 'bout the Mingit Toad, don' ye?"

"Tha's right, Papa," the children said obediently.

The children were roughly Mark and Joel's age, but decidedly less healthy—skin mottled with red sores, hair patchy and stomachs distended from hunger. Getting a good look at Mark and Joel, they turned to each other and giggled, then moved to sit next to their father.

Joel felt the uneasiness he always experienced around the sick or crippled. This whole family seemed ill, not right somehow, and he wanted to leave.

"Ye boys 'ungry?" the woman asked, gesturing for them to sit at the table.

"Set ye'selves down," the man said.

Mark would not meet the man's gaze and kept giving Joel sidelong glances.

"Before we eat could we use your telephone, please?" Joel asked, using his best manners.

"Jes hesh up an' set down," the woman commanded, "while grace is said."

The boys cautiously took their seats as the man began a low-pitched rumbling prayer. "Our God in Heaven, thank'ee for these 'ere eats, though it ain't much, an' will taste like a dog's mangy backside."

The woman slapped his face and he gave her a long, hard look before resuming his prayer in a different tone.

"God, as I was sayin', thank'ee. We's poor an' pitiful wretches like ye'd like us ta be an' all, an' since we's made in yer image, we're sufferin' humbly, jes like yer son, Jesus did. An' I'm thankin' ye fer it an' a fearin' ye fer it, jes like my good wife Mary tells me to, so's ta set a good example fer the childerns.

"Oh, an' if ye'd be s' kind, please protect us from the deadly rogues that 'ave plagued these parts here 'bouts, an' give us good crops. Amen."

Joel tried not to be obvious as he turned to Mark with a questioning look.

"Holy rollers," Mark whispered, "my dad's always goin' on about them."

A plate of greens and burned cornbread was set before each of the boys. Mark toyed with the greens and with a grimace, looked helplessly to his friend.

Joel smiled weakly and put a wooden spoonful of greens in his mouth. He frowned and quickly swallowed the sour, slimy mass.

Mark decided to try the cornbread instead. His first cautious bite scraped the roof of his mouth and cut into his gums and he tried to chew the coarse, bitter stuff more lightly. Unable to swallow the dry gravel, he finally coughed it into the darkness, out of desperation.

"If ye boys ain't 'ungry," said the woman, "leave that food for them that is."

Uneasily, Joel and Mark thanked her and excused themselves from the table. They retreated to the fire.

After several minutes, Mark whispered, "Ask about the telephone."

"Can't you see these people ain't got *nothin'*? If they got no electricity, they sure as hell got no phone."

Junior farted out loud and Mark was suddenly aware of all the noise coming from the family. They smacked, sucked and slurped their food and drink. The woman belched loudly. The man flew into a very liquid coughing fit, and she thumped him on the back a few times until he stopped.

"Yeah, isn't that weird?" Mark had the creepy feeling he used to get watching old *Twilight Zone* reruns.

"Maybe they're Amish," Joel said. "We must have wandered a long way from town. There aren't any people this poor anywhere close to home."

"Maybe you should ask that man to drive us home."

"Retard."

Ebbie's barking startled Mark, and then he heard the sounds of a dogfight. The man caught him halfway to the door.

"Leave it shut," he commanded.

"But my dog—"

The man backhanded him across the face. "Ye' should know better than that, boy. Ye know wha's out there, this hour. I don' know 'bout where yew come from, but 'round 'ere we respect the night."

Ebbie yelped in pain.

Mark, his white face beginning to redden, was working himself up to lash back when Joel stepped in. "Shut up, fool!" he whispered.

Hearing a final yelp that receded into the distance, Mark could only imagine his dog with her throat torn out. Joel tried to smile and punched him affectionately on the shoulder.

The family got up from their meal, the woman and children clearing the table, the man filling and lighting his pipe. His smoke reeked like burning sweat socks. He flew into another coughing fit, spewing phlegm across the room.

"Ye boys better fix ye'selves a pallet with some hay and git ta sleep," he said around the stem of his pipe. "Ye got a long day ahead a ye t'morrow. Ye owe a good day's work for that meal and there's a field out there still needs clearin'."

Mark saw his own shock in the expression on Joel's face. The boys huddled near the fire, trying to draw comfort from one another's presence, and watched the family prepare for bed. The children disappeared beneath the quilt in the corner and the piglet squealed softly. When the adults climbed a crude ladder to their loft, Joel whispered, "Let's go."

Mark was quick on his heels. They fumbled with the door's latch, got it open and dashed out into the night. Utter darkness swallowed them whole. As they stumbled toward the trees, Mark could hear the man shouting after them. Then the cabin door slammed shut and they were alone with the night.

Mark ran blindly, shouting his dog's name until something grabbed him in the dark. He spilled painfully to the ground, skinning his knee. Joel caught up at last, telling him to shut up.

They slowed to avoid vines, low-lying limbs and exposed roots, but stumbled on, the forest's night voices coming at them from every direction out of the blackness.

Mark reached out to grab Joel, who for once didn't shove him away.

"There's no sense us wandering around out here in the dark," Joel said. "I can't see my hand in front of my face."

"We *gotta* find Ebbie!"

"Look, we're just gonna hurt ourselves. Let's settle down somewhere and go to sleep. We'll find her in the morning."

Mark allowed himself to be led to an open spot next to a large tree and they huddled together, their backs up against the trunk.

"What about Billy?" Mark asked.

Joel had no answer, but he lay awake for some time, surprised to find himself wondering what had become of the younger boy.

Soon Mark began to snore next to him and it wasn't long before he was asleep as well.

15

Without disturbing their sleep, a wounded animal crept up on the boys and curled into a ball at Mark's feet. Breathing in the scent of her master, Ebbie took comfort, and managed to leave her pain behind for a while and rest.

16

Billy ran along an animal path until he collapsed, gulping breath while resting against the bole of a tree. His vision was just swimming back into focus when brown arms reached down and lifted him. He gazed helplessly into a deeply tanned face with high cheekbones and angular features. Billy wanted to know if he should be afraid, but the impenetrable, slanted eyes gave away nothing. The man wore a hat made of sticks, and where his hair had not been plucked out, it was long, straight, and black.

Out of the corner of his eye, Billy caught sight of another. This man was smaller and completely bald. He shouted something Billy couldn't understand, and the one holding him replied with softer words. Billy found the gentle voice soothing.

He was placed on his feet and given stale water from a stinking skin. Although he grimaced at the taste, he drank gratefully. The one in the stick hat offered him a piece of what looked like smoked leather. He was so hungry, he nearly inhaled the tough meat and it caught in his throat and he began to choke. The bald man thumped on his back and when Billy didn't cough it up readily, he reached into the boy's mouth with bitter fingers and pulled the meat from his gullet.

The dark men moved off into the trees and the boy, coughing, staggered after them over the broken, rooty ground. Before long, he began to fall behind. As his strange guides faded silently into the woods, already so far away he thought they might not hear him if he screamed, a soft, sucking sound filled his ears. The drain. Out of the darkness of the forest, it winked at him. "No," Billy whispered. The trees began to whirl and the forest voices grew louder and louder, screaming as everything rushed around him and through the drain at his feet.

He teetered on the lip of the drain and it began to pull him down, vertigo spilling him to the ground. Desperate sobs welled within like black, roiling clouds, a storm breaking. With his first tears, the downpour threatened to drown him.

Then he was being lifted by the one in the stick hat. He set Billy on his strong, wiry back, with the slightest of smiles. Billy clung to him like a baby monkey. With his cheek pressed to the soft, sour-smelling leather of Stick Hat's shirt, Billy closed his eyes. The drain began to fade.

17

Joel opened his eyes and blinked at the bright morning. The sun was suddenly eclipsed by Mark's grinning face. "Ebbie's back! She's all cut up, but none of 'ems deep except this one." He took his hand from her flank and it came away red.

"She's tough, Mark," Joel said, yawning. "She'll be all right."

"Yeah, she'll be all right if she can take it easy for a while. Hey, you wanna see something scary? See those big rocks? I was over there taking a pee and there's this big hole in the ground we could've fallen into while we were asleep. And if we'd kept walking. . . ." Mark shuddered.

Although the rocks were twenty feet away, Joel understood his friend's fear—Mark rolled in his sleep. Many were the mornings after they had camped out in his backyard, Joel would awaken to find Mark lying half atop him, or even out of the tent and under his father's car.

Joel stepped between the boulders and gazed into darkness. Smooth limestone walls dropped vertically for about a hundred feet to a dry bed scattered with round rocks, like a bushel of potatoes spilled across a kitchen floor. Moss and ferns clung to the walls like fur on the flank of some great green beast.

"A waterfall cut this," Joel said. "Now there's just a little, trickling spring."

"I bet it's good to drink."

Joel listened to the sound of the water striking the rocks below. "But, dammit, it's comin' outta the wall way down there.

Seems like everything I *really* want's like that—just out of reach."

"Ebbie'll take us to water. All we gotta do is follow her."

"Yeah, but where the hell are we, Mark?"

"What do you mean? We're lost, aren't we? That's where we are."

Joel ignored his sarcasm. "That's not it. None of this, since yesterday, feels right. I can't put my finger on it, but . . . do you *kinda* know what I mean?"

"I thought you said we were just west of town."

"No, dweeb. I'm talking about things like . . . well, we haven't run across any roads or power lines. I haven't heard a single car or airplane since we got lost, and I've kept my eyes and ears open. The only thing that's right is we can still hear those damn cicadas."

Mark seemed confused, a look of uneasiness on his face.

"I can't remember ever in my life looking up and not seeing at least *one* contrail, but look at the sky."

Mark looked up, but before he could respond, a single gunshot rang out, silencing the forest. They froze and scanned the trees.

"That came from over to the left!" Joel said.

Ebbie barked and Mark grabbed her by the collar.

"Prob'ly hunters—what do you think?"

"Maybe we're not lost, after all."

"You think we can get 'em to take us home?"

"Maybe, but we need to be careful—you hear all the time about people gettin' killed by hunters."

Ebbie got away from Mark and took off in the direction of the gunshot. The boys followed, climbing downhill toward a stream that wound around a small ridge. Easing out of the trees, they walked onto a gravel bar that jutted into the water.

Ebbie sniffed her way to the water's edge and began licking something. Joel saw a grease-stained hat resting on the gravel.

"Weird," he said, nudging it with his foot.

To his right a trail of blood led away into shadow. His mouth filled with the ozone taste of fear. Unconcerned, the dog pursued the blood trail behind a fallen tree, and, almost against his will, Joel's eyes followed her.

"Holy shit!" he cried out.

"Oh, *man.*" Mark coughed and turned away to vomit.

Lying at the edge of the gravel bar, his head half-submerged, was the half-naked body of a young man. He'd been gutted like a fish, his viscera draped over a branch of the fallen tree. The gaping hole in his body had been partially filled with smooth river stones.

Mark bolted for the trees, his dog quick on his heels. Joel took another look to freeze the image in his brain before chasing after his friend.

18

Joel started, blinked the image of the savaged corpse out of his mind's eye. He had been waiting in the station for over an hour. His goddam bus was late. The sign above him read, "Terminal Waiting Room." Joel stared at it sourly for a moment. He slouched down in his seat, feeling what the sign suggested to him—that he was just waiting here to die. His stomach started a slow, sickening turn and he closed his eyes against the wave of nausea.

Why the hell had he agreed to go see Moss in the first place? It would have been so much easier to stay home with a bottle and drink away the day.

But that was the long, slow death.

At least with Moss and his family he wouldn't have to own up to anything—they already knew. If Joel could face their knowing eyes, his annihilation would be over quickly, and maybe, just maybe, he could make a fresh start.

Trying to throw off his shakes, Joel squirmed in the cramped fiberglass seat and avoided looking at the others in the terminal. He gripped the arms of the chair, his fingers curling around to the underside where years of abandoned and hardened bubble gum lurked in the darkness. *Fuck. Dee-sgusting, man.* He snatched his hands away and wiped them on his trousers.

The fluorescent bulb directly overhead began to flicker and buzz annoyingly, and he got up and walked across the terminal. He sat heavily in an empty seat and immediately regretted his choice as he caught a whiff of vomit and urine coming from the restroom a scant three feet away. People came and went intermittently through the single grime-streaked glass door that let out to the street. After a time, he began to suspect he was seeing the same people over and over.

Joel watched a grizzled old man hobble through the door and outside. The man was stooped within five or six coats, the outermost a brown corduroy, and looked ridiculous and horribly uncomfortable. Even so, Joel wished the two of them could trade places.

He's probably headed for his favorite spot under the railroad trestle two blocks away where he'll down a fifth of Wild Irish Rose.

The high sounded nice, but suddenly the thought of the sickly sweet, fortified wine turned his stomach and he resigned himself to the dry stint at Moss's. When finally he heard the boarding call for his bus, he had at last become numb to the passage of time.

He wearily got to his feet, grabbed his bag, and followed the others through the doors to the outside where his bus idled on the hot concrete. A fat, sweaty bus driver took Joel's ticket. The man's eyes flicked up to meet Joel's.

"Ya doin' all right, buddy?"

"No," Joel said, "not too good, not too good at all. But don't worry, I won't get sick."

The bus driver's lip twitched in disgust. "If you think you're going to, there's a toilet in the rear."

Joel climbed aboard and hurried to the back, wanting to stretch out on the bench-like rear seats. The interior was dingy and worn, carrying the stink of countless passengers. Joel collapsed onto the seats and spread out. He had no intention of sharing. Joel was impatient for the bus to start moving because he knew the vibration would keep him from having to feel his own shakes. He closed his eyes and listened to the rumble of the engine as one sorry loser after another came onto the bus and found a seat. At last, the bus pulled away from the terminal.

As they bounced along the potholed road, Joel watched an old black man two seats away pull a paper bag from his jacket pocket and take a long swig from the bottle it concealed. *Goddam, but this is gonna kill me,* he thought, dreading having to watch the old man drink all the way to Hewitt.

He looked away, to the other side of the aisle, and his eyes came to rest on a greasy old white farmer. The man lifted an empty Pepsi bottle and spat a stream of brown tobacco juice into it. A strand of saliva bridged the space between the bottle's rim and his mouth until he wiped it away. Fighting the urge to puke for distance, Joel sat up and searched in his bag for the book Billy had given him and began to read.

> And indeed, late in the evening, Matthew Crenshaw and the outlaw came to the home of a man named Harris which, though surrounded by wilderness, was most opulent. There they feasted with Mr. Harris on rare and wonderful foods, and were provided with feather beds in which to sleep. Crenshaw thought that if Mr. Harris was typical of the caliber of Cotten's friends, the outlaw certainly had powerful allies and was perhaps the most dangerous criminal alive.
>
> In the morning, Cotten got them started early. Mr. Harris provided them with fresh horses, and the outlaw gave instructions as to the disposition of their previous mounts.
>
> "But my horse. . . ." Crenshaw queried.
>
> "The horse you ride is now your own," Cotten said.
>
> "Oh, it is much too fine."
>
> " 'Tis but a trifling indication of the bounty to come. We are striking due south now and, weather permitting, will

make the Ghost River by nightfall."

"What will we find at the Ghost River?" Crenshaw asked.

"Within that swamp lies the wilderness fortress of the Mystic Clan. That is where I instructed my confederates to take the stolen slaves."

Crenshaw could contain the question no longer. "Where did these slaves come from?"

"A farm in Adairville."

Now, although elated at the prospect of having located the slaves, Crenshaw feared the worst; worrying that as soon as the negroes saw him, they would give him away. He was concerned that Cotten might read this in his eyes, but couldn't think of anything to say to allay possible suspicion. The more he thought about it, the more impossible the situation seemed to become for him. His mouth became dry while his clothes were soaked through with sweat in spite of the cold. After a time this passed and Crenshaw became more comfortable.

The day became warmer and more pleasant for the men, though more taxing for the horses as the road was a mire. The slow pace at which they moved proved to be a vexation to the outlaw, and he became sullen and withdrawn as the day wore on.

Toward mid-morning, Cotten turned to Crenshaw and said, "It is plain that we will not reach the Ghost River tonight. I must insist on traveling all night."

Crenshaw was confused by this sudden turn of events, fearing that the outlaw was dissembling and intending to lead him into a deadly misadventure. With Cotten in such a dark mood, however, Crenshaw thought it imprudent to question him too much.

Cotten was hunkered down in his saddle, his hat pulled low over his brow. Crenshaw wished he knew what the outlaw was brooding over. Surely he had somehow tipped his hand, and even now his murderous traveling companion was looking for a way to dispose of him.

Finally, after several hours, the outlaw shared out some of his provisions, and they ate a midday meal while in the saddle, Cotten unwilling to lose any time stopping.

After a bit of nourishment, the outlaw was in a more congenial mood and spoke up. "Crenshaw, you must be curious as to how I knew to speak openly with you about speculation. Given a short time with a man and I find know him as one might know his own brother. This is how I knew that you and I are cut from the same bolt. I feel I could trust you with my life."

Crenshaw struggled to suppress a laugh.

"You need only a little practice. I will instruct you in penetrating the thoughts and souls of others. You start by watching an acquaintance's reaction as you tell of villainous exploits. If he warms to you, you press on. Otherwise, you retreat and choose another subject."

Throughout the afternoon, Cotten boasted of the Fraternity's deeds, divulging names, dates, and the sites of their criminal exploits. As the outlaw took the lead, it was an easy matter for Crenshaw to record these particulars in a journal he had secreted in the inner pocket of his greatcoat. He sharpened his pencil many times with his jack knife and wrote as small as possible, anticipating a lengthy record.

Joel closed the book and put it down. His eyes ached from the bright, flickering daylight streaming in through the windows of the bus. Stretching out across the seats, he closed his eyes and was asleep almost immediately.

19

Chasing after Mark, Joel heard his friend's headlong crash through the forest end abruptly. *Oh, Christ. Maybe he fell into another bigass hole.*

"Mark," he called, panting, "are you okay?" Joel heard only Ebbie snarling and he pounded on, dodging whipping branches and grabbing vines.

The dog's angry bark broke up into whining yelps of pain. Joel's stomach went cold. *A bear?* He saw the dog's golden fur through the trees ahead of him. She appeared to be dead, lying in a bramble, blood oozing from the back of her head.

The man was waiting for him just beyond.

"Joel!" Mark shouted, white-faced. "They—"

The heavily muscled arm around Mark's neck tightened. He choked and wheezed.

Instinctively, Joel masked his fear, leveling an expressionless gaze. The man gave him a wide, meaty, almost silly grin.

He sees right through me.

Joel sensed he would never meet a more dangerous man. In the first place, the guy was huge. Well over six feet tall and built like a goddam pro wrestler. Legs like oak trees, thick muscles bulging through stained buckskins. The man's broad, barrel chest rose and fell evenly as he grinned down at Joel. His dark hair was wild and matted, fleshy, red face clean-shaven. His nose had obviously been broken a time or two. But it was the man's eyes that made Joel's heart sink. Small and black, their expression was utterly flat, like the eyes of a fish. *The eyes of a dead man.*

Joel's legs were beginning to shake and he locked his knees, spread his feet apart, and stuck his hands in his pockets in spite of the riot of worms in his gut.

From out of the trees slipped another, smaller man. Wiry and weasel-faced, his crazed expression stalked Joel from across the clearing. Dark eyes bulged wetly, lips skinned back from rotten teeth. His thinning, colorless hair stuck out in mangy clumps. *He looks like a fuckin' rabid dog.*

The men's belts bristled with a variety of antique knives and pistols. Their buckskins were filthy and sweat-stained. If they were costumes, they obviously lived in them. *Freaks—*

"My, my, my," the big one said, snickering and putting a knife to Mark's throat.

The boy's eyes went wide and his lips trembled, but no words would form. Even so, Joel could hear Mark's plea for help.

"Lookee what scrounged itself up fer us," the big man continued, "and just when we need 'em. *Git 'im,* Virg, 'fore he gets away!"

The small man lunged forward and Joel darted out of the way, slipping behind a tree.

"Hey, Wes, which one ye think's got the tenderest meat on his backside?" They danced back and forth around the tree—the man grabbing at him with the speed of a striking rattlesnake, Joel always managing to elude his grasp. Another lunge, and Joel managed to kick Virgil hard in the shin.

Virgil gibbered and howled. "Ye ain't gotta chance, boy—don't ye know who we are?"

"You're some crazy motherfuckers," Joel shouted, "that's what you are!"

"Little hellion," the man said, "we're the Pikes!" He turned his head in a cockeyed challenge.

Did he mean *the* Pikes? No, Joel told himself, there was no way they could be the notorious outlaws he had read about. He pushed it out of his mind. "Damn, you *are* crazy."

"Dammit, quit dancin' wit' him, Virg, an' jus' grab 'im! He ain't nothin' but a boy!"

Joel turned and ran into the brush. Cursing, Virgil thrashed in after him, but the boy scrambled up a tree.

"I'll git ye down from there, I *will!*" Virgil screamed, raising a pistol.

There was a flat crack when the gun went off, but the shot went wide, gouging bark from the trunk beside Joel's head in a woody spray. Adrenaline slammed through Joel's system, his already pounding heart kick-starting like a motorcycle. He leapt for a loop of stout vine, and swung into another tree.

"The mouse's got spirit," Wesley said, laughing.

Virgil started up after him, slipped and fell on his backside.

"Let 'im go, Virg, he ain't goin' nowhere—we got 'is friend."

"Run, Joel," Mark cried. "Get help!"

Wesley struck Mark to the ground, and he lay there, curled into a blubbering ball. Virgil hauled Mark to his feet and he and Wesley started pounding the boy. Mark screamed and sobbed, only becoming quiet when he slipped into unconsciousness.

Joel turned away.

20

Sitting in the lower branches of a sycamore, Joel kept an eye on Mark.

If I get him out of this, that sonuvabitch is gonna owe me. The stupid dumbass has gotten us in some real pretty shit.

Joel glared down at Mark, at his bruised and bloody face, and realized his tough-guy routine was going nowhere. Mark couldn't help what happened and he knew it.

It's just all that blubbering he did—why'd he have to act like such a baby?

That was *a rough beating he took, though, and I'm sure he's all tore up over Ebbie.*

Clinging to the branches, he shook his head to clear it and caught a tantalizing aroma on the breeze.

"Sure smells good, Wes," Virgil said, cocking an eye toward Joel's tree.

"Don' it though? I surely am hungry, how 'bout yew?"

Wesley laughed and looked toward the boy.

This sort of thing had been going on all day. Joel had followed the two men and his friend through the forest, trying to keep a safe distance without losing sight of them. Just about the time he would think Virgil had given up the chase, the man would dash back for him and Joel would scramble up the nearest tree. This became something of a game and, although Wesley pretended to be oblivious to it, he was obviously greatly amused.

Their trek had ended in this small clearing where a worn-out, filthy woman by the name of Myrtrice was busy preparing their evening meal while taking long pulls off a jug. She was missing an eye and her nose hooked almost to her upper lip. Joel thought he'd never seen anyone who looked so much like a fairy-tale witch.

The ropes the Pikes had used to drag Mark through the forest now held him hogtied and the boy hung limp, bruised and defeated, from the lowest branch of a towering maple.

Looks like one of my daddy's stupid, cocksucking deers, Joel thought.

"When's that little-boy stew gonna be ready, Myrtrice?" Virgil asked.

"Yew know good an' well that's venison," Myrtrice said drunkenly.

The two men laughed uproariously. She seemed to reluctantly catch on and began to cackle.

As the light was failing, Joel slipped higher into the sycamore and out of view. Under cover of darkness, and as silently as possible, he worked his way from tree to tree without ever touching the ground. He found a comfortable spot high in Mark's maple and waited for the trio below to fall asleep. Cold and desperately hungry, he listened to them as they talked and passed a jug back and forth.

"Ye know, little brother," Wesley said expansively, leaning back, "ye don' have ta guard my back like ye do. Why ye kin git right out front an' take a man-sized helpin' o' the fight."

"Goddam, big brother, somebody's sure as hell gotta look out fer ye. 'Cause when ye start a-shakin' with the pleasure o' the kill, like ye do, an' yer seed stains the front o' yer buckskins, somebody could easily sneak up behind ye an' slip a knife 'twixt yer ribs."

"Now, Virg, ye listen, an' ye listen *good*—I know ye count on me fer gettin' ye in an' outta scraps in one piece. An' we both know yer takin' away more'n jus' the spoils o' the fight. But, dammit, I gotta know yer gonna be there ta do yer part, an' not wastin' precious time sizin' 'em up 'fore ye do 'em in."

"Aw, stop runnin' yer mouth an' go bury yerself in Myrtrice's cunny."

"What?" asked Myrtrice, her runny eye brightening.

"Ye know I wouldn't poke my *baselgux* inta that filthy old hag."

"Oh," Myrtrice said, drowning her disappointment with more whiskey.

"Yeah I know that thing 'twixt yer legs don' git poked inta anythin'. All *yer* pokin' gits done with knives an' pistols."

"That's my business, little brother, an' yers is yers."

Joel's imagination began to patch the holes in their dialogue, and the awful meaning behind what they were saying began to come clear. Could they really be *the* Pikes? His mind far away, Joel lost his grip and fell, catching himself two branches down.

The brothers looked up when they heard the noise.

"That little bastard's quick, ain't he?" Wesley laughed, popping a cicada into his mouth and crunching down. "Been givin' ye trouble, hain't he, Virg?"

"Yeah, but jus' wait 'til I git my hands on 'im."

Wesley poked at the fire and watched a spray of sparks rush toward Joel's hiding place. The boy quickly pulled his head back behind the trunk and out of the sudden flare of light.

The smaller man pulled out a pipe and began to fill it from a pouch. Wesley took a pull off the jug and searched in a large wallet until he found his own pipe. Virgil passed him the tobacco and spoke so quietly to Wesley for a time that Joel couldn't hear him. Then he put down his pipe, got to his feet, and stretched. He turned to his brother with a grin.

"Hell, Wes, I think I'm gonna hafta take Myrtrice."

"*What?*" she said, showing a gap-toothed smile.

"If'n yer gonna do *that,*" Wesley said, handing over the jug, "ye better fortify yerself first. Ye may want to poke yer eyes out with yer dirk as well."

Virgil took a long pull, set down the jug, and pushing Myrtrice ahead of him, disappeared into the darkness.

Wesley finished his pipe before saying his prayers and crawling into his bedroll to go to sleep.

Joel waited until the big man's breathing deepened and, hoping the whirring of the cicadas would cover the sound of his movements, eased his way down until he was just above Mark. His friend's blackened eyes went wide with surprise and he tried to mutter something around his gag.

"Shut *up,*" Joel hissed, pulling out his pocketknife and beginning to cut the rope. "You want them to hear? Now, when you hit, just get up and run."

Joel cut through the last strand and Mark fell, landing hard. Shedding his bonds, Mark pulled off the gag and tried to get up.

"Run!" Joel shouted, dropping out of the tree beside his friend.

Mark massaged his ankles. "Can't," he said through swollen lips. "I don't feel nothin' but pins and needles in my feet."

Joel heard a loud click as the hammer of a pistol was cocked behind him.

"Don't ye move, boy," Virgil said, aiming his pistol at Joel's left eye, "or I'll blow a hole in ye so big yer head won't fit around it."

"Turn around, little mouse," Wesley commanded. "Take 'is knife, Virg. Myrtrice, git some rope, an' tie 'em knots tight—I'm gettin' tired of this game."

21

Joel woke to a chilly dawn, blanketed by fog. His joints ached from the long night spent tied up on the rough, cold ground. They had taken his knife, but seemed to have forgotten all about searching his pockets. He still had his lighter and was trying to work out how he might use it to help him escape.

Not far away, Myrtrice was hunched over the remains of last night's fire, stirring up the coals. "Oh my haid," she muttered periodically, finally picking up her whiskey and taking a slug. As she moved about, Mark's red tennis shoes flopped awkwardly on her feet, occasionally tripping her up.

The Pikes were just rousing themselves. Wesley yawned and stretched enormously, reaching out and striking Myrtrice on the behind. She stumbled and fell forward into the coals, letting out a sharp cry that echoed eerily about the small circle of trees. Ash and smoke billowed up around her and the Pikes chuckled sleepily.

"Get the coffee, woman," Virgil said, "an' make it strong enough ta bite back."

Myrtrice picked herself up, smacking at the fire in her skirts as she muttered angrily to herself. She tore away the smoldering hem from one of her petticoats and without a word to anyone went back to preparing their morning meal.

"Git them boys some o' that cold stew, woman," Wesley ordered. "Untie that towheaded one, Virg. He kin feed his friend."

"I'll untie 'is hands," said Virgil, "but 'is legs gotta stay tied—the boy's too quick."

Joel was given a wooden spoon and a bowlful of gluey stew. He took a couple of greedy spoonfuls and while chewing, spooned fatty, gray lumps of meat into Mark's eager mouth. He winced as the rough spoon slid over his friend's split lip. After a couple of mouthfuls, Mark refused any more. Joel wolfed down the rest, making himself sick to his stomach. He breathed in deeply and bit his lips, refusing to throw up.

"I have to go to the bathroom," Mark whined.

"Virgil," Wesley commanded sleepily, "git over there an' smack that boy."

Joel chuckled in spite of himself and this earned him a grin from Wesley. Virgil automatically stepped over to deliver the blow.

"But, but—please, sir," Mark said in a timid voice, "I really have to go."

Virgil looked at him blankly, raised his fist.

"You know, urinate?"

"Watch what ye be callin' me, boy." Virgil caught Mark on the chin with a right hook that knocked him senseless.

Joel quashed his outrage and revulsion and forced himself to burst out laughing to see what that might earn him.

"Whaddaya laughin' at?" Virgil asked.

"Leave 'im be, little brother. The mouse's got spirit."

The big man looked appraisingly at Joel, as if seeing him for the first time. In Wesley's expression, the boy saw his opportunity.

It didn't take long for Joel to convince Wesley to untie his legs, and not much longer to convince him to give back his "womanish" knife.

"You might as well untie my friend too. He ain't goin' nowhere."

Wesley looked at him with suspicion in his eyes.

"Don' do it, Wes," Virgil said. "I ain't much in the mind ta go runnin' after 'im."

"Look, Mark's already pissed himself, and he's too scared to do anything on his own, just like Virgil."

"I'll teach ye who's who!" Virgil yelled, launching himself at Joel.

The boy braced himself to take the attack head on, but Wesley threw out an arm to catch his brother.

"Hold up there, Virg."

"Ye heard what he said!" Virgil shouted, struggling against the massive arm. "He cain't—"

"I said *hold!*" Wesley struck him to the ground. "I like the boy."

He turned to Joel and slapped him upside the head. The boy reeled, but kept his feet.

"Yer clever, an' there's somethin' ta be said fer that, boy, but that don' mean ye kin git away wit' bein' disrespectful."

Joel's natural tendency was to meet the man's gaze, but he forced himself to swallow his anger and look at the ground.

Virgil got to his feet and turned toward Joel with the eyes of a lion under the whip.

They spent the next two days waiting in the clearing. *But for what?* Joel wondered. He questioned Wesley, but the man refused to say anything.

He had been allowed to untie Mark, who now sat on his own, away from the others, unwilling to meet Joel's eyes. When he spoke to him, Mark wouldn't respond.

He's just pissed at me for laughing when Virgil punched his lights out. That's what Joel told himself, anyway. But he was starting to get scared. When he looked in Mark's eyes, there was nobody home.

And Joel had other things to worry about. Initially, he expected Virgil to beat the almighty hell out of him at the first opportunity, but it hadn't happened yet—Wesley made sure of that. And now, although the small man's resentment seemed to have simmered down low, the boy kept a wary eye on him. *He still looks like a rabid dog to me.*

Late on the second day, a big-boned, raw-looking fellow with red hair and a hawkish nose entered the clearing and hailed the Pikes. As he approached, Joel could see his face was seamed and weather-beaten, his long, wiry hair tied down beneath a bandanna. He eyed the boys curiously before speaking.

"What 'bout it, Wade," Wesley said to him.

"Flatboat's on its way," said the man, leaning on his long rifle. "Should be 'ere t'morrow."

The three men huddled together, talking excitedly for a time. When Joel tried to get close enough to listen in, Virgil chased him off, threatening to bash in his head. From what he managed to overhear, Joel gathered that a woman would be joining them the next day. They would break camp and by midday arrive at the river.

"I'll be back wit' Sarah Jayne an' clothes fer the boys at first light," Wade called out as he left the clearing.

Watching the two brothers as they whispered by the fire, Joel felt left out. Sitting with Mark and Myrtrice, his mind whirled with ambivalence; he wanted to prove himself, to be a part of the action, to know what the new day would bring; he also wanted to escape, to take his friend and go home. He hoped he was strong enough to face whatever was coming.

22

"What the hell are we waiting for?" Joel grumbled for the fifth time in an hour.

Mark ignored him. He was busy taking in their surroundings. They were waiting on the bank of the Mississippi with the attractive, redheaded woman, Sarah Jayne. *Is she a friend of my mom's?* A layered haze rose from the river, obscuring Mark's vision with a blur of morning mist and flying insects. With the writhing, golden sunlight, the mounting heat promised another miserable day ahead.

"Hey, Mark," Joel whispered, "you know who these guys *are?*"

Mark wondered who Joel was talking about. The only person with them was the woman. He kept on staring at the river.

"The guys who caught us, I mean. Remember me telling you about the great outlaws of the Mississippi and Ohio—the river pirates of the early 1800s?"

Mark nodded. He wanted to respond, but his jaw hurt too much every time he tried to open it. He hoped Joel didn't think he was angry with him.

"Well, that's who these guys are! I mean, the Pikes are really *the* Pikes!"

Mark looked blankly at him and turned away. What Joel was saying didn't make any sense. Best not to think about it.

In the distance, a heavily laden flatboat moved sluggishly toward them on the glassy-smooth, brown surface of the river.

Trees leaned drunkenly from the banks, their limbs dipping down as if straining to pluck the boat from the water.

A black cloud of flies hovered above the cargo, which was piled as high as the boat's small cabin and secured beneath rough canvas. Mark could see four men on board. Two wiry men trailed long poles in the water, one smoking a pipe, the other turning his head to spit a long stream into the water. A husky, bearded fellow leaned against the long stem of a rudder, and, in the bow, a dark man was perched, a rifle across his lap. The boat scene was somehow familiar. Mark seemed to remember an old live-action Disney movie about flatboats. *What was the name of it?* Rat Fink*? Something like that.* He smiled a little. It wasn't until the boat had drawn close enough for Mark to see smoke rising from the lookout's cigar that Sarah Jayne began to call for help.

"Please, if'n ye be God-fearin' men, stop fer us," she shouted across the water, "or surely we shall perish!"

All four heads turned in their direction. The lookout stepped into the cabin, emerging a moment later with another man who bore a spyglass. He studied Sarah Jayne and the boys through it for a while before speaking to the man at the rudder.

"Me an' my boys been left ta the devil, by the devil hisself!" she called out as the boat angled in their direction. "My rogue of a husband took up wit' one o' them slatternly Injun squaws an' left us here ta die!"

"We'd be glad ta help, ma'am," the man returned, "but our provisions wouldn't take us all very far."

"We jus' need a ride a short stretch. Payton's Fort's jus' downriver, an' I got people there."

"Hey, Mark," Joel whispered, "isn't Payton's Fort where we used to go bowling?"

Mark shrugged his shoulders. He didn't feel like bowling.

The boat had drawn close enough for Mark to see the man's

doubtful expression. He wanted to warn them off, but he wasn't exactly sure why. He only knew that he and Joel had become part of something dark, probably deadly, and were only participating out of fear. Their only instructions had been to keep their mouths shut and to follow the woman's lead, *or else.* Mark raised his hand to his face, but didn't touch it. He couldn't bear the thought of another beating.

"All right," the man called out, "we'll take ye that far—cain't leave ye here, wouldn't be Christian. But I have ta warn ye, ma'am, an' meanin' no offense, my boys here ain't had the comp'ny of a woman in a long while. I'd hate ta swear by their manners."

"Thank'ee fer the warnin', but there's nothin' fer it."

Using their poles, the men brought the boat to a stop and held it offshore a few feet. Following Sarah Jayne, Mark and Joel waded out into the river. Once they had been lifted aboard, the men pushed off and poled the craft back out into the current.

"I'm Lester Posey," the man said, collapsing his spyglass and offering his hand to Sarah Jayne. "This is my crew."

"We are so very glad ta meet y'all. I'm Sarah Jayne Plunkett an' these are my boys, Mark an' Joel. We are eternally grateful ta ye fer saving us from this terrible wilderness. Ye cain't imagine what a trial we've had this day an' a half, past."

"Sorry ta hear o' yer suffering, ma'am," Posey said, affecting a deeper tone and an elegant stance, "an' my apologies in advance fer yer discomfort while on board this miserable vessel. I wish we had better accommodations fer ye. Please make yerself comfortable in the cabin, if'n ye like."

The boys were sitting on the edge of the log deck, dangling their feet in the water.

"Yew boys git yerselves up from there an' stay outta the way," Posey said. "Sit down on them grain sacks an' keep still." He gave Mark a sharp look. “Yer daddy do that to yer face, boy?”

“He did,” Sarah Jayne said quickly. “The boy called him a scoundrel for treatin’ me so poorly, and my husband beat him within an inch of ’is life.”

“Poor lad,” muttered Posey.

“He’s my little man.” Sarah Jayne gave him a big, fake smile.

They must be talking about Joel, Mark thought. *My dad doesn’t beat me.* He shuffled over to the grain sacks, plopped himself down near the edge, and gazed at the water. He kicked off the crude leather shoes he had been given to wear and they fell in the river. Sarah Jayne bent down and slapped him across the face. Pain flared like a firecracker, turning his vision red. Sarah Jayne fished the shoes out before they drifted away.

“They killed my dog,” Mark said quietly. He turned and watched the wriggling shapes of the distant hills and trees reflected in the rippling water.

“Half-wit,” Sarah Jayne hissed in his ear.

I don’t know where I am, Mark told himself, *but the water ripples here just the same as it does at home.*

He was beginning to understand what Joel had been trying to tell him three days ago. It was simple, really. He and his best friend—his only friend—had wandered down The New Cut and into another world. His mind shied away from the thought like a skittering mouse in the sudden beam of a flashlight. Again, he found himself drifting away. Unable to take it all in, he could only grasp the minute details of the new world around him; the rocks along the bank, the colors of the tiny insect that presently lit on his arm, the shapes reflected in the rippling water. He turned to watch Joel, who was introducing himself to the man at the rudder.

“Name’s Hank,” the man returned with a nod.

“So, whereabouts on the river are we?” Joel asked.

“Don’t rightly know. We’re gettin’ pretty close ta Tennessee, if'n we ain't there already."

"How long you been runnin' this stretch?"

"Oh, I been on this river off and on, my whole life, I reckon."

"You ever been down to Natchez or New Orleans?"

"Yeah," he said, laughing roughly, "but I cain't say as I recollect a whole lot 'bout it. I do seem ta recall there was this girl—if'n ye could rightly call her that—I knowed down at Natchez-Under-the-Hill. But I was pretty drunk then too." He turned his head and spat a brown, stringy stream into the river.

Joel made his way forward and began talking with another crewman. They were too far away for Mark to hear their conversation clearly, but the drone of their voices, combined with the warm sunlight and gentle rocking, put him to sleep.

Mark's brothers were fighting again. Tab pulled Bob's right arm out of its socket and broke the bone in his left thigh.

"That's a foul, young man!" Mark's father bellowed at Tab. But he wasn't listening.

"Daddy?" Mark called out. "I need to ask your permission."

Bob grabbed Tab with his remaining arm and yanked his head clean off. He stepped back for the kick.

Mark tugged at his father's sleeve.

"That's an illegal move," Daddy shrieked. "Dammit, Bob, it's not time yet!"

But Bob just grinned and let it fly, Tab's surprised expression disappearing out the window and into the hedge.

"I warned you," Daddy said. "You're grounded—fifteen years in your room, buddy boy."

"Daddy!" Mark cried. "Listen to me!"

"Hush, Mark. Be a good boy and fetch your brother's head."

"I need to—" he began, but his father stomped off to prop up Tab's headless body on the couch.

Mark turned toward the slobbering, sucking sound in the

next room. Mama was stooped over the bassinet, feeding his baby sister again—she was *always* feeding the baby.

"Mama," Mark said, "I need—"

She turned her face to him. "Can't you see I'm feeding the baby?"

He could see that her arm was halfway down the infant's throat. Her forearm was purple and red from the sucking of his sister's massive, greasy lips. Mama turned back to the baby.

"But, Mama, I—"

"I really don't have time for this right now!" she said, whirling around and jerking her bloody stump out of the baby's mouth with a pop. She wagged the ragged stump in his face. "Go ask your father."

Mark returned to the other room. "Daddy, Mama said to ask you—"

"Come on, Tab, wake up now," Daddy said, gingerly shaking the corpse.

Mark saw that his brother's head had been reattached with duct tape.

"Mama said I should. . . ." Mark eyed the dark fluid leaking from between strips of the tape. "I mean, I just wanted you to—"

His father wheeled around to face him. *"What?"* His voice echoed and boomed like thunder, lightning crackling about his lips.

Suddenly, Mark couldn't remember what he was going to say. He knew there was *something,* but couldn't remember actually ever having thought it.

Daddy's questioning eyes bored into his as if to say, "If you can't think of anything worthwhile to say, keep your goddam brain *shut!*"

Mark felt his father's anger squeezing the breath from him. Trying to think up something—anything—to say, sweat broke out on his brow and his heart fluttered. His father was red and turning purple. He gritted his teeth and his hands moved forward.

Mark took a breath and opened his mouth. "My shoes—"

"Sweaney's Inn!" called the lookout, waking Mark with a start.

He looked around for his tennis shoes before remembering Myrtrice was wearing them. Beside him, he found the shoes the Pikes had provided and put them on. The moccasins stank and were greasy inside, but they were better than nothing, he supposed.

Everything had changed. The only thing he recognized was the river. A bluff rose to his right. Willows and sycamores grew on both sides of the river and hung low, their roots partially exposed, foliage dipping down to touch the water's surface. Spotted turtles slid off nearby logs into the water with soft ploops.

The river was narrower here and just ahead he saw a cave cut into the exposed limestone of the bluff. Above the mouth hung a crudely lettered sign that read, "Sweaney's Inn."

"I think I've heard o' this place," Hank said. "They gots some pretty women. Ain't that right, Heath?"

Now that they were close enough, Mark could see what the sign offered: *trade goods, eats & likker.*

"Tha's what I hear," Heath said. " 'Sides, we could use some more meal an' I'm 'bout out o' powder."

"I don' know, Heath," replied Posey, "I-I jus' don' know."

Another flatboat piled high with cargo was tied to the nearly horizontal trunk of a willow growing at the lip of the cave. A bearded man wearing buckskins and with long hair spewing from beneath a beaver hat stood at the edge of the rock shelf and waved to them.

"Come on in, friends. We got everythin' ye could possibly

want. We got good Monongahela whiskey, female entertainment an' gamblin'. Ye'd be surprised at what all we trade fer. We got lead, good quality dry powder, an' even our own gunsmith. There's a blacksmith here, too, if'n ye have need o' one."

"Mister Posey," Sarah Jayne said, "me an' my boys kin git on from here if ye'd be so kind as ta put us off at the inn."

"I suppose, since someone else is here ahead of us," said Posey, pointing to the other flatboat. "Pole us on over, boys."

The men bent to their poles while Hank steered them toward the yawning cave mouth.

23

At first, any unexpected sound or movement frightened Billy. The confidence and ease with which the dark men interacted with the forest was contagious, however, and he soon relaxed.

The boy could not understand these strange men, their speech or their actions. They looked something like Indians, so he decided that's what they were. They seemed to be following *something* through the woods, although they were never willing to actually catch up with whatever it was. The word "stalking" came into his mind, but he wasn't sure that it meant what he thought it did, so he pushed it back out. All Billy knew was that he was about to burst from having to keep quiet.

He was sore from endless walking by day and nights lying on the hard, rough ground. They had spent the last three nights under a rocky overhang with only a meager fire for company.

The Indians didn't cook—everything they ate, mostly dried meat and coarse corn cakes, was cold. Billy remained hungry all the time and kept dreaming of his mother's cooking.

For the first time in his life, Billy was spending time away from home. Though it had been a long time since his mother had tucked him in or come to him when he called out in his sleep, each night he would awaken, disoriented and groggy, and cry for her. Then he would hear the whir of cicadas, the crackle of the fire, or the Indians stirring in their sleep, and he would realize he was not at home in his own bed.

At least he was not alone and, although he couldn't understand a word Stick Hat or Bald Man said, their presence kept the winking drain from his mind.

During the day, they moved silently through the forest on their mysterious errand. When they paused by a stream for a simple meal of jerky and water, Stick Hat demonstrated how to load a rifle and then had Billy try it until he got it right. The boy felt proud of the accomplishment, though frustrated that he was not allowed to shoot the rifle.

The afternoon of the third day, they came to a stony ridge with a clear view down one treeless, gravel slope. At the bottom, Billy could see a white tail deer and he said so, nearly shouting with excitement. The buck started, looking in his direction. Hissing angrily, Bald Man raised his rifle and sighted on the animal.

Billy grabbed for the gun as he realized what was about to happen. He was too late. In horror, he watched the gun go to work, the hammer striking a spark that produced a brilliant flash in the pan and a puff of blue smoke. Time stood still for a heartbeat before the hollow explosion inside the barrel sprayed sparks and smoke down-slope.

Billy cheered as the buck bounded away into the undergrowth. Bald Man pivoted, bringing the butt of the rifle around to strike the boy on the side of the head. Billy fell to the ground, dazed, as the man shouted angrily and spat. He raised the rifle to strike again, his face red and full of fury. Stick Hat grabbed his arm. Bald Man shook his companion off, barked something unintelligible, and stormed off into the trees.

The boy began to cry, homesick for his mother and even, strangely, for Teddy. He was confused, scared, his stomach was tied up in a knot, and his head hurt like hell. Although he wanted to trust Stick Hat, he could not read a man whose face seemed to show no feeling.

Stick Hat knelt beside him and roughly lifted him to his feet.

He slapped the boy—that was all—and Billy knew he'd really screwed up. He understood that this sort of thing would not be tolerated.

24

The deafening volley nearly took Posey's head off, his neck seeming to disappear in an explosion of red. His head dropped back like one of those carnival clowns you hit with a baseball, but he was still standing. Sarah Jayne drew a knife from her bodice, stepped forward and cut through the remaining ligaments. She pushed the stumbling body into the muddy river and, with a grin, dropped the head to the log deck.

Mark was unable to move, as if he were pinned to his grain sack. The ringing in his ears was replaced by a terrible din—the cave mouth vomited a cacophony of clashing steel and firing guns, as a small army of pirates assaulted the crew of the tiny flatboat.

Mark looked for his friend. Joel's face was frozen with a look of childish terror, and then he was plunging into the river, swimming for the rocky shore.

Virgil rushed onto the deck and grabbed Hank by his red beard. The wiry man thrust a pistol under Hank's chin, pulled the trigger and a roaring crimson flower of blood and tissue bloomed from the back of his head. Letting the dead man drop, Virgil turned to Mark, and licked his chops.

Mark turned away. The horror rising in him was huge, all-consuming, and he refused to feel it. He was afraid that if he did, he'd never feel anything else. The thick smell of gunpowder and death caught in his throat and made him gag.

He saw Sarah Jayne plant her knife in the middle of Heath's

back. A black man's broken sword bit deeply into the crewman's leg, nearly severing it. Wesley stepped in and split Heath's forehead with a stone tomahawk. As Sarah Jayne turned to Wesley with a smile, half her pretty face vanished in a haze of red. The big man pushed her dead body into the river.

Riddled with musket balls, a crewman spun drunkenly, dropped his Bowie knife and fell. He rolled onto his stomach and disgorged blood into the water.

Sitting in the middle of the action, Mark felt apart from it all, as if he were watching a violent television program. With a hollow thud, a musket ball plowed a smoking gash into the brown oak at his feet and, feeling curiously ignored, he turned to see where it had come from.

He saw the cutthroats crowding together on the cramped deck, lining up for a chance to cut down the last of the crewmen.

Wesley let out a deep, inhuman bellow, lifted Heath's dead body above his demonic, red face and threw it, knocking the remaining crewman overboard along with several of the pirates. The big man walked calmly to the edge of the roiling water, pulled one of his pistols, and shot the man through the neck. He threw his head back and Mark watched as intense satisfaction rattled his frame. A dark stain spread from the bulging crotch of his breeches. It took Mark a moment to understand what he had just seen. Then he swallowed hard, trying not to gag. Wesley adjusted his crotch and looked around.

"Git these bodies outta here," he said. "Clean off this deck an' 'em rocks 'fore they stain."

As Wesley scanned the bank and trees, the pirates set to work, clearing away the evidence of the fight and looting the cargo—grain sacks, a couple of bundles of furs, barrels, wooden crates, and several rifles.

"Joel?" The big man shouted. "Ye been shot? Ye dead somewheres, boy?”

As the silence stretched on, Mark looked around, wondering if he should worry about his friend. Suddenly, he began to quake violently and lost control of his bowels.

25

Crouched behind a lean-to of damp, mossy boulders near the cave entrance, Mark peered at the gathering of pirates within the cavern. The scene was eerily distant, a feeling very much like what he experienced when he had scarlet fever two years ago.

The room bellied out a hundred feet across and fifty feet high. Stalactites grew down in clusters from cracks in the ceiling, while the floor was scattered with the broken remains of stalagmites and other loose stone. Graffiti decorated the walls—names, dates and maybe a dirty limerick or two—and the ceiling was stained with soot from fires and torches.

Throughout the afternoon, Mark had tried to keep to himself. The pirates must have known where he was all along, but they didn't seem to care. They probably weren't thinking about him at all. They were drunk with liquor and victory and bloodshed. *There was nothing like that in the Disney movie, that's for damn sure.* He closed his eyes against the red-spattered memories.

Mark was getting cold and bored. He could stand to sit by the fire, or maybe even watch some TV. But he wasn't sure it would be allowed, and he didn't want anyone else to hit him, so he just listened to the pirates talk.

"Here's to Sarah Jayne!" A tall, lanky man with tangled brown hair held up a sloshing mug. "She were a fine, brave woman."

Pirates murmured their assent.

"An' she had the finest little cunny in Tennessee!" a small, ratty fellow hollered.

"As if ye ever got within arm's length of it, Zeke!" someone shouted. Laughter rippled through the cave.

"An' Oliphaunt! Don' fergit him!" called a voice from the back of the chamber. There was a weak response from the outlaws. Evidently, Oliphaunt hadn't been as popular as pretty Sarah Jayne.

"If Oliphaunt hadn't been so damn drunk, he wouldn't've drownded," Wade said loudly. He showed a big smile in the firelight. There were a few murmurs and nods of agreement.

Mark could see that Wesley was becoming irritated by the talk. The big man glared angrily into the fire.

"If Wes wasn't s' *damn* reckless, Oliphaunt would be alive right now," a man challenged from across the room.

There was sudden silence. The men nearest the speaker moved away from him.

Virgil looked to Wesley. "Whaddaya think, big brother?"

"I think we kin make do wit'out Earl," Wesley said, his voice echoing deeply within the stone cavern.

The crowd pulled back to make room for the coming fight, leaving a small child and two chickens exposed in the ring with the combatants. A dark-skinned woman, gibbering in mixed Spanish and English, crossed the circle, shooing the chickens ahead of her and plucking up the child as she went.

Virgil took the blade his brother offered, and Earl, pulling a Bowie knife, came forward to meet him. Wade stepped up behind Earl and gave him a shove and the man stumbled, almost losing his balance. Virgil knocked his knife aside, swung a rock against the side of his head, and Earl fell.

With the cheers of the others, Virgil lifted the man.

Is he already dead? Mark wondered. *He's limp as a noodle.* Virgil hauled Earl to the edge of the fire and pushed him in. The cheers died down quickly and those near the fire drew back, shielding their faces from the spray of sparks that flew up. Virgil chuckled and kicked the burning man a few times.

Mark looked away. *Well, he's dead now.*

"Git 'im outta there," Wesley growled. "He's stinkin' up the place."

Wade grabbed Earl by the collar of his buckskin shirt and dragged him across the floor, leaving a glowing trail of coals. Virgil hefted the smoking body to his shoulder and, whispering in his ear, slipped out into the darkness.

Mark crawled out of his shelter and stepped into the cave. The cutthroats didn't notice him until he was shouldering his way into their midst. The boy sat cross-legged in Virgil's place, and stared intently into the fire.

Sitting high in the branches of a sycamore, Joel was attempting to cook an eight-inch bluegill he had managed to catch with his hands. Since he was afraid a proper fire would give him away, he had taken a sharp stick, speared the fish through the middle and held it over his Zippo's meager flame.

This is stupid, he berated himself. *The fish is a hundred times bigger than the flame, dumbass.*

Steeling himself, he took a bite of the tepid, raw fish and began chewing. With a grimace, he spat out the reeking mouthful and watched it fall through the limbs of the tree. The white mash landed on Virgil's forehead as he passed beneath.

Fuck. Joel's stomach knotted up, and he had to grab the tree trunk to keep his balance. Virgil wiped off his head and glared up into the night. Joel ducked out of view, nearly dropping the fish and the lighter.

"Goddam birds," he heard the man mutter. Joel squinted down at him. *Oh Christ. He's carrying a dead guy.*

Virgil shifted his burden to his other shoulder, and mounted a switchback trail that took him to the top of the bluff where he was on a level with Joel. The boy watched him disappear into the billowing smoke that had been rising from a hole in the rock ever since the pirates had retired to the cave with their spoils.

Joel watched and waited, expecting the man to emerge any second, coughing and choking. When, at length, he didn't return, curiosity got the better of him and Joel swung off the end of a limb and onto the top of the bluff. He edged over to the windward side of the hole and tried to peer in. There was nothing to see, but he could hear voices drifting up with the smoke.

"Why hello there, boy," Wesley said, his voice muffled and distant. In a much higher, playful tone he added, "Sit ye'self down. Virgil won't mind!"

"I jus' wish I could watch some TV," Mark said, sounding small and pathetic.

"Dammit, Wes," a new voice complained, "that boy jus' ain't right. Kin we tie 'im outside ta a tree or somethin'?"

"Leave 'im be, Wade. The boy ain't worth the effort, an' 'sides, he's funny."

Mark was startled when Virgil appeared from somewhere within the cave. A gruesomely hairy naked man voiced the question Mark was too afraid to ask. "Where'd *yew* come from?"

"Shut the hell up, Laris," Virgil snapped as he stepped up to the fire. "Mind yer own goddam business or I'll make ye put some clothes on."

Virgil turned to take his seat and found Mark sitting in his place. Speechless, he could only stare.

"Look, Virg," Wesley teased, "the boy's got yer seat."

"I'd prefer ta think that my seat's done caught me a little boy."

Virgil edged around the fire, grabbed Mark by the front of his shirt, and lifted him off his feet. The man's stubbled chin brushed the boy's face, and his breath was thick with a stench like decayed meat.

Mark's body began to tremble, as hard as if he were lying naked in the snow. He looked into Virgil's crazed, red-rimmed eyes. "I-I know you're n-not listening to me. I-I know y-you don't want anything to do with me, but I just have to say this thing."

"He's funny," Wesley said, chuckling. "Let the boy speak."

Virgil stared at Mark, eyes narrowed. "I ain't got time fer this, boy. I'd jus' as soon kill ye—"

"I-I been smokin'—Joel makes me do it. And he dared me to steal a girlie magazine from Marvin's Market and I did it. And I feel real-real bad. I don' wanna get a whippin'."

"Oh, ye're gonna git a whippin', an' then some. I'm gonna beat you 'til ye're *good* an' tender." Virgil hauled his fist back. Mark closed his eyes.

"*Hold* up now, Virg," Wesley said.

Virgil turned to his brother, a look of surprise on his face. "He ain't good fer nothin' else, Wes!" He looked to the others. "We gonna feed this boy? He ain't gonna earn 'is keep."

The crowd murmured its assent.

"He makes me laugh," Wesley said.

"Which one o' ye's gonna take care o' 'im?" Virgil asked the crowd. "How 'bout yew, Laris? Ye look like ye're ready fer some fun wit' 'im." Laris let out a hyena cackle and waggled his naked pelvis at Mark. *His dick looks like one of those worms in a bottle of tequila,* Mark thought.

"He's my *dawg,* now," Wesley said, raising his voice so all could hear. "He's quiet an' keeps ta himse'f, so I done decided. An' *nobody's* gonna whip *my* dawg."

The small man dropped Mark roughly, and the boy stumbled

and fell on his butt. "Leastwise, he's *gotta* sit somewheres else."

Wesley gave Virgil a hard look, and the little man stomped out of the chamber.

The breeze changed, blowing smoke into Joel's face. He coughed and rubbed at his eyes, circling the chimney and listening for Virgil's returning footsteps. Several times the man's silhouette formed in the roiling smoke. As quickly as it formed, it dissipated, and Joel, crouched ready to run, would relax a bit.

He's not coming back.

"Leastwise, he's *gotta* sit somewheres else," Virgil's voice came to him from deep within the bluff.

Now, although he couldn't see through the thick smoke, Joel knew there must be a passage off the chimney that led into the lower cavern.

Squeezing his eyes tightly shut and holding his breath, Joel rolled onto his belly and dangled his legs down into the hole. He felt along the wall until he found a place to rest his feet, then wriggled down the hole and put his weight on the narrow ledge.

The rock crumbled beneath him. Clawing for a grip, Joel fell backward into the smoky pit, stifling a scream. He fell forever—landing on a ledge six feet below the top of the chimney. The breath and his scream were knocked out of him. Panicking, his eyes burning and lungs aching for air, he got to his feet and searched frantically for an exit with his hands. He stumbled and fell through a black opening.

Choking and coughing, tears running down his cheeks, he caught himself on the wall and felt his way forward. Someone or something large bumped into him in the darkness.

Joel cried out, his heart leaping into his throat. Although he cowered down on the floor, he was struck again, this time in the head. Lashing out at his attacker, he caught it in his arms and relaxed a bit, realizing it was something swinging from above. Confused, he stepped back, pulled out his Zippo and struck the flint. The sparks ignited the wick and the space filled with a flickering, orange glow.

"What the fuck—"

Staring, it took him a moment to figure out what he was seeing through the blur of watery eyes. A log had been wedged between the walls near the ceiling. Hanging from it were several sides of meat, sparkling with tiny beads of liquid, curing in the smoke. He reached for the brown-stained surface of one of the sides and came away with tiny crystals. Although he didn't touch it to his tongue, his mind said, *Salt.*

"It's a smokehouse." He was startled by the banality of it. He had expected a torture chamber, at the very least.

Joel's mouth watered at the sweet, oily scent of the meat. He got out his knife and began to cut into it, but the rind of the meat was tough and the side swung away from him. The thought of hugging the half-carcass in order to cut off a chunk was sickening. That and the smell, which started to tip over the edge of tantalizing into cloying. There was just something—wrong about it. He choked on the smoke, and backed away.

As he retreated, Joel noticed a torch jammed into a crack in the wall. He touched his flame to it. The room brightened and he felt his way along the sweaty walls. Holding the torch off to his right, he set the sides of meat to swinging as he hurried across the chamber and entered a dark passage. Gratefully taking a breath of clearer air, Joel followed the winding tunnel toward the sound of distant voices.

26

Gunshots from the river. Startled, Billy screamed and leaped into the air. The next shot whistled under his outthrust arm. Bald Man grabbed him by the back of his shirt and roughly yanked him down.

The boy and the Indians crouched down on the trail, peering through the holes in the undergrowth in search of their attackers. Billy began to cry and Bald Man struck the tears from his eyes, startling him into silence.

Against the sunrise, through the thinning trees, he could just make out the thin brown ribbon of the river and the dugout canoe from which their attackers had spilled. The Indians pushed Billy ahead of them into the undergrowth that fringed the trail and raised their guns to fend off the attack. The boy curled into a fetal position, sneaking glances over his shoulder.

In his peripheral vision, he saw Bald Man rise and fire. Suddenly blood and bone spattered the boy's knee and the Indian slumped backward, the flintlock falling beside him. Billy stared at the bloody shard of bone on his leg, unwilling to look over at Bald Man.

As he watched, a drop of blood oozed slowly from the tip of the bone onto his leg, and his whirling mind slowed enough for him to think. If he touched it, he would scream and then Stick Hat would strike him. But there was something Stick Hat would want him to do—he picked up Bald Man's rifle and began reloading.

Stick Hat fired and traded his flintlock for the one Billy held ready. As the boy fumbled powder and shot into the hot barrel of the rifle, he glanced up and saw the white men silently zigzagging, keeping low as they ran from tree to tree, their rifles held ready. Stick Hat pulled the trigger and there was a flash in the pan, but no more. With an angry hiss, he threw down the rifle and grabbed the one in Billy's hands. The attackers were almost upon them, their lead shot slapping holes through the leaves.

Stick Hat didn't stop to remove the ramrod the boy had left in the barrel and hastily fired upon the closest attacker. The man was charging toward them, knife drawn, when he stopped in mid-stride and fell, the ramrod suddenly blooming from his chest.

The attackers hesitated, hunkering down to reload. In the brief pause, Billy struggled to load again. One of the attackers moved off to Billy's right, another to his left, circling to flank.

Stick Hat slapped him to draw his attention back to the task at hand.

There was a great blast as the three remaining men fired at once, disappearing behind a cloud of blue smoke. A bright red hole appeared in Stick Hat's upper chest and he fell over, landing hard on his back, hissing between clenched teeth.

A voice barked a command and the attackers began retreating toward the river. Billy watched the two men move out of the woods from either side. They rejoined their companions at the canoe and the party soon vanished downstream.

"Allez!" Stick Hat commanded, pressing a deerskin bag of dried fish into Billy's hands and thrusting the boy away from him.

"No!" Billy shouted, "I *won't* go, and I don't like stinky fish."

Stick Hat closed his eyes and became limp, exhaling loudly. The boy clutched at him, shook him, but got no response. He began to cry. The drain rose up in his mind's eye, and he forced himself to stop sniffling, hoping it wouldn't see him. But it did. The drain gave him a long, slow, meaningful wink. He turned and ran toward the river. He had to find help.

When he looked over his shoulder, he saw Stick Hat open an eye to watch him go.

27

"Have you seen the river?"

After leaving the smokehouse, Joel had quickly become lost in the tangle of passages. He was in a breakdown chamber, the terminus of several tunnels, trying to decide which way to go when the small voice startled him.

"What?" Joel raised his torch to get a better look. A frail, dirty child stood in the aperture of the tunnel to his left. The boy's skin was pale, as if it had never felt the touch of the sun, and his eyes had the large, unblinking gaze of a nocturnal creature.

"Ye know," the boy said in a conspiratorial whisper, "the *river.*"

"Look, I'm *lost,* can you tell me how to get out of here?"

"Naw." The boy's voice was thin, emotionless. "I ain't never even *seen* the river."

"Why not? It can't be that far."

"Us childerns ain't allowed up top." The child turned and darted back down the passage, calling over his shoulder, "An' ye cain't make me go up there neither!"

Joel tried to follow, but soon fell behind as he passed into a chamber filled with an orange glow and the smell of smoke. It was a wide room with a high, sooty ceiling. Shadows milled about small fires, women and children naked or dressed in rags. The place reeked of unwashed bodies, spoiled food, and illness.

In his school library, Joel had read about this cave and the outlaw mob based here. He knew about their "bloodthirsty piracy" along the Mississippi and Ohio rivers. But what he'd read didn't include much about daily life at the cave, let alone what went on deep inside.

He knew a law-abiding community would be a much safer place for him in this day and time. However, his books had also told him that there were no other settlements within fifty miles of the cave. And to move away from this area was to move that much further from home.

I should just take off and start looking for the way home.

Then he thought again about how bad Mark looked after the Pikes had beaten him.

No, I can't just leave Mark here. I've got to try and help him get home. No way he could survive here on his own.

As Joel wandered across the chamber, looking for a way out, he stumbled across a naked woman sitting in the dark with a toddler at her breast. He stopped dead in his tracks and stared at her breasts and immediately felt the swelling in his pants. The woman shooed him off and he moved on, readjusting his crotch.

At one end of the chamber, a great snoring pile of adults and children were curled together sleeping, and, at the other, a human pyramid teetered toward a hole in the ceiling. The crying of a baby echoed harshly.

Joel spotted a tunnel at the far end of the chamber and was making his way toward it when he realized he had yet to react to the strangeness of this place. A feeling of emptiness overcame him. To his horror, a lump formed in his throat, and his eyes began to sting.

I thought I was tougher than that. A couple a people murdered and I go all to pieces and run.

"Goddammit!"

His tough facade held for only a moment before crumbling

to dust. Joel collapsed to the tunnel floor where he lay in a heap, weeping.

28

Sitting atop the bluff, Mark swung his legs back and forth over the edge and watched the river slide by far below.

Laris walked out of the cave, put his hands on his hips and rotated his pelvis vigorously, taking a deep breath. Mark's eyes widened—the man's furry buttocks were painted bright blue.

"Laris," trumpeted Virgil's voice from inside the cave, "Wes says if'n yer gonna run 'round nekkid like that, do it inside the cave."

Laris turned and walked slowly back toward the cave, glancing up at Mark just before he disappeared from sight. Mark quickly looked away.

Don't look at him, the boy told himself. *If I don't look at him, he won't see me.*

A thin, squealing voice caught his attention. Looking around for its source, he heard it say his name. He squinted into the bright morning and saw a tiny, flailing, hopping form on the opposite bank, a hundred yards away. This time, he heard the voice clearly say, "Mark, that you?"

He turned away and tried to imagine what his mother would have fixed him for lunch. A "monster" cheese sandwich on white bread with mustard, fishy-smelling corn chips, and lemonade. *Yeah,* he thought, *that sounds real good right about now.* His stomach growled noisily and he tried to ignore it.

Down at the cave mouth, he could see the outlaws had stopped what they were doing to look across the river. A knot of men gathered about Wade as the man pointed. Mark felt a distant uneasiness rise up within him.

"It's me—Billy!"

The small boy had removed his yellow shirt and was waving it over his head, apparently trying to draw as much attention to himself as possible. Below, Wade had beckoned Virgil to the water's edge and was pointing at the distant boy.

"Fucking retard!" Mark said. He scrambled to his feet and scampered down the switchback trail. Reaching the bottom, he untied one of the canoes floating amidst the rocks at the water's edge, grabbed a paddle, and started out across the river.

"Where the hell ye goin' wit' that dugout?" Virgil yelled.

"Better leave 'im be," Wade said. "He's Wes's dawg, remember?"

Virgil clouted the man solidly on the head and Wade tumbled into the river.

The canoe was heavy and responded sluggishly to Mark's paddling. He worked frantically, at first making only circles as the current pulled him downstream. Virgil burst out laughing and the other outlaws followed suit.

And then Mark thought back to summer camp and everything was okay. If he'd done his chores, in the afternoon he could spend some free time with his friends. They enjoyed taking the canoes out on their own to do a little fishing. With these memories, he began alternating sides with his strokes and the little craft straightened out.

"Billy, the current's carrying me downstream," Mark shouted. He pointed to a rock jutting out into the water. "I'll meet you there."

The small boy ran, his short legs kicking up dust as he tried to keep pace. He tripped and fell on the stones by the water's edge, picked himself up and, with bloodied knees and a limp, ran on.

29

Joel had been watching the cave, the pirates, and especially Wesley for the past half a day. When he saw the big man heading out of the cave alone and into the trees south of the bluff, he followed. He waited in the brush just off the path Wesley had taken, giving the man plenty of time to do his business. Within minutes, Wesley returned the way he had come, buttoning his trousers. Joel, holding a pistol at his side, stepped onto the path, blocking the way.

"Where'd ye git that pistol, Little Man?"

He doesn't seem surprised to see me.

Joel tried to twirl the weapon on his index finger. "I dunno, way back in the cave somewheres," he said, taking on Wesley's accent and manner of speech.

"Ye been back *there?* Don' ye know there's cannibals in there an' the ghosts of those we done killed? Why, Little Man, if'n ye ain't scairt o' that, ye jus' might be of the right grit, after all. Now, if I's ta take ye under my wing. . . ."

Joel looked at the man, unsure of himself. He laughed to fill the silence and Wesley grinned at him.

"Is that thing loaded?"

"Nossir—I didn't know how."

"Yer sure a queer one, Little Man, but yer tough an' I like ye. I'm givin' ye the run o' the place, the cave an' ever'thin'. An' if anyone gives ye trouble, ye jus' tell 'em ta come talk ta me. Now, c'mere an' let me show ye how ta load that."

30

Where the hell did Billy come from?

Joel was knocking around a gully just south of the cave bluff, exploring the pirates' horse corral, when Mark and Billy caught up with him. He had tried not to think about what became of the little boy. But now, here he was, just like at home, popping up where he was not wanted.

"Where you been, Billy?"

"I been with Bald Man and Stick Hat."

Joel looked at him blankly. "Who?"

"Bald Man and Stick Hat, they're those brown men we saw near my creek—'cept Bald Man's dead now."

"Slow down, Billy. What the hell are you talking about?"

"You remember—those guys who stopped you from picking on me with that bug."

"God, that was *days* ago! Hey, I bet those were Indians."

"Yeah, only they got guns instead of bows and arrows, and instead of feathers, Stick Hat wears a stick hat."

"Dumbass."

"Don't call me names! I came to ask you to help. Stick Hat's hurt real bad—he can't move—and we need to help him. And I asked Mark, but he ain't right. So will you help?"

Joel thought about it—a real live, yet incapacitated and unthreatening Indian—that *would* be something to see.

"How far is it, Billy?"

"I dunno. I think I walked for two days."

"Well, we're gonna need some supplies, then. We should steal a dugout—we can't drag Billy's Indian all the way back—and food for at least four days."

"I can go and get what we need," Mark said, "I'm the big man's dawg. I make him laugh. 'Sides, if I get caught, nobody's gonna do anything 'cause they're scared of Wesley."

"Goddammit, Billy—all you gotta do is keep the oar in the fucking river and point us in the direction we're 'sposed to be going! I've told you over and over, every time you get us out into the current you're just sending us back the way we came!"

"I'm tired, Joel, and I'm hungry."

"*Tired?* You're not doing any of the work—quit your *goddam* complaining. Me an' Mark's doing all the rowing!"

Joel shook his head, disgusted with the little boy. They had been traveling upstream for a day and a half now, and the expedition was turning out to be a royal pain in the ass.

Joel was getting hungry too. Billy had a goddam bottomless pit for a stomach and kept getting into their sack of supplies when Joel wasn't looking. They had brought dried-out cornbread and jerky, not nearly enough of either, and now it was almost gone.

And Joel was tired. Last night when they slept in the tall grasses that grew along the bank, the little boy had kept him up half the night with his goddam whining. Every time Joel managed to drift off, Billy would yell "Mama!" and wake him up.

"I don't care if you're about to fucking starve to death, Billy, if you eat any more of our food, I'll throw your ass in the river."

Joel had no complaint about Mark, however. His friend just rowed and rowed, mechanically, never saying a word.

"Hey, guys," Billy said, "that's it!" He pointed out a rock formation shaped like a squatting toad and steered the boat for it.

The Mingit Toad, Joel thought, though he could clearly see it was just rock.

They dragged the dugout up onto the bank and moved cautiously along the river. Showing off, Joel pulled out his pistol and held it out before him, trying to appear nonchalant. To his irritation, neither of the other boys seemed to notice.

"Wesley says I have to go on an 'adventure' with him and a bunch of his men," Joel said. "It'll be like nothin' I ever done before—like stuff I only dreamed about. I know folks'll get killed and that could mean me. But I'm real excited too—I've never ridden a horse before. That's why I was down at the corral, giving the horses a look."

"You think your daddy's gonna like you doin' that?" Mark asked.

Joel realized that Mark didn't even know where he was. That was all right—Joel just needed to talk about it. He didn't need to be understood.

"They're river pirates an' they're killers. I read all about 'em. I always wanted to be that tough. But, before, it was just a game. Now it's real and I don't know if I can do it. It ain't right and I'm scared too. I'm not sure I wanna miss out on it, though."

"You'll like Stick Hat, Joel, even though you can't talk to him. He pretended like he was dead to get rid of me, but I knew it was only 'cause he had to. He should be here, somewhere."

"He *damn* well better be, after hauling my ass all this way."

"There's Bald Man's gun! Ewww—and there's Bald Man! *Yuck,* lookit the flies!"

"He's dead, you stupid, little dicknose!"

Joel turned, prepared to throttle him, but the smaller boy was running toward a tree.

"Stick Hat!"

Joel ran a few steps to catch up and that's when he saw the shoes.

"Nikes?" he said, staring at the Indian's feet.

Stick Hat was propped up against the trunk of the tree, his hat lying crushed and broken by his side. Between patches of deerskin, Joel made out the bright orange Nike symbol on the sides of the shoes. The pistol, forgotten, fell by his side.

They can't be, he thought, *not here. Maybe I'm not where I think I am. No, I must be—I've read about some of these outlaws, I know who they are. He must've gotten them from someone else. If that's right, then it could be there's an easy way in and out of this place.*

The Indian was smiling weakly at Billy. The small boy tried to hug him around the neck, but Stick Hat gently held him off, indicating the wound in his shoulder.

From the shadows behind him came a rhythmic thumping and a dog's whimper.

"Ebbie?" Mark said.

His dull eyes brightened as he moved around to get a better look. Joel could see she was thin and dirty, her coat matted. There was a crusty scab over her right eye. Mark carefully wrapped his arms around her and stroked her back as the dog feebly licked his face.

Joel knelt down at Stick Hat's feet and inspected the sneakers. Pointing at them he said, "Where did you *get* those?"

The Indian shrugged, shaking his head. "Je ne comprends pas."

"Jen nay comprend pah," Mark said, repeating Stick Hat's sentence.

"You understand him?" Joel asked.

Mark didn't answer. His eyes were turned inward once again as he mechanically petted his dog.

★ ★ ★ ★ ★

During the half day spent getting Ebbie and Stick Hat into the dugout and downstream to the outlaws' bluff, Joel tried to question the Indian about the Nikes. His efforts with English were frustrated; no matter how loudly or slowly he spoke his questions, Stick Hat just stared at him, or shook his head. Joel finally turned to his friend for help.

"It's French," Mark said. "He's speaking some kinda French. I'll talk to him—I took French last year."

"You can't do any worse than I have."

"Tray be-in, mishure. Maresee ay voo. Ill fay bow. Shem may pell Mark. Jen say pah. . . ."

A worried look crept across the dark man's face. Joel quickly realized that Mark was merely repeating the stock phrases all first-year French students learned.

"You failed French, didn't you?"

"Yeah."

They put in upstream and out of sight of the cave, and hid the canoe under low-lying limbs. Mark lifted Ebbie onto the bank while Joel and Billy helped Stick Hat. They stumbled across the rocks near the water's edge and rested in the shade. Joel pulled the last of the dried meat out of their supply sack and passed it around.

"Virgil makes this jerky. I've seen where he does it." Joel tore at the leathery meat with his teeth. It was good. A little sweet, like pork. "We should wait here 'til dark. Then I can sneak us into the cave."

"What are you so scared of?" Billy asked.

"I ain't scared of *nothin'*, you little homo, at least not for me or Mark. You and the Indian are different."

"Why? What'd *we* do?"

"Just shut the hell up!"

Stick Hat suddenly spat out the tough meat, grimacing.

"Qu'est-ce que c'est que je mange?"

Joel gave the Indian a dirty look and turned to Mark.

"I don't think he likes it," Mark said.

Joel filled a waterskin before they headed for the back entrance to the cave he'd found earlier. The sun was a hot red ball sitting on the horizon as they set out, but had vanished by the time they arrived at the opening to the tunnel.

"I know a little room in here where you can hide out," Joel told his friends. "The Indian can stay there too until he can get along on his own."

A look of astonishment crossed Stick Hat's face when Joel lit his Zippo.

"It's a lighter," he said, smiling at the Indian, "nothin' special." He pulled a candle out of his sack and lit it.

Ebbie sniffed warily at the entrance, but was unwilling to enter. Mark finally picked her up and carried her in.

The tunnel gradually grew larger as it wound back into the hill. Leading the way, Joel trotted ahead and then suddenly turned to his right to demonstrate how he could vanish into the bare rock.

"It's not until you're standing right next to this passage that you can see the opening," he said.

A short distance within was a small, dusty chamber.

"You should be safe in here. I found this room when I was wandering around looking for a way out. There weren't any footprints on the floor so I knew no one ever came in here. If you follow the main passage a little farther, there's a little waterfall where you can get a drink. Just behind that is an opening that leads up to Virgil's smokehouse where there's meat. Just keep going up and to the left.

"Oh, and I found these in a storeroom somewhere back in there." Joel pulled several candles out of his pockets. He handed these and the waterskin to Billy.

"You're not leaving us, are you?" Billy asked. "Stick Hat's hurt, we gotta help him."

"He'll be all right, Billy." Joel pressed the Zippo into his hand. "Don't worry. You just stay here, out of sight, unless you need food or water. There's no telling what they'd do if they found you. I'll only be gone a couple of days."

31

Surprised and unable to think of what to say, Billy watched silently as Joel turned and walked away. Although he didn't really like Joel, with Mark so weird and Stick Hat injured, the bully was the obvious leader. Now, the little boy had no one to turn to but himself, and was afraid that wouldn't do him any good.

"I'll be right back," Mark said, snatching the Zippo out of Billy's unresisting fingers. "Take care of my dog."

"Hunh?" Billy turned to face him, but Mark was already headed down the passage, the lighted Zippo held out before him. "Mark, where you going?"

There was no answer. He was already gone. Billy was going to chase after him, but then realized there would be no one left to take care of Stick Hat.

For several minutes, Billy stared blankly into the darkness that had swallowed Mark up. The lighter had left an afterimage, a tracer that described the movement of the flame as Mark left the chamber. Billy watched until the worm of light vanished.

32

Joel startled awake, suddenly staring at the cavernous ceiling of yet another bus station. The sickly light and sour smell of unwashed humans took him right back to the pirates' caves on the river. He blinked once, twice, and rubbed his eyes.

The family walking toward him looked like they were right out of the backwoods of Tennessee. In fact, except for their modern clothing, they looked a lot like some of the denizens of Wesley Pike's private Hades. The harsh fluorescent lighting inside the bus terminal gave their skin a faint greenish cast. Zombies. *I'm in a fuckin' zombie movie.*

"How ya' doin' buddy?" the balding fellow said—*the father,* Joel thought.

Joel looked away. *Give the guy too much attention, and he might launch into a hard-luck story.* A perverse little smile quirked his mouth. *You wouldn't want to eat my brain anyway, zombie-boy. It's pickled in alcohol.*

Across the depot an elderly couple sat side by side in a decaying fiberglass booth, their expressions weary and haggard. A trail of cracked and stained linoleum led the way to the front door. Joel considered getting up and following it outside.

"Don't'cha recognize me?"

Joel gaped at the man. "Moss?"

"Yeah, it's me. I know the package looks different, but surely you didn't expect me to stay the same."

Joel laughed uncomfortably as he rose and shook Moss's

hand, realizing that, yes, he had expected him to stay the same. Moss was seven years older than Joel and the extra years had taken a toll on him. He was sporting a large bay-window gut and his thinning hair had gone almost completely gray.

This was very awkward and Joel needed a drink, right now, to smooth things out.

"This is Lynn," Moss said, smiling as he turned to the plump brunette standing beside him. "And this is my girl, Rachel, and my boys, Brian and Caleb."

Joel smiled uneasily and found himself reaching for the pint he normally kept in his coat pocket. To disguise his effort, he shot a hand out to shake Lynn's hand while pushing his hair back with the other.

"Lemme get that bag for ya, Mister Biggs," said Caleb. He was the youngest, maybe about eight. A round-faced, red-headed boy, he reminded Joel of Billy as a child. It felt strange—Billy never called him Mister—and made him feel old.

"You know that bag's too big for you, Caleb," Lynn said. "Brian, help Joel with it."

"Yes, Mama," the other boy droned. The lanky, black-haired boy reluctantly picked up Joel's bag and headed out toward the parking lot. He was twelve or thirteen—about the age Joel and Mark had been when they followed The New Cut that day. Joel sighed, jammed his hands in his pockets. *If I could start over again at twelve, would I blow it this badly? Oh, probably.*

Caleb jogged after his brother. "What's wrong? Too heavy for ya?"

"Go to hell, dicknose," Brian said, punching him on the arm.

"Language!" Lynn warned. Then she turned to Joel. "You'll have to forgive Brian. He's been quite a handful lately."

Moving into the brilliant daylight, Joel's eyes watered and threatened to brim over. He quickly wiped the tears away and looked to see if anyone had noticed.

Rachel was eyeing him curiously. She was a pretty teenager, even though she carried herself with her head down and had a rather sullen expression. Her blond hair was so pale it was almost colorless, but it gave her an ethereal, waiflike appearance. Her eyes, half hidden behind ragged bangs, were a wide, wounded green. She had a small gold ring through one nostril, and her full mouth was painted a glaring scarlet. As they walked across the parking lot, she was hanging back, no doubt too cool to walk with her parents.

Stumbling, Joel realized how much his shakes were screwing up his coordination.

God just get me to their place without letting me embarrass the hell out of myself.

The cracks on the linoleum floor inside had followed them out onto the worn asphalt parking lot, where several rusted vehicles were parked haphazardly, as if abandoned.

"That's our van over there." Moss pointed to a run-down tan vehicle resting within a crumbling rectangle of yellow paint. He unlocked the door and got in and Lynn sat in the front passenger seat beside him. Caleb slid the side door open and motioned for Joel to get in. "No, you first," Joel said, and the boys both tumbled in. Joel tripped on the running board and banged his head as he fell forward.

"Ow!" he yelped grabbing his forehead.

The boys laughed and Lynn smiled sympathetically, extending a hand to help him in. Seeing Moss's pitying expression in the rearview mirror, Joel wanted to flee. He glanced over his shoulder at Rachel. She wasn't laughing, and she wasn't pitying. Her expression held curiosity, and something else he couldn't quite pinpoint.

"You okay, Joel?" Moss asked. "It'll get better, don't worry."

What the fuck would you know about it?

Rachel got in and they pulled out of the parking lot, turning onto a narrow, two-lane highway.

Lynn turned to him as if she'd just remembered something important. "I had an uncle was an alcoholic," she announced, brightly. "But he got A.A. and lived 'til he was eighty-five years old!"

Joel stared at her a moment not knowing what to say. He wanted to jump out the open window beside him. Instead, he swallowed hard and said quietly, "I am too."

"Geez, Mama," Rachel mumbled from the rear of the van, "sometimes you say the dumbest things."

"What was that, young lady?" she asked, losing her smile.

"Rachel, don't you take that tone with your mother," Moss barked.

They rode the next several miles in awkward silence. Joel felt like he was the center of a cruel universe. His breath caught in his throat and he loosened his shirt collar, carefully avoiding eye contact with the others.

To fill the silence, Moss began to blather, rambling on and on about buying their house, what he'd been doing since college, that sort of thing. But Joel heard none of it. As they moved out of the small town of Hewitt into open farmland and eventually along country roads surrounded by forest, Joel escaped, traveling back to the virgin wilderness in which he and Mark and Billy had found themselves after walking along The New Cut. It had been brutal there, and sometimes terrifying, but the future was a wide open space, big as the blue, unpolluted sky. He wasn't trapped in a whirlpool of self-destruction, then.

Moss's voice jarred him from his reverie. "So whaddaya think of our little homestead?" The road carried them upward and when they broke from the trees, Joel could see a cabin standing amidst thick oaks and towering maples. To either side of the green front door were rock gardens with red and white petunias. Plastic toys were strewn throughout the yard and a rope swing hung from the stout limb of one of the oaks.

"Nice—*real* nice," Joel said.

But what it reminded him of was not so nice at all. Although it was a lot more solidly constructed, it looked something like the cabin where he and Mark had taken shelter their first night in the 1800s. They had had no idea when or where they were, and the family living in the cabin had taken them by surprise.

They got out of the van and took the flagstone walk to the front door. The inside of the Phelps' cabin was one large room and Moss stood in the middle of it and pointed at things.

"That's the kitchen," he said indicating an area to his left full of counters, table and chairs, and exposed shelving, all clustered around a wood-burning stove.

Joel didn't want a tour. His nerves were shot and his gut was writhing from withdrawal cramps. Standing beside Moss, he found himself to be the center of attention, as everyone watched for his reaction. All he wanted was something to lean up against, maybe a chair to sit in, or hell, he would just lie down on the cool floor if they'd leave him alone.

"That's the living room, where we do our living." Moss indicated the area to his right. "You'll notice we don't have no television," he said with a great smile. "Hope you don't mind. It's just we don' believe in it—ain't that right, childrern?"

"Yes, Papa," they said in unison, sarcastically.

This was all so meaningless—Joel didn't care, didn't give a shit where anything was, except maybe the bathroom. His needs were very simple right now, but he knew there was no way they were going to be satisfied anytime soon.

Brian climbed a ladder and dropped Joel's bag onto the floor of the loft.

"The loft's cut into four sections. Three bedrooms and a storage space. That one's yours—Rachel gave it up so you could have your own. She's a good girl."

Joel realized that if his stay here was to be at all tolerable, he had better shape up. It wasn't the Phelps' fault that he felt like shit and, although he realized he didn't care much about these people and their home, he ought to try and be civil. He had to get through this somehow.

"Thank you, Rachel," Joel barely managed to mutter.

" 'S'okay," she said sullenly, turning away.

"Rachel here is full of that trendy teenage angst," Moss said, beaming.

"Moss," Joel said, suddenly sympathizing with the girl, "that's the dorkiest thing I've ever heard you say."

Rachel burst out laughing as her father turned red. The boys were giggling and Lynn slapped her husband on the back.

"He's right," she said, "and you know it."

Moss's attitude seemed to implode and then he too was laughing.

"Sorry, buddy," Joel said, then took a deep breath—he needed to say something, show his gratitude at this point, but wasn't sure how. "Didn't mean to embarrass you in front of your children. Tell you the truth, I'm just not too sure about myself all the way around. I can't say I'll be much fun, although I'm grateful that you invited me here. If you can put up with me for a while, maybe I'll come out of my shell."

"Try and make yourself at home. Me and Lynn and the children will leave you pretty much to yourself if that's what you want. You just let us know."

"You children go on now," Lynn said. "Do your homework or something. Dinner will be ready in about an hour." Then she turned to Joel. "Hope you're hungry." She headed for the kitchen. "We've got beans an' cornbread an' turnip greens," she called out over her shoulder. "Don't worry, though. We're not vegetarians—I put country ham chunks in the beans."

"Sounds great," Joel said.

"C'mon, let's go on up to the top of the hill," Moss said, "an' I'll show you the sights."

"You know, Moss, I'm feelin' kinda rough. I really don't think I'm up to it."

"C'mon, buddy." Moss grabbed Joel by the arm and steered him out the front door of the cabin. "It'll do ya good." Moss smiled reassuringly, but his grip on Joel's arm remained firm.

After a hundred yards and a lot of huffing and puffing on Joel's part, they reached the summit, which gave them a broad view of the farmland below, lit by the yellow afternoon sun and dozing beneath a soft blanket of haze.

"How much of this is yours?" Joel asked, to be conversational.

"Couldn't afford anything flat—just the top of the hill, here, that nobody else wanted. I have cleared off a little spot over there," he said, gesturing, "where I hope to grow a little something."

Then Moss indicated three large humps situated near the center of the cornfield below. "Those are Indian mounds."

In spite of himself, Joel perked up at this. "Oh, you know something of the history hereabouts?"

"Nope, nothing really. Guy who sold me the property pointed those out. Hell, for all I know there's a bomb shelter under there."

"But they *are*—really, they are Indian mounds, prehistoric Indians."

"No shit?"

"Yeah—sure looks that way. History's my field, especially local history."

"Is there much of that?"

"Sure there is!" Joel chuckled and realized this was the first time he'd shown any good humor since arriving. He'd have to work on that. At least the nausea and cramping were gone. Now he just had to get over his shakes. "I guess you don't remember when we were kids, you sent me a history book you stole from the school library. It was called *The History of Matthew Crenshaw and His Adventure Exposing the Great Land Pirate, Jarrett Cotten and the Mystic Clan.* You said it was a real cool story. You were right. It was that book that first interested me in history. The copy you sent me was lost, but I recently got a new one. I've been reading it again and brought it with me."

"Maybe I'd remember if I saw the book."

As they talked, Joel caught a hint of their old friendship and began to see the Moss he remembered from childhood. When he was a boy, Joel had spent as much time as possible with the Phelps family. It was a welcome respite from his life at home with his drunken father. Old friends of Joel's mother's family, the Phelps were considered family themselves. He grew up knowing Moss as "cousin Moss," his mother as "Aunt Kate," even though they weren't actually blood relations. Though he was a good bit older, Moss had never treated Joel like he was a nuisance. He had been a surrogate big brother, sharing his interests with Joel, and he was one of the few people Joel had ever trusted. In the Phelps home, Joel wasn't glancing over his shoulder all the time, waiting for a curse or a blow. He had discovered that he was intelligent and capable of learning. He had learned to read for pleasure and to be fascinated with life itself.

Then they'd lost touch when Moss went off to college.

"Joel," Moss said, turning serious, "I hate to lay this on you—our problem and all—but as you may have noticed, we're having trouble with Rachel. You know the type of thing, finding marijuana in her room, her skipping school to get drunk with her friends, and, generally speaking, just a sour disposition. If she gets on your nerves, I'll speak to her."

"No, please don't. Look, I don't want to be more of a problem than I already am."

"But you're no problem at all!" Moss said, smiling. "It's our pleasure, *really.*"

"Moss! Joel! Dinner!" Lynn called. "C'mon now, 'fore it gets cold."

As they headed back down the hill to the cabin, Joel listened to the dry crunch of fallen leaves and realized that autumn had arrived. The smell of wood smoke brought back sweet, but uncomfortable memories.

"Sorry," Lynn said as they entered the cabin, "but the beans are kinda burnt."

"I'm sure they're fine," Joel said.

"You can say grace if you want to, Joel," said Moss, taking his seat with the others, "but keep it to yourself."

Joel snickered as he sat down, recalling the strange prayer of the man in that other cabin, where he and Mark had spent their first night in the past. "Our God in Heaven, thank'ee for these 'ere eats, though it ain't much, an' will taste like a dog's mangy backside."

For a moment the others stared at him and then they burst out laughing.

"Now that's my kind of prayer," said Moss.

"I guess that means you don't think much of my cookin'," Lynn said, sticking out her lower lip.

Joel laughed nervously. "No—I, uh . . . sorry. Hell, I haven't even tried the food yet. It—it's just somethin' I heard once. No offence, Lynn."

As she served the children, he remembered the culture shock he and Mark had experienced that night in the cabin with the frontier family. At the time, he was an average twentieth-century boy who had never gone hungry before. Suddenly he was thrust amongst people who survived on little or nothing. Joel looked at the food on his plate and smiled. How incredibly strange it was that the Phelps were serving him cornbread and greens.

"It's been a long time since I had cornbread and greens." *Did we have cornbread and greens that night? Do I just think we did, because I'm looking at it right now?*

"Well I hope you like mine as much as what you had in the past," Lynn said.

"Believe me, I can't help but like 'em better," Joel said, smiling. "Reason it's been so long is how bad they were last time."

"Oh, I'm sorry, Joel," Lynn said. "You don't like cornbread and greens, do you? I knew I shoulda asked you first."

"I'm sure I'll like 'em just fine. Please, everyone just go on with your dinner and don't worry about me."

"I don't like cornbread an' greens either," said Brian.

"Me neither," Caleb said, whining.

"You boys like 'em just fine," said Moss with a warning look.

Joel accepted a steaming plate, and could see that the pinto beans were indeed burned. Taking a mouthful, he forced himself to smile.

"They're just a little bitter," Lynn said hopefully.

"They're *fine,*" he said. *Compared to a dog's mangy backside, anyway.*

He tried the cornbread and found it to be sweet and crunchy. The greens were delicious, rich with the flavor of smoked pork. Every time he put beans in his mouth he tossed in some greens or cornbread to cut the bitter flavor. He ate everything on his plate, surprised to find himself quite satisfied.

The others were much slower eaters and continued in silence for some time. Joel watched, fidgeting uncomfortably until he could take it no longer.

"Thank you for the wonderful dinner, Lynn—it was *delicious,* really. I need some air though, so if you don't mind, I'll go outside and sit on the stoop."

"Just make yourself at home, Joel."

He rose and carried his dishes to the sink, feeling their eyes on him, then moved to the front door and stepped out. He sat down on the step and looked out into the quickening dusk. Small insects buzzed around his head, nipping at his ears. Taking a deep breath, he exhaled heavily, feeling much of his tension seeping away.

Joel was just beginning to relax when Moss appeared beside him. He couldn't help feeling angry with himself for being on guard in his "cousin's" presence, and he could think of only one way to cure the problem—he had to take a chance, had to let someone in. If he didn't do it now, he knew he never would. Joel grinned uneasily, wanting a tall drink.

"Moss, I wanna take you into my confidence about something. I need help deciding how real this thing is that's been bothering me. Maybe we'll decide it's just my drinking. If not . . . well, one way or the other it's got to come out."

"I'm flattered that you would choose me," Moss said taking a seat beside him.

"I'm just gonna jump right in there and you'll have to catch up the best you can. I—I hope you won't just think I'm crazy and call the men in the white coats." Joel tried to smile.

"Nah," Moss said, looking a little worried.

"When I was a boy, me and a couple of friends got lost in the woods one day and wound up back in the 1800s."

Joel saw Moss lift an eyebrow.

"Me and Mark Ryder were both twelve years old at the time, and Billy Howard was six or eight. We were exploring along a creek when we got lost."

Joel paused for a moment to let this sink in. He watched the branches of the trees twisting in the wind. Moss shifted uncomfortably, but remained silent.

"We lost Billy pretty quickly and he ended up with some Indians. Mark and I found a family living in a cabin—that's where I last had cornbread and greens. We ran away from them and were captured by the Pikes. You ever heard of them?"

"What Pikes?"

"You know, Wesley and Virgil Pike, the Mississippi River pirates."

"You're nuts. Those guys—"

"Yeah, I know. That's the hard part. And you'll never find any evidence in the history books that we spent any time with those guys. Not that we would have made any impact on recorded history—we were just children."

"That's crazy," Moss said. "You can't be talking about *the* Pikes."

"Yeah, those are the guys. There's no room in their story for three little boys, is there? But I know we were there. I just can't prove it. I've spent a great deal of my adult life looking for evidence."

Moss started to say something, but Joel hushed him.

"Please, let me finish. Mark and I were caught by the pirates and used as bait to lure a flatboat into an ambush. They killed everyone aboard, slaughtered them and then stole everything they had. We'd never seen anything like that. Mark wasn't the same for days and I—I don't know."

Joel shook his head to clear it of the memory.

"After that we were taken to the Outlaw Cave, you know the one on the Mississippi near the northern Tennessee line?"

"Yeah, just up from Reelfoot and across the river. It's part of an historic park now."

"That's right. Well, in the meantime, I decided it was best to get in good with Wesley, if we were to have any hope of getting away."

Joel turned away, chewed his lip. "There's more, but I guess that's a good start. I know that's all pretty hard to believe."

"But—"

"No, don't say anything. I know—it's become hard for me to

believe, too. But, here's the thing, and I'm not real sure how to say it. As horrible as that experience was, it seems like it was the only part of my life that had any real meaning. I'm not saying that I'm any great picture of a man, but what growing up I did was in the month or two I spent in the 1800s."

"Joel, I—I don't know what to say."

"You don't have to say anything, Moss. Just think about it for a while, would you?"

"Sure thing, Joel."

"And do me another favor. Don't tell Lynn, or anyone else."

"No problem." Moss's brow knitted, and he shot Joel a sideways look.

"What?" Joel asked.

"I remember—my mom told me your friend Mark Ryder vanished one summer. Everybody thought he'd been kidnapped by a sex pervert. As I recall, you had been missing for a time, too. Some thought you two had both decided to run away from home together."

Joel was surprised at the stab of pain that shot through his heart. When he spoke, his voice was harsh and ragged. "He got left behind."

"Weren't you questioned about Mark's disappearance?"

"Yeah—I told my dad, Mark's parents, even the police who were looking into it that I didn't know what happened to him. I guess they believed me."

Moss patted Joel on the shoulder and they went in the house.

After the Phelps family had all retired for the night, Joel lay in bed trying to read the Crenshaw book. He started nodding off almost immediately and the book fell from his grasp as he fell asleep. His dreams returned, as they often did, to Wesley and Virgil Pike.

33

One way or another, this "adventure" is gonna kill me.

Although Joel had been excited at the prospect of riding horseback, after the half day he had suffered in the saddle, he never wanted to lay eyes on a horse again. His legs ached, his butt was sore as hell, and his balls throbbed like a toothache. *No wonder cowboys were always yodeling.*

"Ye wan' some o' this jerky, boy?" Virgil asked.

"Yeah, thanks." Joel thought that chewing on the tough meat would at least take his mind off his aching butt for a while.

"How 'bout yew, big brother?" There was a peculiar leer on Virgil's face when he asked the question.

"Ye know I never partake," Wesley said, pulling a johnnycake from a pouch and munching on it.

How about that, Joel thought, *a bloodthirsty pirate that's a vegetarian.* He kept himself from smiling.

"I want ye ta lay off the boy, Virg."

"I ain't but offerin' 'im somethin' ta eat."

"Ye know what I mean."

The sound of a shot caused Joel to jump in the saddle.

Wesley reined his horse and looked back along the line of mounted men. "Goddammit, *Perry!*" he said, seeing the telltale smoke that rose from the brown-haired man's rifle.

"I was shootin' a crow!" Perry said, sitting as straight and tall as he was able.

The big man rode back along the line. "I tol' y'all no *goddam* noise!" He reached out, pulled the man from the saddle and threw him to the ground. Before Perry could gain his feet, Wesley had dismounted and grabbed a fistful of brown, greasy hair. He pulled the man upright and punched him hard in the throat. Red-faced and clawing at his neck, Perry fell and writhed on the ground.

Virgil whooped and hollered, nearly falling out of the saddle.

Wesley turned away and mounted his horse. "Let's move on."

Joel quickly put out of his mind the realization that he could displease the big man as easily. If he allowed himself to worry about it, he sensed he would instantly become the sort of person that irritated Wesley.

Joel was glad he was near the head of the column of forty men so he wouldn't have to watch Perry for long. As the pirates rode past, some chuckled at the dying man, some crossed themselves and some just looked away.

" 'Twas jus' as well. I saw one o' Perry's brood outside the cave jus' this mornin'. I'd've wrung its scrawny little throat if it hadn't slipped into the river and swum 'way. I'd warned 'im 'bout breakin' that law *many* times. Perry weren't a good father—he weren't rearin' 'em right no how." Wesley glared around, waiting for someone to challenge him.

"Yew tell 'em, big brother." Virgil cackled, while the rest of the party remained silent.

"Don't ye see, boy," Wesley said to Joel, "I cain't have childerns running wild on the bluff an' drawin' the 'tentions o' unwelcome eyes ta our li'l op'ration. There's fifty men an' more an' their fam'lies as makes their livelihood outta that cave, takin' what's theirs ta take off the folks haulin' their riches downriver. We got a good thing going, spent a long time building it up, an' I ain't gonna let some caterwaullin' brat spoil all my careful laid plans." Joel nodded, keeping his eyes down.

"Plans my ass!" Virgil said. He cackled again and his brother shot him a hard look.

The brothers fell silent and Joel could hear the men directly behind him talking.

". . . ridin' the Natchez Trace wit' Mason. We was hauntin' this spring 'long the Trace, an' one afternoon three men an' their pack horses come 'long fer water. 'Course we was all blacked an' we jumped outta the cane an' demanded they surrender their money and property. One o' the pack horses got spooked an' run 'way. We took what we could, a pitiful small take, off'n the men an' horses what was lef' an' was in a pretty big hurry ta make our escape. I heard tell later, from a man I knowed up in Nashville, that the horse that run off was carryin' eleven thousand in gold coin. So, the party caught up with the horse, made it back home and drank a toast ta our ineptitude. Now ain't that somethin'?"

"Somethin' I'd fergit if I was you," his companion said.

"Life is fer laughin' an' havin' a good time. Death is nothin' but serious, an' if ye cain't laugh at yerself from time ta time yer halfway there."

They can slaughter an entire boatful of people for some grain and stinky old skins, but at least they've got a sense of humor. Joel blinked the wave of unreality from his mind.

By the time Wesley called a halt, Joel was so tired and sore from riding that he tumbled out of the saddle and nearly fell to the ground. Taking the reins, he led his horse to a stream where Wesley was watering his own. *Fuck. I'm walking like John Wayne with a stick up his ass.*

"Ye ain't done much ridin', have ye boy?" Wesley asked, noticing Joel's stiffness.

"No, I ain't. Not much anyway."

"Well, stretch yer legs some. Takes the stiffness out."

Joel left the horse drinking at the stream and walked into the trees to get away from the others. He did his best to work the stiffness out of his body, but he was so sore he could hardly move. He didn't feel much better by the time the big man called for everyone to mount up.

"Ye be careful with that horse, boy," Virgil called out, "it ain't yers! Hell, it ain't none o' ours, neither—it's stole!" A few men laughed loudly.

When Joel was feeling fine he had a difficult enough time reaching the stirrup. Now, in pain and trying to hide his discomfort from the others, it was almost impossible. He put his foot up on the stirrup, grabbed the horse's mane, pulled and jumped. The saddle slid off the horse and knocked him to the ground.

Virgil howled his laughter so hard, tears sprang from his eyes. Joel felt his cheeks burn as the other pirates joined in.

"Goddam! Don't ye know nothin' 'bout ridin', boy?" Virgil threw a little rock and hit Joel in the back of the head.

Joel tried to ignore him. He lifted the heavy saddle and struggled to put it back on the horse. He was too short to maneuver it into place and when it fell to the ground once again, the pirates laughed even harder.

"Ye ain't good fer nothin', boy, know that? Nothin'!" Virgil spat on the ground in disgust.

"Help 'im with 'is saddle, Virg. An' tighten that cinch back up, or I'll give ye another whippin', right here an' now!"

Virgil scowled at his brother, but obeyed. As he was putting the saddle back on, he muttered under his breath. Joel knew the man was talking about him because he heard his name a time or two. When he was done, Virgil stomped off to his horse, mounted up, and trotted off without a word.

"Virgil," Wesley called out after him, "where the hell ye goin'? Virgil? *Goddammit!*"

34

As the flame began to flicker, it set up a strobing effect and Mark imagined he was moving in slow motion. Did he, or did he not see a salamander boy scuttle across the path? He tried to aim the Zippo in the direction the thing had squirmed. It shifted in his hand and the hot metal burned his palm. He cried out, dropping it, and still lit, the lighter skittered across the rock, coming to rest under a boulder. Mark chased after it, squatted down and reached an arm into the space beneath the rock.

Curses from his left.

In the corner of his eye, there was a sudden wisp of smoke, or long gray hair. Startled, he spun toward it, choking back a cry. No one was there.

Mark tried to ignore his imagination as he reached for the lighter once more. *Anything could be under there, you know. A rat. A big spider. A whole nest of centipedes.* His fingers brushed the still-warm lighter. He grasped it and withdrew his hand in a hurry.

Despite the chill air, Mark removed his shirt and wrapped it around his hand to protect it from the lighter's heat.

A flash of green light from behind.

He held the lighter before him and headed deeper into the cavern. Something tickled his ears; a soft giggling.

Did that laughter come from voices or from falling water? The waterfall Joel had mentioned shouldn't be too far away. He was becoming thirsty just thinking about it.

"Unlike 'is brother, he's always hungry," came a man's voice.

Mark paused by the passage from which the voice emerged. He looked in and, seeing nothing but darkness, he thrust the lighter into the opening. Inside were a pair of dirty, raggedy men, one a skinny, balding fellow in rotten buckskins, his companion taller and hairier but shirtless and barefoot.

"Ye kin see it in 'is face," the balding man went on, shielding his eyes from the light.

His companion glanced over at Mark and then back. "It's the hunger o' the spirit. I once saw 'im tear a man's throat out wit 'is teeth."

"Hello," Mark said as he passed between the two and moved off down the tunnel. They smelled like Joel's father did when he'd been drinking.

The men stared after him. "Oh, tha's jus' Wesley's dawg."

Mark wandered down the passage toward an orange glow coming from a chamber in the left-hand wall. As he got closer, the air filled with a pungent aroma that stung his eyes and took his breath away.

Inside, a massive, green-stained metal boiler sat atop glowing coals. A copper tube snaked out of the top and looped over into a barrel. With a finger, he traced the length of the metal snake and knelt to examine the barrel. This was the source of the smell. It was large, like one his mother used to catch rainwater, and toward the bottom was a spigot.

A couple of empty, earthenware jugs waited nearby on the stone floor. Along the wall were stacked more jugs, all corked and sealed with wax. Curious and thirsty, he picked one up and heard liquid sloshing around inside it. He pulled out the cork and took a tentative sniff. His eyes filled with tears and his nose began to run. It reminded him of kerosene.

Lifting the jug, he took a small sip and coughed on the foul-tasting liquid. It burned like hell, hitting the back of his throat like flaming gasoline, and he gagged.

Stupid, he thought, replacing the cork. He set down the jug and headed out of the chamber and down the tunnel.

As he skirted a gaping hole in the stone floor, Mark saw hands flailing toward the rim of the chasm.

"Hey, boy, c'mere an' gimme a hand," the darkness called out to him in a strained, female voice.

Mark peered down at the grasping hands. They belonged to a thin, pale woman in rags, her eyes squinting against the light he was holding. She wobbled back and forth within the opening, as if unsure of her footing.

Although the sight of her was unsettling, Mark instinctively reached out to help her. The woman seized his wrist tightly. She swayed back, taking Mark with her.

"Let go!" he shouted as he fell forward.

He toppled through the opening, planting a violent kiss on her forehead. Salty liquid filled his mouth as his teeth broke through her skin. A chorus of horrified moans filled the darkness below as he struck something that screamed, something that thrust into his gut, and at last landed atop a weeping, groaning pile of broken flesh.

In the dim, yellow light, he disentangled himself, pulling a limp arm off his chest, fractured bone protruding from the skin in bloody daggers. He kicked a bleeding torso from atop his legs and stood up.

Where's the lighter?

An underfed body lay across his path, skull dented in and leaking blood, back arched and trembling. He jumped clear of it and scanned the floor for the Zippo. The heap of bodies looked like one tortured, twisted creature, groaning from many mouths, bleeding from countless wounds. Mark thought, for some reason, there were probably similar things in hell.

He felt lucky to have survived the fall. His mouth hurt a bit, but still, he was all in one piece. Now, if he could just find the lighter.

Scanning his surroundings, he found his shirt and pulled it on over his head.

A grunting sound came from his right, and he turned. A stone formation was crouched against the wall. Or was it a statue? It seemed to be straining, a peculiar look on its immobile features. A foul odor greeted him and he turned and walked across the broad chamber in the opposite direction.

A withered dog, missing both hind legs, dragged itself after him. Mark stopped to look at it, and it snuffled up to him, eagerly wagging the entire rear half of its body in greeting. Mark bent to pet its head. Beneath its dry, sparse fur, its skin was rough with scabs and sores.

In an alcove, Mark saw a woman eating the side of a child's face. About to turn away from the horrible sight, Mark realized that she was just licking him clean.

That's a damn sight better, he thought, laughing.

He came to a stinking, brown pile heaped behind a wall built from broken cave formations and logs. A wiry, dark man whose arms and legs jerked like a gigged frog's emerged from behind the wall and motioned Mark over. "Have a bite to eat?" he asked. When Mark approached, the dark man held out a hand full of reeking filth. Mark grimaced and shrank away. The man plucked a pale lump from the mess—in the poor light it looked like a giant grub worm—and popped it into his mouth.

"Oh God!—that's *so* gross!" Mark clapped his hands over his mouth, trying not to puke.

"Wha's a matta boy?" The man plucked another lump and offered it to Mark. "Don'tcha like mushrooms?"

"Mushrooms?" He laughed at himself and accepted a handful. Walking away, he selected one, brushed away its coating of

horseshit and took a tentative bite.

Not bad, he thought with surprise, *and I never liked mushrooms before.*

His foot struck something that skittered across the floor with a metallic ring. His mind said, "Zippo," and he chased after it. The wan, yellow light gleamed off its polished surface, and he snatched it up, relieved.

The lighter held before him, he began circling the wall until he found an opening that led into a dark tunnel. When the sounds of human activity had faded behind him, he sat on the floor and closed the lighter. Plunged into darkness, he had nothing but himself.

At first, the silence was a physical thing that pressed in on him. Then he was able to pick out distant sounds from the utter blackness—a shout or cry, the trickle of water, a slight breeze.

Alone.

The word rose unbidden in his mind, trailing memories of Joel and home after it. He didn't like being alone in the dark; even Billy and his Indian would be better than this.

Where are you, Joel? he wondered. *I wish you'd hurry up and come back. I don't want to play this game anymore, I just want to go home.*

Huddled into a ball, Mark put his head in his arms and wept for himself, for what he had suffered at the hands of the Pikes and for being torn from his own world.

I've got to take care of myself now. This isn't a game anymore.

35

"C'mon, Little Man—wake up."

Joel opened his eyes to see Wesley leaning over him. He didn't know where he was, at first, then remembered that the outlaws had set up camp for the night in a small wooded gully. Utterly exhausted, Joel had fallen asleep without bothering to get anything to eat.

All around him, the others snored loudly and he wondered why no one else was up. It was still dark. Stars flickered between the branches of the trees.

Wesley went over to the far side of the clearing and roused Wade. Joel couldn't hear what they said, but presently Wade nodded and pulled his blanket back over his head and Wesley headed back his way.

"Up, Little Man. We ain't got all night. Virgil's got some coffee boilin'. Go git yerself a cup an' be ready."

What time is it? he wondered, slowly getting to his feet.

His knees popped loudly in protest, and Virgil glanced over with a grin that seemed to say, *I know what you're made of.* Joel's legs and back were stiff and aching, and he gingerly stretched out the worst kinks before making his way to the fire.

"Ye think ye kin stand much more o' this, boy?" Virgil asked. He handed him a steaming tin cup.

"I'll be all right." Joel almost dropped the scalding drink. Juggling it in both hands, he set it down on a log and blew on it till the coffee was cool enough to sip. He hated coffee, but not wanting to look bad, he forced himself to drink, trying not to grimace at the taste.

"Jus' a little stiff is all."

Virgil mumbled into his cup. Joel imagined he heard the man say, "Dumbass." *But that couldn't be,* he told himself.

Wesley suddenly appeared on Joel's right. "Ye jus' wait, Little Man. I'm gonna show ye the power o' superstition. Ye didn't know the Pikes was demons from hell, did ye?"

Come to think of it. . . .

"Git that coffee drunk, Little Man. Virg, go unhobble the horses." The big man grabbed up a saddlebag and followed his brother.

Joel held his breath, gulped down the foul liquid and walked over to where the Pikes were saddling up their horses. He picked up a blanket and began saddling his own, the way he'd seen the others do. When he was done, Wesley nodded his head with satisfaction and then checked all the straps and cinches to make sure everything was tight.

Reluctantly, Joel mounted the horse, gingerly easing himself into the saddle. His butt was a great dull ache, and, although he was still excited about the "adventure" Wesley promised, he wished there was some other way of getting there. He followed Wesley out of the clearing and into the night. Virgil brought up the rear.

The air was chill and dry and a gentle breeze blew across their path. In the woods to either side, frogs trilled loudly and the crickets competed with the cicadas for his attention. Joel realized that as the week had progressed, the crickets had begun to drown out the cicadas.

These cicadas only come out every thirteen years, yet they're here now just as they are back at home. Is it a coincidence?

He got the crazy feeling that his ill-fated trip down The New Cut and the cicada invasion were inextricably linked.

If they all die out—gone for another thirteen years—will I be stuck here until they come back? Of course not, that was nutty. But was it any more nutty than everything else that had happened?

Joel looked toward Wesley, but instead of an answer, he saw only the man's massive back. In the heavens, from which answers to such questions were supposed to come, there was only the Milky Way.

A gust of wind whipped the branches overhead, bringing a slight chill. He shivered, both from the sudden cold and the wind's lonely voice. Then the wind shifted direction and came up from behind, bearing with it the sour scent of Virgil. The man smelled like a wild animal; one that would just as soon tear his throat out as look at him. Joel was afraid.

36

In the weak light of dawn, Joel sat on a tree stump hidden from the trail.

"Wait here," Wesley had told him. "Ye'll be outta harm's way, but ye'll git ta hear everythin'. Now, I want ye ta report ta me on what all's said by the posse. Ye hear me, Little Man?"

The Pikes had moved on up the trail about twenty yards and hid in the brush. Joel had been waiting for over an hour now, occasionally chewing on a strip of Virgil's jerky.

He was just nodding off when the sound of hoof beats reached him. He perked up and leaned out from his hiding place to peer down the trail to his right. A large party of armed men on horseback was moving up the hill. Joel estimated there were about sixty of them altogether.

He glanced to his left toward the Pikes' hiding place just as they stepped out onto the trail. When the posse was abreast of Joel, he heard the lead rider call a halt. His men glanced uncertainly at the Pikes. The outlaws stood defiantly in the middle of the road, their hands on the butts of their pistols.

"It's *them!*" someone whispered.

"The Pikes—it's the *Pikes!*"

Joel heard the name, whispered in alarm from man to man. Taken by surprise, the party recoiled, horses shifting nervously as voices rose in pitch and volume.

Obviously shaken, the lead rider turned in his saddle and shouted, "Silence!"

"They's demons from hell itse'f," someone said.

"Look at *that* one," said another, pointing at Virgil. "He's eatin' a baby's *leg!*"

Joel looked to see the wiry outlaw chewing some of his jerky. The man dramatically ripped off a chunk and chewed.

"The big one's got the color o' the devil."

"They ain't demons, they's haints."

"An' I hear ye cain't kill 'em 'cause they's already dead."

"Silence!" the leader bellowed at his men, looking none too confident himself. He turned to the Pikes. "Lay down yer weapons an' lie down in the road!"

Joel could barely make out Wesley's low rumbling. At first he thought Wes was laughing. He wasn't. He was growling. The big man slowly walked toward the posse, picking up speed as his inhuman growling grew louder. The rumbling became a horrible scream, and Wesley charged like a blood-crazed bull. The riders began to break up, a confused and fearful shouting rising from their ranks. Those in the front scattered off the trail and those in the rear of the column turned and fled back the way they had come.

The leader, all afluster, shouted orders to the wind. Swearing, he raised a pistol and sighted on Wesley. The big man roared louder and ran straight at him. The leader fired and the shot went wide. Almost on top of him, Wesley let out a massive, *"BOO!"*

The posse leader's horse reared, nearly throwing its rider before bolting off down the trail.

Wesley pulled his pistols and tossed them aside, then fell on the road, laughing.

Virgil came walking up, cackling madly. "One o' these days, big brother, ye gonna git us killed."

Could I ever be like these guys? They're so damn tough and they're not scared of anything! Well shit, Wesley calls me Little Man, so I guess he thinks I'm tough enough.

"Like I don' tol' ye, Little Man, we's demons from hell!"

37

Billy was startled by a sudden scraping and a flash of light, brilliant in the darkness. He caught brief glimpses of Stick Hat trying to light tinder with his flint and steel. With a meager flame, the Indian lit one of the candles and the chamber leapt into view.

Billy put out a hand and touched one of Stick Hat's Nikes. "I hope Mark won't be long."

The Indian smiled at him.

To pass the time, Billy started a game, drawing figures in the dust on the cave floor. He drew a stick figure, pointed first to it and then to himself, saying, "Billy."

Stick Hat nodded his head and then began his own drawing, a stick figure, twice as tall as the one Billy had drawn and wearing a hat. "Willawic," he said, pointing to himself and then to the drawing.

"Stick Hat," Billy corrected, with a mischievous smile.

The Indian smiled back, nodded his head and said patiently, "Willawic."

Billy gestured toward Willawic's wounded shoulder. "Does it hurt much?"

The Indian shook his head.

Billy drew the Nike symbol in the dust and then pointed to the shoes. Willawic gave him a questioning look.

"Nikes. My mama was gonna buy me a pair, but she never did." He spelled out N-I-K-E-S in the dust, pointed to the shoes again and said, "Nikes."

Willawic took off one of his shoes and turned it around to show Billy the heel. "Nikes," he said, pointing to the word printed on the shoe.

Billy grinned. "That's right. Wow! Now you can read and everything! You're *real* smart."

Willawic began drawing in the dust, periodically looking up to make sure Billy was watching. He drew something that, to Billy, looked like a map. After studying the drawing for a moment, Billy thought he recognized the Mississippi river within the crude topography.

Willawic swept his arms around as if encompassing himself, Billy, the cave, and everything. Then he stabbed his finger at a point on the map next to what Billy had decided was the Mississippi river.

The boy nodded his head enthusiastically. "Hey, this is working. We're talking!"

Willawic pointed to himself and then to a spot above the northernmost end of the Mississippi.

"Is that where you're from? What is that, Canada or Alaska or something?"

The Indian shook his head.

The boy studied the map and finally pointed uncertainly to a spot he thought was closest to home.

"At least I *think* we're from around here somewhere."

Next to the picture of himself Billy drew a picture of Joel—a stick figure with a frown—and Mark—one with crazy spirals for eyes. He pointed to himself and the two boys and shook his head, throwing up his arms and making an exaggerated frown. "I think we're lost."

Billy then pointed out several spots around the one Willawic first indicated and shrugged his shoulders with obvious confusion. Willawic nodded his head, as if understanding. He put a hand to his chest and then placed that hand on Billy's shoulder.

Billy smiled, suddenly flooded with relief. *He'll take care of me,* the boy thought, *I'm really not alone.*

38

Billy heard a loud clatter and a hissed curse from the corridor outside. Ebbie gave a soft bark and got up stiffly to investigate. Taking a lit candle, he followed after her and found Mark struggling to drag an overloaded tow sack around the corner.

"Get back, Ebbie," Mark said. "You're in the way. I'll pet you in a minute. Now, go on."

"Mark, you're back."

Mark gave him a look of exasperation. "What a genius! Climb on over this thing and help me push it inside."

Billy did as he was told. "Whatcha got in there? Something to eat, I hope."

"Oh, I got all kinds of neat stuff in here."

The two wrestled with the bag, reshaping it so that it would pass through the twisted entrance to the dusty chamber.

When they had it where they wanted it, Billy looked up, panting, and said, "Hey, Mark, I gotta ask you something."

"Yeah? Whaddaya want?"

"Where are we?"

"In a cave, simp—jeez!"

"No, no—I mean where *are* we? I mean, these people are real weird and there's nothing like this near home. And I don't recognize anything, and people shoot each other here and kill each other and don't say anything about it. It's not like Cowboys and Indians on TV, Mark, but it is, kinda. Where are we?"

Mark said nothing for a moment, and then answered with a

shake of his head. "Don't ask stupid questions, Billy. Just help me with this sack. I think you'll like what I brought."

"Oh, all right."

Willawic sat up, curious, coughing on the dust the boys were stirring up.

Billy tried to open the bag, to see what was inside, but Mark pushed him away. "Hold your horses. Santa's got presents for everybody!"

As Mark crouched down before the bag, the dog curled up beside him. He scratched behind Ebbie's ears, pulled a couple of bones from his pockets and gave them to her.

The first thing he pulled from the bag confirmed Billy's suspicions that Mark had lost his mind. It seemed to be a set of wooden teeth. Mark snapped them opened and closed, making lunges at Billy and laughing.

"Stop!" Billy giggled. "I wanna see what else you got."

"I have food, but you may not like it very much."

He pulled out a cloth sack of dried fruit, one of dried fish, and two sacks of dried beans. Then he produced potatoes that were wormy, bread that was dried out, and mushrooms that were still caked with horseshit.

"Yuck! I'm not eatin' *that.*"

"Hey, I did what I could. Starve if you want to."

"What about water? The stuff in that skin stinks!"

"Sorry, but all I got's in skins. And I bet it stinks too."

Billy wrinkled his nose.

"You might like this better." Mark rolled out a small keg.

"What's that?"

"It's whiskey, dumbass," he said with a smile.

"I can't drink that, I'm not old enough."

"Who's gonna stop you—your mother?"

The boys laughed.

Next out of the bag were cigars. "You gotta have cigars with your whiskey," Mark said, passing one to Willawic, "it's the *law!*"

The Indian nodded his appreciation and lit it with the candle. The chamber soon filled with noxious smoke, and he put it out, fanning the air and coughing. The boys laughed.

Mark pulled out candles and torches, a folding knife, a pistol and a couple of blankets.

"I did what I could to find some bandages for Stick Hat."

"His name's Willawic."

"Willawic? That's weird. How do you know that?"

"We been talking," Billy said with a smile.

"Talking? Like English?"

"No, like stick figures in the dust, dumbass."

As if to illustrate his point, the Indian pointed to himself and said, "Willawic," then to the older boy and said, "Mark."

"Hey neat, he really *can* talk to us."

"Yeah, kinda. And he can read too!"

"Well, anyway, all I could find for bandages was this rotten cloth." He pulled out a strip of dirty, moldering fabric. "And I've got gunpowder and lead balls for the pistol. That is, if the gun ain't broke, and I think it is."

He handed the pistol to Willawic. The Indian took one look at it and tossed it aside.

"Yep, it's broke all right." Mark grinned sheepishly at Billy. "Oh well, at least we've got the rifles."

The two boys piled the lead balls into a neat pyramid and placed a pouch of gunpowder next to it.

"But I saved the best for last. You're gonna love it."

"What is it?"

"Oh, I dunno."

"C'mon, Mark, lemme see."

"It's just something to help us pass the time, that's all." He

reached into the sack and pulled out a pumpkin.
"We can make a jack-o'-lantern!"

39

"That was *so* cool!" Joel cried up at Wesley. "I've never seen anything so neat in my whole life! You're some real fucking shit, scaring those pussies off like that. You came running at 'em like you weren't scared o' jack shit and—what a bunch o' pantywaists—they took off like they were being chased by some big, fucking tank—you know one o' the ones with the huge flamethrowers or something. Yeah—that's it—you were like some big motherfuckin' armor-piercing round shot out o' the biggest goddam cannon the world's ever seen. No—an intercontinental ballistic-fucking-missile. Fifty megatons o' radioactive death!"

Wesley could only stand and gawk down at the boy as Joel ranted. Virgil seemed ready to smack some sense into him, but Joel knew Wesley would never allow it.

"Goddam, boy," Virgil said, "if you don' stop, yer shit's gonna fall right out yer mouth."

"How did you—I mean what did you—what—why did—why were they so scared of you? You don't even know those guys, do you?"

"Never seen 'em before in my life," Wesley said.

"But—I don' understand."

"He done tol' ye," Virgil said, "the Pikes is demons from hell."

"Yeah, right. . . . You may not know them, but those guys sure know all about you two."

"Tha's right, Little Man, and they's scared o' us, all right. An' that fear's a powerful tool. I been tryin' to show ye how it's used. Ye build y'self a wicked reputation, an' half yer work's already done fer ye."

Joel was excited and flying high all day. In his eyes, Wesley shone like a movie star. Not one of those wimpy pretty boys either—Wesley was the real thing. Joel saw in Wesley the kind of badass he'd always wanted to be. *He's fucking invincible,* Joel thought, looking at the big man. *Bullets just slide off him.*

By noon they'd met up with Wade and the rest of the outlaws and were on the trail again. They rode for an hour and a half and Joel, riding next to Wesley, ran his mouth. For the first couple of hours, Wesley swelled under the nonstop barrage of flattery. It was obvious to Joel that the big man didn't understand much of what he said, but that didn't seem to matter.

"Now listen to me, Little Man," Wesley said at last, gritting his teeth, "ye better hesh up now. We's gonna be lyin' in wait offa the trail fer a bit. Don' know jus' how long. If I hear ye talkin', I'm gonna hafta smack ye. Ye listenin' to me, Little Man? Now, make sure yer pistol's loaded, an' git yerself hid an' outta the way. We all gotta be ready fer anythin', ye hear?"

Behind an embankment along the road, the outlaws hunkered down and waited. They loaded weapons, sharpened blades, and traded whiskey and stories back and forth among themselves. Joel kept to himself and did little but watch Wesley as the big man moved about. He had always known about the power of fear, had been *the bully* and used that to his advantage. Wesley, however, had turned it into an art form.

Their eyes met and the big man's grin seemed to say, "Now watch this." Wes stood up and cleared his throat loudly and everyone turned toward him.

"Boys, I don' hafta tell none o' ye what a good thing we got goin' at the cave. The posse is on its way ta try an' put an end ta that. This here's our chance ta defend our livelihood, an' rightfully so. Well, *goddam,* we cain't let 'em jus' take it from us! An' after what we do here today, we ain't gonna have no more trouble!"

The men roared their assent.

From his station among the trees growing on the slight embankment beside the road, Joel recognized the leader of the approaching armed party. The way the posse had panicked before, he figured they would still be running. He started to feel a grudging respect for the man. He must have regrouped his men and picked up the outlaws' trail. *Well, you'll soon be runnin' like rabbits again,* Joel thought with a smile.

Joel had been so wrapped up with thoughts of Wesley, he wasn't thinking about why the pirates were here. As the posse drew abreast of the outlaws, Joel abruptly realized that there would be no running this time. They were riding into a massacre.

This is exactly what the Pikes wanted. They used themselves as lures and made sure the posse knew exactly where to find them. Oh Christ—

Wesley gave the signal and half the outlaws rose up and fired their weapons. Through the blue cloud of powder smoke, the boy saw several men fall beneath the storm of lead.

Ohmygod, he thought, his mouth agape. There was no thought of firing his pistol.

The posse leader's head opened several new, red eyes and the man slid from the saddle. The surviving horsemen drew weapons and cast frantically about for targets. They shouted to one another to get off the road and out of the line of fire, but the road was clogged with panicked and dying men and horses, and escape would not come easily. As one man wheeled his mount, the horse lost its footing and tripped over another fallen horse, and crushed its dying rider. Another man scrambled on foot to get away, slipping in the blood and entrails of one of his comrades. A knife whistled out from the underbrush and split his throat.

In the hiatus of gunfire, the pirates, wielding steel, fell upon the rioting posse like angry spectators at a bloody parade. A wild and fearsome cry broke from the body of the melee, the Pikes at the screaming heart of it. Joel watched from the embankment, his pistol, forgotten, hanging limply from his fingers. He found himself the sole spectator and it was all he could do to keep from running.

Joel saw Virgil stalking each of his victims like the predator he was, quickly zeroing in, killing with sudden brutality. Without a sound, he seized a wounded man lying on the road, opened his jaws like he was about to scream from the bottom of his soul, and ripped out the man's throat. Bits of flesh were caught in Virgil's crooked teeth and blood drooled out of his mouth onto the dusty road.

Then the smaller Pike was hidden from view as the battle swarmed around him. Joel watched as a pirate's lower jaw was torn away by a pistol shot, and then his attacker fell, his throat cut from behind.

With calculated ease, Wesley rushed up behind a man wearing a military uniform and shoved the barrel of his pistol up between the soldier's legs. The man's eyes went wide and then Wesley pulled the trigger. The soldier fell, holding his crotch and screaming, blood spraying through his fingers in garish ribbons. A slow smile spread across Wesley's face. As he turned toward Joel and took his hand away from his crotch, the boy saw the massive bulge in the front of Wesley's breeches.

His eyes met Joel's across the bloody ground and the boy saw a question forming in the big man's red face. A confusion of fears boiled up in his mind and, before Wesley's question seemed fully formed, Joel lifted his pistol and ran toward the diminishing fight, firing his weapon at an innocent tree.

Stumbling over the dead and dying, Joel felt a sudden, hard punch on his left arm and then he was on the ground, rolling and thrashing as the pain in his arm became the whole world.

40

Joel was drifting off to sleep, his pain subsiding a little, when Wesley came over to check on him. Virgil ambled up behind his brother, watching around the big man's shoulder as he checked the splint Wade had fashioned for the boy.

"You doin' all right, Joel?" Wesley asked.

I'm fucked—he's calling me Joel. He nodded his head, trying to anticipate what Wesley was thinking and running through all the possible explanations he might give for his actions. He was going to have to think fast if he was going to get out of this one.

"He says he's all right—leave 'im be. Shit, Wes, ye sure are actin' queer. And, what the hell was that speech all about?"

"It was fer the boy."

"The boy? What the hell? Ye ain't his goddam school marm!"

"Ain't school learnin', little brother, what I was tryin' ta teach 'im."

"Jus' words, goddam words! An' they're wasted on the boy! Jus' lookit 'im, Wes, he didn't *learn* shit!"

Joel felt Wesley's eyes on him.

"So tell me, *Little Man,*" Virgil asked, "is that yer arm hurtin' ye, or is it yer conscience?"

"Don' toy wit' 'im, Virg. Say what ye mean."

"He *knows* what I mean, Wes. Ye did a whole lot o' *nothin'* out there today, didn't ye, boy?"

"I was lookin' fer an opening—ye know—to get right in there wit' the killin'. It's jus—"

Virgil spat. "Yer yella, boy, a coward. Admit it!"

The accusation hung in the air like the blade of a guillotine. Joel's mind was a blank, no words would come to him. He was on the verge of panic when the idea struck him.

Flattery had worked well enough until now. Perhaps, it would carry him a bit further.

"I didn't wanna say nothin'," Joel began, hoping the words would come to him. "But while the whole thing was goin' on, I-I couldn't help watchin' the master at work."

A great smile slowly spread across Wesley's face.

"Aw shit, Wes, ye ain't gonna—"

"No—now, Virg, let Little Man have 'is say."

"Wesley, I been studyin' how ye move around the men, git what ye want, make everybody serve ye. And in the battle today, I couldn't keep my eyes off ye. Ye were truly inspired—an' inspirin'! I never seen anybody move like that, master over all ye surveyed."

Virgil spat and walked away.

41

Joel's eyes flew open. The cheap digital clock beside him read six a.m. *I'm lying in Moss's loft. Not on my back in a pool of blood.*

He rubbed the old scar on his left shoulder and sat up. *Shit. I feel worse than I did last night.* He still couldn't untie the knot in his gut, and although the weather was not particularly warm, he was already glazed with a feverish sweat. He swung his legs over the side of the bed and cautiously stood up. His shakes had settled down to an electric sizzle and his coordination seemed to be returning, though his nerves were still raw. *Keep it cool, now. Don't bite your hosts' heads off because you're all fucked up.* Joel rubbed his greasy face with his hands. *Why did I dump all that shit on Moss last night? I said too much. Christ, I shouldn't have said anything at all. He probably thinks I've lost my last functioning brain cell.* When he was sure he wouldn't fall on his head, he started down the ladder.

"Moss is out front painting the lightning strike on the big oak tree," Lynn said before Joel was even all the way down. "He should be through pretty soon."

Accepting a cup of coffee from her, Joel sat in the living room and tried to gather himself together. Before he'd finished his coffee, Moss returned from painting the wound in the tree and cheerfully insisted once again that fresh air and exercise would do him some good.

"It's just a little hike. Me an' the children are all goin'," Moss said. "You don' wanna be left out do you?"

Joel rubbed his temples. *Yes, Moss, that's exactly what I want, I want to be left out, left alone, left to die, so get out of my fucking face!*

Of course, he didn't say it. After a moment, Joel heaved himself up and followed.

The morning sun burned the mist off quickly as they walked down the western side of the Phelps property, headed for a creek. Caleb and Brian ran ahead, while Rachel hung back.

"This here's the real reason we bought this property," Moss said, indicating the gurgling, crystalline water.

"Hm," Joel grunted. He was still feeling pretty raw.

"It's real nice, ain't it?" Moss said.

"Unh-hunh."

"So whaddaya think of our little farm?"

"Real nice." Joel didn't look up as he walked along, but he could tell Rachel was watching him. He glanced over his shoulder at her, and they exchanged a dark look. The corner of Rachel's mouth quirked up. Joel realized that she'd been dragged along on the hike just as unwillingly as he had.

"Were you comfortable last night—sleep well?"

Moss's voice grated on his nerves like sandpaper. "Sure," Joel mumbled.

"What?" Moss said a little too loudly.

"I said, *'Sure.'* "

"I mean, no tellin' how bad off that bed is, the way Rachel gyrates in her sleep."

"It's all right."

Moss breathed deeply and looked away. Joel knew he should open up, but couldn't. He just wasn't in the mood.

They waded out to a gravel bar in the middle of the stream. Joel ground his teeth together as cold water filled his shoes.

"See all these smoothed-off river stones?" Moss asked, picking one up. "You find some of 'em in the damndest shapes. Me an' the children like to make a game of it."

"I found one, Daddy," Caleb said, "looks like a giraffe."

"No it don't," Brian said, "looks more like a walrus."

"You know, you're right, Brian," said Caleb, "it *does* look like you."

"Your face!" Brian punched him on the arm and Caleb ran to search the other end of the gravel bar.

"Here's one that looks like a dead muskrat," Rachel said, holding it up. Joel glanced over at her, and his eyebrows shot up. She was holding a dead rodent by the tail, a little smirk on her face. He noticed, then, how full her lips were. Joel looked down in embarrassment. *She's just a kid, for Christ's sake. Don't be a fuckin' pervert.*

"That's 'cause it *is* a dead muskrat," said Brian.

"Oh," she said, swinging it gently back and forth. "Is it?" Joel wondered uncomfortably why she was looking at him.

"Put it down, Rachel. That's repult-seev." Moss shook his head.

She let its tail slide slowly out of her hand and the dead animal struck the gravel with a dull thump.

"Here's one looks like a potato! Doesn't take much to do that," Moss said, clapping Joel on the back and laughing.

"Whatever," Joel said.

Moss has turned into such a hick. Just like his fat cow of a wife.

Wait a minute. That's not fair. God, I'm being such an asshole.

"See what you can find, Joel." Moss's voice was gentle, and Joel felt like even more of a shit.

He stared at his friend, then picked one up at random. "This looks like—I don't know—a fossilized dog turd."

Moss, Caleb and Brian burst out laughing, and Joel winced. He didn't like the stupid game, his nerves were fried from lack of drink, he wasn't enjoying the company, and he had a periwinkle in his shoe from wading out to the gravel bar. He just wanted to go back to the cabin, lie down and take another nap.

"Here's some Indian money," Caleb said running back to his father. He held the fossil out for Moss and Joel to see.

"The Indians didn't really use that stuff for money," Joel said with a snort.

The boy lost his smile, looked at his feet and turned away.

Way to fucking go, you goddam drunk.

"No, wait a minute," Joel said. "It's even cooler than that. Let me see that."

Caleb handed him the stone disk.

"What this is, is a fossil of sea life that existed here when this whole area was under the ocean, millions of years ago. What do you think about that? It's millions of years old!"

The boy had regained his smile. "That's pretty cool."

"Thanks, Joel," Moss said. "I know you're not feeling too good."

" 'S'okay."

"Listen, this afternoon I've got to go into town to pick up this sports car I bought. It's real powerful. I've always wanted one like it. When I come back, we can take it for a spin on some of the windy back roads—what do you say?"

"Sure."

Joel went and sat on the bank. Rachel sat on the opposite bank and stared at him until Joel leaned back on the grass and closed his eyes just to get away from her. Moss and his boys mucked about in the river, splashing each other until they were soaking wet. After an hour or more of turning over rocks, chasing minnows, crawfish, and salamanders, Moss nudged Joel with his shoe.

"Well, I guess I'd better get back on up the hill. If I don't help Lynn with some chores she's gonna have my hide."

Joel followed him, huffing and puffing his way back up the

hill and arriving at the cabin sheened with sweat in spite of the cool autumn weather. While Moss went about his chores, splitting wood and reglazing a couple of windows, Joel lay on the couch. It wasn't long before his eyelids grew weights, and he started drifting off. As he washed under a warm tide of sleep, Joel wondered if death would be half as pleasant, and if so, what he was waiting for.

42

As Joel stepped around the corner leading to the boys' hideout, he saw a wavering light coming from within. Ebbie started growling.

Stupid damn dog.

The first thing he saw was a half-rotten jack-o'-lantern, a candle guttering within it. The wide, toothy grin sagged, black-edged with mold.

Ebbie rose and greeted him with a single bark and Joel patted her on the head. To his right, he saw Stick Hat training a rifle on him. The Indian lowered the gun and lay back down. Mark and Billy were bedded down beside each other on the floor to Joel's left.

"Joel," Mark said, stirring sleepily under his blanket.

"What happened to your arm?" Billy asked, yawning. He rose and examined the older boy's splint and sling. "That's gruesome!"

Joel glanced down at his arm. It was bruised from the shoulder to the elbow. It had originally been purple-black, but now it was fading into lurid reds and greens. *Looks like a goddam sunset.*

"I got shot, in a battle."

"Did *not!*"

"I did *too,* you spaz! Now, jus' shut the hell up, willya? I'm hurtin'. Wes says I'm lucky—musta been hit by a spent bullet, 'cause it didn't go deep, but it sure as hell bruised me up and might have cracked the bone!"

"Jeez, Joel," Mark said, "he didn't mean nothin' by it."

Joel looked at Mark with surprise. He'd never known him to take up for Billy before. He almost said something, had opened his mouth to speak when he thought better of it.

It's the pain making me irritable. His arm throbbed with a deep ache and he had difficulty concentrating on much else. *I wish I had a painkiller, even one lousy Tylenol.*

"Damn," Mark said, "I'm sorry you're hurting. Is there anything we can do?"

Joel was surprised again. *Something's happened to him—he's not so whacked out anymore.* "Not unless you've got any aspirin."

"Sorry, no aspirin, but we do have *this.*"

He turned away, and when he swung back around, he was holding a big jug. Joel grinned as he pulled the cork and allowed his friend to help him lift the heavy jug. He took a long gulp of the whiskey, coughing and spilling the fiery liquid down his shirtfront.

It tasted awful. His mind suggested "moonshine." But then, as he'd heard his father say so many times, "When you're hurtin', the taste don't matter, as long as it does the trick." And even though his father had been talking about a different kind of pain, Joel decided he was right, just this once.

"Shooowee," Billy said. "That stuff's all over your shirt. You're sure gonna stink."

Joel almost came back with something smart, then thought of how Mark might react. Instead, he smiled—at Billy, Mark, or himself he wasn't sure.

Beginning to relax, Joel took another drink, not coughing as much this time. A heavy warmth was spreading from his belly and into his chest and arms. He closed his eyes. His head was beginning to buzz a little. *No wonder my dad likes this shit so much.* Mark popped something into his mouth.

"A cigar? Where the hell did you get it?"

"Back in a storeroom somewheres." Mark whipped out the Zippo and flipped it open. "I was wandering around, found all kinds of stuff. Had to stay low, to keep from being caught—had a couple of close scrapes, lemme tell you. Virgil damn near walked right up to me. But, hell, I kinda know my way around here now. There's a whole bunch of storerooms for food, ammunition and even a place where they sometimes keep horses. And you know what, Joel? That whiskey you're drinking was made right in this cave. It was! I saw the still."

Joel bit the end off of the cigar and spat it out the way he'd seen TV cowboys do. Mark offered him a light. He took a big puff of smoke and immediately began coughing. Stick Hat grinned and Mark laughed.

"Yuck!" Billy said, making a face. "I don't think I like cigars much."

"Oh, I don't know." Joel puffed hugely and tried to sound like a plantation owner. "Ah do s'pose it's an *acquired* taste." He launched into a coughing fit and everyone laughed, even the Indian, although Joel was sure the man didn't understand a word they were saying.

"Look—" Mark reached into the bag by his side. "I've got some potatoes, some beans, even bread!"

"Thank God! 'Cause I'm starving." Joel looked at the food and laughed. "Shit, Mark, how do you expect me to eat that stuff?"

"Well, it ain't much, I admit."

"Ain't much? I can see something moving inside those potatoes and just how, exactly, do you plan to cook those beans?"

"If you leave them in your mouth a real long time," Billy said, "they get soft enough to chew up and swallow. But if you just swallow them without letting them get soft, they give you the farts something awful."

"Yeah, and he stunk this little room up to high heaven. If anybody'd lit a match, we all would have exploded." Mark grabbed his throat and made a face.

Joel chuckled, thinking that he liked this new Mark.

"Hey," Billy said, "we been talking to Willawic!"

"Willawic? Who's that?"

"You know," Mark said, "the Indian—Stick Hat."

"Is that his name?"

"Yeah, we can talk to him now, kinda. And *I* taught him how to read." Billy puffed up.

"No shit?" Joel raised an eyebrow.

"Yeah, it's true," Mark answered, "well, sort of. Billy started it. He an' Willawic were trying to talk by drawing stick figures in the dust. I tried out my French on him. I've had to relearn just about everything I know. It's not the same as at school, and I can only understand about one word in ten, but I *can* talk to him—well, kinda."

Joel stared at his friend a moment. "Wow. I'm really impressed, Mark."

Mark swelled, smiling a little self-consciously.

"Really, I mean it. That'll sure help us a lot, too."

"Yeah, Mark, that's real cool," said Billy. "What I did was real cool, too, wasn't it?"

"Yeah, sure it was, but I wanna hear more about this battle." Mark patted Billy on the back.

"Yeah, Joel, tell us. How'd you get all shot up?" Billy was practically hopping with excitement.

Joel looked at his left arm uncomfortably. "Looks an' feels straight 'nough," Wade had said, "but wear this jus' in case the arm's broke."

Joel looked away. "I'm sorry, guys, I don't think I feel like talking about it much, right now."

When he rode out with Wes six days ago, Joel had suspected

that he was about to participate in something *wrong*. But he'd been so excited about the adventure, he'd pushed his fears to the back of his mind. He'd never expected the experience to fill him with such horror. Now when he closed his eyes, he saw the violent, bloody images that had been burned into his brain that day. His sleep was tormented with the screams of the dying posse men.

"Oh come on," Billy said, *"please?"*

At any other time, Billy's whining voice would have pushed Joel over the edge. But, from everything that had happened, he was in too much pain and too tired to lash out. Instead, he reached out and put a hand on the small boy's shoulder.

"Later, Billy, later. I promise."

43

From a hole high in the ceiling of the entrance chamber, Joel could see everything below. Laris, his naked body painted with red and white stripes like a candy-stick, strutted through the gathering of outlaw revelers, leading a train of prisoners taken during the "adventure." The drunken pirates tore at the prisoners, doused them with wine, urine, and feces. The captives were spat upon and smeared with handfuls of phlegm and ejaculate. They were burned, beaten with knotted ropes and clubs, slashed and pierced by sharp tools and weapons.

Joel closed his eyes against the nightmare. He heard a noise from behind and turned to see Mark. His friend knelt beside him and peered down through the hole.

"Christ," Mark whispered, the color draining from his face, "these guys are . . . I don't know, Joel . . . must be the worst men that ever lived!"

"Yeah, something like that." A wave of nausea hit Joel in the pit of his stomach as he stared at the blood trailing behind the captives. "That shit's like what the Iroquois Indians used to do to their enemies. It was cool to read about, but to actually see it. . . ."

"Are they all crazy, Joel?"

Joel looked up when he heard the raw edge in his friend's voice. "I don't know." Horrified, but strangely compelled, he turned and looked back into the chamber below.

Laris wound his entourage about the fire in the center of the chamber, coming to a stop before Wesley. "Naked, fer yer pleasure, they all are, dear Captain. On behalf o' our great company, I ask ye ta have yer way wit' them."

"Laris, git the hell out o' here. Cain't ye see I'm eatin'?"

As the painted man trotted off with his charges, Wesley tore another hunk of meat from the pig roasting in the fire.

"Hey, Joel, you remember telling me about how these guys would roast you like a pig with your dick in your mouth?"

"Yeah, what about it?"

"There's a pig down there, roasting with its dick in its mouth." Mark's laugh was forced.

"So there is," Joel said flatly.

Virgil, herding before him a group of ragged women from the depths of the cavern, entered the massive chamber. Squealing children followed after them.

Shouts and screams boomed across the chamber as the outlaws rioted, each man fighting for his own woman. Virgil stood in their midst and laughed. The victors dragged their winnings away, wrestling them into submission and then copulating in the dust.

The children wandered aimlessly, with dogs, chickens, pigs, and a screaming spider monkey. Two boys grabbed a dog's tail and ran along behind as it yelped and snapped at them. The girls played with corn-husk dolls in an open space by the entrance.

A bearded pirate wove his way unsteadily between revelers to the fire.

"Rufus!" he cried drunkenly to a friend, clapping him on the back with excessive force, "how in hell are ye?"

Rufus stumbled forward under the blow, his mug sloshing its contents across his shirt. "Goddam, Gower! What was that fer?" Without waiting for an answer, he clouted his friend on the head with his empty mug.

"It was jus' a friendly peck, goddammit!" Gower slammed an arm into Rufus's crotch, grabbed his testicles and bore down.

A long, piggy squeal emerged from between Rufus's clenched teeth as he sagged against Gower. "I thought we was friends," he barely managed to say as he drew a knife and thrust it between Gower's ribs.

Gower coughed and fell back, releasing Rufus's balls. Rufus clutched at his crotch and curled into a fetal position on the ground.

"We was," Gower wheezed. Plucking out the knife, he rolled toward his friend and planted the blade in his ear. Both men spasmed and seemed to expire simultaneously.

Joel shook his head and looked at Mark, refusing to believe what had happened. When he saw his friend's face, twisted with shock, Joel knew his eyes had not deceived him.

The screeching spider monkey caught Joel's attention as it capered over to Virgil. The man was lifting a whiskey jug to his mouth when the animal climbed up his leg. It chittered noisily and urinated down his thigh.

"Goddammit!" Virgil howled as those nearby guffawed. He scowled at them and seized the howling monkey by its tail.

"Burn in *hell,* ye hairy goddam beast!"

He ripped it screeching from his leg and flung it underhanded into the heart of the fire. It made a high-pitched, pitiable scream as its hair ignited. The monkey leapt from the inferno, a living, shrieking comet. Pirates pointed and howled with laughter. Cursing, Virgil snatched a cudgel from his belt and knocked the little creature back into the fire. This time it wasn't coming back out. As the animal roasted, Virgil let out a deep belly laugh.

Mark grabbed the lip of the hole, white-knuckled. Joel saw tears in his friend's eyes, reflecting the orange firelight.

"He's one *goddam mean motherfucker,*" Mark whispered.

Joel lowered his head. "Yeah, he's a scary one. He's crazy,

Mark, crazy as hell and more dangerous than you know—worse than any of the rest of 'em."

Mark turned to face him. "Joel, we gotta get out of here."

"Where would we go? There aren't any other settlements for miles and miles. And besides, if we went looking, we'd only be moving that much further from the way home."

"Well, can't we just leave? Even the woods would be better than this. You can help us there. You always said you could get along fine in the woods, living off the land."

"That was bullshit, Mark, pure bullshit. No matter what I said, there's no way we could survive out there. It's full of dangerous Indians, wild animals and these *goddam* outlaws. And what would we eat? I can't hunt for shit, and neither can you."

"What about Stick Hat—I mean Willawic? I bet he can hunt—he could hunt for all of us."

"He's hurt. He's had a bullet go right through his shoulder and he can't move that arm."

"He's gonna get better."

"But how long's that gonna take? How long before Virgil decides to come after us?" Joel looked earnestly at Mark. "But you do have a point. If we can just hold out till Willawic gets back on his feet. . . ."

"At least we can get away from this, right now." Mark pointed down through the hole at the party below.

"Let's go up to the top of the bluff. The view's great from there."

Joel stood beside his friend on the top of the bluff and looked down at the cold-wiggling stripes of moonlight as they played on the surface of the river. Clouds scudded across the dark-blue sky, obscuring patches of stars. A cool breeze filled their loose cotton shirts and whispered through the cracks in the rock.

"Lookit that wilderness," Joel said. "There's *nothing* out there for hundreds of miles."

Mark gazed out at the silvered blue landscape, and then turned to his friend. "Home's out there somewhere, ain't it?"

"It's not so much some*where,* but some*time.* Our home won't be there for, what, almost two hundred years."

"It's strange to hear you finally say that," Mark said with a shiver. "I know you were hinting at that on our way here, and I've been trying not to think about it. But shit, there's no escaping it." He looked at Joel. "Somehow, I wish you hadn't said anything, though. I feel like, maybe, it could've still been a dream or something if you hadn't just now made it real."

Joel smiled at him, a hollow expression that barely touched his lips. "I know what you mean, and I'm sorry, buddy." He reached out and put an arm around his friend. "We gotta face it, though. And, if we can figure out how we got here in the first place, maybe we can figure out how to get back."

"I don't have the slightest idea where our creek comes out on the Mississippi, do you?"

"No. But shit, someone had to come that way before, 'cause Billy's fucking Indian's got on a pair of Nikes."

"Maybe he can help."

"That's exactly what I've been thinking. You better get to work on your French."

They watched as two outlaws emerged from the cave and staggered onto the rock shelf below, throwing punches at one another. The men fought their way to the water's edge, tumbled into the river and vanished from sight.

"I think I've got Wesley fooled, for now. *He's* not after me. But Virgil, he's something else. I need your help, Mark. You can be the eyes in the back of my head—help me look out for that maniac. He means trouble."

Mark's eyes went wide. "He'd just as soon kill me as you, Joel."

"Yeah, but you're Wesley's dawg. Nobody's gonna bother you, not even Virgil. You've got free run of the place. They all think you're nuts and they're probably afraid the evil spirits that made you that way'll rub off. Let 'em talk, it gives you that much more freedom." Joel patted Mark awkwardly on the shoulder. "Besides, it ain't you he's got it in for. He's out for my blood, Mark."

Mark looked uncomfortable, stared at his feet. He looked down at the river.

Downstream, one of the combatants emerged, sodden, from the water. There was no sign of the other.

"You don't have to say anything, Mark. I understand—you weren't with us for a while there, but it sure is good to have you back."

"Thanks."

The boys were quiet for a time and Joel heard only the sounds of the wind, night birds, and crickets. When he realized that the cicadas were gone, a great void opened up in his gut and he felt his hopes falling into it. He was certain that he would never see home again. He decided to keep that to himself.

"Look, my arm's hurtin' bad. I need to get back down there and drink some more of that nasty-ass whiskey."

44

Billy was surrounded by darkness. He couldn't see his hand waving just inches away from his face. Like a substance filling the space around him and obscuring all light, he could feel the blackness.

He and Mark had been on their way to a storeroom deep in the cave to get more powder for Willawic's rifles when it happened. They were skirting a treacherous drop-off. Mark was in the lead, carrying the lit Zippo, when he lost his footing. He hadn't even cried out as he fell.

At least I'm not alone, Billy thought. Mark was lying unconscious at the bottom of the pit. His breathing, a soft snoring, could still be heard. The little boy could almost imagine Mark was just taking a nap. He wished he could believe that. In the second before the lighter had gone out, Billy thought the pit looked to be fifty or sixty feet deep, if it had a bottom at all.

Billy had been certain at first that Mark was dead. He'd called out to him for what seemed like forever, with no reply at all. His own blood was pounding so hard in his ears that he couldn't even hear Mark's breathing. But then he'd called out one more time, and Mark had answered. To Billy's horror, Mark seemed to have gone crazy again. Nothing he said made any sense.

No, not crazy. After a while, Billy decided that Mark was talking in his sleep. Each time he spoke, his voice began quietly, then became loud enough to be understood.

He's starting up again. Billy strained to hear.

"No, Mama, you can't take it from me. I already asked Daddy, and he said it was okay. From now on I'm not asking anyone. I'm just gonna make up my own mind!"

"Mark, wake up. Turn on the lighter." A sleepy mumble, and then Mark was snoring again. *He must have hit his head so hard. . . .*

Billy felt trapped. He was too fearful to move, afraid he might wind up beside Mark in the bottom of the pit. His tailbone was sore from sitting motionless so long, and his eyes ached from straining to see something, anything.

Carefully, he reached out, one hand at a time, patting at the rock around him. *Just to make sure,* he thought, relieved to find all the rocks where he expected them to be.

His fingers traced the sloping flowstone lip of the pit. As he leaned forward, running his hand along the slick, moist surface, he slipped and pitched forward. Billy could suddenly see himself in his mind's eye—see himself falling and falling and falling. His heart missed a beat, and he felt a dizzying sickness. He lost his bearings, his sense of orientation—was he leaning into the pit, or was his butt sliding out from under him? His whole body flinched and he caught himself as he was falling to one side.

Panic.

The sloping rock was like a huge drain, one that led down, down into darkness and pain and death.

"Mark!" he cried, panting with the flood of adrenaline. "*Please,* wake up!"

The darkness seemed to swallow his words. Below, Mark had become quiet again. Billy wasn't sure which he liked better: Silence, or Mark's confused ramblings.

Tears threatened to spill.

I've got to learn how to be brave, like Mark and Joel. Billy choked back his tears. *I wish Willawic was here, or Ebbie. They'd know how to find the way out.*

But the Indian's wounded shoulder had kept him from coming along. Billy wished he could at least have the dog for company.

Waiting alone, in the utter black, the boy could only keep his panic at bay with the thought that Mark would eventually wake up.

He just has *to.*

45

Joel scrambled after Wesley and the small group of pirates making their way to the corral.

"But I promise I won't get in the way," he said.

"Ye cain't go an' that's that," said the big man. "Yer arm needs time ta heal up."

"Oh come on!"

"Dammit, Little Man, don't make me smack ye. We's jus' goin' bill collectin'. It ain't like we's gonna have any fun."

It wasn't that Joel really wanted to go on another "adventure." He just didn't want to be left behind, and alone, with Virgil.

Watching the group mount up, Joel kicked at the dust in the corral. As they were departing, he desperately sought the words that would convince Wesley to take him along. But they wouldn't come to him and before he knew it, they were gone.

When he turned to head back toward the cave, Virgil was standing just outside the fence, not six feet away, a hungry smile upon his lips. Joel became still and they stood regarding one another through the rails of the fence, the noonday sun beating mercilessly down.

"Well now," Virgil said.

Joel shuddered at the look in the man's eyes and wanted to run.

"Yer school marm's gone, an' now yer all alone in the schoolyard wit' the bully."

He ain't much bigger than me, Joel thought, *and I've taken on plenty of kids older than me. 'Course, Virgil grew up on the frontier. And he's crazy.*

"Whatcha talkin' 'bout, Virg? You thinkin' 'bout doin' somethin', or are you just full of horseshit?"

The man snarled and lunged, trying to grab him through the fence. He got a handful of shirt. Joel threw himself backwards, twisting away. The shirt ripped and Joel landed flat on his butt. He jumped up and ran as Virgil struggled through the fence and gave chase.

Joel stumbled on an exposed root and fell on his face, eyes blinded by the thrown-up dust. His splinted arm was twisted beneath him, and he cried out in pain.

Virgil was on him in an instant. He grabbed Joel by the collar and belt and lifted him off the ground. Kicking and screaming, Joel was carried away by Virgil Pike.

Billy woke up lying on his side on the hard rock. He opened his sticky eyes and suffered a moment of absolute panic—he couldn't see. With a little scream, he rubbed his eyes, blinked, and then remembered where he was. In the bowels of the cave, in the pitch darkness. Mark was in the pit next to him, probably dead or dying. Tears welled up in Billy's unseeing eyes.

"Mark?" he called out. "Mark, you alive?"

There was no answer. Billy wrapped his hands around his knees and put his head between his shoulders. He had no idea what to do.

Then he heard something. Not very loud, but definitely there. A soft grunting, and a scrabbling, like claws. *There's something in here with me!*

"Mark! Help! Mark!" Billy shouted. Again, no one answered. But the grunting got louder, the scrabbling more urgent.

Billy had to get out of there. But he was terrified to move.

What if he were surrounded by pits like the one that had swallowed Mark alive? But he couldn't stay still and let some *thing* eat him for dinner, either. He cautiously reached out a hand, feeling for solid ground.

Something grabbed Billy's wrist. He opened his mouth and screamed.

Dumbass, Joel told himself for the umpteenth time, *should have known better than to go down to that corral.*

He coughed on the thick smoke, and his spasming chest made him swing gently back and forth. He was in the smokehouse, hung upside-down from the log overhead, and his hands and feet were numb from the ropes that bound him. Dizzy, he felt his head was going to burst under the pressure of the blood filling it. He bumped into one of the sides of meat hung alongside and he could almost taste the salt coating its sweating, brown surface. Joel's wounded arm ached terrifically, but at least Virgil had not hogtied him—the pain of that would have been unbearable.

"I gotta shit," the small man had told him, "but when I git back, I'm gonna carve ye up, eat ye, and then shit some more."

Images of Virgil committing cold-blooded murder came back to him again and again—Virgil with another man's blood drooling out of his mouth, Virgil shooting a man in the head at point-blank range, Virgil eviscerating a teenage member of the posse. Fear mounted as scene after scene played across his mind, along with horrifying new scenarios in which he was the victim.

The sound of footsteps broke his anxious reverie. A sudden charge of fear shot through him and he looked toward the sound, straining against his bonds and trying to see through the thick pall of darkness. He managed a clumsy "Shit!" around his gag.

The footsteps grew closer and, as he struggled, he began to

swing wildly, colliding with the sides of meat and the chilly wall. A wavering orange light appeared in the distance.

Fuck me up the butt, he thought, *it's Virgil!*

He saw the man looming through the smoke, carrying a great blade in one hand, ready to fillet him.

"Shit-oh-shit-oh-shit," he whimpered, tears of fright drooling into his hair.

The wavering form grew closer and by the flickering torch in the man's hand Joel could almost see his angry face.

"Hi, Joel!" Mark said, holding a guttering torch aloft. "Whatcha doin'?"

"God," Billy said, coughing, "it's really smoky in here."

"We finally found the smokehouse," Mark said, cheerfully, "came up for some jerky. Want us to let you down?"

46

When Joel struck the floor of the smokehouse, Mark laughed, remembering a time when their roles had been reversed.

"Can't feel nothin' but pins and needles in your feet, can you? It hurts, don't it?"

"You hear that?" Joel asked.

"Yeah, I hear footsteps," said Billy.

"I don't hear anything," Mark said, still chuckling. "You know I fell down this big ol' pit and got knocked out. Billy was stuck in the dark 'cause I had the lighter. He thought he was gonna die until I woke up and climbed out and scared the shit out of him. Take a look at this!" He pointed at a bruised swelling on the side of his head. "I nearly cracked my skull open—"

He bit his tongue as Joel yanked him off his feet.

"Come on, goddammit!" Joel snapped. "Virg's coming back and he's in a foul mood!"

Angry growls and barked curses chased the boys down the nearly vertical shaft that opened at one end of the smokehouse. The sounds of Virgil's pursuit echoed eerily along the stone walls.

"Oh little mouse!" Virgil said, changing his tone. "Joely, Joely, Joely!"

The boys traversed a small chasm and then started down the chimney again. Near the bottom, the walls narrowed, forcing them to move single-file until they came to a crack in the wall that led to a five-foot drop to the floor of another tunnel.

"Hurry up, Joel!" Mark cried.

"Hang on, I only got one fuckin' arm."

"He's gonna get us!" Billy shrilled.

"I'll go first and then help you and Billy down." Mark wedged the torch into a small crack and then jumped, a blast of adrenaline making him unsteady on his feet. He leaned against the wall and reached up for Billy. The small boy kicked him in the ear.

"Sorry." Billy's voice was breaking up. "I-I think I'm gonna pee."

"Not on me, you're not!" Mark yanked the boy from the crack and dropped him roughly on the floor.

Billy got up and ran. A few steps carried him outside the pool of light cast by the torch. Mark was turning to help Joel when he heard a thud and Billy's yelp of pain.

"Dammit, Billy," Mark called over his shoulder, "stay where you are and don't move. You wanna fall in a pit like I did?"

Mark was wrestling gently with Joel's splinted arm, trying to help him work it through the crack. It popped free and Joel slipped, landing on Mark. They stood and when Mark retrieved the torch, he saw that his friend was pale and sweaty from the pain and exertion.

"When I gits done wit' ye, little mouse," Virgil hollered from above, closer than Mark expected, "there ain't gonna be 'nough lef' ta bury!"

Billy ran back. Blood was running from his nose and there was a large wet spot around the crotch of his pants. "C'mon, guys, we gotta run and hide!"

As the boys ran along the corridor, Mark wondered if Virgil could track them by following the scent of Billy's blood. They could separate, he decided. That way Virgil would have to choose between three trails of footsteps.

But I sure as shit wouldn't wanna be at the end of the trail he chooses.

Glancing behind, he saw Billy and Joel struggling to keep up and he stopped to wait. As they continued, Mark periodically slowed to let the other two catch up.

The sounds of Virgil's pursuit at times seemed distant and then close, as if he were almost upon them. *Must be a trick of the tunnels,* Mark thought, because when he turned to look back, expecting to see the man right on their heels, there was only darkness.

"Little mouse, gonna hang ye by yer own tail!"

When he saw the hands flailing in the hole up ahead, Mark stopped short and turned to Joel, whispering, "There's a hole with a woman in it."

"What the hell are you talking about?"

"No time to explain. Here, take the lighter. You guys jump behind that bunch of rocks there and hide."

"But—"

"Dammit, Joel, there's no time!"

Billy had already jumped off the path and Joel followed, crouching down out of sight. Mark scuffed up their footprints, confusing the trail, and then scuffed his way toward the hole in the floor.

When Virgil came around the bend in the tunnel, Mark didn't give him time to focus on him. He dropped the torch, and leapt through the hole into waiting hands.

The human pyramid collapsed, taking him with it. He heard somebody say, "Not again!" as he rolled to the floor and stood up shakily. He stepped back from the groaning pile of humanity and looked up through the hole in the ceiling at Virgil's cursing silhouette.

"Oh well," Mark said, "I'm lost again."

★ ★ ★ ★ ★

Joel was shocked when his friend leapt into the hole. But he and Billy didn't have much time to react before Virgil took their attention, staring down into the hole and swearing a blue streak.

"He must be okay," Billy whispered, "since Virgil's cussing at him."

"He was addled to start with," Joel whispered back. "I don't think that bonk on the head did him any good."

Virgil finally headed back the way he'd come, muttering angrily to himself. As the little man passed their hiding place, Billy made an involuntary whimper and Joel slapped a hand across the boy's mouth.

They waited long after the man's footsteps and curses had faded away before venturing out. Stepping over to the hole, they peered down. Thirty-five feet below, Mark stared back up at them.

"I'll catch up with you later," he said, "at our hideout."

"Are you all right?" Billy shouted. "That's a long fall!"

"Shut the hell up, asswipe!" Joel hissed, glancing over his shoulder, "You want Virgil to hear? He ain't that far off."

"Sorry, Joel."

"C'mon now, we gotta get outta here." He picked the flickering torch up off the ground and led the way.

"You know," Billy said, "Mark's our hero!"

"What?"

"Mark's our hero."

"Whaddaya mean?"

"Well, you saw what he did. Jumped, what—like six hundred feet or so? He could've died! And he did that to get Virgil off our trail. He took a big chance. He's our hero!"

"Yeah, I guess you're right. I hadn't thought of it that way. Remind me to give him a big ol' kiss when we see him again."

They were almost to their hideout when they heard Virgil roaring as he ran, his footsteps echoing loudly along the corridor. The boys wheeled to look, and Virgil came charging around a corner.

Billy backed up against the wall to keep from being trampled, and Joel took off running, heading for the back way out. Virgil's fingers were snagging the ends of his torn shirt when Joel burst through the opening and made a quick turn to his right, dropping the torch. Virgil charged through the cave mouth and kept going, pushed by his own momentum. He stumbled and fell as he whipped his head around looking for Joel. The boy had a head start climbing up the rocky bluff, and he took advantage of it. His splinted arm slowed him down as he scrambled for the top. Virgil was up and after him again, climbing the cliff face like a spider.

This is gonna hurt like a mutherfucker, he thought as he rushed across the flat, stony top, *especially if this is the wrong spot. But not nearly as much as what Virg will do to me.*

Joel scrambled for the edge of the cliff and threw himself off. Relief flooded him as he looked down and saw the green river directly below. He hugged his left arm and braced himself. He hit feet first and knifed down into the water, but his left elbow hit the surface and a monster wave of pain blasted up his arm. Joel blacked out.

Moments later, he came to, bobbing to the surface and choking on a mouthful of water. His arm throbbed like one big toothache. Crying out in pain, he held his wounded arm to his side and began to sink. He kicked with his legs and rose back to the surface.

Looking up, he saw Virgil racing down the switchback trail. He reached the bottom and jumped into a dugout, paddling upstream to head the boy off. Joel swam for the opposite shore. His clothing weighted him down and his arm pulsed with fresh waves of agony.

Virgil fought the current to reach him, paddling furiously and screaming curses. Joel willed his legs to kick harder, his good arm to stroke faster.

". . . you!" The wind brought the single word, full of menace, to Joel's ears.

Joel pushed himself, flailing his limbs, as the current began pulling at him. It wore him down and he began to sink. With all he had, he kicked back to the surface.

The man was close enough now for Joel to hear him shouting, ". . . ye *dare* drown on me, boy! Don't ye *goddam* dare!"

Joel knew he was as good as dead—if he didn't drown first, Virgil was sure to kill him.

But Virgil was slowing up, running out of steam, gradually falling behind.

Feeling gravel under his feet, Joel hauled himself up and began to slog his way toward the distant shore. Seeing the current had carried him some fifty yards downstream, Joel cut upstream across the gravel bar. When he was halfway to shore, the bar gave out and he plunged under water again. He kicked back to the surface and continued swimming for the opposite bank.

Gradually the river bottom came up to meet him again, and he crawled through mud and silt up onto the bank. He collapsed, gasping for breath, the pain in his arm pounding away at him. He could only hope that Virgil had tired himself out so much he would abandon the chase.

Little chance of that.

His eyes focused on worms wriggling out of the mud. His cheek was on the cold clay, mouth open and gasping for breath. He wondered if there were any worms near his lips and that got him moving again.

Joel spat out mud and propped himself up to get a better

look downstream. Some two hundred yards away, Virgil had abandoned the dugout and was pulling himself ashore. The pirogue wandered off, carried by the current. Joel glanced back the way he had come. He guessed that, in thirty minutes, he had swum more than a quarter of a mile.

Joel fought his way to his feet and stumbled forward. He squeezed between stunted saplings, their twisted limbs decorated with debris from past floods. Immediately, he came up against an almost vertical wall of eroded clay and stone. He tried to scramble up, but it crumbled beneath his fingers and toes. Crouching low, Joel skirted the wall, moving upstream until he came to a small, deep-walled creek that emptied into the river. He sloshed his way into it and found a root sticking out of the bank with which he could haul himself out. He swung up onto a mossy knob that supported a massive cottonwood.

Hiding behind the great bole, he inched his way forward to get another glimpse of Virgil, but the man was nowhere to be seen.

Joel turned to the forest that loomed behind him. In the half-light, beneath the canopy of leaves, it was not a welcome sight. He felt small and powerless, like he did the first time he emerged from The New Cut into the virgin forest. And, this time, he was alone.

Virgil's gonna find me if I don't keep moving. I don't see him, but I know he's back there.

Joel followed a narrow animal path that wound into the forest. When it passed into a briar patch, he considered crawling in to hide. But he realized it would provide more pain than protection and would ultimately trap him. Virgil would only have to wait for him to come out.

As he hurried along, the vines reached for him, thorns hooking into his shirt. "Shit!" he hollered, pulling a long, wicked thorn out of his arm.

That's it, you dumbass, just go ahead and tell Virgil right where you are.

He heard a branch snap to his left and nearly peed his pants. Heart pounding, he whipped around to look, but there was nothing to see. In the distance, something fell from a tree and an animal cried out, sounding almost human. Joel's hearing became hypersensitive as he strained to identify each new sound. Most were animals, but those left unexplained ate at him. *Virgil could be anywhere. Anywhere.*

He was hungry and thirsty, and he cursed himself for not getting a drink from the river when he had the chance. His arm throbbed painfully, and his legs and feet were one colossal ache.

There was a sharp click in the distance. *A pistol being cocked!* A burst of adrenaline, and Joel threw himself to the forest floor.

Wait a minute, Virgil doesn't have a gun! Probably a damn *deer stepping on a* damn *twig.*

I hope.

Joel sat on his butt and took a deep breath. He realized he should slow down, take more care to be quiet.

The sun was vanishing behind the slopes of distant hills, and what sky could be seen through the webwork of tree branches overhead was orange and vermilion.

After scouting about for a place to hole up for the night, he found the ancient ruin of a massive tree. Its hollow trunk towered forty feet above the forest floor. Its blackened, jagged top, blasted by lightning years before, came within easy reach of the lower limbs of neighboring trees.

A good escape route.

The only other way in was a gaping hole some five feet off the ground, where a limb had rotted away. With his good arm, Joel leapt for it and hauled himself up. He dropped down inside, hoping he wasn't about to land on a bear. But his feet never touched the bottom. Something had him by his bad arm and he jerked to a stop, pain cascading into his shoulder and chest.

"Owgoddammitsonofabitch!" he sputtered. But it wasn't Virgil who held him. His splint had caught on the bottom of the entrance hole. Eyes watering with pain, Joel twisted himself around until the splint tore free.

He fell on his butt, landing on soft, spongy moss and leaf debris. His movements stirred up flakes of rotted wood and excited the whitish glow of foxfire. He began to itch as a horde of beetles crawled out of the wood to inspect him, their sticky little feet scratching at his skin.

Joel bit off the scream rising in his throat. He brushed the insects away, but they crawled right back on and he was forced to try to ignore them. Eventually, they seemed to lose interest and went back to their wooden nests. Resting his head on his good arm, Joel curled up in a ball and closed his eyes. He was more exhausted than he'd ever been in his life, but he couldn't relax. *What if Virgil looks in and finds me here? I can't climb out of the top of this tree quickly. I'd be like a fish in a barrel. What if those bugs crawl in my hair? Shit, what if they go in my ears?*

Fuck it. They can set up housekeeping in my goddam nose if they want to. I don't give a shit anymore. With a great exhalation, Joel drifted off to sleep.

There was a sudden, loud tapping outside on the trunk of Joel's tree. The sound jolted him awake, and he hauled himself up to peer cautiously out the hole, squinting in the filtered morning sunlight. Startled, a red, black and white bird flew away.

It's only Woody the Dicknosed Woodpecker.

Relieved, he dropped back down, aware of the emptiness in his belly. He also became aware of the close, dusty smell of his hideout. The wood was dry and flaked if he brushed up against it, and his skin itched miserably from all the wood dust that had worked its way inside his clothing.

Joel struggled out of the tree, bumping his injured arm several times. The pain ran like electrical shocks through him and he regretted his choice of a hiding place. Getting in was one thing, but getting out was like working some pain puzzle. And the worst thing was that it had all been unnecessary—Virgil was nowhere to be seen and Joel didn't have to use the escape route.

Of course, the bastard might be watching me right now.

Joel walked away from the sun, assuming that would take him back to the river. He wished he could walk silently like the Indians did. For all the noise he was making, he could've been an elephant crashing through the jungle.

He followed the sound of gurgling water and soon found a spring surrounded by a cluster of stones. He tore moss and ferns from the rocks to make a place for himself, flopped down on his belly and stuck his face in the water. It tasted better than it had any right to, and he drank until he was sick to his stomach. His parched throat began to loosen and he made a soft sound to check out the equipment as he straightened up.

An iridescent dragonfly lit on his arm and he watched it poke about the hairs of his wrist. At one angle, it was an intense, unnatural green, at another, a deep, electric blue. He thought the insect was one of the most beautiful things he had ever seen, and when it rose and began to fly away, he followed. Unwilling to take his eyes off it, he stumbled along and would have missed the berry bush if the dragonfly had not lit upon it.

Thanks, Mr. Fly.

As if in response, the creature lifted from its leaf, fluttered about his head, and flitted away.

Joel gorged himself, staining his hands and face purple with blackberry juice. He went back to the spring, and rinsed himself off.

I wish I had a canteen so I could take some water with me. Or even one of those god-forsaken, stinking water skins.

Joel listened to the forest. The wind was up, rattling the leaves in the trees and hissing through the underbrush. The insects were rioting. And had he ever listened to the birds before, really listened? God, they were so loud and there were so many different voices. *Are they talking to each other, or do they just want to fuck?*

Feeling that he had put an entire night between himself and his pursuer, Joel was beginning to relax. He lay down on a mossy slope and had just dozed off when a sudden itch—not of the body, but of the mind—awoke him.

Joel wasn't sure what it was, but whatever, it was persistent. Like a mosquito after his blood, he could swat at the feeling and it would just flit away, only to return again.

He sat up suddenly, the hairs on the back of his neck standing on end. Was he being watched?

Virgil!

Joel bolted to his feet, glancing desperately in all directions. Realizing he was out in the open, he looked for a way into concealing undergrowth. He crouched down and scrambled for the brush.

Turning, he caught a glimpse, a glint of sunlight off what might have been an eye and what looked like a warty back. He focused on the knobby trunk of a hackberry tree. Was that it? Was Virgil hiding behind the tree? Joel hit the ground, craning his neck to see beyond the blowing weeds. There was a croaking, or was that two trees rubbing against each other in the wind? He saw a brownish, lumpy shape bounding through the grasses beneath the hackberry.

Ol' wiley Toad, he'll git ye every time.

Royce's words popped into his head like an unwanted guest. Joel thought that old coot, holed up in that cabin with his family, was nuts talking about that frog thing.

The Mingit Toad is a giant toad, easily as big as yew, or even me, an' he'll steal yer soul if'n ye look 'im in the eye.

The boy eased into the crisscross shadows beneath the trees, filled with curiosity and fear. *Could it be,* he wondered, *could that old coot have been speaking the truth?*

"No fucking way," he muttered, trying to dispel the fear that bred in the silence. "That's totally nuts."

The forest seemed to gather up his words and throw them to the wind.

Joel wanted to get a look at the thing, whatever it was, whatever the truth. But. . . .

An' don' think ye kin git a looksee, an' jus' look away quick-like. Nossir—even Injuns ain't that quick.

Was he tracking the toad, or was the toad tracking him? And just how big was this thing, anyway?

He's been known ta lasso small childerns wit' 'is long, black tongue, reel 'em in, an' swaller 'em down.

He remembered Royce making that long slurping sound.

Joel eased toward the hackberry, moving as quietly as possible. The grasses bent and swayed beyond the tree, as if something fairly large were moving. Crouching low, he sidled up to the base of the tree. When he was in position, gripping the warts on the bark, he held his breath and listened. A soft, almost human grunting came from the other side. He'd take a quick look, a real quick look, and then run away.

Sneak up on ye an' jump out at ye when ye least 'spect.

Joel leapt out, adrenaline racing through his body, his nerves sizzling and his eyes bugging for a glimpse of the monster.

An' bang!

There was Virgil, squatting over a fresh pile of shit, his breeches down around his ankles. He looked up, as surprised to see Joel as the boy was to see him. Joel gave him a shove and Virgil toppled backward into his pile.

The boy leapt away and was running full tilt by the time Virgil's cries of rage filled the trees.

47

Joel had been gone for more than a day and the boys wondered if Virgil had caught up with him. Was he even still alive?

"We should go find him," Billy declared as they sat in their hideout chamber, watching Willawic chanting. "Maybe he needs our help!"

The color drained from Mark's face. "We got no idea where he is. He could be anywhere. And what are we gonna do if we run into Virgil, Billy?"

"Kill him!" Billy grabbed a flintlock and stuck out his chin.

"We'd prob'ly get lost and die ourselves before we ever even found him. And Joel can take care of himself. 'Sides, this is his fight. He'd prob'ly be mad if we tried to help." Mark frowned as he spoke, then leaned forward and put his chin on his knees.

Billy watched him carefully. He still thought they should go after Joel. But something about Mark's scared, troubled eyes told him he'd never convince the older boy of that.

"I know, Mark! Let's go huntin'! That way we'll have some fresh meat when Joel comes back!" Billy brandished the flintlock, which was longer than he was.

To his delight, Mark thought that was a fine idea.

In the late afternoon, they slipped quietly out the back of the cave and into the woods beyond. They followed a faint trail, their untrained eyes scanning the trees and brush for game.

"I don't see nothin'," Billy said, struggling to keep the heavy flintlock against his shoulder, like a soldier. "Maybe we should make a whole bunch of noise and scare 'em outta hiding."

"Flicto," Mark said, "we just got out here. If you're patient and quiet, we'll find something."

"Whaddaya think we ought ta shoot, Mark? A cardinal, maybe? They're real pretty and red—they ought to taste real good, maybe like red chicken." The boy licked his lips in anticipation and lost his grip on the rifle. It fell backward over his shoulder into the weeds.

"Shut the hell up, Billy, you'll scare everything off." Mark, watching the other boy struggle with the weapon, shook his head. "Now, you can't just shoot anything that comes along—it's *got* to be something ugly. Think about it, the only things that are good to eat are ugly—pigs, chickens, and shrimp—they're ugly—oh, and lobsters, they're the butt-ugliest of them all and supposed to be the best eats."

"They're red, like cardinals." Billy paused to think about that. "Hey, Mark, where you think we could find lobsters? Can we shoot some in the river?"

"Moron."

The rifle fell again, this time scraping Mark's shin and landing on his toe. He yelped and swore under his breath as Billy lifted the weapon.

"If you can't do any better than that, I'm gonna take it away from you."

"Whaddaya mean, 'take it away'? *I'm* the one who knows how to load and fire it!"

"Yeah? Well you sure as hell don't know how to handle it."

"You're so big and tough, *you* try carrying it."

Mark took the flintlock from him with a disdainful smirk. As soon as he hefted the weapon, he began tottering. Billy laughed at him as the older boy shifted his grip and carried it across his shoulders.

I bet he wishes he'd kept his big mouth shut, Billy thought.

"Hey look, there's a possum," Mark said, unshouldering the rifle. It was so cumbersome, he couldn't steady it.

Billy crossed his arms and snickered.

To sight along the barrel, Mark leaned way back.

"Possum ain't no good to eat. You know anyone who eats possum?"

"I've heard of it." Mark grunted out the words. " 'Sides, it's ugly."

The barrel bobbed up and down, swayed back and forth, as the boy aimed toward the branch on which the animal was perched.

"Dumbass," Billy said, as Mark pulled the trigger.

There was a click, a snap and a few sparks. That was all. Billy burst out laughing, Mark dropped the rifle in disgust, and the possum scurried up the tree.

"It ain't loaded! God, you're such a flicto, Mark! Pick it up and let me show you how it's done. Tilt the barrel over here." The younger boy was eating this up and took his time loading the weapon, occasionally glancing at Mark with a smug expression.

When they were finished, the boys scanned the forest for a likely victim.

Billy grinned and pointed. "There—a robin! Hold the barrel for me and do as I tell you. Now—a little to the left. Higher, higher—there."

When Billy pulled the trigger, four things happened at once: Mark, hunched over, his face directly over the pan, got a face full of burning powder; Billy's shoulder was dislocated by the recoil; the rifle discharged its ball; and, in a spray of feathers, the robin was picked up and thrown thirty feet.

Mark clutched at his face, howling. Billy, rolling on the ground and screaming with pain, inadvertently popped the joint back into place.

The pain in his shoulder subsided and Billy got to his feet. Seeing Mark, his face stained black and speckled with little red burns, he broke out laughing.

"What're you laughing at?" Mark demanded, stomping off in search of the robin. "Little shit."

Abandoning the flintlock where it fell, Billy trailed after, rubbing his shoulder.

"Son of a bitch," Mark said in an awed voice.

"What is it? Lemme see."

Mark turned, holding what was left of the robin up to his face by one of its twiggy claws. "I can *see* you," he said, peering through the golf-ball-sized hole in the body of the bird.

48

Joel had no idea how far behind Virgil was, but he knew in the pit of his stomach that the man was still back there.

He ain't got a gun, but I'm sure he's got that big, fucking knife he always carries.

At first Joel had thought crawling through the tangled underbrush would be an easy way to lose Virgil. But now, he was beginning to feel it was a mistake—he was becoming a part of the tangle.

While sawing through obstructing vines with his Swiss Army Knife, the boy grew impatient. *This little thing ain't for shit!* He gave the blade a disgusted look. Then he smiled.

Virgil's knife is bigger, but I bet it don't have a toothpick!

He chuckled, then stopped himself, sensing that this was a dangerous thing to do. When he laughed, Joel had the feeling that, no matter where Virgil was, the man would hear him.

He stumbled through his cut in the curtain of vines. Joel gasped, backpedaled away from the edge of a monstrous sinkhole. A sinkhole filled with twisted, mummified corpses.

His heart lurched. Joel bit back a shout. He took another step back, staring at the horror he'd almost pitched into. But on second look, they weren't corpses at all. The sinkhole was filled with deadfall; twisted, fractured wood, dry leaves, and tangled vines. His eyes and his fear-stressed imagination had turned it into a charnel pit.

Joel shuddered, and turned to leave. But the vines and brush had closed behind him. He'd have to hack his way out again. *Maybe right into Virgil's lovin' arms.*

He turned back around, and considered the sinkhole. *Looks like a really good place to break a leg.* It would be difficult with his splinted arm, but he might just make it across—that is, if the rotted wood didn't give way beneath him.

Joel stepped carefully onto a fallen trunk and eased his way onto the twiggy jungle gym. Thinking it was best to spread out his weight, he got down on his hands and knees and crept along the length of the dead tree. *So far, so good.* But the trunk was thinning, and its branches creaked and popped beneath his weight. When a branch broke with a dusty snap and painfully jerked his injured arm, Joel chose another wooden path, the massive roots of another downed tree.

The roots looked like an emaciated and unnaturally twisted corpse. Joel hesitated before touching it, almost expecting to feel decayed skin. He glanced around, looking for a stronger handhold, and had the sudden, gut-wrenching impression that he was crawling over a mountain of corpses. For just a moment, his nostrils were filled with the smell of rotting flesh. And then it struck him—they looked like the piles of dead the Germans left in their concentration camps after World War Two. He was surrounded.

The thought took him off guard and he slipped, falling into the open arms of the "body" beneath him. With a cracking and groaning, the limbs wrapped around Joel and squeezed. He cricd out with thc pain in his arm.

He thrashed against the wooden embrace, slipping still deeper into the fetid hole and becoming ever more tightly wedged beneath the weight of many limbs.

As Joel's panic crested, a scream rushing to the surface, his mother's advice came back to him—they'd been at Pawley's Island when he was very young and she'd cautioned him about the undertow. "The more you fight it, the deeper down it'll pull you. Just relax, and you'll bob right to the surface."

Joel stopped fighting, tried to calm himself and control the pain. Carefully, he worked at the bars of his wooden prison, loosening them one at a time. His panic ebbed as the limbs released him, the wood becoming lifeless once again. Joel met with little resistance, his small frame easily slipping in between the intricately woven branches.

A loud crack, and Joel froze. The limb he was straddling snapped. He plunged downward, crashing to a stop only inches from the jagged end of a broken limb. He threw himself away from it, and his splinted arm smashed into a heavy branch. Tears of pain streamed down his face. Sucking in panicked breaths, his arm throbbing, he hugged himself and rocked back and forth until the adrenaline was all burned off.

As he stared at the jagged point below him, an idea formed in Joel's head. Working his way to the stinking floor of the sinkhole, he pulled out his knife and began sharpening broken branches.

Waiting in the darkness like an ant lion in its pit, Joel had been calling out to Virgil every few minutes for the past three hours, confident that, sooner or later, he would be found. He was starting to lose his voice.

At last, he heard the sound of Virgil crashing through the vine-tangled forest and cursing. Joel's stomach twisted with fear and more than a little excitement. *It's gonna work. I'm gonna get him.*

"Here I is, little mouse!" Virgil's voice called from the far side of the sinkhole. Joel couldn't see him through the thick tangle.

"I think I broke my leg," Joel whimpered hoarsely, drawing on the pain in his left arm to make it sound convincing. "I don't care what you do to me, just get me outta here!"

"Why, of course I'll help ye." The man's tone was unctuous. "Ye jus' wait right where ye be, an' I'll come fetch ye."

Joel heard limbs snapping as Virgil crawled out onto the tangle.

"Where ye be? Dammit, boy, I cain't see ye!"

Joel maintained the strain in his voice. "There's a way down in the middle."

He saw the man's silhouette crawling from branch to branch above him. His nerves rattling, Joel readied himself, tensing at each creak and groan of the wood, at each of Virgil's curses as the man slipped, caught himself and continued on.

"I can see you now—come straight down."

"Goddam wood's all rotted!"

"Hurry, Virgil—I'm hurtin' awful bad."

"I'm gonna have ye, boy. But it'll take me some time, so hesh yer mouth."

Virgil reached out with his left leg, testing a branch, and then put his full weight on it.

There was a loud crack as the limb gave way. Virgil crashed down, tumbling as he broke through the branches. Joel aimed a sharpened limb squarely at his back, but the man bounced off a log just before reaching him, and the spear missed its mark. The stake pierced Virgil in the side and he screamed, choking and coughing on the downpour of broken twigs and wood dust.

Joel let go of his weapon like it was a poisonous snake and struggled out from under Virgil. He grabbed a branch and hauled himself upward, scrambling up the ladder like jumble of logs and branches. Thrashing and screaming, Virgil hurled useless curses after the boy.

Joel felt wooden hands grip his leg and a surge of adrenaline propelled him upward. Kicking violently, he freed the leg, almost losing his shoe. Hurling himself up through the tangle, he screamed for all he was worth, terrified of being dragged down to die with Virgil.

At the top, Joel paused to rest, balanced in the tangled wood like a spider in its web. He looked down at Virgil. He could just barely make out the shape of the man, splashed with red, impaled like a bug on a pin. With a flush, Joel realized it was probably Virgil, not the limbs, who had grabbed him. *That's the last time you'll ever touch me, you ugly fuck.*

But he wasn't dead, not yet. Virgil's leg kicked, his arms reached up for Joel. "When I git outta here—"

The man broke off with a ragged scream of pain.

"I don't think so, Virg." Joel carefully made his way to the edge of the pit without looking back. "I don't think you're going anywhere."

49

"Y'all keep yer mouths shut an' listen to me," Wesley said, his voice echoing within the cave.

Mark could see that the big man was upset. The boiled-shrimp red of his face had darkened to an angry crimson, and his forehead was knit up like a bulldog's. He looked like a demon. Mark expected him to spit fire at any moment.

"Now, all up and down Shillelagh Trace, our men 'ave been strung up. I wouldn'ta believed it if I hain't seen it wit' my own eyes.

"Bob Horne was asleep when they come fer 'im. Broke 'is door down, and twenty men shot 'im dead right there in 'is bed. Horne's wife tol' us she'd been washin' 'is brains out of 'er hair all day."

There were a few murmurs of shock from the crowd.

"This 'ere same Tennessee volunteer militia chased Wiley Cooke into a cane break an' then surrounded an' burned it down, 'im wit' it. Ebenezer an' Fredericka Zootaburt got all tore up by dawgs, the militia standin' by jus' a'laughin'."

The outraged muttering grew louder. *As if you assholes didn't do six worse things than that every day before lunch,* Mark thought.

"An' that lil' operation wit' the slaves—all gone an' our men wit' it—all hanged, dead."

Wesley paused, took a deep breath and a long drink of whiskey.

"What we gonna do 'bout it?" Laris asked, idly stroking his

erect penis with a palm full of honey.

"We'd o' took off after 'em if it hain't been they was a hunderd men to our ten."

"I heard they's this notable," said a fat, hairy black man, "name o' Thomas Fellowes headin' up this volunteer militia, hired by the governor of Tennessee."

The name, Thomas Fellowes, was familiar to Mark, but he couldn't remember where he'd heard it.

A tall, skinny man to Mark's right said, "I heard Fellowes was scalped by injuns but the sumbitch didn't die. Some ol' rootwoman who found 'im wanderin' the woods tol' him to drill holes in his haid and he did it, right through his skull! An' that didn' kill him neither."

"Horseshit!" someone yelled.

The man glared around. "He did it wit' a fishin' knife, an' new skin, wit'out hair, grew out o' the holes an' covered the top o' 'is head. Ugly as a bear's arsehole, they say he is, an' meaner'n shit too."

"Wes, some o' the men been hearin' gun shot off ta the west the last few days," said Wade. "You think it might 'ave somethin' ta do wit' this 'ere militia?"

"Naw, they's comin' from the other direction. Pro'bly some o' our own, tired o' the wormy beef we been eatin'."

It was probably me and Billy hunting, Mark thought.

The big man pulled out his pipe and loaded it.

"Dawg, fetch me a flamin' faggot fer my pipe."

Mark gave him a blank look. "You mean like Laris?" He watched the naked man swatting at a horde of flies with his free hand.

"That boy jus' ain' right, Wes," Laris said, letting the juice run off his hand into the fire.

"Get me some *fire!*" Wes boomed.

Mark almost fell into the flames in an effort to do the big

man's bidding.

All were quiet while Wesley lit his pipe.

"We need lookouts at the Four Corners, day an' night. Everyone keep fresh powder an' shot an' don' stray far from yer rifles. All wimmen an' childerns below. Stockpile what ye kin. We'll be ready or there'll be hell to pay!"

Joel took a deep breath and walked into the cave. The outlaws were assembled, but it wasn't another drunken, hell-raising party, thank God. He saw Wesley in the middle of the room, towering over the others. He made his way through the crowd toward the big man.

"Paint my ass blue and call me Laris," Wesley said, grinning. "Where in hell ye been, Little Man?"

Well, y'see, Wes, Virgil wouldn't stop trying to kill me, so I dropped his ass in the world's biggest briar patch, and the last time I saw him, he was pinned through the middle like a goddam bug on a corkboard. . . . Joel felt a crooked smile tug at his mouth. Of course, he couldn't tell Wesley he'd murdered his brother. But weirdly enough, he wished he could. He knew that if he'd killed anyone but Virg, Wesley would have been proud of him.

"I's back in the cave, tryin' ta scare up some cunny."

"Fer three days?"

The big man looked surprised and the others laughed.

"Have any luck, boy?" came the voice of a dead man.

Joel froze. For a horrible moment, he thought he would puke on his shoes. *No. Fucking. Way.*

The outlaws parted, and Joel saw the impossible. Virgil, shirtless, propped up on a blanket-draped rock. A soiled bandage around his middle, fresh blood seeping into his bedding.

"But you're—" *dead,* Joel finished in his head.

But Virgil was obviously not dead.

How could Virgil have gotten back before I did?

The firelight flickered, casting demonic shadows on Virgil's face. The man was smiling, but his eyes were filled with pure, flame-blue hatred. Joel could hear Virgil's voice in his ears, knew what the evil little man was thinking as if he were reading his mind. *I'm gonna git ye, boy!*

A sudden shiver wracked Joel's body. *He's a demon. He really is. He can't be killed. And when he catches me. . . .*

Bullshit. He knows these parts, is all. He knew a shortcut back. And he must not be as bad off as I thought.

Joel spat on the ground, trying not to look utterly terrified. He wondered if Virgil would give him away. Maybe he'd already told Wesley what happened. On the verge of being caught in the lie of the century, Joel's belly crawled with angry worms and sweat popped out of every pore.

"But I'm what, *boy?*"

There was a long pause, a charged silence as everyone waited for Joel to respond to Virgil's question. He looked to Wesley, but could read nothing in the man's expression.

"Uglier'n usual. Naw, I couldn't find no cunny back there I'd care to have."

Everyone laughed and there were murmurs about Joel still being a virgin, still being a little boy, after all. Wesley clapped him on the shoulder.

"Don't ye fret none, Little Man. I'll go drag ye out a real woman." Wesley headed off into the cavern, leaving Joel behind.

The crowd was breaking up, still laughing. Across the chamber, Joel saw Mark headed toward him. But Virgil didn't move from his bloody nest. Joel could feel the man's cold, murderous eyes on him.

"Joel, you're okay!" Mark said. "How'd you get away from Virgil? And how in hell did he get that hole in him? Did you do that?"

"Shush! You want the others to hear? Let's get out of here."

"But Wes has gone to get you a *real* woman," Mark said with a snicker.

"Not now."

As they turned a corner, passing out of earshot and into another tunnel, Joel collapsed against the wall. His legs gave way and he slipped to the floor, hugging his knees and trying to catch his breath.

"You'll never believe it," he said, turning to his friend. "That crazy bastard chased me all over hell. I was down in this fallen-tree-pit-kinda-thing and I stabbed him with a stake I carved. I didn't think he'd be botherin' us no more."

"He crawled back here about noon today."

"That's impossible." Joel grabbed Mark's leg and shook it. "I tell you I stabbed him real good. I watched that stake go right fucking through his gut. And, Mark, I left him miles and miles from here. How could he get back before I did?"

"Well, he is all messed up, but he ain't totally outta commission." Mark helped Joel to his feet. "He won't be troubling us for a while though. C'mon, let's get back to the hideout."

"That guy ain't real! Nobody could survive that wound and crawl back here—there's no stopping him!" He tried to give Mark a gallows grin, but only managed a tight grimace. The pit of his stomach was cold and painful. Once again, Joel's mind suggested to him that maybe, just maybe, Virgil wasn't human. Unexpectedly, Joel gagged. He swallowed hard, refusing to puke in front of his friend.

They reached the tunnel that led to their hideout. Joel felt his legs go rubbery and he sagged against the wall again, deflating like a sail losing wind. Mark looked helplessly at him. Joel wished he could say something reassuring, but his throat had gone dry.

"Billy's bored," Mark finally said. "He's making noises about roaming around wherever he wants."

"Shit." Joel mouthed the word without much enthusiasm. "Wesley's got a law about children staying inside the cave."

"Well, it's a good thing Ebbie's taken to Willawic like she has. Just that rope around her neck wouldn't've been enough to keep her from following me—hell she's chewed right through stuff like that before—and Willawic hadn't been up to chasing after her."

"Damn, Mark, if that dog of yours starts roaming around, someone'll snatch her up and make a stew outta her."

"Yeah, I know." He fidgeted from foot to foot. "Oh—we know how to hunt, now—Billy and me. We learned how to shoot one of them flintlocks and shot a robin all to hell. Well Billy did anyway. We got it in the hideout, 'long with a whole bunch of other stuff we shot. We kept it all except for the stuff we ate."

A slight smile crept into the corners of Joel's lips. "You're full of shit."

"Oh yeah? C'mon inside, and I'll prove it to you."

50

When Joel sauntered into the hideout the next day, Mark could see he was feeling a lot better. He'd regained his cocky swagger, and the fear had faded from his expression. Mark found himself weirdly grateful for that. Somehow, nothing he'd seen so far had been as horrible as the hopeless terror he'd seen in Joel's eyes.

Joel grinned and clapped him on the shoulder. "Hey, Mark, I met this girl! She's kinda pretty, an' I think I could get her to let me fuck her real easy, no problem."

"Ew!" Billy said, shrilly. "You mean stick your dick up her butt an' pee?"

"God—you're such a homo!" Joel spit in his general direction.

"Girls are gross. They give you cooties."

"Shut the hell up, dumbass. Go an' play with your Indian."

Mark turned and regarded the man. Willawic was crouched in the dust, chanting. It seemed as if, while awake, that was all the Indian did these days.

"I think what he told me was that he's calling on spirits to help him heal," Mark said. "Then again, maybe I made half that up."

"Well, it's damned queer how much he does it."

"So, tell me about her," Mark said. He sat next to Ebbie and scratched her belly. When her leg began kicking, he chuckled.

"Like I said, she's pretty. And I saw her titties!"

"Bullshit!"

"I did so. They're kinda small, but they're there, all right."

"What did they feel like?" Mark squeezed imaginary breasts in the air before him.

"I didn't touch 'em yet, but I'm gonna, next time I see her."

Mark looked down at Ebbie's withered brown nipples and wondered how much they were like those of a girl. *Nah. They gotta be better than that!* He grinned.

"And I'll kiss her too."

Mark lost his smile. "Goddam, Joel, that's really gross!"

"Whaddaya mean? Kissing's not so gross. I might even use my tongue."

"Oh man, that's even worse. That's like lickin' somebody's butthole."

"To hell with you, Mark, you're getting as queer as Billy."

"Hey, at least I'm not talking about licking somebody's skanky ol' mouth."

"What the hell are you talking about?"

"Joel, don't you know these people don't brush their teeth? Wesley has breath like a dead walrus. I bet she doesn't even know what a toothbrush is."

Joel paled. "Shit, I never thought about that."

51

Joel's palms were slick with nervous sweat as he, Mark, and Billy wove between the outlaws gathered on the rock shelf around the evening fire. They came to a stop before Wesley.

"This is *my* dawg," Joel said to the big man. "His name is Billy."

Joel held the younger boy on a makeshift rope leash. Billy was down on all fours, wagging his rear end enthusiastically. He sat up, his hands held before him like a begging dog, and panted with his tongue out.

Laughter and derision rumbled through the gathering. Wesley chuckled, eyeing Joel intently.

"Damn, Wes," said a pock-marked outlaw named Dunbar, "it's bad 'nough ye got these boys runnin' all over creation, like as not ta give us away."

Several men nodded, murmuring cautious agreement. Joel looked nervously around and then turned back to Wesley. "He ain't gonna be no problem—he'll behave himself. You'll see."

"Let the boy 'ave 'is little pet," Laris said with a toothy smile. "What's wrong with y'all? Don'tcha remember, when yew was jus' a boy, wantin' that special *something* by yer side?"

"It's damn queer is what I think," said another man, named Puett.

Wesley stopped chuckling and gave Puett a slow, meaningful stare.

"Not Wesley havin' a dawg," Puett amended. "Th-the boy I mean."

Wesley relaxed, leaning back, and everyone was quiet for a moment. The river exhaled a cool breeze, bathing them in rank breath, and a screech owl called from off in the forest.

Finally, Earl Ray, a big burly black man, stood up and stabbed an accusing finger at the boys. "It *ain't* right an' it's damn disrespectful ta Wesley."

"Shet up," Laris said, clouting Earl Ray on the arm.

"No way!" Mark said, facing the black man. "It ain't disrespectin' nobody! Sure, he got the idea from Wesley, but, if anything, he's honoring him. You know Joel would give his left nut to be like Wes."

Joel kicked Mark in the shin. Wesley rumbled out a laugh.

The other men argued back and forth, their voices growing so loud that Joel couldn't understand any of it.

"That's it," Wesley's deep voice boomed. "Y'all shet up! I've done made up my mind. Little Man, ye kin 'ave yer dawg—long as ye look after 'im an' keep 'im out from under foot."

The shouting died away, the sound of the night breeze loud in its wake. Silence gathered about the outlaws as they returned their gaze to the fire, the only disturbance a luna moth which flew in too close to the flames. Its wings caught fire and it dropped, like a blazing stone, into the glowing coals.

Joel sat by the fire, Mark and Billy at his side, and glanced around at the outlaws. He picked up a stick, wedged it under his foot, and began to whittle a point.

No one had said anything for the past five minutes and Joel wondered if it would go on like this all night. The air was cool and the river pirates had built their fire well out on the shelf of rock before the cave. From the darkness beyond the orange dome of light came the rhythmic chirping of crickets and the shrill cry of frogs. A living thing slipped into the unseen shallows with a ploop, while farther out, something disturbed the silvery surface of the river. A glow of turquoise rimmed the hills across the water as the day passed into night.

Billy fidgeted at Joel's feet. He seemed to have tired of his mock panting and was now quiet for the most part.

The breeze shifted direction, blowing sparks between silhouetted figures and smoke into Joel's eyes. He thought to get up, but knew the smoke would only follow him—it always worked that way.

The smell of the fire was thick in his nostrils, bringing him a sense of well-being as he was reminded of times when he and Mark had camped out in his backyard. There was also a delicious fear, as he sat with his back to the darkness, watching the raw energy of the fire eating at the logs.

There was no telling what waited in the darkness beyond the safety of the fire's glow. Odd, half-heard sounds penetrated the ever-present crackling of the fire, whispering of something that might at any moment reach inside the comfortable orange dome of light and warmth and snatch him away without a trace.

I have to be careful not to get too comfortable here. Something's gonna happen sometime—something's gotta break and I've gotta be ready when it gets here.

"Goddammit, Pinrod, grab yer own goddam balls!"

Joel looked up, startled to see one silhouette slugging another.

"I ain't—oof!" the Pinrod silhouette said, struck in the gut and stumbling back and falling over two more burly black shapes.

The shapes fell upon him, pistoning arms and curses. Finally, they left him lying senseless, and resumed their places by the fire.

"Make room, make room!" cried a retinue of Virgil-bearers. Three shapes vacated a flat-topped boulder and the man and his bedding were deposited there.

Mark tapped Joel on the shoulder and leaned over to whisper, "C'mon, let's get outta here."

The boy was ready to agree when Virgil's gaze lit upon him and he knew he dare not.

"Goin' somewheres, boy?" Virgil asked.

The crowd was silent, waiting to see what would happen next.

"I sure hope not," he continued, grinning like a snake. "I's thinkin' mebbe I finally got some time ta git ta know ye, now that I's laid up like this. Why don't ya sit with me a while?"

The boy sat, squirming beneath the weight of the crowd's expectant gaze.

Virgil's grin widened, exposing the brown gaps in his uneven teeth. "Tha's a good boy, doin' jus' as 'e's told."

The crowd laughed. To Joel it seemed the automatic laughter of a king's courtiers.

"Now, Wes, ye better remind me—which one is yer dawg, Mark or Joel?"

More laughter—even Wesley joined in.

Be cool, Joel told himself, *just let it go.*

"Now, Joel, you better remind me," Mark asked, "which one is it does the thinking, Virgil or Wesley?" Joel gasped, amazed at his friend's nerve. *This place has sure as hell changed him. And me.*

Wesley let out a guffaw and clapped Mark on the back. Joel watched Mark's gaze flick from him to Virgil. The small man's face darkened as the pirates' laughter trailed away. The shelf of rock seemed suddenly very crowded.

"*Goddam* yer mouth, little boy! It's 'bout ta git ye a *whole* mess o' hurt!" Virgil half rose, grimacing and reaching for his wounded side.

"Look's like you're the one who's hurting, Virgil," Mark said, "not me. Just how much hurting do you figure you can do, anyway?"

"Are you drunk?" Joel whispered to his friend.

"Little, bastard, yer gonna regret this! Soon as I'm up an' able, I'm gonna kill ye. Ye hear? *Kill* ye."

Mark ducked his head down, like a turtle retreating into its shell.

"Watch the way ye be talkin' ta my dawg," Wesley growled.

Virgil eased himself back down onto the boulder, raising his cup and drowning his rage in a big gulp of whiskey. Immediately, one of his retinue refilled the cup.

"That's the problem wit' these boys, Wes, they ain't got no respect, don' do nothin' but live offa our hard work an' run their fool mouths like they ain't got the sense ta recognize death when they see it."

Wesley leveled a gaze on Virgil that would make most men wet their pants. "Now lookee here, little brother, I knows yer drunk and hurtin', so I'll let it pass, this once. But yer treadin' thin ice."

Virgil drained his cup and spat into the fire, the alcohol igniting in a *whoosh* of flame. In the brilliant light, the man aimed his manic gaze directly at Joel. Suppressing a shudder, the boy cringed inside.

"Come on out with it, Virg. What're you tryin' to say?" Joel tried to sound relaxed, but his heart was hammering. He couldn't shake the image of Virgil impaled at the bottom of the sinkholc.

"Ye ain't tough enough. Ye ain't o' the right grit—neither o' ye. An' it seems nobody 'roun' here knows it but me. Ye cain't shoot a gun, an' ye cain't kill. Ye cain't ride a horse, an', shit, ye cain't even find cunny in a cave full of wet, warm holes."

The crowd laughed and Joel felt his cheeks flush.

"No, but I'm pretty good with sharp sticks," he said coolly, holding up the wood he had whittled. "Ain't I, Virg?"

The small man rose up, his face darkening again, but then stopped with a short, sharp cry. A red flower started to bloom on the bandages around his middle. Wesley glanced from his brother to Joel, eyes narrowed.

"Ye ain't but *shit!*" Virgil ranted. "Yer nothin' but a weak little *boy!*"

A huge brown beetle, the size of a prune, landed on the rock next to Virgil. The man snatched it up and shook it toward Joel.

"Boy, yer as low an' useless as this goddam bug!" At that, he popped the beetle into his mouth and crunched down hard. He chewed deliberately and slowly, all the while staring at Joel. He washed down the grisly mouthful with a big slug of whiskey.

I'm gonna chew ye up, his beetle-stained grin seemed to say. Joel grimaced, shuddering at the idea.

Another beetle, the size of two prunes stuck together, buzzed past Joel's head and landed at his feet. Without thinking, he stabbed it with his sharpened stick and popped it into his mouth. As Virgil watched, the color of his face deepening yet again, the boy chewed slowly and carefully. Trying to ignore the foul taste and the insect's last, desperate writhings, he kept his cool gaze on his adversary.

Virgil's angry mouth worked silently, as murmurs of surprise rose all about him. Wesley laughed and clapped Joel on the back.

"Sorry 'bout that, Little Man, I fergot 'bout yer bruised wing."

" 'S'okay, it's feeling much better, lately."

Across the fire, Virgil had gotten to his feet and was stumbling toward Joel, clutching at his bloody side. The boy made ready to run, certain that not even Wesley was going to be able to hold the little man back.

But at that moment, a horse broke free of the darkness, clattering explosively onto the rock shelf. The rider was torn and bloodied, his mount trembling and blowing foam as he dismounted.

"They's a militia," he panted, "comin' straight fer us, not one day back."

The red anger drained from Virgil's face, and he paled. The crowd's sense of expectation vanished and the air was full of a different kind of tension.

That's the break we've been waiting for, Joel thought, *that militia's gonna come in here and save us all. We gotta be ready, and we gotta take Billy's Indian with us.*

Mark grabbed Joel by his good arm and led him into the cave. Billy, still attached to the makeshift leash, trailed along behind them.

Just inside, Joel pulled away into the shadows and vomited.

52

Joel had been trudging along beside Wesley for half the morning as the big man strode about the cave and the bluff, directing preparations for their defense against the impending attack of the Tennessee volunteer militia. Now, sheened with sweat from the heat of the day, Joel stood with him on the rock before the cave mouth. The shelf and cave were filled with river pirates, their attention focused on the big man's red face. Joel was hoping Wesley would put him in charge of something.

"Wade, yew an' some o' the boys bring up some more powder kegs," Wesley ordered.

Wade nodded, gesturing for others to lend a hand.

"An' git them new barrels from the dry chamber up top. I don' wanna take no chances with damp powder.

"Harbinson, take a wheelbarrow, go wit' Wade an' wheel out as much shot an' flint as ye kin find an' start dolin' it out ta the men, then set up a station back in the cavern where the men kin git what they need when they run out. Make sure ta tell everybody where it is, now.

"O'Keefe, set these here men ta linin' up them boulders across the cave mouth—we kin defend the place from there, an' climb up top through the chimney if'n we have ta.

"Manley, I want ye up top wit' as many men as ye kin muster. Dig a trench along the edge o' the bluff an' build a battlement of wood, stone, whatever ye kin find. Our best shots will fire down from there.

"Lansdale, git the horses corralled in the cave. We might need 'em. Once ye git 'em all inside, cover the back entrance wit' plenty o' brush.

"Carlton, make sure Myrtrice's got food an' drink laid in—plenty o' whiskey. I'm postin' everyone ta reg'lar guard duty—a man every fifty yards. There's a whole lot o' work, so let's be at it."

This might be the eve of some great battle out of one of his history books. Joel knew from his reading that there was a big battle at the cave around this time. After that battle, the cave would not be used by outlaws for several years, but he did not know whether the pirates or the militia would come out on top. He did know that a lot of men would die on both sides.

He had no way of knowing if this would be that particular battle, but there was sure a lot of excitement in the air and he liked that. Something important was about to happen and he was actually going to be a part of it. He was as exhilarated as he was scared shitless. He saw his hands were trembling and he thrust them into his pants so no one would notice.

I've gotta see this. I'm never gonna get another chance to see a real battle like this again! But then, this is the perfect chance to escape—at some point in the fighting we're gonna have to slip away to the other side.

"Joel," Wesley said, turning to the boy. "Since yer arm's broke, I want ye ta organize the wimmen an' take care o' the slops."

Seeing Joel's expression droop, he clapped him a little too hard on the back and sent him sprawling in the dirt. The boy winced and automatically rubbed his splinted arm as he dragged himself up.

" 'Twas a joke, Little Man!" Wesley laughed. "But quit actin' like yer arm's hurt. Take that goddam stick off an' see if it works!"

53

Joel was exhausted. After working most of the night with the pirates, he and Mark returned to their hideout in the early morning to find Billy, Willawic and Ebbie were gone.

"Where the hell could they be at this hour?" Mark asked.

"Hell if I know."

"Well I ain't going looking for 'em—I'm too damned tired."

"Before you go to sleep, help me out of this thing."

"Hand me your knife, then."

Mark began carefully cutting.

"How's it look, Mark?"

"Well, it's all purple and blue and green and stuff. Looks like a frickin' sunset. Hold it up and swing it around. How's the elbow?"

Joel gingerly moved his arm in a circle. "Kinda stiff is all."

Mark poked lightly around the puncture wound at the center of the bruise. "That hurt?"

"Not *too* much."

"You're cured!" Mark said, lying down on his blanket. "I'm going to sleep."

Joel collapsed heavily on his own blanket.

Somehow, during their argument, Joel's hand had found its way into Virgil's mouth and now the man was bearing down with his teeth. Joel reached out with his other hand to push him away, but instead of Virgil's face, he grabbed Billy's leg, and then he was awake.

"Goddammit, Billy—get off my hand!"

Mark sat up. "What's going on?"

"Nothing," Billy said. "Go back to sleep."

He stepped over Mark and set down a brace of rabbits. Willawic followed Billy into the chamber, carrying more rabbits, a couple of squirrels, and a pouch full of bobwhite eggs.

On her way over to Mark, Ebbie paused to lick Joel on the face. Her tongue reeked of dog shit and he immediately thought of the dog licking her own ass. He spat and pushed her away, and she let out a slight whimper.

"Careful with her," Mark said angrily. "She's not all healed up. C'mere, girl," He hugged her around the neck and she wagged her tail as he ruffled her ears.

"Where you guys been?" Joel asked around a yawn.

"Huntin'," Billy answered simply. "Whadya think?"

Joel stared at all the dead animals and wondered if they could eat them all before they rotted. "Hunting? Are you guys nuts? You coulda been killed! Goddam, the woods are crawling with river pirates. You can't be sneaking around out there at night, shooting guns—you're liable to get yourselves shot!"

"Oh, don't worry about us. We haven't been using no guns. Willawic and me's been trapping. We've been out every night for a week now. Didn't you know?"

"You mean like that meat Willawic made for us last night was stuff you guys caught?" Mark asked.

"Yep—caught it ourselves!"

"Still," said Joel, "with Willawic hurt and all—"

"Oh, he's a lot better now. His shoulder's still stiff, but he can bend his arm pretty good."

"I guess maybe he'll be thinking about leaving soon." Joel eyed Willawic. "We still gotta find out where he got those Nikes. It's our only connection to home—if we can figure that out, we're home free. Mark, you better get to work on your French."

"I've been trying. But I can't figure out the right question."

"Well you better figure something out quick. We might wake up one morning to find he's gone, taking our one chance to get home with him."

"I don't think he'd do that," Billy said.

"Why not?"

"I dunno. I think, maybe, he likes us or something."

"It wouldn't take a genius to figure out we're in trouble," Joel said, "and maybe he figures he owes us."

"Maybe," Billy said, curling up beside Willawic. "I'm too sleepy to think about it. See you in the morning."

Joel watched as his friends settled down to sleep. He tried to imagine Billy and his Indian slipping silently through the trees, past Wesley's sentries, without being caught. He shook his head, looking at the small boy with wonder, a touch of jealousy, and newfound respect.

54

Mark had spent the better part of the morning in a small chamber molding lead shot as Wesley had instructed him to do. He was becoming weary of working over the hot fire and his mind was beginning to wander. He felt someone watching him and the hairs on the back of his neck prickled.

He looked up and there was Laris, standing in the entrance. The naked man's eyes smiled at him. It seemed a slippery glance, one that slid over Mark, leaving an oily film in its wake.

"Howdy, Laris," he said forcefully. "What's up?"

"I was jus' watchin' my boy," the man said in an unctuous way. "I hope I didn' startle ye none."

Mark smiled to conceal his nervousness. "It don' bother me none, as long as that's all it is."

The smile slithered from Laris' eyes to his thin lips, reminding Mark uncomfortably of a poisonous snake. He got the idea that Laris' act was well rehearsed.

"I was jus' watchin' ye work."

Laris took a step forward. Something in the man's face caused Mark's heart to hammer in his chest.

"I was jus' watchin' yer butt move while ye was bent over."

Mark's mouth went dry and his face stiffened, felt like it might shatter at any moment.

"It's nice—nice an' round, an' tight as a baby's butt. Jus' as pink too, I bet."

Mark wanted to run but his feet had taken root where he stood.

"I could paint it," Laris cooed. "Yeah, I could paint it bright red an' then we could run—run together."

His moist eyes glistened, and his tongue darted from his mouth like a hungry eel.

"An' when we were done runnin' an' were all nekkid an' sweaty. . . ."

Mark's stomach knotted up and gooseflesh swarmed over his body. The palms of his hands were sweaty and he rubbed them uselessly against the sides of his legs.

"C'mere, boy." Laris sidled closer. "Let's get nekkid together."

He reached out a trembling hand and Mark backed away. Laris followed until Mark was backed against the wall.

Run! Mark's brain screamed at him. *Run, you idiot!* But his legs wouldn't obey. The man smiled his slippery smile and an eager light came into his eyes. Paralyzed, Mark watched helplessly as Laris traced a finger along his cheek. And then the man had seized his arm and his lips were parting ever so slightly, his face drawing nearer.

Mark closed his eyes, clenched his teeth. *No no no no no no no—*

A shot rang out and something wet splashed his cheek. Shuddering, he looked up to see Laris, a hole in his face, sliding to the stone floor. Across the chamber, Wesley stood in the opening, his pistol still smoking. Without a word, he lowered the gun and walked away.

55

Sitting with the outlaws by the evening fire, Mark and Joel listened as Virgil told the tale of how his side happened to get pierced. Every once in a while, the man would glance over at Joel.

Is Virg trying to get a rise out of him? Mark wondered.

"An' I tell ye," Virgil said, leaning forward and groaning, "I had 'is throat slit, blood was a-sprayin' ever'where, but that ol' bear had jus' enough stren'th lef' in 'im 'fore 'e died to pick me up an' hurl me 'gainst this big ol' tree. One o' its dead limbs—not the bear's, but the tree's—pierced me clean through my guts."

"Liar, liar, pants on fire!" Mark said. "That's the biggest pile of bullshit I ever heard in my life. Goddam, Virgil, even you can lie better than that. And if everybody around here wasn't so damn scared of you, they wouldn't believe you either!"

In the silence that followed, Mark was surprised at his sudden outburst. It felt good to stand up to someone as awful as Virgil. *I wish some of the bullies back home could see me now. It's me they'd be afraid of then, not Joel.*

"Yer funny all right, boy," Virgil said. "I've heard tell o' jesters over in Europe, that's got free reign ta say anythin' they want 'bout anybody they want. They kin insult anyone at all an' there's nothin' nobody kin do 'bout it. But," he said, leaning toward the boy, "even they's been known ta go too far an' lose they heads—lose 'em ta the executioner's axe."

The verbal sparring between Virgil and Mark had been going on for the last few nights. The men gathered about the fire seemed to have become increasingly uncomfortable with it. Tonight, they shifted nervously as their eyes sought distraction as far from the scene as possible, and some got up and drifted quietly away into the night.

"Jester?" Mark asked. "Who needs a jester with you around?"

Wesley burst out with a belly laugh, clapping Mark on the back. He stood and gave his brother a helpless shrug. "He's jus' a dawg," he said, then walked off into the darkness.

Mark smiled victoriously as he watched the wiry man's face turn an ugly shade of red. Beside him, Joel pulled at his arm insistently and muttered something, but Mark ignored him. He sneered at Virgil.

"You're like some super dumbass Igor to Wesley's Dr. Frankenstein—always picking the wrong brain. *Your brain!* You think you're some shit, like some mama's boy King Kong trying to fight Godzilla who's a hundred times bigger and nuclear powered too. You've got this little-bitty brain from the 1800s while we got these great big twentieth-century brains. You can't hope to win. Joel proved it—and you can't take it—you half-assed Davy Crocket wannabe."

"Mark," Joel hissed, "shut the hell up."

Baring his teeth, Virgil pulled out his knife and began digging out large chunks from the log on which he sat.

"You think you're some shit, some bad-ass, mean mutherfucker—too bad you can't wait around about a hundred years or so to see Hitler—he killed millions, tortured 'em, gassed 'em, shot and burned 'em, and then made soap and lamp shades out of 'em. But you—you let a couple o' boys—"

"Mark!" Joel shouted.

Mark rounded on him. "Can't you see I'm saying something here?"

"We gotta get outta here!" Joel insisted, shaking his friend.

"Just a minute." Mark twisted out of Joel's grasp. "I'm almost through."

"No, Mark, *now!*" Joel grabbed him by both shoulders and swung him around. "Everyone's gone. We're *alone* with Virgil!" Mark saw how pale Joel was, the beads of sweat on his face, the sick terror in his eyes.

Mark looked around at the nearly empty chamber, his boldness draining away fast. It left him entirely when he turned back and met Virgil's raging eyes as if for the first time. The man flipped the knife in his hand and threw it. Mark's guts went cold as the blade grazed his cheek. A warm trickle of blood collected on his chin.

"Better listen ta yer friend an' go while ye kin, *little boy.*"

Numbed, Mark allowed Joel to lead him away.

"You gotta stop getting Virgil so angry. He's gonna kill you if you don't stop."

"Yeah, I know. I don't know what comes over me. It's like when I got Wesley there to back me up, the words just spill out."

"Yeah, but Wesley walked out tonight." Joel gazed at his friend, a mixture of concern and admiration creeping across his tense features. Shaking his head, he grinned. "Mark, I gotta lot of respect for anybody who can stand up to Virgil like you've done—even with Wesley at your back, it takes a lot of balls. And I'm impressed as hell."

Mark grinned sheepishly, turning away, embarrassed by his friend's candor.

"But I'm gonna tell you something else and you're not gonna like it." Joel's grin disappeared and he looked Mark straight in the eye. "I think it's stupid as all hell."

The smile fled from Mark's face when he saw what was reflected in Joel's eyes. It was fear of death, plain and simple, and he realized with a creeping chill—*the cold of the grave,* he thought—just how close he had come to dying tonight.

56

Mark and Joel forced their way through the crowd gathered at the mouth of the cave. Squinting against the light of the rising sun, Joel swallowed nervously as he peered between the boulders lined up across the cave entrance. The line of men on the opposite bank of the river had arrived during the night. The first of the pirates to awaken this morning had seen them and immediately roused the others. Jeph, the pirates' lookout, hung from a tree at the river's edge. There was an electric tension in the air as the outlaws whispered among themselves.

"Sonuvabitch," Mark muttered, "it's the militia, ain't it?"

Joel nodded his head, grunting in agreement.

"Mus' be eighty ta a hundred men, or more," said Harbinson.

"We's got the cave an' the ridge," Wesley said.

Across the river, a din rose from the volunteer militia that seemed to mix with the humid, almost heady, morning heat. Joel could make out only syllables at first. Occasionally a word made its way over the water and eventually whole phrases. As the mob gained their wind, Joel could hear entire sentences.

"Yew killed my wife!"

"Yew run off wit' my niggers!"

"I remember that stupid bastard," Harbinson shouted, laughing. "I *did* steal his niggers."

". . . burned me out, ruint me!"

"Thieving bastards! Ye took my daughter down ta

Natchez. . . ."

". . . drown ye like the river rats ye are!"

". . . burn ye out an' send ye ta hell!"

"Hell? Is that where we're going?" Wesley said, laughing.

"They shore talk big, don' they?" said a pirate to Wesley's left.

Turning toward him, the big man said, "Carlton, git off yer lazy ass an' do what I tol' ye!"

The man hopped over the wall of boulders and ran off toward the water's edge. Immediately, several shots sounded on the far shore. The lead balls splashed into the river and the pirates laughed.

"What the hell're y'all shootin' at us anyways?" Wesley shouted. "Corks and harsh words? Oh, how that hurts!"

The pirates laughed at Wesley's joke a little too hard.

Joel saw Carlton scamper back up the hill. He stopped just short of the barricade of boulders. "Uh, Wesley, what the hell was I 'sposed ta be doin'?"

"Goddammit!" Wesley roared. "I give ye an order, I 'spect it ta be remembered. If'n I see ye 'gain today, I'm gonna rip yer fool head off!" Wes stepped over the wall like he planned to kill Carlton then and there.

Carlton clambered over the barricade and darted inside the cave, vanishing into the crowd.

Across the river, the line of militia parted and several men struggled to roll something large to the water's edge. Joel, trying to make it out, shielded his eyes from the glare of the river. He caught sunlight glinting off a metallic surface. "Wesley, they've got a cannon!"

The big man strained to see. "Goddammit!" He pounded his fist against a boulder. "That ain't fair—the bastards." Wesley turned and shouted up toward the top of the ridge. "Wade, we got us a cannon back in there anywheres?"

"Naw," the man called back, "not one that ain't broke."

The cannon's first shot fell short, not thirty yards away, sending up a spray of water that pattered about the shelf.

"Oh shit!" Mark said. "Let's get outta here, Joel, before we get blown up."

"Wait a minute. I gotta see this."

"And get killed?"

"I can't leave *now.*"

"At least get out of the line of fire."

Joel looked from Mark to the militia and nodded. The boys scrambled over the rock wall and off to the left, tucking themselves into a thicket.

Noticing the boys, Wesley scowled and pointed back into the cave. "Joel, take my dawg back inta the cave or up top. I won't 'ave ye gittin' all shot up."

Joel was about to object when the next shot blasted into the shelf at the waterline, spraying everyone with water and fragments of stone.

"C'mon, Mark," Joel said, grabbing his friend, "let's get inside before we get blown all to hell."

They headed toward the back of the entrance chamber, where they would be able to see the action in relative safety. Their route snaked among pockets of men, some waiting for the inevitable attack, some busy with last-minute preparations. Halfway across the crowded chamber, the boys spied Virgil, hobbling along with a cane. To avoid the man, they cut back, heading for the opposite wall.

"I gotta see this, Mark. I may never get to see a real battle again. We've *got* to keep an eye on the fight anyway because at some point we're gonna have to slip away to the other side. We just have to wait for the right time."

"Hey guys!" a small voice called out to them.

Joel turned to see Billy approaching. The dust on his face

showed the recent tracks of tears.

"What the hell are you doing?" Mark hissed. "Don't you know the shit's about to hit the fan? Go back down with Willawic, *right now!*"

"W-Willawic's gone. He took off with everything he had. I don't think he's comin' back."

"Sonofabitch!" Joel shouted. "There goes our chance!"

Billy ducked his head, trying to hide his face from the older boys.

A look of sick fear came over Mark's face. "Where the hell is Ebbie? Where's my dog, Billy?"

"Willawic took her," Billy whispered, looking down.

"Fuck! Fuck! That goddam thieving Indian bastard!" Mark's face was beet red, as were his eyes. Joel could tell his friend was fighting back tears. He turned away.

"I'm sorry," Billy said, biting his lower lip. Joel watched the little boy uncomfortably, then put a hand on his shoulder.

"It's not your fault. I think he'll come back, Billy. He probably cleared out just for the fight, then he'll come back when it's all over. And don't worry about him, he'll be okay—he's an Indian."

Joel looked sideways at Mark, who was wiping his eyes angrily on his shirt. "And I know he'll take care of Ebbie. You wouldn't want her around during this shitstorm, anyway."

"He'd better," Mark growled.

Billy sniffed noisily, wiping his nose on his shirt.

"C'mon," Joel said, "let's go up top. We'll be able to see everything from there." He took a torch from beside the fire at the center of the chamber and led the way.

A concussion at the entrance, a storm of stone fragments, and the screams of wounded men frightened the boys into a darkened side passage.

"Hurry!" Joel called out, as a horn sounded from outside.

"They must've hit the shelf!"

Behind them a crackling burst of gunfire blended with the angry cries of the outlaws, creating a great roar that warped and twisted as it bounced around the irregular walls.

The sounds of hell, Joel thought.

As he turned a corner, a wiry arm grabbed Joel and he dropped the torch. By its sputtering light, he saw only the brilliant pinpoint reflections in Virgil's eyes as he was drawn up face to face with the man.

"Ye've had it now, *little mouse.*" Virg's saliva was like liquid anger, spraying Joel's face and burning his eyes. "Yer 'bout ta take yer last breath!"

Like a snake coiled to strike, the small man's fist drew back. There was a blur and Joel's head snapped back, his lips exploding, white hot against his teeth in a wash of metallic blood.

"Stop!" Billy screamed. "You're hurting him!"

"What should I do, Joel?" Mark shouted.

His voice sounded oddly distant. Dreamlike, Virgil's fist pistoned forward again and again, blasting against Joel's mouth like cannon fire and knocking out a tooth. Wanting to slip to the floor and on into darkness, he hung limply in Virgil's grasp, just waiting for the next blow.

"Oh, little mouse, little mouse," Virgil said, shaking his head in mock pity. He held Joel like a sculptor examining his work. "Ye really cain't fight, kin ye? Guess yer jus' not a man after all."

As if seeing a flaw in his masterpiece, the man drew back for another blow.

"Let him go, goddammit!" Mark hurled a rock at the side of the man's head.

Virgil dropped Joel and grabbed his bloodied ear. He roared, cursing as he whirled around. Mark threw another rock and Virgil struck out at him with his cane. The boy ducked, rolled out of the way. Virgil drew back for another strike.

Joel got to his feet unsteadily and shook his head to clear it.

"Mark!" he cried as the cane struck his friend's left temple. He ran and jumped, landing on Virgil's back and pounding away at the small man's head.

Billy was running back and forth, screaming at the top of his lungs.

"Goddammit!" Virgil slammed back into the wall, knocking the wind out of Joel. He lost his grip on Virgil's shoulders. Sprawling to the floor, he saw Virgil wheel on Mark, lift the boy by the shirt collar and slam him against the opposite wall.

"I kin git yer friend later, but right now I'm fixin' ta bash yer brains all over this 'ere wall." Virg dropped his cane, and hauled back his fist. Mark closed his eyes.

Billy stood nearby, chest heaving, tears rolling down his face. His fists were clenched, his body trembling. Suddenly he darted forward and grabbed Virgil's cane. As Virgil's fist connected with Mark's cheek, Billy jabbed the cane into his wound.

Virgil screamed. Or, more accurately, he threw back his head and howled. Joel had never heard a human being make a noise like that. *Of course, Virg ain't exactly human, is he?* Joel shook his head to clear it.

Virgil swung his fist down, but Billy danced out of the way. He dropped the bloody cane as if it were a snake. Virgil stepped back and pulled his pistol.

"No!" Mark screamed.

Virgil pulled the trigger. There was a deafening blast, drowning Billy's scream. The rock behind his head exploded into shrapnel. Billy hit the floor like a sack of potatoes.

Their ears ringing, everyone stood stock still. Joel and Mark, their mouths hanging open, stared aghast, then turned toward Virgil.

The man, bleeding profusely, steadied himself against the

wall and tried to return the power of their combined gaze. His eyes wavered but a moment and that was all Mark seemed to need—he was on top of the man in an instant, all clawing fingernails and thrusting fists and feet, sharp spiking knees and elbows.

"Goddam murdering bastard!" he screamed, digging the fingers of one hand into Virgil's left eye, while clawing at his throat with the other. The man screamed and thrashed wildly, trying to protect his face.

Joel slammed his foot into Virgil's groin and he sank, rolling into a fetal position. Howling, Mark leapt on the man again, spiking him hard in the side of the head with a sharp elbow. Virgil shot a fist up, catching Mark under the chin and the boy sprawled backwards, senseless.

Joel rushed the man, just in time to catch a fist with his face. Joel's vision blurred and he found himself lying on his back, staring up at Virgil as the man strangled him, a lunatic grin on his rabid-dog face. Joel's head was pounding and his eyes felt like they were bulging out of his head. His chest hitched, over and over, his lungs trying to suck in oxygen that wasn't there.

"I said stop it, little brother!" he heard Wesley's voice commanding. "Let the boy go—*now.*"

"The boy's poisoned ye," Virgil roared, almost incoherently, his vise-like grip tightening on Joel's throat. "He's too damned smart. The little bastard 'as turned ye 'gainst yer own brother. He almos' killed me, an' he makes a fool outta me. Ever'body laughs. I gotta kill 'im, Wes."

The boy felt himself receding into deep, velvety darkness. It wasn't that bad, really. His lungs didn't hurt anymore.

"Ye cain't have 'im, Virg. He ain't jus' a boy—there's somethin' inside 'im ye'd best not eat. If'n ye don' let 'im go, *now,* little brother, that's *it*—I've had it!"

Wesley's dark silhouette rose up behind Virgil's mask of fury, and then everything went dark.

Joel came to, lying on his back, the big man fussing over him. To his right, Virgil lay in pool of blood, a bullet hole in the left side of his forehead.

Joel sat up, shaking. He turned to one side as his body quaked with a violent retching that caused his sore throat to seize up. Nothing came up but the burn of stomach acid.

"Ye'll be all right," Wesley said.

Still shaking, Joel pointed to his mouth and shook his head to tell Wesley that he couldn't speak.

The stupid death of Virgil Pike.

History had told him that Wesley Pike had killed his own brother, but had not elaborated on the circumstances. Nor had it informed him that he, Joel Biggs, had been their bone of contention.

"Git ye'self up, Joel, an' git up top. Take the dawgs up wit' ye." The big man turned to leave, and then paused. "Ye made me kill my own brother, but I'll settle that score wit' ye later. I promise ye that." He hurried out of the tunnel, heading for the shattered entrance.

Mark knelt next to Billy, crying.

"Come on," Joel said gently. "There's nothing we can do for him now. He's gone."

Mark stroked Billy's bloody hair. "He was just a little guy," he murmured. "How could that fucker kill such a little, bitty guy?"

"I ain't bitty," Billy said, frowning, eyes still closed.

"He's alive!" Joel screamed.

"Billy!" Mark yelled, helping him sit up. "I thought Virgil shot you through the head!"

"I think maybe he did," Billy said, gingerly touching the back of his skull.

"No, look!" Joel pointed to the bullet hole in the wall. "It just hit next to him, and sprayed him with a whole bunch of rock chips." He picked a shard out of Billy's matted hair. "See?"

"OW!" yelled Billy. Mark laughed, then hugged him.

"We gotta go," Joel said. "Can you walk, Billy?"

"I think so." The little boy got to his feet, and wavered a little. Mark wrapped his arm around Billy's waist.

Joel hesitated, then squeezed Billy briefly around the shoulders. "I'm glad you're not dead, you little shit."

"Me too," Billy grinned.

Joel led them into Virgil's smokehouse and up through the chimney.

They emerged from the wood smoke into the heart of a maelstrom of violence on top of the bluff—whirling smoke, gunshots, shouting, the smell of blood, men rushing about, and above all the hideous screams of the wounded and the dying from the fight below. Joel stood in the midst of the chaos, addled by its ferocity. Noxious fumes clogged the air, and he was somewhat surprised to see by the position of the sun that it was already well past noon.

Looking over the edge of the bluff, he saw a flotilla of rafts and flatboats sliding downriver to the cave mouth. On the shelf, many of the volunteer militia had taken refuge under the overhang, but the pirates still held positions behind several boulders and were firing upon them. As he watched, the militia seemed to draw together and then with a shout they swarmed over the boulders and fell upon the pirates. Joel saw many drop.

All along the switchback trail lay the bodies of men who had died trying to storm the ridge top.

"Git back from there, fool," Wade snapped at him. "Wes'd have my head if I was ta let ye git killed."

Joel stepped back to rejoin his friends. Now he saw volunteers rushing through the trees to the west, trying the long, rugged slope to the top. Some of the pirates had gathered along that edge of the ridge and were training their muskets on them. Their shots rained down, dropping the Tennessee volunteers as they ran.

"Joel, we're gonna die," Billy said, "we're gonna die!" The little boy clung to Joel's hand and trembled, tears running down his face. "Everybody's shooting at us!"

Joel saw his own fear in Billy's face. He crouched down with him and Mark in a crevice in the stone while the battle raged on about them.

The intensity of the battle diminished with the growing dusk, and the boys remained in the broad crack in the stony ridge top until nightfall. A quiet settled over the battleground, interrupted only by sporadic sniper fire and the demoralizing cries of the wounded.

Joel watched the militia's sentries, backlit by a luminous mist, marching along the opposite bank. From his position within the cleft of stone, he heard the pirates murmuring. Pipe and cigar smoke began to replace the stench of burnt powder. The pleasant smells from the cookfires became confused with those of spilled blood and open wounds. Billy was huddled in a miserable little heap at the bottom of their foxhole. Mark squatted next to him, a faraway look on his face, his hands covered with Billy's blood. He'd spent the past few hours picking slivers of stone from the skin of the little boy's scalp.

A figure stood up among the pirates, for a moment silhouetted plainly against the night sky. Several voices called out for him to keep low and, as if on cue, Joel heard a shot from the river below. The man ducked down as he ran toward the chimney.

"Wesley Pike!" a hollow voice called from down at the river. "This 'ere's Thomas Fellowes, an' I's appealin' ta what decency ye might 'ave. Lay down yer arms an' surrender, 'fore there's more killin'."

Joel knew that name, Thomas Fellowes, from the Crenshaw book. The events in the Crenshaw book wouldn't take place for another twenty years. *Probably not the same man,* Joel decided.

"Run 'long home, Granddaddy," Wesley sang out, " 'fore ye gits yerself hurt!"

"If'n ye surrender now, I'll see y'all git a fair trial. But I cain't hold back my men forever, Pike. They've lost too much an' they's angry. I won't vouch fer their behavior if'n this goes on much longer."

"If'n ye don' stop yer whinin', I promise ye my butchers won' make yer death a quick one."

"I'm sorry ta see yer reputation's well deserved, Pike—meaner than mean an' jus' plain dumb."

"Tomorrow we'll see who's who!" Wesley turned away.

"I'm sick, Joel," Billy said, tugging on the older boy's shirt sleeve, but Joel didn't respond. "I don't feel good. I think I'm gonna spit up."

Joel was wondering what was going to happen to them. If they tried to cross the river now, they'd be shot down like water rats.

"Joel." Billy gave the older boy's sleeve another, more insistent, tug. "I gotta go somewhere an' puke."

"Stay down, Billy. You can puke when it's all over."

"I can't wait." Billy turned away. "I gonna—"

The sour reek of stomach acid permeated the air around them.

"All that's comin' up is juice. I haven't had anything to eat all day. I wish Willawic was here."

Joel turned and looked at the boy. Billy's face, rimmed in orange light from the cookfires, was pained. Mark patted him on the shoulder. Billy leaned against him, just a little.

"He'll be back, don't worry. I'll take care of us until he gets back, I promise. You stay here with Mark, and I'll go get us something to eat."

"Hey, Joel," said Mark. "Try to find a bandage for Billy's head, would ya?"

"Sure, Mom."

Mark half-heartedly flipped him off.

Joel edged along the ridge, halfway expecting a bullet in the back at any moment.

"Git down, Little Man."

He was surprised to hear Wesley's voice, and more than a little afraid. He wasn't in a hurry to find out how Wes planned to repay him for Virgil's death. Joel turned and headed in the opposite direction, toward the cookfire that had been set up on the far side of the ridge top. From the fire, sparks and smoke coiled about each other as they ascended into the night.

"Ain't nothin' left," said the cook, stooped over to clean out a huge pot. "Shoulda got in line wit' the rest o' the men."

Joel sagged and started to turn away. The cook's expression softened. He reached into his apron and offered Joel some jerky.

"Jerky?" Joel asked, uneasily. "Where'd you get it?"

"Off that flatboat we took las' week. It ain't much, but it'll fill ye up. Now, if'n it ain't good 'nough fer ye, then. . . ."

"No, no—I don' mean to seem ungrateful or nothin', I'm jus' tired is all."

The man nodded his head, fishing around in his supplies.

"Can you give me enough for Mark and my dawg too?"

The cook smiled and handed over several long strips of dark, leathery meat. "And here." He handed over a crumbling handful of cornbread. "I was gonna throw this ta the dawgs—the *real* dawgs," he added with a smile.

Joel smiled his thanks, accepting the crumbs of cornbread.

"Wash it down wit' this." The cook handed him a small jug.

"Thanks, I appreciate it."

Joel turned, heading back through the dark blue night to where Mark and Billy waited.

"Here." He handed the other boys strips of jerky. "It's not Virgil's jerky. I think it's beef."

Biting off a big mouthful, Billy chewed rapidly.

"Slow down," Joel said, handing him a piece of cornbread. "Believe me, it'll only make you sick if you don't chew it up real good first."

Billy grunted around his mouthful and chewed more slowly.

The boys ate in silence. The food satisfied Joel's physical hunger, but did nothing for his weariness. He took several deep gulps from the jug, hoping it would help him sleep. Mark, eating in silence, took the jug and drank deeply. He'd been mentally checked out since before the battle. *Probably worried about his damn dog,* Joel thought.

"Whiskey?" the small boy asked.

Joel nodded. "You don't want any, Billy."

A shadow stood up and a shot sounded from the river below. The shadow tumbled backward, landing heavily, and was still.

"Goddammit!" Wesley roared from somewhere in the night. "Keep yer goddam heads down! We cain't afford ta be losin' no more men."

Mark and Billy had fallen asleep, leaving Joel alone. The little boy was curled up against Mark's back, his thin arm holding on tight to the older boy. Joel was struck by a quick pang of jealousy. No one had ever trusted him like that, and he had the feeling that no one ever would.

The cries from those in pain had diminished to moans drifting eerily out of the darkness. They surrounded him, passed through his head and he wondered if tomorrow his own cries might be among them. He tried not to listen, tried to shut out the sound, and hoped sleep would come quickly and take him away from this waking nightmare.

She came out of the darkness and, without a word, sat beside him. Joel saw she was about his age, and prettier than the other girl—he couldn't remember the other one's name, now. This girl's breasts were much fuller and she sat so close, they rubbed against his arm.

She put her arm around his shoulder, grasped his hand, and placed it on her breast. Joel's breath caught in his throat and he was instantly erect. He massaged the small nipples through the thin cloth of her shift. Her hand dropped to his lap and she leaned forward to kiss him, her lips parting.

That's when he saw her teeth. The firelight outlined the broken edges and wide gaps in her idiotic smile. Several teeth fell from her bloody gums even as he watched. They were nose to nose when she let out a blast of noxious breath and, his stomach souring, he retched. He desperately wanted to escape, but he couldn't; no matter where he moved, the girl was always there, right in his face.

Jerking upright, Joel saw it was almost morning. By the thin, predawn light, he saw a wet spot in his pants and was disgusted with himself, horrified to think that he had actually been so aroused by a dream so disgusting.

"Joel," Mark said, "you awake?"

"Yeah, I uh—" he began, hastily covering the wet spot in his crotch with his hands. "Hey, where's Billy?"

"He's over there, pissing over the edge."

Joel whirled around in a panic. "Billy, get down!"

"Not *there,* spazmo." Mark smiled. "Over there." He pointed behind him.

Walking toward them from the back of the ridge, Billy was trying to retie the front of his breeches.

"Damn," said the little boy. "We're still alive!" Mark and Joel looked at each other, and burst out laughing.

57

Wesley and Wade were crouched together talking near the western precipice. Joel, pretending to dump scraps from his plate over the edge, got in close enough to eavesdrop.

"We cain't hold the cave," the big man said urgently.

"Whaddaya wanna do, Wes?"

"Well, I been thinkin' o' a way we could git away. It's gonna take a powerful distraction fer us ta do it though."

Wade nodded his head.

"Tell ye what we's gonna do. We's gonna let that next wave git ta the top."

Clearly incredulous, Wade seemed to have a hard time holding his tongue.

Joel hurried back to his friends. "Things're probably gonna get rough around here."

"Maybe now's the time to go over to the other side and surrender," Mark said.

"If we're not real careful about that, we might get shot—as deserters by the pirates, or as pirates by the militia."

"I didn't think about that."

"I wish Willawic was here," Billy said.

"Yeah, me too," Joel said. "Maybe he could figure a way out of this mess. The way I see it, the only thing we can do is hang loose and wait to see what happens."

Watching from his hiding place among the rocks, Joel could

imagine their attackers' point of view—somehow, a group of twenty-some-odd young men had managed to run all the way up the long, slow northern slope without losing a single man. And now they were charging onto the ridge top looking for targets to fire upon, but finding none. They looked to each other for answers. Boulders littered the otherwise empty expanse of stone and from behind one of these, Wesley Pike's voice boomed out, shattering the stillness.

"Ye boys is surrounded, an' if'n ye wants ta go on livin', lay down yer rifles."

The volunteers, their eyes still nervously scanning the ridge top, became still, then slowly and carefully placed their weapons on the bare stone and stepped back from them.

The pirates rushed from their hiding places and beat the helpless volunteers senseless. Joel looked away.

"We's got some o' yers up here, Mister *goodie* Fellowes. Tell yer men ta hold their fire while I talks ta ye."

Joel heard Fellowes shouting commands, and Wesley stepped up to the edge of the ridge.

"Didja git ta wonderin' what happened ta 'em after they didn't come back? Or didja figure they got killed, jus' like all ta others ye sent up here?"

Wesley grinned wickedly, squinting his eyes against the noonday sun.

"Ye better listen, an' listen good. Now that we's got somethin' o' yers, somethin' yer gonna want back—it's time ta dicker."

Muted sounds of outrage floated up from below, a "damn ye ta hell" or two reaching Joel's ears.

"Now, now." Wesley adopted a patronizing tone. "There's no call fer ye ta git all riled up. When things was goin' yer way, ye didn' hear *us* complainin'—ye didn' hear us moanin' or whinin'. Nossir! We jus' laid down an' died, without a word. We was bidin' our time, an' now it's our turn."

The pirates shouted their approval and hurled taunts down at the men below until Wesley silenced them with a gesture.

"We ain't bargainin' wit' ye, Pike!" Fellowes shouted. "Ye ain't got nothin' ta bargain with. Those men ye got lef' their homes an' loved ones ta come here an' fight knowin' full well—"

He was cut off by the indignant cries of his men.

"Fu'the'more, we's got ye surrounded an' it's only a matter a time 'fore we storm the top."

"Nothin' ta bargain wit'?" Wesley's voice was a low, bear-like growl. He stepped back from the edge and gave the signal.

Joel watched as one of the prisoners was led to the edge of the bluff. He was a tall, skinny guy in his late teens, and he looked scared to death. A big, beefy pirate named Shanahan had him by the back of the neck, a pistol to his temple. Angry murmurs rippled through the volunteers. Shanahan looked over his shoulder at Wesley, grinning. Wes gave the slightest flick of his hand, and Shanahan shoved the kid out into space.

The boy screamed, his arms and legs pinwheeling as he fell. Some of the militia called out his name—*Seth, thought Joel, his name is Seth*—as his body described a long, slow arc, which ended on the rock shelf below. His scream was cut off by a sickening, explosive smack. Broken bones sprang from his body like jagged switchblades, and his blood splashed the rocks.

"*That's* what I got ta bargain wit'," Wesley shouted over the sudden burst of gunfire from below. He waited for it to die down before speaking again. "A man every twenty minutes 'til ye withdraw 'cross the river."

Joel knew that his reaction a month ago would have been to look long and hard at the dead man, to take in every detail. But now he just felt sick and sad. He turned away.

"Holy fucking Christ," Mark muttered into his hands.

"Joel, is he dead?" Billy tugged on the older boy's sleeve. "He's dead, isn't he? He's gotta be dead. Did they kill him?"

"Shut up, Billy. Of course he's dead."

"No I'm *not* gonna shut up, Joel!" Billy's eyes were wide and he dug his fingers hard into Joel's arm. "I'm *not* gonna shut up, and yer gonna tell me what's going on. I don't understand—why did they do that to that man—*why?* Why are we here? Why can't we go home? Where's Willawic? I wanna go *home!*"

The edge of hysteria in the boy's voice was sharp and his words cut deeply. All three boys looked at one another, their eyes tearing. No one was ashamed, and no one laughed.

No one said a word.

Horns and gunshots rent the air as the attack began on three sides. As a number of foolhardy volunteers scrambled up the switchback trail and others climbed the huge sycamores that rose up beside the face of the bluff. Those remaining on the shelf of rock kept up a steady fire to keep the pirates down.

Mark and Billy followed Joel as he scrambled from one hiding place to another, watching each battle with a sickened curiosity. As they peeked from behind a low, squat boulder, Mark craned his neck to see and a bullet nearly parted his hair. He squawked and fell backwards into the dirt. Joel punched him in the shoulder. "If you're gonna tag along, at least keep your heads down!"

To the north, the volunteers crept up the rocky slope, providing each other covering fire as they went.

The attackers had moved the cannon to a rocky prominence. The first shot whistled harmlessly over the pirates' heads, crashing into the rocky soil of the western slope and exploding well ahead of the volunteers charging up that side.

Wesley gave the order to roll a massive boulder down the west side. Joel squinted. To his horror, he realized that there was a man lashed to the side of the rock. His head was slumped to his chest and he appeared to be unconscious, or dead. But as six of the outlaws heaved away at the massive stone, the man tied to it began shouting. His screams were cut short. The sight of his pulverized body rolling down to greet them took the fight out of his fellows, and those who weren't diving out of the way hesitated. Some even ran. The pirates fired down upon them.

Another prisoner, a short, pot-bellied fellow with two black eyes and a broken nose, was shoved onto the ridge by laughing pirates. A powder keg half filled with lead shot was tied to his back. The fuse was lit and the man was thrown over the bluff, a shrieking human bomb. He slapped into the rocks below with a sound that echoed across the river. Although he was obviously dead, his fellows rushed to his aid. The keg exploded and a storm of lead shredded the onlookers. *Looks like it's rainin' blood,* Joel thought, feeling nothing.

The cannon fired again and the shell slammed into the ridge top. Miraculously, it hit no one, but ricocheted over the west side and exploded, raining fiery hot metal onto the retreating volunteers. A roar of laughter rose up from the pirates.

At the north side, an assembly line had been set up to prepare explosive kegs; one group of outlaws removed half the powder from each, replacing it with lead shot; another cut and rammed in fuses; while those at the edge of the incline lit the makeshift bombs and rolled them down among their attackers.

The first bowled over a couple of men before exploding. Others, bounding down the slope, exploded over the heads of the attackers, showering lead shot and splintered wood.

The militia had finally taken control of the main cave entrance and the pirates, retreating from the battle below, came through the chimney, joining their fellows on the ridge top.

The cannon fired again, but the shot was low and struck a sycamore. The tree snapped in two and fell, taking the men in it down and sweeping others off the switchback trail.

Volunteers poured out of the chimney and onto the top of the bluff. They made a circle and fired on the backs of the pirates. Several outlaws fell before they could whirl and fire on their attackers.

Wade ordered a group of outlaws to pursue the volunteers down the chimney and clear out the passages to the westward entrance.

"That's fine," Wesley said. "But jus' chase 'em off an' let 'em find their way back out again. They'll tell Fellowes 'bout the chimney."

"But, Wes," said Wade, "they'll jus' come right back wit' a whole mess o' men."

"Hell, they cain't get through the chimney but one at a time. Now, listen—what I want ye ta do is round up some men an' git ta work blastin' the big tunnel that leads ta the west entrance. Guard that passage off the chimney that runs down ta the back-door. We wan' 'em thinkin' they's found a way in, but I don' want none o' them bastards finding their way ta our escape route."

The militia was retreating on all sides and, as Fellowes tried to regroup them along the river's edge, the smoke cleared and the air became still.

"Lookit 'em run, Wes!" Wade cackled.

"Shit," the big man said, "they ain't really runnin'. They're doin' jus' what I wan'. They's all gonna gather 'long the river an' storm the cave. Once they start in, that's when we make our move. If we play our cards right, he an' 'is men'll git lost deep in the cave while we all make a run out the back."

Wade caught sight of Joel. "What about the boy an' the dawgs?" he asked.

Wesley looked at Joel, started to say something, but then shook his head. He turned away and looked over the edge to watch the Tennessee volunteers filing toward the front of the cave from the north and south.

"Mister *goodie* Fellowes," Wesley called over the edge. "I's changed my mind—now, we'll be sendin' 'em back ta ye every five minutes."

Another man was hurled screaming into space and crashed on the rocks below. Wesley waited until the uproar had subsided before speaking again.

"Let's see now—that leaves nineteen. If'n ye wants 'em returned in one piece, ye gots ta git yer men 'cross the river."

"My men're roarin' mad, Pike," Fellowes shouted, "I *cain't* jus' git 'em 'cross the river that easily!"

"Wade, how much more time 'fore the next man goes over?"

The man pulled out his pocketwatch and looked at it, then raised four fingers.

"What? Ye say four minutes? I don' think that's 'nough time fer 'em ta git 'cross the river, but they *might* save the next man."

"Goddammit, Pike, yer the devil hisself! An' if I don' kill ye today, I assure ye, there *will* come a time."

"An' I assure ye, there's only three'n half minutes lef'!"

Fellowes could be heard arguing with his men and, after a time, the sounds of shouting and a fistfight drifted up the bluff.

"Two minutes, gentlemen!" Wesley called out sweetly.

"It'll take me a half hour, at least, ta git my men rounded up an' everythin' in order. Ye gots ta give me more time."

The big man pretended to consider this. "Cain't do it, Fellowes. One minute!"

"But half my men're still 'round the far side o' the bluff! An' the boats're all a tangle!"

"Ye sure gots a problem, don' ye? Yessir, ye surely do."

Despite Fellowes' relentless arguments, Wesley would not respond. When Wade gave him the signal, Wesley leaned over the edge and spat. "Time's up!"

58

Morning light streamed in through the small bathroom window of the Phelps' house as Joel sat on the toilet reading the Crenshaw book.

> By early evening they came to the town of Wallace where Matthew Crenshaw had a friend, Thomas Fellowes—

Joel was so startled to see the name "Thomas Fellowes" that he dropped the book on the floor and reached out for balance, his left elbow striking a row of toiletries on the shelf beside him. They fell to the flagstone floor with a great clatter.

"You all right in there?" came Lynn's concerned, motherly voice.

"Yes, Lynn. I made a little mess, is all."

"I guess my beans and cornbread didn't go down so well after all. Don't worry about it. I'll get in there with the mop when you're finished."

Oh God, now she thinks I've got projectile diarrhea, or something. Joel reached down and picked up the book.

> By early evening they came to the town of Wallace where Matthew Crenshaw had a friend, Thomas Fellowes, who was the proprietor of the general store. While Cotten went to the Walker Tavern to refill his brandy flask, Crenshaw went to the general store and confided to his friend that he

was traveling under an assumed name in the company of Jarrett Cotten. He further explained that he was pursuing evidence for an arrest warrant against the outlaw and enlisted the aid of Thomas Fellowes in preparing a statement. The statement would attest to Crenshaw's presence in the store that day and recount his conversation with the proprietor. Fellowes agreed and Crenshaw left to rejoin the outlaw and continue their journey.

My Thomas Fellowes? Joel wondered. *It could be he survived. Then again, it could be another with the same name—neither name was uncommon in the 1800s.*

He reopened the book and continued to read.

(The testimonial of Thomas Fellowes, former Captain of the Tennessee Militia, as provided to Deland Carter, Sheriff of Madison County, State of Tennessee.)

No—It says he was captain of the Tennessee Militia. What are the odds that there were two captains of that militia with the same name?

State of Tennessee, Shelby County, 1833

The man going by the name of Matthew Crenshaw requested that I, Thomas Fellowes, make this statement attesting to an incident which occurred in the township of Wallace in the state of Tennessee on the twenty-seventh of November, 1833. The gentleman in question, while passing through the town in the company of Jarrett Cotten, came to see me on a matter of great urgency.

Before I continue, I must state and attest that I have known the man going by the name Matthew Crenshaw (hereafter referred to as Crenshaw) since he was a youngster. I do know his true name, and that he is now well beyond his thirtieth year. Furthermore, I should say here that prior to the date aforementioned, I knew the name Jarrett Cotten as belonging to one who was an infamous outlaw.

My friend sought me out in my General Store to speak privately, saying that he was passing himself off to Jarrett Cotten as Matthew Crenshaw, a man of desperate temperament; and through this deception, hoped to put himself in good stead with Cotten. Crenshaw said he told the man he was a complete stranger to the territory and told me that if I were seen with him, to feign unfamiliarity.

He was pursuing Cotten after the man had stolen two negroes from the farm of Crenshaw's good friend, Hume Stogdon, in Madison county, Tennessee. Being under the guise of an outlaw, Crenshaw hoped that Cotten would lead him to the stolen negroes.

Crenshaw wanted to be seen by me on this day to leave some record of his passing, being afraid Cotten had seen through his deception and was soon to do him in. I agreed to prepare this letter and gave him a loaded pistol so that he could defend himself if Cotten turned on him. We were together but a very brief time before he rejoined Cotten.

This is the extent of my knowledge on the subject, but it has been suggested to me that Mr. M. Ryder and Mr. J. Biggs—

Joel burst from the bathroom, holding his pants up with one hand, ran into the kitchen area where Lynn was canning peaches. She backed away from him, a yelp of fear escaping her lips, but he got in close to her and held the book open.

"What does that say?" Joel demanded.

"What. . . . Where?!"

"There," Joel said, pointing.

"But . . . it has—"

"No—just read it from the beginning of the paragraph," he said, pointing to the previous paragraph.

"This is the extent of my knowledge on the subject," she read haltingly, "but it has been suggested to me that Mister M. Ryder and Mister J. Biggs were witness to a good deal more and if found, would be of great assistance in this matter.

"If it serves the cause of justice, then I freely give this account of the events thus known to me. Penned by my hand and entered into record at Alexandria, Tennessee, on the tenth day of May, 1833.

"THOMAS Q. FELLOWES

"(SEALED)"

M. Ryder and J. Biggs—She saw it too! Joel's heart was hammering, his head swimming. He suddenly felt a little sick.

"But what does it mean?" she asked. "Was that an ancestor of yours?"

"I don't know," he said, and then returned to the bathroom to wipe himself.

59

By late afternoon, the boys were the only ones left on the ridge top. Bodies lay scattered about them, and the air was thick with flies and the smell of death; coppery blood, feces, sweat and terror.

The volunteers hadn't tried to retreat. Fellowes had tried to make them, but his frantic, bellowed orders to man the canoes had been shouted down by dozens of angry, bloodthirsty men. They would not be denied their revenge, no matter what happened to their comrades. Faced with a full-out assault, the pirates had flung all the captives off the ridge top at once, driving them with guns, knives, and bullwhips like a pack of human lemmings. For a moment, the sky had rained screaming, pinwheeling men. Then they hit. The sound alone was enough to make Joel not look down. He imagined the shelf below to be painted red, the broken bodies like twisted and discarded children's toys, and shuddered.

Joel now stood on the west side of the ridge and watched the outlaws pour out of the back entrance on horseback and bolt into the trees. As Wesley shot out of the cave, he turned and looked to the top of the bluff.

"I'll be back after ye, Little Man," he shouted.

Wesley, after me?

Somehow, he couldn't bring himself to be afraid, although he knew he probably should be. Thinking he might never see the man again, Joel felt strangely sad.

Whatever else Wesley is, Joel thought, his eyes stinging with unshed tears, *he looked after me, and was, sort of, my friend.*

"You're one cool motherfucker, Wesley," he said as the big man vanished into the trees, "even if you would pass for the devil himself."

He remembered what Wesley had said about him to Virgil—"He ain't jus' a boy—there's somethin' inside 'im you'd better not eat."

Was he afraid of me? Is that why he treated me so well?

A cold shiver crept over him, and Joel knew he would never forget the electric taste of fear that was Wesley Pike—the most dangerous man he would ever meet. He felt a dizzying mix of relief and exhilaration at the thought of having survived his encounter with the Pikes—like the time a car had hit him while he was riding his bicycle. The bike was ruined, but he had gotten up and walked away.

Then he remembered that the big man had no other appointments to keep with history. Fascinated with the outlaw, Joel had gone to the library last fall and looked up all he could about Wesley Pike. There was some mention of his name surrounding events after this point in time, but there seemed to be serious doubt among historians that he had survived this battle. There was some suggestion that the later appearances of Wesley Pike were in fact made by the outlaw's older brother, Jamus Pike.

I guess I won't be seeing you, Joel thought.

He turned away and walked across the ridge top to join the other boys on the east side, arriving just in time to see the tail end of the volunteers' charge, a wild screaming tide that washed into the cave mouth.

Based on what he'd overheard Wesley say, Joel tried to envision the scene within the bluff—the volunteers fanning out to secure every passage, the last of the pirates hanging back just long enough to blow up the few tunnels that connected to the back entrance.

Less than an hour later, a sorry-looking stream of the outlaws' castaways—women, children and old folks—poured out and pooled on the rock shelf, herded by volunteers with rifles.

"Might as well give ourselves up," Mark said, "now that the shooting's over."

Billy and Mark started down the switchback trail. Joel paused, lost in thought, looking at the river. "Yeah, it's better than wandering around—"

He saw the volunteers shoving the old and feeble men and women into the river.

"Wait a minute, guys."

"No, c'mon, Joel, they're our saviors!" Mark said.

"No, let's watch 'em for a minute. I'm not sure I trust these guys."

Mark seemed about to respond when a scream clearly caught his attention. Looking down, he watched the volunteers methodically clubbing those of their victims who did not drown readily.

"Oh man," Mark whispered, "oh *man.*"

"Why are they so mean?" Billy said. "Everybody's mean here."

Joel said nothing. He stood as if paralyzed, staring at the scene below. Again and again, the volunteers herded the old and infirm off the edge into the river, stabbing, shooting, or clubbing any who gave them trouble.

"Something's *really* wrong here," Joel said. "I thought they were gonna save us from the bad guys."

Another group of volunteers were separating and lining up the women and children. The men appraised the captive women, made their selections and led—or dragged—them away. They marched the children away, out of sight.

"We'll be okay, Joel," Mark said. "See? They're treating the women and children all right."

"I dunno, we don't know where they're taking them or what they're doing to them."

"If we don't give ourselves up, what are we gonna do for food?"

"Yeah," Billy said, "I'm already hungry."

"I thought you two knew how to hunt."

"So?" Billy asked.

"So—let's get a rifle, powder, and shot from one of these dead guys and take off."

60

In the light of dusk, Mark waded through the shallows near the bank of the river. He was trying to catch up with Joel and Billy, who were crouched behind trees at the water's edge.

Joel turned around and shushed him and Mark looked to see what they were watching. The volunteers had herded the surviving women and children into the pirates' empty horse corral. Outside the enclosure was a tree, its numerous low-lying boughs laden with corpses.

"I think they're killing off the ones that are sick, full of demons, or just plain ugly," Joel whispered.

"We oughta run in there and start shooting," Mark said. "Kill every one of 'em and set all the prisoners free."

"That'd be great if we had M-16s," Joel hissed. "But with these shitty flintlocks, you're lucky if your single shot hits the target."

"Oh yeah, I didn't think about that."

"Dumbass."

"I'm hungry," Billy said. "Let's go hunting."

"It's getting too dark to hunt," said Joel.

"Willawic would do it."

"Yeah, well he's a damn Indian—isn't he?"

One of the men seized a blond woman by the hair and began dragging her toward the river. She kicked and screamed until he clouted her on the head.

"He's coming straight for us," Joel said.

"Let's get outta here."

"Yeah, Joel, let's get outta here," Billy whispered, tugging at his sleeve.

"Not now, he'll see us."

The man swung the woman around and she fell on her backside between a pair of willows at the river's edge, not fifteen feet away. He fell upon her and pulled up her skirts. When she screamed, he clamped a hand on her throat and cast a glance over his shoulder. His fellows seemed to be making a strong effort to mind their own business. He ripped open the front of her dress, baring her small breasts. After fumbling with his pants for a moment, he shoved himself brutally into her.

Seeing the woman's breasts, Mark was excited—he wanted to get a better look, but it was all wrong, too frightening. Her face was turning blue and he knew that if the rapist didn't release her soon, the man would be having sex with a corpse.

"Do something, Joel!"

"Whaddaya want *me* to do? They'll see me and then we'll get caught."

"Shoot him!" Billy said, clutching at Joel's shirt.

"Fucking idiot!" He shook the boy off and crept quietly along the water's edge, drawing his pocketknife. The man was grunting, pounding into the woman, and didn't seem to hear the boy approaching. Joel jumped from the water and lunged onto his back. He quickly drew the blade across the volunteer's throat.

Blood sprayed from the wound so fast and heavy it didn't look real to Mark; more like a special effect in a horror movie. The man clutched at his neck and tried to get to his feet, but he stumbled, garbled noises coming from his ruined throat. He collapsed, rapidly weakening as his life bled away.

"C'mon," Joel said to the woman, who was trying to catch her breath, "you're safe."

She took one look at him, at the blood covering his hand,

and began to scream anew. Springing to her feet, she ran back toward the corral, flailing her arms and shouting for help.

"Goddam, Joel," Mark said when his friend returned. "You killed him, I mean you *really* killed him."

"Shut up!" Joel hissed. There was a fearful light in his eyes and he was shaking. "We gotta get the hell outta here and fast!"

Mark grabbed Billy and they swam out into the river. Joel followed and the three boys disappeared into the growing dark.

61

Mark and Joel had left Billy sleeping in the crotch of a tree in the forest and then slipped through the night to spy on the Tennesseans once again. The volunteers' bonfire was a living column sprouting from the rock shelf and supporting the sky. At its base, a log exploded, and like an earth-bound comet, it spewed glowing fragments toward the stars. Dark silhouettes writhed about it, men and a few of their female captives, dancing. Long shadows leapt away from them, rolled over the spot where the boys were hidden, and climbed the new face of the bluff.

Joel watched a couple of the men rolling another keg of whiskey from the cave. They were greeted by a cacophony of whooping and hollering. A discordant rabble near the battered cave entrance took up a ballad and wailed away at the silent wilderness.

Mark tapped Joel on the shoulder and pointed. They watched three men emerge from the cave and approach Thomas Fellowes, who was sitting on a log smoking, about fifty feet away from the boys. Fellowes set down his pipe.

"Sir, we's been back in there 'bout as far as ye kin get, an' we think it's pretty much cleaned out. The place mus' surely be possessed o' some evil spirits. We saw corpses lying about, pregnant with living brood. There was a room in there full o' nothing but gnawed human bone. An' toward the top, there was a chamber hung wit' long pig. Do ye think we ought ta take 'em down an' give 'em a decent burial?"

"Naw, Joe," said Fellowes, "You an' Forrest git to work firs' thing tomorrow wit' those kegs o' powder. Blast the entrance and that oughta be enough."

"Yessir."

The men walked off and Thomas Fellowes went back to smoking his pipe.

Fellowes didn't really look all that bad, Joel thought. He was the type of tall, stern, weatherworn man he had always imagined frontier lawmen to be. Moments later when the fire flared up, however, Joel got a good look at the man's scalping scar. It was beet-red, starting in the middle of his brow and spreading out to encompass much of the top of his head. In the flickering light, his nature seemed to waver between the malignant and the benign.

Joel found himself unable to fit the legend to the man—the stories the pirates told of Fellowes painted a picture that fit this gruesome apparition, but the troubled man beneath the scar, the one Joel saw sitting and smoking by himself on the fringe of the fire's light, belied his appearance.

Somewhere, someone produced a fiddle and began sawing out a jig that jangled the nerves. Volunteers grabbed up female prisoners, like so many sacks of potatoes, and began whirling them about, drunken leers smeared on their faces. Others simply dragged their women off into the darkness.

"Mark," Joel whispered, "you know something? The only difference between these guys and the pirates is that they do their raping in the dark, where their buddies won't see 'em."

A knife fight broke out—the combatants grotesquely keeping time with the meter of the jig. There was a lunge and a slice and one of the men stumbled back, his throat spraying blood. Desperately clutching the wound, he dropped his knife and stared wide-eyed at his opponent before falling to his knees.

Jolting applause and jeering laughter sprang from the drunken crowd as the man crumpled and died.

" 'Ay watch this!" a man shouted. He was kneeling behind a trussed pig. "This 'ere pig's cleaner'n any o' them rank wimmen y'all dragged out."

He opened his pants and was preparing to plunge himself into the animal when a man to his right pulled out a pistol and shot him dead.

The crowd fell silent and the fiddler abruptly ended his jig. All eyes were on the killer.

"This unholy place's gotten ta us all," he said, calmly reloading his pistol. "Decent men engaged in unnatural acts! I'll be glad ta be quit o' this place! God 'ave mercy—" He placed the gun to his temple and fired.

62

"I'm glad Billy wasn't with us last night," Joel said, thinking of the murder/suicide they had witnessed. "He definitely didn't need to see that."

He and Mark were hiding at the edge of the forest, watching the volunteers rise. A few of them were already up, busily preparing food and coffee, while others stumbled about holding their heads, or barely managed to drag themselves to the river before vomiting.

"These are just farmboys," Joel said, turning away. He watched a flight of birds against the early morning sky. "They don't know how to handle all this death and destruction."

Mark looked at his friend, a puzzled look on his face. "What about us?"

"I guess—" Joel began. Then he shook his head and laughed a little too hard. "What've we seen here that we haven't seen a million times on TV?"

"Yeah, but that ain't real." Mark's cautious grin somehow reminded Joel of the cracks in his mother's "good" china, the stuff that hadn't been used since before she died.

Uncomfortable, Joel decided to change the subject. "You know, I've read that the piracy along the river died down about 18—"

The explosion was so loud, Joel felt like a wedge of sound had been driven between his ears. The boys instinctively flattened themselves on the ground, shielding their heads as a great gout of smoke and debris shot out of the cave mouth.

"What was that?" Billy asked, stepping up behind them. "That was a 'splosion, wasn't it?"

"No, that was just your butt, Billy," Joel said, "you farted."

"Did *not!*"

Mark and Joel broke up laughing. They stumbled out of the trees to get a better look.

"It was Mister Fellowes and his men blowing up the cave entrance, dumbass."

The hungover volunteers were clutching their heads and screaming. They saw Thomas Fellowes standing on a rock outcropping above the corral. An angry crowd gathered about him. Crouching low, the boys crept closer, scurrying over to hide behind a stack of firewood near the corral.

"After the debauchery o' last night, leading ta the death o' three fine men," Fellowes said, his fists on his hips, "y'all should be thankful the evils o' the cave can no longer plague ye."

"Ye had no right!" shouted a young, blond man. "Ye shoulda taken a vote."

"It were draggin' ye down the path—" Fellowes began.

"We had the right ta clear out the cave, our own damn selves," interrupted a burly, hirsute fellow. "The filth as what lived here, robbed us fer years, an' we had a right ta their cache."

"Jeb's right—the spoils o' war," said the blond man. "But we kin still git in through the hole up top o' the bluff."

"Hold on, now," said an older, graying man, "Fellowes is right—this is an evil place. Why, the evil liquor pulled outta that devil's den an' poured down the throats o' them good, Christian men, polluted 'em an' drove 'em murderin' mad. Did not the good Lord bury Sodom an' Gomorrah 'neath fire an' brimstone? 'Twas the Lord's judgment, rightfully passed—Satan's den *had* ta be buried."

Jeb grabbed the older man by the shirtfront and thrust his

face forward until they were nose to nose. "Goddammit, Preacher, I didn't sign on fer no revival meetin'. We was *cheated!* I ain't gonna listen ta no preachin' over this 'ere. We was all tol' there'd be salvage ta be had." He punctuated his words by punching the Christian in the mouth. The man fell to the ground and Jeb kicked him repeatedly.

Fellowes jumped down and pushed his way through the men. He caught Jeb by the shoulders and pulled him away. Jeb twisted out of his grip, turning to face him.

"Get *down,* Billy!" Mark hissed.

"I can't hear," Billy whined, ducking down behind the woodpile. "Can't see neither."

"You don't need to hear this, Billy," Joel said.

"This ain't worth killin' each other fer!" shouted Fellowes. "This man ain't done nothin' ta deserve this."

Jeb glared at him and raised a fist.

"I led y'all here," Fellowes continued, "an' I'll own that there was a lot said when we was tryin' ta raise this militia—things as jus' weren't true. But truth is, we came here ta clean out the pirates, an' clean 'em out we did. The entrance to the cave is blocked—they ain't comin' back."

The crowd grumbled angrily, but no one was willing to say anything directly. Fellowes stood straight and tall.

Jeb lowered his fist. "Ye've had yer day, Fellowes. From now on, *my* word is law. The men're wit' me. We kin call a vote, if'n ye like."

"No need. I kin see what's happenin'."

Jeb turned and walked off without another word.

Billy had climbed on top of the stack of firewood. Joel grabbed the boy by the pants and yanked on him. "Get *down,* Billy! Someone'll see you!"

Billy and half the woodpile tumbled down, exposing all three boys. Thirty faces turned in their direction.

"Oh shit," Mark said, and Joel had to agree with him.

63

"Here he comes again," Joel said, pointing to the hunchbacked albino he had dubbed "the White Ghoul."

Mark turned and nodded, feeling a shiver of dread.

Is he coming for us this time?

The White Ghoul lowered the tiny, night-black round glasses he always wore and scanned the children with his red, filmy eyes. His colorless hair floated around his head in the slight breeze like dead seaweed in a backwater. He selected a scrawny little girl, slung the screaming child over his shoulder and hauled her away. Mark was ashamed to breathe out a sigh of relief.

Ever since yesterday, when the boys had been placed in the corral, they had watched the man harvest his crop of little girls and boys. Periodically, he stopped by the enclosure to make a selection. No one knew what he did with the children, for they never returned.

But it was rumored. . . .

Mark shuddered, unable to help himself—he knew the man was not *really* a ghoul, and *surely* they were not flaying the children alive—*I haven't heard any screams*—or, as the outlaw women had suggested, "carted 'em off ta 'is hell 'neath the gravestones." But he knew something was happening to them, and his imagination was going wild. Every time the pale man appeared, Mark wanted to scream.

Like all the prisoners, Mark's hands were tied behind his back and his legs were hobbled by a length of rope. An additional layer of split rails had been added to the corral and tied in place. Five guards watched over them day and night, rifles held at the ready.

None of the other prisoners would speak to the boys. Mark had tried to talk to them, but they turned away whenever he approached. The children from the cave were a quiet lot. They were all bunched up, clinging to one another and so camouflaged with filth that if it weren't for the occasional sob, cough or moan, Mark might have taken them for an aggregate of stone and mud.

The thick, cloying stench of feces, urine, and body odor was oppressive, and Mark breathed as shallowly as possible through his mouth. Even so, he could almost taste it.

From the huge oak just outside the corral, the militia had hanged all of the captured outlaw men, as well as many of the females. Mark tried not to watch them swaying gently in the wind.

All afternoon, his bladder had been aching—he waited as long as he could before urinating, because it was humiliating to do it out in the open, where everyone could see him. He knew he couldn't wait much longer. His stomach was an empty aching, but he didn't expect their jailers would feed them any time soon.

Mark sat in the reeking mud next to Joel, Billy's face buried in his chest. At first he had been embarrassed to comfort Billy, but soon realized that it was comforting to him as well. Thankfully, Joel hadn't made a joke of it.

Mark looked up with a start to see Thomas Fellowes staring at them through the rail fence. Joel seemed to notice him too, and the man nodded his ugly, scarred head.

"Did they ever finish building that B-2 Spirit Bomber?"

"Hunh?" Mark asked, his jaw dropping. His brain couldn't

make sense of what Fellowes had said. Beside him, Joel's mouth also gaped.

"You know," Fellowes prompted, dropping his heavy accent, "the Stealth Bomber?"

"Uh, yeah," Joel answered. "How—how do you know about that?"

"Oh, I'm an airplane nut from way back. Used to fly too—had my own Cessna."

"But—" Joel started.

"When you were caught, I saw them take your Swiss Army Knife. I'll try to get it back for you, but it might take some doing." An eagerness settled into the man's features, his eyes brightening. "Now tell me something—how'd you boys get here anyway?"

"We were wandering down Brown's Creek," Joel said. "I guess we just got lost."

"Brown's Creek? Do you mean the Brown's Creek in Dexter, Tennessee?"

"Yeah. You know it?"

"Damn straight I know it! I used to live right on it. The Howards were my neighbors—you know them?"

"That's me!" Billy said. "My mom and me's Howards. Are you the one Willawic got his Nikes from?"

"Nikes? What do you mean?"

"Never mind," Joel said. "You just be quiet, Billy, we're talking to this guy."

"Missus Howard is Billy's mom," Mark said, "and if it weren't for her we wouldn't be here. She straightened the creek in her yard and we went exploring in it."

Suddenly Mark's eyes widened as he recognized Fellowes. "I know you—you're the Fellowes guy who ran off on his wife."

"Yeah," Joel said, "my dad said you just up and disappeared one day."

"I sure did." Fellowes laughed. "But not like everybody must've thought. You see, a tornado pulled down an old oak tree that stood on the property line between me and the Howards. I got some tree surgeons in to cut up the wood, but I had to pull the stump myself. I had to dig down about eight feet. When I looked up, my house was gone."

Mark stared in amazement—the longer he looked at the man, the less gruesome Fellowes seemed, and the more the Mr.-Fellowes-the-neighbor showed through.

"Goddam, I just can't believe it," Joel said. "You don't know how good it is to see someone from home!"

"Actually, I do." Fellowes looked down and chuckled. When he lifted his head again, his eyes were moist. "You know, we're not the only ones who disappeared from that neighborhood. There was this alcoholic woman lived up the street a ways, name of Myrtle or Myrtox, or something like that—she vanished without a trace. No one thought much about that. But then there was this accountant lived next to me on the other side. Don't remember his name, but I used to see him jogging up and down the street all the time. His disappearance made it in the paper."

"Can you get us outta here?" Billy interrupted. "It stinks real-real bad!"

"I'll try, but don't get your hopes up. Jeb's in charge now."

Fellowes stood and walked over to the captain of the guard at the gate. "Harris, I need these here boys ta help me haul some wood."

Harris scratched his head and squinted. "Jeb tol' me not ta let anyone but 'im an' Thorpe take any o' the prisoners outta here."

"Shit! 'Course, I know there's been a change o' command an' all, but surely, Harris, ye know Jeb couldn't a meant *me.*"

"Well . . . damn. All right, Fellowes, but don'—"

"Harris, goddam yer wormy hide!" Jeb's bass voice boomed as he walked up to the two men. "Wha'd I done tol' ye?"

"But I—"

"I tol' ye they's spoken fer."

"I jus' need 'em fer a hour or so," Fellowes said.

"Ye ain't got no business wit' 'em childerns," Jeb said, his eyes narrowing with suspicion, " 'cept, maybe, *unnatural* business. What 'bout it, Fellowes?"

"You know what your problem is, Jeb?" Fellowes said. "Too much testosterone."

That brought a smile to Mark's lips.

Jeb gave the man a blank look, and Fellowes turned and walked away.

64

"I've seen your Indian in the woods," said Fellowes, his voice coming out of the twilight.

"Willawic?" Billy turned toward the voice, his wide eyes looking for the man through the fence rails. "You've seen Willawic?"

"If that's what he calls himself, yeah," came the disembodied reply. "He's been keeping an eye on you."

He'll save us!

Through the tears filling his eyes, Billy scanned the edge of the forest for the Indian. All he could see was the quickening dusk gathering in the trees.

"Mister Fellowes? Did he—did Willawic have a dog with him? A yellow dog?" The desperation in Mark's voice made Billy sad for him.

There was a soft chuckle from the shadows. "Yes, I b'lieve he did."

Mark made a noise, something between a squeak and a laugh.

"See, Billy," Joel said, "I told you he'd be back! Say, Mister Fellowes, how did you know he was with us?"

"Well, it seemed pretty obvious. I saw the Nikes and remembered what your young friend here asked me this afternoon."

"What are we gonna do?" asked Mark. "How are we gonna get out—we were hoping he'd be able to help us get home."

"Good idea, the Indians probably know a great deal more about this area than we ever will. I'm going to try to create a distraction so you boys can escape and get to him."

"Can you do that?"

"Shouldn't be a problem. They already consider me a trouble-maker."

"But if you do that," said Joel, "they'll catch you and you won't be able to come with us. I really think Willawic knows how to get us home."

Fellowes seemed to be thinking about that. "You know, it would be nice to fly just one more time. But . . . I don't see any other way." There was another pause. "Joel, here's your knife."

Billy watched the pocketknife sail through the air and land in the mud next to Joel's left foot. He looked in the direction from which the knife had come, but there wasn't anybody there. A moment later Fellowes appeared at the corral gate.

"Harris, I mean ta have a woman," he said, shoving the man aside, "an' ye'd best not stand in my way!"

"Ye ain't gettin' in, Fellowes."

The guard grabbed him by the shirt, but he pushed him back. Harris threw a punch and Fellowes ducked beneath it.

The other guards turned to watch the altercation, shouting their enthusiasm.

Joel spun around in the mud and retrieved his knife. He had the blade out in a split second.

"Mark, I'll hold the knife while you cut your ropes. But be careful—it's real sharp."

Billy glanced back and forth from the knife to the fight. Mark was going too slow!

Fellowes struck Harris in the gut and the man doubled over.

The rope came off Mark's wrists and he grabbed the knife and started to work on Joel's.

Harris rammed his lowered head into Fellowes, knocking them both to the ground.

The other guards had left their posts. Billy thought they

would jump in and stop Fellowes, but they formed a cheering ring around the men.

"Gimme the knife back," Joel said, "and hold still while I cut the ropes off your legs."

The men were rolling on the ground, struggling to slug one another, grappling for an advantage.

"Now Billy," Mark said.

The little boy was suddenly free of his bonds.

We're gonna get caught—we're gonna get caught!

Harris whipped out a wicked-looking blade and thrust it into Fellowes' shoulder. The man cried out and drew his own knife. The voices of the crowd got louder, vicious with blood-lust.

"Let's get outta here!" said Joel, heading for the back of the corral.

Billy tried to hurry, but the mud sucked on his every step. Catching up with the others, he saw Willawic waiting to help them over the fence. Ebbie danced back and forth behind the rails, whining with excitement. Mark and Joel climbed halfway up and reached down for him. Billy held out his arms to them—and someone grabbed him from behind. He was hoisted yelling and kicking into the air. He saw Mark and Joel's horrified faces receding into the twilight as his captor slung him over a bony shoulder and started to run in the opposite direction. Billy tried to wriggle free, but the man's grip was like a vice. "Let me go, dammit!" Billy screeched.

"Hesh," said a hissing, nasal voice. "Jus' hesh now, boy." Billy twisted his head around, and found himself staring into the bone-white face of the White Ghoul. His eyes glinted blood red in the failing light. He gave Billy a death's head grin, revealing long, yellow teeth.

Billy opened his mouth and screamed.

65

No one's chasing us, Mark thought. But, still, they ran. Willawic would not stop, didn't even look back to see if the boys were still with him. He just kept running, a rifle held in each hand. *Is he trying to lose us?*

"Hey!" Mark yelled, for the tenth time. "We've gotta go back for Billy! That freak's got Billy!" Willawic didn't even turn around. Mark had shouted in English and French, even thrown a little rock at the Indian, but he wouldn't answer. *I thought he cared about Billy,* Mark thought bitterly. *Stupid me.* He couldn't bear to think about what might be happening to the little guy.

The boys struggled to keep up as the Indian disappeared into the trees. Mark was worn out and was having a hard time in the growing dark.

"Ow—fuck!" he cried, stumbling and falling over a log.

"Wait up!" Joel called to Willawic.

Mark sat up, rubbing his shin. Ebbie rushed to his side, licking his face. He squeezed her tight, rubbing his face in her neck. He hadn't had the chance to properly greet her yet. He thought he'd never been happier to see anyone or anything in his life. "We'll find Billy," he whispered into her fur. "We have to."

Mark saw Willawic, winding back through the trees toward them. The Indian grabbed him by the arm and lifted him roughly to his feet. "Allons-nous."

"Jay mort!" Mark said.

"Nous y allons!"

The Indian turned and jogged off once more.

"C'mon," Joel said. He tugged at Mark's arm and set off after the Indian.

Finally, when knives of pain were piercing Mark's sides and he felt like his lungs would explode if he took another step, Willawic slowed down. He dropped down low, motioning for the boys to be quiet. Mark narrowed his eyes. There was a cookfire flickering in a distant clearing. Mark could hear voices, raised in anger. To his surprise, Willawic crept closer. He and Joel had no choice but to follow.

It was a large clearing. Lean-tos lined the perimeter. A few people milled around close to the fire. As they moved even closer, Mark realized with surprise that they were children. Two men stood nearby, engaged in a heated argument. One was a hatchet-faced volunteer named Samuel. The other was the White Ghoul. Mark's heart began to hammer.

"Get him!" Joel hissed to Willawic. "Shoot that ugly sumbitch and find Billy!" The Indian answered with a smack to the side of Joel's head. Joel muttered a curse, and then fell silent.

"I need the boy," Samuel was saying. "Nobody else'll want him. He's comin' with me, an' that's that." He reached into the shadows behind a tree and hauled out a long-limbed, skinny boy. As the firelight flickered on the kid's face, Mark recognized him. He'd seen him plenty of times before, in Wesley Pike's caves. He'd seen him in the filth of the corral. He was one of the first kids the White Ghoul had carried away. Mark thought his name was Jeremiah.

"No!" The White Ghoul took a step forward. His nasal voice was surprisingly strong. His eyes flashed hellish crimson in the firelight.

"What the hell ye mean 'no,' rev'rend?" Samuel snarled. "I'm takin' this little animal off yer hands. Ye oughter be grateful ta me."

"Reverend?" Joel whispered, saucer-eyed. Ebbie whined, and Mark shushed her.

"He ain't an animal. Jeremiah's a child. A human child. An' if ye cain't make him yer son, if ye cain't take him into yer heart and raise him up and love him like yer own, ye cain't have him." The White Ghoul cocked his head like a bird of prey, fixing Samuel with his demonic eyes.

Samuel took a step back, but he didn't release his hold on Jeremiah's wrist. "I'll raise him up right," he mumbled.

The White Ghoul drew himself up to his full height. "I know what ye want him for, Samuel Rickets. I heared ye talkin' wit' yer cronies. Ye plan ta use the lad as a slave in yer fields. I'm tellin' ye now, I won't let that happen."

Samuel spat on the ground and glared. "An' who's gonna stop me?"

In a fluid, reptilian motion, the White Ghoul pulled a hunting knife from a sheath strapped to his thigh. Quick as a snake, he had the point under Samuel's chin. "Jus' because I'm a man o' God don't mean I won't carve ye up like a spring lamb," he hissed. Samuel's eyes went wide, and he let go of Jeremiah's arm. The boy scrambled off into the nearest lean-to. The White Ghoul closed the distance between himself and the man, thrusting his face within inches of Ricket's.

"And I looked, and behold; a pale horse, and his name that sat upon him was Death." He grinned, revealing long, uneven teeth. "I'm about as pale as they come, son."

Samuel Rickets turned and ran.

Two surprising things happened then. Willawic stood and held up a hand to the White Ghoul, who sheathed his knife and hailed him back. Then Billy burst out from a lean-to and grabbed the White Ghoul's other hand. When he saw Willawic, he squealed with joy and ran to him. Willawic strode into the clearing, holding Billy in his arms.

"What the hell's going on?" Joel demanded, his voice shaky. Other children began to emerge from the lean-tos; children Mark had assumed were gone forever. Most appeared marginally clean, their hair brushed, their faces washed. *Probably for the first time in their lives,* he thought.

"Mark! Joel!" Billy hollered. "This is the rev'rend Micah Grouse! He's not a White Ghoul at all!" Hearing this, the reverend threw back his head and laughed.

Mark shifted from foot to foot. "Why did you grab Billy?"

"I saw you boys makin' yer escape, an' I thought there was no way the little 'un could survive on the run with ye." He smiled. "But from what he's tol' me, he's survived a lot worse."

Willawic set Billy on his feet. The little boy scampered back to the pale man, who patted him on the head. "The rev'rend's been taking kids out of the corral an' adoptin' 'em out to the volunteers," he said happily. "He wasn't eatin' 'em or anything! But I told him I don't need to be adopted, I've already got a mama."

"Is that true?" The reverend Micah fixed his unnerving gaze on Mark.

"Yes, sir. We're all on our way back home. Willawic here's gonna help us."

The reverend nodded. "He's a good man, that one. He shot a deer an' gave it ta me ta feed these here childerns."

"Why, um . . . why did you just come in and grab kids, and take 'em away like that? We all thought you were. . . ." Joel's cheeks went red, and he looked down.

"I'm sorry fer scarin' ye. I jes' wanted ta get as many childerns out as fast as I could. I had ta get 'em away from that place. The devil holds sway in that camp, boy. We may have driven Wesley Pike out, but 'is evil covers that land like poison."

The other children surrounded Reverend Micah now. He patted the head of a feral-eyed little girl, who leaned against him.

"I'm only adoptin' these younguns out ta the decent volunteers, y'see. I won't let 'em go ta jes' anybody. I'm takin' five or six of the unfortunate babes home myself." He grinned like a jack-o'-lantern. "I jes' hope the wife don't kill me."

"The wife?" Joel mouthed to Mark. Mark kicked him on the shoe.

There was a noise in the distant woods, and Willawic looked around warily.

"I reckon ye'd best be on yer way," the reverend said. "Ye wouldn't want some of the bedeviled to catch up with ye."

Mark and Joel agreed. Reverend Micah gave them some dried meat and berries in a leather wallet. Billy ran to him and gave him a fierce hug. "You're awful nice for such a scary-lookin' guy," he said.

The reverend looked down at him and nodded gravely. "I thankee, little one," he said. "Bein' scary has its advantages in such a savage world."

As they followed Willawic through the trees toward the river, Mark looked over his shoulder. He could see the white oval of Reverend Micah's face in the moonlight as he waved good-bye.

It was full dark. The river was black as oil. The Indian dragged a dugout from the underbrush and pushed it out into the water, steadying it while Joel and Billy climbed in.

Mark froze, suddenly filled with uncertainty. He wished they could have spent the night with Reverend Micah, in the warm circle of light around the cookfire. He stared across the water, the sliver moon a thin scribble on the river's surface. Willawic and Joel began paddling into the wriggling light. Suddenly the river seemed miles wide and menacing. Ebbie looked from Mark to Willawic and back again, whining uncertainly.

Joel turned around. "C'mon."

Something dark wiggled in the glassy smooth shallows near the dugout and leapt with a splash.

Mark sucked in his breath. "Look out!"

The words were out before he had thought about it. He didn't like the way they were thrown back at him, hard echoes bouncing off the trees on the opposite bank.

Joel was still looking at him with a "What's up with you?" look.

"Guess it was just a fish jumping." Mark shrugged, smiled apologetically.

"Come *on*. You don't wanna be left behind." Willawic let out a low whistle, and Ebbie barked once and jumped into the water. She started swimming for the canoe. Joel turned back around, and Mark was suddenly alone with the wilderness and all its dangers at his back, the dugout moving away from him. Abandoning one fear for another, Mark splashed in after the dugout.

The water shocked him—it was cooler than he expected. His clothes filled up quickly and dragged on him as he swam out into deeper, darker waters. The current tugged at him with a cold, lingering grasp that said, "Let go, and I'll take you away."

An owl called hollowly from the trees ahead, disturbing the stillness and startling him out of his funk. Mark fought his way toward the canoe. Willawic and Joel were already lifting a dripping Ebbie into the boat. She looked at Mark and woofed softly.

"Climb in," Joel said, reaching for him.

Mark's friends and a chill breeze awaited him in the canoe. His gooseflesh stood out in the moonlight.

"Freezing your balls off?" Joel asked with a grin.

Mark shot him an angry look. Ebbie leaned against Mark, her wet, smelly fur against his wet, smelly clothes.

"Too bad we can't have a fire tonight, hunh?"

"You're kidding," Mark said, hugging himself.

"Nope, sorry. Someone might see us. But you *really* needed a bath, lemme tell you."

Reaching the far shore, they dragged the dugout onto the rocks. Willawic led them to a tiny clearing about fifty feet from the water's edge. Once he was away from the river and within the shelter of the trees, Mark began to warm up.

They shared some of the food the reverend had given them. As they munched, the boys took to guessing what Mrs. White Ghoul might look like.

"I'll bet she's real pretty," Billy said. " 'Cause he's so nice."

Joel grinned. "She's probably another albino. Don'tcha think, Mark?"

"Yep. I'll bet she's white as milk, with eyes like rubies. And I'll bet the Rev thinks she's the prettiest thing in the world."

"I bet they've got a bunch of little albino kids!" Joel said. "And they're so pale they're clear!"

"Yeah! You can see their guts and everything!"

Billy's eyes went wide. "You really think so?"

Mark and Joel looked at each other, and burst out laughing.

After their meager dinner, the boys huddled together, watching the Indian clear the ground to make a smooth place to sleep.

"Hey," Joel said, "let's tell ghost stories!"

"No way!" Mark said, hugging his clammy dog. "No fucking way."

66

Joel awoke to a heavy fog. Willawic and Billy were already up. Seeing that he was awake, the Indian offered Joel a handful of seeds, roots and berries.

Ebbie was scratching at a rotten log, gobbling up bugs. Joel made a face.

He shoved Mark with a foot. "Wake up, dumbass!"

His friend moaned, turned over and opened his eyes, yawning. "This fog is really spooky."

"Yeah," Joel said around a purple mouthful of huckleberries, "I like it a lot."

"Well it's gonna make it hard to find our way." Mark accepted the food Billy offered him and began to eat.

"No it won't," the little boy said. "Willawic's leading the way, and besides, if someone was following us, they couldn't see us in this fog."

"You think they're still back there?"

"I don't think they ever were," Joel said.

That seemed to cheer Mark up a little.

Joel stood up and stretched. "Hey, guys, we're starting for home today!"

"You don't know that," Mark said. "I don't think Willawic's understood a damn word I've said. For all we know, he's taking us back to his home where they're gonna turn us into a bunch of fucking Indian slaves."

"He wouldn't do that!" Billy said.

"Yeah, retard. Settle down—don't be such a stick in the mud."

Mark grumbled, turned away, and unbuttoned his pants. "I gotta pee."

The sun was breaking through the fog as Willawic lifted Billy to his shoulders and set out into the trees. Joel hurried after them shouting, "Wait up! He's still taking a piss!"

Mark was buttoning his breeches as he ran to catch up.

The fog burned off quickly and the day was bright and crisp. The world was full of vibrant color and, as the Indian set an easy pace, Joel found himself beginning to loosen up and enjoy the morning. Was it his imagination or did Willawic know the lay of the land? His stride was confident, as if he knew exactly where he was going. He must truly know what the boys were after.

They were going *home,* and the thought of it lightened Joel's step. He just wished he could talk about it with the Indian to confirm what he already knew in his gut.

The forest was so beautiful, so different from the way it was at home. Joel wondered if he would miss it. Probably not. At least he got to see the virgin forest. No one from his time, to his knowledge, could claim that—except Fellowes. And Myrtrice. Not that a drunken old whore like that gave a shit.

Joel couldn't remember ever feeling so truly alive before. Everything was just as it was supposed to be. He had his friends, he had survived a great adventure, and had become a part of history. It was like he had climbed inside one of his books—just what he'd always wished he could do. He would have memories to last a lifetime.

Billy turned around and, with a mischievous grin, stuck his tongue out.

"The little shit," Mark said. "I'm walking around with goddam rocks in my motherfucking shoes, wearing clothes that never dried out last night while *he* gets a free ride!"

"Hey, lighten up!" Joel said. "This is great! When was the last time you got to take a hike in the untamed wilderness of the 1800s with a real, live Indian as your guide and protector? Listen to the birds! They're all saying to each other, 'Wanna fuck?' in a thousand different languages."

Mark was trying to hide his snicker, but Joel heard him.

"Hey, I'm feeling good. What's wrong with that?"

"Nothing."

"Well Willawic—"

"Shit." Mark spit into the underbrush. "Willawic, Willawic, Willawic—that's all I hear from Billy, and now I'm hearing it from you too. He's just a dirty ol' Indian."

"What're you talking about, Mark? You could learn a lot from that guy. He knows how to live off the land, hunt and trap. I bet he knows how to make all kinds of stone tools—you know, arrowheads and shit. And fight! Shit I bet he could beat up anyone in our time. Lookit the way he moves through the forest. He knows what he's doing, he's part of the land."

Willawic turned around without stopping, a grin on his face.

Does he know we're talking about him?

"And he took care of your dirty ol' dog, didn't he? Do you really think she woulda survived the battle at the cave, Mark?"

"Yeah, I guess he is kinda cool." There was a smile on Mark's face.

"No shit. Hey—we should take him home with us! He could teach us all kinds of stuff!"

"Yeah, sure—I bet he'd freak seeing a car!"

The boys laughed and Joel was glad to see that Mark seemed to be coming out of his foul mood.

By early afternoon, Mark was really beginning to resent the fact that Billy got a free ride while he and Joel had to hoof it. Of course, he couldn't imagine Willawic giving *him* a piggyback through the forest.

His cheeks burned at the idea. Was he such a wiener or was it just petty jealousy? Either way, it was damned embarrassing. Mark cast a sidelong glance at Joel.

"What's wrong, Mark? You're all red."

"Uh, nothing—mind your own business."

"Jeez, Mark! Who peed in your Wheaties?"

"There aren't any Wheaties here." He turned away and trudged on, grinding the brittle sticks and leaves beneath his feet. Ebbie bumped his thigh with her nose a time or two, and Mark patted her head, his expression softening a little.

Willawic took Billy off his shoulders and set him roughly on the ground. He turned and, without a word, handed Joel one of the rifles. Ebbie tucked her tail between her legs and whined.

"What's up?" Mark asked.

Willawic's head whipped around and he glared at the boy.

"Why did he give *Joel* a gun?"

"Don'tcha know nothing, Mark? Jeez, just shut up!" Billy whispered.

"But what's going on!"

Willawic slapped a hand over Mark's mouth. The boy smelled pine sap on his palm.

What—are he and Joel gonna shoot me—in front of Billy? As soon as the thought popped into his mind, Mark knew it was ridiculous.

"Silence!" the Indian hissed, his French marred by his strange accent.

But why. . . .

The Indian released him and slipped between a pair of thorny honey locusts and into the shadows beyond.

"What am I supposed to do?" Joel whispered.

Mark shrugged his shoulders dramatically.

"Follow him!" Billy said, almost without a sound. "Dumb-ass."

Joel made as if to smack him and then started after Willawic. Mark turned to follow but Billy held him back.

"They might need help," Mark said.

"Willawic? Are you kidding? He's an Indian. He knows how to hunt."

"Oh, is *that* what he's doing? God, I thought maybe it was some of the militia after us."

"Gee—I never thought of that."

"You mean, maybe it *is?*"

Mark heard a growl, low and vicious. He spun around. Billy gasped and grabbed him.

A cougar emerged from the shelter of the trees, ears laid flat against its skull, lips skinned back from white, gleaming fangs. Mark saw a bloody gash on the mountain lion's flank.

"Willawic!" Billy cried.

Slowly and deliberately, the cat crept forward, its eyes locked on Mark's.

Mark was frozen where he stood. He felt a warmth spreading out from his crotch.

Snarling, the cat bunched its legs beneath it for a leap.

The animal jerked as a double blast of sound jolted Mark from his paralysis. Billy screamed and Mark watched the big cat drop, as if in slow motion.

Willawic and Joel came running back, their rifles smoking.

"Gee, Mark," Joel said, "did you wet your pants?"

"N-no—when Billy grabbed me, I guess he must've slob-bered all over my pants, or something."

"Hey, it's no big deal, Mark, I'da been scared too."

Willawic wasted no time in lifting the mountain lion to his shoulders and carrying it off into the trees. Curious, the boys ran after him.

67

"Hey, Mark, you want another kitty cat cutlet? I'm stuffed."

"Not me. That first one tasted like gamey shoe leather. No wonder nobody eats cats."

"Dogs'll eat 'em," Billy said, making a "gimme" gesture to Willawic. "I'll take it if Mark doesn't want it. Owoo!"

Willawic took the stick on which the gray catsteak had been cooked and poked it into the ground beside Billy. The boy blew on the meat, trying to make it cool enough to eat. Ebbie lay at the edge of the firelight, contentedly chewing on a big piece of mountain lion. The sight made Mark grin. *If that mean ol' gray tomcat down the street from me could see this, he'd die of a heart attack!* The thought of home gave him a sudden, unexpected pang.

"Allay vu mon mayzon?" Mark asked Willawic.

The Indian laughed. "Certainement."

"Sairtaymont?" Mark asked, confused.

"Oui. Ça me plaît à visiter votre maison."

"What's he saying, Mark?" Joel asked.

"He said it'll be his pleasure to take us home tomorrow!"

"But what does visitay votruh mean?"

"Maybe it means we should have a party when we get there."

"Ask him about the Nikes again."

Mark thought for a minute and then pointed at Willawic's Nikes. "U ay luh persone key donnay votruh shay-vo."

"What did you ask?"

"I asked him, *where is the person who gave you the shoes.*"

Willawic thought, his face a mask of confusion. "Cheveaux?" He paused a moment and said, "Cheveaux?" Then he looked at his shoes and his face brightened. "Ah . . . chaussures!"

"Wee!" Mark pointed at Willawic's feet, flushed at the thought that he was finally being understood.

"Voulez vous aller le voir?"

"Wee!" Mark said, his heart performing a double flip. "May wee!"

"What is he saying, what is he saying?" Joel asked.

"He asked if I wanted to be taken to the man who gave him the shoes. I finally did it, Joel! I came up with the right question to ask him—he knows *exactly* what I'm talking about!"

68

The red clay of the trail was imprinted with hundreds of hoofprints, but it was hard and dry now. Joel estimated it had been a couple of weeks since anyone had passed this way. It was a clear and easy route and Willawic and the boys were making good time.

Yer yella, boy, a coward! Virgil's voice mocked in his head.

For a moment, Joel froze in his tracks, his heart skipping a beat. Then he began to recognize bits and pieces of the trail and a deep shame overcame him. Suddenly, he was on the verge of turning around, even if it meant going back alone.

He looked up to see Mark staring at him. "C'mon, Joel—whadya stop for?"

Willawic stopped, turned, and looked up from the new stick hat he was weaving as he walked. Billy sat down on the trail, took off his shoes and banged the rocks out of them.

"Nothin'—I was just thinking there might be a better trail on the other side of that hill."

"Why would you think that? What's wrong with this one?"

"I dunno. I . . . just thought maybe we could find a way that doesn't wind around so much."

Willawic turned back and walked on, Billy at his side.

"Jeez, Joel, you can really be a goober sometimes, you know that?"

It's just up ahead around the curve in the trail. But if I don't follow, they're gonna start asking questions.

As he started walking again, he kicked at the cracked clay. His foot struck a small stone and it flew into the air, hitting Mark on the thigh.

"What was that for?" Mark asked, wheeling around.

"Sorry."

I bet the ground's still all roughed up and there might be blood in places. There'll probably be bullet holes in the trees and maybe some blood-stained clothes and stuff.

Billy started singing, "There was an old lady who followed a fly—"

"Billy, you want someone to hear us?" Mark said.

"I don't care! And Willawic doesn't either."

Still hanging back, Joel looked half-hopefully at the trees. *I could just run. They'd have to follow me—they wouldn't leave me all alone.*

"There was an old cat who swallowed a, uh, a horse. I don't know why, it's stupid of course."

Aw, hell, what's a little bloody ground?

The trail climbed a slight rise as it curved and Joel was thankful the maples on either side obscured what lay beyond.

Concentrate on Mark—talk about what we'll do when we get home.

"There was an old house who swallowed, uh—dammit! What should it be, Mark? Swallowed a what?"

"Swallowed my dick!"

"That's gross! There was an old house that swallowed Mark's dick, I don't know why, but *that's* real real sick."

Mark laughed.

"Hey, Mark," Joel said, a little too loud and happy, "when we get home, whaddaya say we go in on a subscription to *Big Hooters* magazine?"

"Yeah—hey, if we put up a mailbox on your tree house, do you think they'd deliver it there so your dad wouldn't know?"

"No way. We'll get a post office box."

"That's gonna be *so* cool. It'll sure beat having to rip 'em off from Marvin's. What else will we do?"

"I don't know. Why don't you think something up?"

"Let's get some army men and play war in The New Cut! We can carve all kinds of ledges and caves and castles and shit in that muddy bank and have this big ol' motherfuckin' assault!"

They were rounding the curve in the trail and Mark's eyes lit up with excitement as he talked. Joel kept his eyes locked on Mark's face, grinning in spite of himself.

"Wait a minute, Joel. Maybe that's not such a good idea, after all. We could get lost again."

"Yeah, I see what you mean."

"You know what else we could do—Oh man! What the fuck happened *here?*"

Without thinking, Joel turned to look. His stomach went cold, doused in ice water. "Jesus," he whispered, unaware that the word had escaped his lips. "Jesus *Christ!*"

Willawic was frozen in his tracks, staring, Billy beside him with his mouth hanging open. Ebbie hid behind Mark's legs, whining.

Two buzzards dropped atop a mutilated corpse and began to tear at the remaining flesh. The wind shifted, bringing Joel his first whiff of the battlefield's virulent stench of decay. A storm of flies filled the clearing, blurring the scene into unreality.

There was blood on the ground, but it had dried into dark stains that were not particularly disturbing. But the corpses. . . . They were gutted, their throats torn out, most of the flesh ripped from their limbs. Their clothing, tatters of stained cloth, were tangled with shreds of dried tissue. Buzzards floated like black ash, circling above the carnage.

The buzzing of the flies got louder and louder, drilling into Joel's head. He stumbled forward into the midst of the corpses.

A couple of buzzards flew heavily away. Others glared, but refused to leave their gruesome meals.

"Where are you going?" Mark asked, grabbing Joel by the arm and swinging him around. In the distance, Joel could see Willawic leading Billy away. Ebbie followed behind them. Even this far out, he could see that her body language was hunched and fearful.

"What's going on?" Mark demanded. "Do you know what happened here?"

Joel shoved him and Mark fell to the ground, staring wide-eyed. Joel walked out into the middle of the battlefield. He looked wildly at the corpses surrounding him on all sides.

Mark was shouting something at him, but Joel didn't hear. He was distantly aware that his mouth was hanging open, but he couldn't think to close it. There was a tangle in his head, a riotous confusion which left him unable to do anything but stare. A tight knot of pain lodged in his throat. He tried to cry out, to scream, but it just hurt too much.

"Mark, I—" Joel started, but couldn't go on.

Feeling his knees weaken, he tried not to collapse, tried not to give in, but the riot in his head erupted. The explosion forced a single, agonized howl and hurled him to the ground. And then he was crying in great uncontrollable sobs that wracked his body.

"Joel, what's wrong?" Mark knelt beside him and laid a hand on Joel's shoulder.

"It's all my fault."

"What are you talking about, Joel? Nothing's your fault."

"This is what happened on that *big adventure* Wesley took me on." The sarcasm scalded Joel's throat like vitriol.

Mark seemed to stumble on his words. Then he gripped Joel firmly by the shoulders and turned him around.

"Listen up, Joel—we're just little boys."

He looked up, ready to punch Mark's lights out, until he saw his eyes.

"Little boys?"

Mark laughed. "Yep, just like Billy."

Joel wiped his eyes and nose, turned his head and spit. "Well if we get back, don't tell anyone at school about this or I'll have to break your arm again."

"All right," Mark said. He helped Joel to his feet and led him out of the battlefield.

69

Mark had fallen behind again. He heard the others talking excitedly around the bend and hurried to catch up. Just beyond the turn in the trail, he found his friends clustered around Thomas Fellowes.

"Luck of the damned," Fellowes was saying, obviously in response to something Joel had asked. "There's no other way I could've found you."

Willawic had lowered his rifle and was watching the conversation with interest. Ebbie danced around Fellowes, sniffing him. The man reached down and scratched between her ears.

"But how'd you get away?" Mark asked.

"I killed Harris, and then I killed Jeb. After that, I just walked away and the volunteers let me. I figured it would only be a matter of time before someone else got up the nerve to stand up to me."

"Is that *it?*" Mark asked.

"Well, that's all I'm gonna tell you."

"I guess that'll have to do, then," Joel said.

"God," said Fellowes, "I'd give my left arm to have a cold brewski and a cheap, greasy, hamburger."

"Yeah," Billy said, "I wanna go to Burger King!"

"Not Burger King! There's this greasy ol' place down on the Old Shillelagh Road called Cutie's—now *there's* a place you can get a serious burger." Fellowes patted the little boy on the head, making him smile.

"So how's that hole in your shoulder?" Joel asked.

"Bad! My bones stopped Jeb's knife, and the wound's not too deep, but the blade nicked my clavicle and that hurts like hell. I don't wanna talk about that either, and I'll thank you not to remind me."

"Sorry."

Fellowes waved it away. "So you think your Indian knows where he's going?"

"He knows exactly where he's going," Mark said. "I've talked to him."

"Willawic's gonna take us all home!" said Billy.

"Well then, we'd best be gettin' on about it." The man gestured down the trail. "This the right direction?"

Willawic nodded and led the way.

"What makes you so sure about him?"

"He talks French," said Mark, "and so do I."

"Yeah, he and Willawic finally figured out what each other was saying."

"Are you sure he knows what you're saying, or do you just hope he does? I've dealt with these Indians a lot more'n you have, and I know they can seem mighty agreeable when they want to." He ran a hand over the red lunar landscape that covered the top of his head.

Mark looked at Joel. He didn't like where this was leading. All he knew was that the Indian was going to take him to the one he got the shoes from, and that had to be good enough. But how could he explain that to Fellowes?

"Trust me, Mister Fellowes. Me and Willawic's got it all worked out."

The burning orange light of the sunset peered through the tops of the thickly crowded trees to Mark's right. To his left, the sky was purpling and a half moon had risen. All around, darkness gathered in the nearly impassable forest and the trail thinned, nearly disappearing in the shadows ahead.

Willawic was passing into those shadows and the others followed. Mark took a deep breath and released it slowly. *Relax,* he told himself. *There's nothing in the woods out to get you. Willawic knows what he's doing—probably just hunting for a place to camp for the night.* He looked to Ebbie for reassurance. She seemed content and relaxed. Surely no mountain lion, no bear, no pack of scalp-hunting Indians were nearby.

As they entered the trees, Mark saw fireflies rising from the forest floor, their pulsing lights dispelling some of the gloom. He was glad to see these friends from home, and he only regretted he didn't have a jar in which to catch them.

First time I've seen you guys this year.

He reached up to carefully catch one of the fluttering insects. Making a cave with both hands, he peered in at the firefly. It flashed, filling his hands with its greenish glow. Laughing, he let it go and found that the trees had become trees again and were no longer menacing. Joel and Billy laughed uproariously as Ebbie snapped up fireflies, smacking her black lips as she munched them down.

Willawic stopped in a small clearing and set about starting a fire. He sent Billy to collect firewood and Mark and Joel joined in. Fellowes sat heavily, groaning to himself and gingerly probing his wounded shoulder, apparently unable to forget the pain after all. Ebbie sat next to him, sending out waves of dog empathy. *She really is a good girl,* thought Mark. *Even if she eats bugs.*

He set down an armful of wood near Willawic. The Indian was hunched over dried grass and twigs, setting flint to steel. He blew as the first sparks caught, nursing them into flame. Sparks burst skyward, like short-lived orange cousins to the greenish fireflies.

The smell of smoke filled the ring of trees as Willawic carefully placed the burning tinder under a small pile of twigs. Systemically he fed his fire heavier and heavier wood until a welcoming blaze filled the clearing.

Mark smiled and sat, leaning forward to absorb all the warmth he could. Billy and Joel sat next to him and the boys watched the crackling flames.

"Lost my damn pipe," Fellowes said, "and I could sure use a smoke, too."

"Smoking's yucky!" Billy said, "I wish we had some marshmallows."

Willawic took the last two mountain-lion steaks out of his shirt. He had wrapped them in cat skin, forming a wallet to keep them fresh. Setting the steaks to cook on sticks over the fire, the Indian sat back on his haunches and watched the others.

"So tell us about how you got scalped," Joel said.

"God, Joel, that's not very nice," said Mark. "Maybe it's a bad memory or something. You don't know."

"Well, it ain't a good memory. I don't mind telling you about it, though. Christ knows if I was a boy, I'd wanna hear it. There's not all that much to tell, really."

Fellowes shifted, trying to get comfortable.

"I guess I oughta start back at the beginning. I got here about 1807, which makes it, what, 1811 now—have I really been here for four years?"

"I thought it was 1811 or 12," Joel said, obviously pleased with himself.

"So you said you looked up from digging out that stump," Mark said, "and just found yourself here?"

"Yeah, but I didn't know where *here* was. At first I thought I must've bumped my head and was seeing things, 'cause I didn't recognize anything around me.

"I started wandering around, heading back toward where my

house *should* have been. When I couldn't find it, I figured I'd just gotten lost somehow."

"My house disappeared too," Billy said, "and I went running all over the place looking for it."

"Well, it didn't take me long to figure out that I wasn't just lost—I thought maybe I'd wound up on another planet or something, you know, like in science fiction."

"How long did it take you to figure it out?" Joel asked.

"A while," Fellowes answered, chuckling, "but I guess it wasn't until that first time I got attacked by Indians that I really knew."

"Damn!" Joel said. "Is that when you got scalped?"

"Yeah," said Mark, "did they cut you to the bone?"

The man laughed, his weather-beaten face crinkling around his smiling eyes. Ebbie rested her chin on his knee, and he absently stroked her golden head.

"Well, Willawic wouldn't do anything like that," Billy said, quietly.

"No, I didn't get scalped that first time. You see, I'd found the remains of a deer carcass an' had started a fire with my butane lighter to cook some of the meat. I guess the fire, or the smoke, attracted 'em, 'cause the next thing I knew, I was up to my neck in whooping and hollering redskins."

He laughed and the boys joined in. Mark leaned toward him, caught up in the man's tale. Billy and Joel were also staring up at the reflected firelight gleaming in Fellowes' eyes.

The man pulled up his shirt sleeve, revealing an ugly, round scar on his bicep. "When they attacked, I took an arrow straight through my arm."

"Ew," Billy said, wincing, his face screwed up in a grimace, "did it hurt?"

The others laughed at the little boy.

"It hurt like hell! Luckily, it went straight on through, the arrow didn't get stuck—that would've left me defenseless. Here I was wrestling with these two Indians when I've never wrestled with anyone in my life—Christ, I was only a frigging insurance salesman.

"But I had the lighter still in my hand, adjusted to give me a big flame so I could start my fire. So I lit it an' the next red face that popped up in front of me got a snout full of burning butane. He screamed and ran. I lit up the other guy's hair and he ran off too. Goddam, but that would have been funny—seeing this Indian hauling ass through the trees, streaming flames behind him—if it weren't for the frigging hole in my arm and all the wounds I got from their blunt tomahawks. Goddam, that hurt."

"Thomas Fellowes," Joel said dramatically, "insurance salesman and Injun Igniter Extraordinaire!"

The four broke up laughing, the sound filling the small clearing. Willawic looked up at them and smiled, obviously enjoying their amusement. Then he went back to tending the steaks.

"I guess I wandered for about a week, living off the land—my years as a Boy Scout had never been handier—before I came up with a plan. I headed west an' ran into the Mississippi. I saw a log floating by and I jumped in, swam out to it and climbed on. I knew that if there was anybody besides the Indians here I would find them in New Orleans—that is, if I made it there at all, I was getting damned hungry."

"Wow! What was New Orleans like?" Joel asked.

"I never made it, I got to Natchez first—or Natchez-Under-the-Hill—they wouldn't let me up top. I guess I looked pretty bad.

"That town scared the shit out of me. It was nothing like I expected. From reading books, even from museums I'd gotten the idea that this era should've been romantic somehow—like if it was a movie, it would star Errol Flynn, all swash and adventure. But it wasn't. It was ugly. Ugly and brutal."

They all fell silent for a moment. The only sound was the crackling of the fire and the hissing of mountain-lion fat dripping into the hot, orange coals. Willawic took the steaks out of the fire. He cut and served them, smiling weakly, as if apologizing, Mark thought, for the meager portions. Ebbie sniffed the air hopefully. Billy slipped her some dried fish.

"I decided to head back to Tennessee, to Nashville, along the Natchez Trace. I hooked up with a farmer returning to Tennessee after selling his goods down in New Orleans—he and his sons were looking to add as many honest folk to their party as they could get, the Trace being a dangerous road to travel."

"Cool beans!" Joel said. "I've read all about the Trace."

"It ain't nothin' like what you've read, boy, let me tell you. I've done my share of reading on it, too, but there was nothing cool about it."

He shook his head, smiling, his gaze far away.

"There was a lot of walking—I ain't never been so tired in all my life—and it was tense, stressful work too. We expected attack around every corner—attack which never came, thank God. All the way to Nashville, I was told some scary shit about all manner of men. Fear was a constant companion. Each and every one of those honest men was scared to death of the outlaws, like pitiful little animals, hiding from the predators that haunted the Trace.

"People in our time complain about crime in America being the worst it's ever been." He paused and spat into the fire. "But they don't know. They have no idea. People back home—they're safe as babies in cribs compared to people here. And that trip's what done it for me. That trip showed me lives ruled by fear, and I asked myself, 'Should anyone have to live like that?'

"I decided I was gonna do what I could to change the quality of life in these parts, fight for truth and justice and all that other idealistic bullshit. Well, hell, years later, I find myself leading a group of farmers and getting myself outsmarted by none other than Wesley Pike."

He stopped and the wind seemed to go out of him.

"So how'd you get scalped?" Joel asked.

Fellowes laughed. "Aw, you don't wanna hear about that, do you?"

"Yeah!" the boys said, in unison.

"Well, about two years ago I'd gotten myself appointed constable for this tiny-ass borough called Upperbutterson, bordering on Chickasaw territory. Seeing as we were infringing on their hunting grounds, killing and driving off their game, the redskins were not disposed to being friendly toward us.

"Two springs back, the Indians apparently decided they'd had enough and started raiding our borough and another one just down the Tennessee River. As constable, it was my duty to defend the settlement, so I rounded up all the able-bodied men and instituted patrols to watch for Indians in the woods by day and night.

"I don't remember a lot, 'cause it was a bad head injury, but it happened while I was on patrol. One night I fell asleep when I was 'sposed to be on guard. The next thing I knew, an Indian's got me 'round the neck and he's cutting this big ol' strip outta my head. I'm tellin' ya boys—I've never felt pain like that before or since in my life. It felt like he was rippin' my damn brain out. When I started to fight him, he whacked me upside the head with his tomahawk, and the lights went out."

"How'd you get it fixed?" asked Billy.

"Well, I'd heard from James Robertson up in Nashville about a way to cure scalping—he had to perform the operation on his son, and it worked. You see, the skull is two layers of bone with some tissue in between. If you drill holes here and there just through the top layer of the exposed skull, over time the tissue will grow out of the holes and form kind of a scalp. It ain't pretty, but it's better than nothing."

There was an uncomfortable silence. Billy had both hands wrapped around his head and a slightly sick look on his face.

"But what I wanna know," Fellowes said, leaning back, "is what you boys are gonna do first when you get home."

"I dunno," Joel said, "take a bath, probably."

"Yeah, you *need* one!" Mark said. He fanned his nose, laughing. Joel shoved him and he toppled over.

"I'm gonna hug my mama," Billy said, "and then I'm gonna shoot Teddy with one of Willawic's rifles. You know I know how to load and use one, don't you?"

They all laughed but Willawic, who turned to them and smiled. Mark and Joel poked at Billy until he tumbled over sideways, giggling.

"Who's Teddy?" Fellowes asked. "And why would you wanna shoot him?"

" 'Cause he's fucking my mama and he's a jerk."

Mark and Joel grabbed each other and rolled in the leaves, laughing.

"Goddam," Mark said between gales of laughter, "goddam B-Billy." He fell all over Joel again, holding his sides. "When did *you* get guts?"

"I've always had 'em. It's just with everybody around me being so mean, I had to get mean too."

Joel almost fell in the fire he was laughing so hard. Fellowes, chuckling, reached out with his good arm and pulled the boy back. Mark saw tears streaming down Joel's face.

"I can't—I can't—" He took great whooping gasps of air. "I can't—oh shit, I can't stop laughing!"

This broke everyone up again.

"Are you laughing at me?" Billy scowled.

Joel looked like he was going to be sick. "No, Billy, it's just the look on Teddy's face when he sees you holding that flintlock on him."

"*If* I can hold it up." Billy giggled.

"Come on now," Mark said, after they had calmed down, "let's get serious. When I get home, everything's gonna be different. I ain't gonna smoke or steal stuff anymore, and I'm not gonna wait around for anybody else—I'm making my *own* mind up from now on! If nobody likes it, well, that's fine. I'm gonna decide what's best for me."

Joel looked at him appraisingly. "I bet you will, Mark."

"I think," Fellowes said, his eyes focused faraway, "I'll take my Cessna up and fly no place in particular—just fly 'til I run outta gas and land at the nearest airport. That is, if my wife hasn't sold it. Hey, I'll tell you what, boys. When we get home, I'll take us all out flying. Maybe we'll all fly up to Nashville for the State Fair. Must be coming up on September pretty soon."

"That'd be *great,*" Joel said.

"Yeah, we'll have a blast."

"Do you miss your wife?" Billy's voice was high and clear in the night air.

Fellowes hesitated, rubbed his chin. "When I first got here, all I thought about was survivin'. Not much else crossed my mind. And besides, me and the wife were havin' trouble right before I left. We were even thinkin' about splittin' up. But after I'd been here a few months, I started missin' her. I mean, so bad it hurt. All I could think about was the way she felt, the way she smelled, how fine it was when we were young and first together." He threw a twig into the fire, then another.

"Then, just like everything else back home, she didn't seem quite real anymore. The hurt went away, and the want. To tell you the truth, I don't think about her that often anymore. But you know what? I'd like to see her. Just to find out . . . to find out if there's anything left between us."

The older boys stared into the fire, looking uncomfortable. Fellowes let out a harsh laugh. "Of course, she'll probably take one look at me and run like hell. I look like somethin' from a goddam zombie movie."

Mark and Joel laughed.

"No she won't," said Billy. "Not if she really loves you. If she loves you, it wouldn't matter if the Indians cut off your whole face."

Fellowes smiled, and gave the little boy a quick, hard squeeze around the shoulders.

Mark lay back in the weeds. Ebbie got up from Fellowes' side, stretched, and lay down next to Mark. As he listened to the others talk about home, their voices blending with that of the night, he drifted into an untroubled sleep.

70

Rolling over to remove the rock that had poked him in the ribs and disturbed his rest, Joel saw Billy, Willawic, and Ebbie disappearing into a predawn fog. He wasn't awake enough to call out to them, and was on his way back to sleep almost immediately. It was probably just a dream anyway.

Sometime later, he was awakened by the sun on his face.

Across the clearing, Mark was yawning and stretching. "Where's Billy and Willawic?"

"I saw 'em walking away into the fog—but I thought it was a dream." Joel rubbed the sleep from his eyes and looked around the sun-dappled clearing.

"Maybe it wasn't," Fellowes said. He was sitting by the remains of last night's fire, stitching a torn seam in his breeches. "I've been awake for half an hour and I haven't seen 'em. Both rifles are gone too. And the dog."

"They must be off hunting." Joel got to his feet and started for the trees.

"Now don't wander off, boy."

"I won't. I just gotta pee."

Joel followed a thin trail into the trees, stepped behind a bush, and relieved his bladder. When he'd finished and was about to head back toward the others, he spotted footprints leading deeper into the forest. "I found their tracks," he called out to Mark and Fellowes. "I'm gonna follow the trail a little ways and try to catch up with them."

As he progressed, the trail narrowed and dead trees leaned into the path. Thorny vines reached for him, nicked his arms, and dug into his shirt. Joel slowed, dodging the tendrils. Shielding his face, he turned around and walked backward, plucking out the spikes as he moved, only to have more embed themselves in his clothing with every step. Just as he decided to go back, a mass of the vines tumbled out of the trees and landed in the path before him. Glancing over his shoulder, he saw, in his peripheral vision, an opening behind him. Steeling himself, he yanked free of the thorns and dove for it.

The pain lasted only a moment, and then he was falling. Fleshless, skeletal hands—the limbs of dead trees—caught him up in their woody grip, rolled him into a ball, and hurled him down slope.

"Mark! Fellowes!"

Landing on his back in a crackling web of dead vines and limbs, Joel at last came to a stop, torn and breathless, the smothering twigs clutching him fast in their greedy embrace.

For a moment he didn't move, afraid any motion would send him crashing deeper. He sneezed wood chips and dust. This sent him into a coughing fit and he spasmed so violently the vines threatened to drop him to a ground he could not see.

He groaned, gingerly touching himself to see if he was still whole. His probing fingers found a gouge on his left forearm and, with the pain, he sharply sucked in his breath.

He looked up and saw his friend standing not forty feet above him. Then Mr. Fellowes was beside Mark and they were talking.

"Can you get out?" Fellowes asked.

Joel began to push at the wood surrounding him, but he couldn't get any leverage. This underbrush, if it could be called that, was the most thickly knitted he had ever seen.

Taking a good look at his surroundings, he could see that all the trees—no, *all* the vegetation around him, was dead. Not only was it all dead, he thought, but it looked like the dead, each withered shrub a spine and twiggy ribcage, the trees upright corpses. Panic clutched at his heart. For a horrible moment, Joel was convinced that this was the same deadfall where he had trapped Virgil. He imagined that Virgil was below him, dead like the trees and bushes, waiting for him to fall into his bony arms. Joel squeezed his eyes shut, gritted his teeth. *Don't be a fuckin' moron.*

"How far am I off the ground?" he called out.

"Oh, about two feet I'd guess," Mark said, chuckling. "How'd you get down there anyway?"

"I jumped, dumbass, whaddya think? Now come on down and help me outta this—I'm stuck!"

"Who's the dumbass?"

Mark sat on his butt and slid down the steep slope. Fellowes didn't hesitate to follow, sliding down on his heels, holding his left hand out behind him for balance.

An odor of rot and corruption drifted up from below. Again, Joel's vision blurred with panic. Maybe it wasn't Virgil down there waiting for him, but it could be somebody else, some grinning, decaying corpse. . . .

But now Fellowes was wading out into the dry tangle, Mark following quickly after. Joel's relief was cut short when he noticed that his companions were sinking deeper with every step. By the time they reached him, Mark was up to the hips in it, Fellowes to the knees.

The man pulled on the wood that bound Joel, but it resisted, reluctant to surrender its catch. As he moved, Fellowes continued to sink, vines slipping around his legs to draw him down.

"Goddamsonofabitch!" He stumbled forward. "I can't hardly get a grip without something being yanked out from under me."

"Hey," Mark called out, "lemme go! This stuff is grabbing

me too. I can't move anywhere but down."

"I'm sinking!" Joel tasted sharp fear on his tongue. "*Help me!*"

Struggling to reach his friend, Mark fought against a strong tide of eager fingers. As Joel watched, Mark seemed to gain less and less with each effort—the boy pushed forward, only to be dragged back, and inexorably down. Joel looked to Fellowes, but saw only his shoulders and head sticking out of the tangle.

"I can't see you now, Joel." Mark's frantic high-pitched voice was distant, a mere squeak without resonance.

"I'm here," Joel cried, his panicked words sounding like they were cast down a long, padded hall.

"Everybody hold still!" Fellowes shouted. "If we all thrash around, we're only gonna get ourselves stuck but good. It's like wooden quicksand."

Joel froze, but still felt himself gradually slipping downward. "It's not gonna stop! I hope there's air down there—I'm having trouble breathing already."

There was a thrashing where Mark was going under, his voice, though muted, full of panic.

As if from another room, Fellowes called out, but Joel couldn't understand what he was saying. And then he too had gone under, the silence from below swallowing him up.

Joel wanted to take a deep breath before he went under, but instead, he screamed.

He choked on the dust, coughing and flailing as he was drawn down into darkness. Using his hands, he located the other two.

"Don't worry, we'll get outta this," came Fellowes' flat voice.

They pushed at the wooden world surrounding them, forming a tunnel as they moved through the sticks. Joel thought it was like working with fluffed up excelsior.

"There's a goddam stick up my butt!"

"Mark, shut the hell up!" Joel felt a rage of frustration. "All you do is complain."

"Do not."

"Pipe down, both of you! It's not helping any."

Joel bit off his sharp reply and forced himself to take a deep breath. He gagged on a lungful of reeking stench and dust.

Suffering pokes and jabs from every side, they crawled ever downward—the only direction the tangle allowed—eventually coming upon other small, cramped tunnels. The only light was provided by occasional pencil-thin rays penetrating the knot of vegetation and sharply defined by the wood dust floating in the air.

"I ain't going any further," Mark said, coughing. "I'm staying here 'til Willawic finds me."

"Goddammit, Mark, you get up off your ass and follow us or you'll never get out of here!"

"I can't take it anymore. I can't breathe, it stinks in here, I can't see, I got dust in my eyes and in my mouth, and I'm gettin' all scratched up. I feel horrible! I ain't gonna move no more!"

"You listen to your friend, Mark. You give up now and you don't have far to go—hell, you're already buried. Just grab the end of Joel's shirt and move along behind him. You don't have to think about it, just *do* it!"

Joel would never suffer the embarrassment of giving up like that, but he knew just how his friend felt. Something inside was telling him to lie down and give up. Or was it this place? Was Fellowes feeling it as well?

"Don't worry, Mark, I won't fart," he said, trying to make light of the situation.

Joel put his hand down on a bundle of leather-wrapped sticks. When he pushed on it, the sticks cracked, the sack collapsed, and he fell forward, stopping inches away from the skull of a desiccated fawn. It exhaled a dust cloud that reeked of decay.

So that's what's been stinking so bad. No that couldn't be it—that little thing couldn't stink up this whole place.

"Mister Fellowes, there's a dead animal over here."

"I've seen 'em too. Just leave it be, boy."

The claustrophobic darkness that nearly shut out the light squeezed Joel and his companions through the cramped tunnels. Dust collected in Joel's eyes and he rubbed them and blinked. He felt soft fleshy spots beneath his hands—*Fungus?* he wondered—which left his palms damp and sticky. He wiped them off on his bare forearms and where he spread the dampness, he broke out in a burning itch. Then his eyes started to burn too, and tingle, like they were swarming with ants.

"Goddam!" Mark shouted. "This sucks!"

"Feels like we're crawling through a patch of stinging nettles!" Fellowes said. "There's another dead animal up here. I can't see it real good, but it looks like it's got mold or fungus all over it and it's half-dissolved. I think this place is eatin' away everythin' with acid or something. It's like we're crawling around in some kind of thing's big ol' belly."

Tears were streaming down Joel's face as he blinked again and again. "Don't rub your eyes!" he shouted. "I can't hardly see, my eyes are swole up so bad." The shrill edge of panic in his voice embarrassed him.

"Hang on to my shirttail, Joel," Fellowes said. "It's too dark to see much anyway."

As the passage got bigger, Joel found he could get his feet under him. "You're not making this tunnel anymore, are you Mister Fellowes?"

"No, we just broke through into this one. It gets even bigger up ahead."

Forcing his swollen eyelids open, Joel could see light up ahead and a snarl of dark shapes, perhaps the rotted trunks of great trees, crisscrossing their path.

A rotten corpse came out of the wall of sticks to Joel's right and he screamed. It fell between him and Fellowes. The man whirled around.

"What happened?" asked Mark. "I can't see anything."

"It's this stinking, rotten dead guy!"

Fellowes bent over the grisly shape. "Take another look, Joel."

"Oh, jeez, I'm such a dumbass—it's just a stupid log."

"Maybe you're not such a dumbass. Look at this branch." The man pulled a piece of wood out of the wall and held it in the thin light. "It looks like a stick, but see here on the end there's the knob of a ball-joint and I'll bet. . . ." He broke off the knob. ". . . yeah, bone marrow."

"It's all mixed up," Mark said. "That ain't right—trees don't have that."

"Mark, it's like when we found that skull in The New Cut. I swear to you when I hit it with that stone, it sounded like a rock and it chipped like a rock. But when we pulled it out of the mud, it was bone."

"Yeah, and that same day, when you pulled those leg bones outta the bank, I coulda swore they were roots—they had twigs and shit hanging all off 'em."

"And when I was diggin' that stump just before I got lost, the roots down deep in the dirt were shaped like skeletal hands, finger bones and all. I thought it was real weird, but nothing to get too excited about."

"It's *real* strange. Whaddaya 'spose it's all about?"

"I don't know," said Joel. "I haven't ever seen anything like it before—it's not like you see this kind of thing happening all over the place. This is probably limited to a small area and if The New Cut is included in that area, then maybe we're real close to home."

Mark's voice was thin, frightened. "Was this—did this shit used to be alive?"

The boys looked to Fellowes. He paused for an uncomfortable moment. "I ain't gonna pretend I know what's happening. I—"

The log-thing reached up and grabbed Fellowes. He was jerked savagely to one side, crashing through a thin wall of the dead wood. Joel and Mark grabbed his legs and tried to pull him back, but all they could do was hang on. As suddenly as he was seized, Fellowes was released and the boys helped him to his feet.

"What the hell?" Fellowes rubbed his shoulder.

"Some tunneling bear," Mark said, "I'd guess."

"Bears don't tunnel, stupid."

We all know that wasn't an animal. Joel pushed the thought out of his mind, unwilling to focus on it.

The smell of decay had become so overpowering that Joel had to breathe through his mouth to keep from gagging. Even so, it filmed the inside of his nose and mouth, and left a bitter taste on his tongue.

They turned and looked at the massive snarl of shadowy trunks and splayed roots that loomed in the darkness, stretching toward the dim light above.

"Is it a trick of my eyes," Joel asked, pointing, "or are those trees moving?"

Fellowes considered the jumble of roots and trunks. "I don't care if it gets up and dances a jig—if we can climb up that mess, we might just get outta here."

"I ain't climbing that shit," Mark said. "If Joel said it moved, it moved."

"Then you can just wait here in the dark, *alone.*" Fellowes pushed the webwork of twigs and branches out of the way, moving toward the towering snarl.

Pushing his fear aside, Joel followed the man across the damp, twiggy floor. His feet sank into the spongy morass with an unpleasant squishing.

Mark scrambled after them.

Fellowes waded out into a thick, black mire at the foot of the snarl of roots and trunks. As he moved, bones and bits of rotting hide bobbed to the surface and drifted toward Joel. Watching them queasily, he saw worms wriggling in the thick soup.

"You only have to be in this crap for a second," Fellowes said.

"C'mon, Mark," Joel said over his shoulder, "I'll give you a piggyback. At least one of us won't have to walk through this shit."

Mark eagerly climbed on and Joel set off into the gore. Like warm axle grease, it oozed into his shoes, and he thought he could feel worms wriggling between his toes.

Fellowes was in the darkness where the roots wove together, looking for footholds. "C'mere, boys, and give me a boost up."

"Push Mark on up first."

With their help, Mark reached and grabbed at a stout root and hauled himself up. Joel put his hands together and Fellowes stepped into them and reached for Mark. Once Fellowes was up, he lent Joel a hand.

Trying not to think about crushing the worms, he quickly wiped off his hands on a root. He reached for Fellowes and the man lifted him.

Mark was twenty feet up, and Fellowes was rapidly closing on him. Beyond, there was a hole in the twisted canopy of dead trees. Joel desperately wanted to reach it but couldn't get a firm hold; each time he tried to lift himself, his slime-coated hands and feet slipped.

"Goddammit!"

"I'm sorry, Joel," Fellowes said, returning for the boy. "I know full well the animals that made that soup down there were alone when they died. We ain't getting outta here unless we help each other."

Mark and Fellowes gave Joel what assistance he needed, and the three climbed out of the gloom into the brighter tangle above. Struggling up the twisted tree, Joel caught a warm puff of fresh air and breathed in gratefully. Above awaited a halo of daylight. Feeling like he was crawling out of an open sewer, Joel climbed up into the brightness and stood beside his companions on a fallen trunk. The trunk lay horizontally in the tops of several trees and created a path that led off into the distance.

Joel saw that a great expanse of the twisted, dead wood lay about them on three sides, waiting to claim new victims. Looking back over his shoulder, he saw a low hill about a hundred yards away. The thought of having to cross that distance over the wasteland of dead wood dashed his elation at having escaped the quagmire below.

"It's gonna be a real bitch getting outta here," Joel said.

"This sucks." Mark snapped a brittle branch between his fingers. "It really fucking sucks."

Just below him, Joel could see the skeleton of a small animal caught up in a confusion of vines. Bones littered the tangled landscape—individual bones hung in vines, entire skeletons impaled on sharp stake-like branches. "If I see another bone I'm gonna scream!"

"Calm down, boy. Somethin' ain't right here I grant you, but whatever it is, it hasn't gotten us yet. We're getting outta here, don't you worry none."

"What do you suppose killed everything?" Joel whispered. No one answered, perhaps because they hadn't heard him, or perhaps because they didn't want to speculate. *It could have been radiation,* Joel thought. *Or poison, like Agent Orange. Or a tree disease.*

Or something worse. A whole lot worse.

"Hey, Joel, is that the little hill where you fell down?"

Joel squinted. "Yeah, but it doesn't look as high as I thought."

"Isn't that Willawic standing on it?" Fellowes asked.

"Yeah," Mark said, "and there's Billy and Ebbie with him. But how are we gonna get to 'em?"

"We'll just walk along this log," Joel said, holding his hands out for balance and heading toward Billy and Willawic. "It looks like it goes quite a ways in the right direction."

When the trunk became too thin to support their weight, they found trunks nearby that bore scratches left by large animals climbing out of the tangle.

"Follow the scratches," said Fellowes, "I bet they were left by either a bear or a cougar. If they could get out, we can."

As they moved, they could hear chopping in the distance, above them.

"Willawic's choppin' a little tree down for you!" Billy shouted. Ebbie barked urgently, her voice thin and brittle in the strange, unnatural air.

When they were at the foot of the hill, the chopping ceased. Joel heard a twisting groan and watched a sapling fall toward him. The Indian moved it into a better position and braced his end. One by one, the three climbed up the hill, using Willawic's tree for support.

"So whaddya find down there?"

"Nothing all that exciting," Joel said, panting and looking at his companions with a smile.

"Yeah," Mark said, laughing. "Nothing much, except that we're probably real close to home."

71

Skirting the valley of dead trees, the party had reached the top of a ridge when Joel was startled by a booming voice.

"Mister goodie Fellowes!"

Joel's insides turned to water. They all stopped and turned toward Wesley Pike. Joel saw Fellowes' eyes go wide and the man reached out as if seeking balance. Willawic leaned on one of his rifles, standing stock still. Ebbie bared her teeth, a low growl starting in her throat.

Wesley was standing at the edge of a drop-off between a pair of massive oaks. He held something in his right hand and rubbed it with his thumb, while his left hand rested on the butt of a pistol.

"Y'all're damned hard ta track down," he said, his voice heavy with sarcasm. "I had a devil of a time followin' ye!"

Wesley moved very slowly, circling to the left, closing the distance between himself and Fellowes.

"I hope ye had fun destroyin' my li'l op'ration, 'cause I aim ta see it's the last fun ye ever have."

"Shit," Mark whispered, "I thought we'd seen the last of that sonuvabitch." He put a hand on Ebbie, who was pressed to his side, growling like a chainsaw.

"The boys and the Indian ain't got nothing to do with this. You can let 'em go."

"Bullshit, we're in this together!" Joel said to Fellowes. Then he turned to Wesley. "You took care of me and I thought you were so cool, but you're the cruelest motherfucker I ever seen."

Wesley's laugh began as a soft chuckle and built until it echoed off the distant hills. "An' yer jus' now seein' it? Seems like ye've changed yer colors, Little Man. I remember seein' a cruel streak in ye as went plenty deep."

"Least I've learned to be ashamed of it."

"Gotta be cruel ta live in this 'ere wilderness."

"Yeah, well, I don't live here."

"Not anymore," Wesley said with a scary smile.

Turning toward Willawic, he raised his free hand. The hand whipped forward, flinging a stone the size of an apple. It struck the Indian in the forehead and he fell.

Billy screamed, rushing to the Indian's side. Ebbie barked wildly.

"That's one," Wesley said.

Joel saw the pirate raising his pistol toward Fellowes. Fellowes fired his rifle from the hip and the pistol disappeared from Wesley's grasp. The big man bellowed, wringing the pain out of his hand as he charged, head down. In a half-crouch, Fellowes stood still. The outlaw was almost upon him when Fellowes dropped and rolled forward to meet him. Wesley tumbled over him, slamming into the ground.

Mark grabbed a handful of stones and pelted Wesley in the head and back. Fellowes sprang to his feet and dove for the outlaw, using the butt of his rifle against the side of Wesley's head. As Wesley was rising, Joel jumped on his shoulders to keep him down. One of Mark's stones struck Joel in the head and he tumbled to one side, dazed. Ebbie danced around the fight, snarling, snapping at Wesley's legs.

Looking up from the weeds, Joel saw Wesley getting to his feet. Fellowes swung his rifle, catching the outlaw in the backs of his knees. Wesley bellowed, but kept his feet. He spun on Fellowes and grabbed the rifle. He yanked it from his hands and, swinging it like a club, caught Fellowes in the gut. Fellowes doubled over, sinking to his knees, and Wesley raised the rifle to strike him on the head.

Joel saw Mark struggling to raise Willawic's rifle. It wobbled in his grasp and then he fired. Wesley screamed, dropped Fellowes' rifle and grabbed his thigh, where a red, meaty hole the size of a peach blossomed. Clutching his wounded leg, he fell onto his side. Ebbie lunged forward and latched onto his ankle, shaking her head viciously. With a curse, Wesley kicked her hard with his other foot and knocked her flying. Ebbie hit the ground heavily and lay gasping for breath.

Fellowes was rising, stumbling and coughing, holding his gut as he tried to get his feet under him.

Mark handed the rifle to Billy, who struggled to reload it.

Joel rushed the pirate, ready to plant his foot in his gut. Wesley seized the boy's raised foot and bore down, twisting. Joel fell onto his back, kicking his foot free of the man's grasp. He landed a hard blow to the outlaw's nose. Wesley bellowed and the ground trembled. From where she lay, Ebbie let out a tremulous howl. Joel kicked Wesley's gaping wound and the pirate dropped to all fours.

Mark rushed in and snatched up the rifle that Wesley had dropped.

Holding a large stone in his right hand, Fellowes moved toward Wesley as he crawled for the trees.

Blood spraying from his nose, the outlaw rose to his knees, then to his feet. He limped his way uphill, following the steep edge of the ridge, Fellowes close on his heels. Ebbie, back on her feet, walked stiff-legged and growling next to Fellowes. Her hackles were up, her tail down. She seemed more than angry. She seemed terrified. For some reason, Joel didn't think it was Wesley she was afraid of.

"Come on," Joel shouted, starting after the two men, "bring

me that rifle."

"It's not ready yet!" Billy said.

"Well hurry it up!"

Joel wove in and out of the trees, trying to keep the men in view. Mark, carrying the empty rifle, was close behind his friend.

Wesley turned on Fellowes, pulling a stone tomahawk from his belt. "I'm gonna scalp ye," he snarled, "and this time, it ain't *ever* gonna heal up."

Fellowes staggered back and put a tree between them. They danced back and forth, Wesley taking swings at the man. The weapon whispered through the air, bit chunks of bark out of the tree and came within inches of his face. Ebbie ran back and forth, barking.

Joel and Mark closed in and Fellowes broke and ran. Wesley pounded after him.

Billy came running toward the older boys. "It's ready, it's ready!"

Wesley stopped and raised the tomahawk to throw at the other man's back.

"Get down, Mister Fellowes!" Joel shouted.

Fellowes dove to the ground. The tomahawk whistled harmlessly overhead and tumbled over the drop-off.

"Goddammit, Little Man! I'm gonna skin ye, but good!"

As the outlaw's words echoed, the ground shook once more. Joel trembled violently. *Wesley's not human. He's a fucking force of nature.* He swallowed back a manic giggle.

Wesley pulled a broad-bladed knife from his boot. He rushed Fellowes as he was trying to get to his feet. The big man grabbed Fellowes from behind and put an arm around his neck. He used the knife to cut off the man's cheek. Fellowes screamed, a torrent of blood pouring down his face and drenching his shirtfront. Wesley lost his grip in the slippery fluid and Fellowes fell back, twisting free. Ebbie darted forward and sank her teeth into Wesley's calf. The outlaw jabbed at her with his knife, catching her in the shoulder. Ebbie yelped and let go.

"Ebbie! Get the hell away from him!" Mark screamed. She ran to him, still keeping her eyes on Wesley. She began shaking violently.

Billy stumbled and fell, and the rifle went sliding forward. Joel rushed back for it and, struggling with the unwieldy weapon, ran toward the fight.

Fellowes came up with a knife from his boot and took a swipe at the outlaw, missing his belly by inches.

Wesley roared, and the trees shook, showering leaves. Joel could feel the man's deep bass voice rise up out of the ground through his feet.

The outlaw lunged, and Fellowes cut his wrist. Wesley switched his blade to the other hand and thrust forward into Fellowes' upper chest. Fellowes pivoted as the knife tore through his shirt and into muscle, and the blade pulled free.

Joel rested the barrel of the rifle on Mark's shoulder and drew a bead on Wesley's chest.

The big man grabbed Fellowes' knife hand and swung in at his belly. Fellowes yanked back, and Wesley's blade merely cut into the cloth of his shirt.

Joel inched the barrel over, trying to keep the rifle aimed at the outlaw's chest. Joel could see the bead on the end of the rifle hovering over Wesley's heart.

The outlaw charged into Fellowes and the two tumbled over, dangerously close to the edge of the drop-off. Locked in the outlaw's embrace, his arms constricted, Fellowes gouged uselessly at Wesley's skull with his knife. Wesley raised his blade in the air, to plunge it into Fellowes. He turned so that his back was presented to Joel.

Joel pulled the trigger, just as Willawic reached down to take the rifle from him. The explosion was so loud, the world rumbled about him and the earth began to move. Joel could feel his guts shaking like Jell-O. How much powder had Billy put in that rifle?

He was so surprised at Willawic's sudden appearance that he hadn't seen what happened to Wesley. Joel looked up in time to see the two men tumble off the edge of the ridge.

He got shakily to his feet and looked up to see a new ridge rising up out of the earth in the distance. He heard Mark say something but it was drowned out by a great rumbling. They were all knocked off their feet as the ground bucked. Joel was dimly aware of Ebbie, howling and tearing at the ground with her teeth. Willawic pointed to the distant hills and said something Joel couldn't hear. The boy saw muddy-gray, roiling water rise in the distance and swallow a string of hills.

"Shit, we gotta get outta here!"

A great oak crashed behind them, its top sweeping smaller trees off the edge.

"Mister Fellowes!" Mark called, crawling to the lip of the drop-off. "There he is!" he said, pointing down.

Joel moved to the edge and looked over. One hundred feet away, Fellowes was lying on his back, bleeding and unconscious or dead. There was no sign of Wesley.

The water rushed in and bore Fellowes away.

"Help him!"

"Mark, we can't! He's gone."

Willawic grabbed Billy and swung him up onto his shoulders. Abandoning his rifles, he ran from the onrushing water. Joel grabbed Mark and tried to drag him off in the same direction.

"No!" Mark twisted out of Joel's grasp and, sitting on his butt, scrambled down the hill. Ebbie, who seemed to be having some kind of fit, stopped thrashing and looked up as Mark went down to the water. She lurched to her feet and followed him.

"Mark, get back here!" Joel screamed.

The water was rising swiftly. Mark tried to follow Fellowes along the water's edge, but the man was quickly swept out of sight.

"Stupid goddam sonofabitch!" Joel shouted after his friend.

A tree rushing along in the current struck Mark from behind. The boy fell headfirst into the water and came up sputtering as he was swept along in the current, and then Joel lost sight of him.

"Mark!"

He scrambled down the hill after his friend, but the water was rising fast to meet him, and he found himself retreating. He caught sight of Mark just as the boy went under. Ebbie began to bark, a high, hysterical yipping. She hesitated at the water's edge for a moment, stepping from foot to foot. Then she leapt into the raging torrent after Mark.

"Willawic!"

Joel hauled himself back up the hill, but when he reached the top, the Indian was nowhere to be seen. He ran in the direction Willawic had taken, catching up with him as the Indian was struggling to carry Billy to the top of the next hill.

"Where's Mark?" Billy asked from his perch.

"Carried away by the water!" Joel said, puffing.

"What? No, he can't be!"

"It's true, goddammit—I saw him go in, but I couldn't get to him in time."

Still skirting the valley of dead trees, they ran along low, rolling, rocky ground. A crack formed in the earth to their left and the ground at their feet heaved upward ten feet. They fell flat on their faces on the new shelf. The water quickly filled the area below as they got up and ran on.

To his right, Joel saw the opaque, gray water filling the valley. The dead wood swirled about, and he saw an animal's skeleton being carried along in one of the tangles. The landscape was now beginning to look vaguely familiar.

They moved to higher ground and slowed, finally coming to a stop on a rocky outcropping. Joel looked at the body of water covering what had been the valley of dead trees.

"During the earthquake of 1811," his encyclopedia had told him, "the Mississippi River ran backward, forming a lake which survives to this day."

"Reelfoot Lake," he said numbly. "We just survived the New Madrid earthquake of 1811."

"Isn't Reelfoot Lake real close to home?" Billy asked.

"Yeah, 'bout ten miles from where we live. But we can't leave Mark behind."

72

"Come *on,* Joel. If we don't go with him now, Willawic's gonna leave us!"

Billy could see Joel was in no shape to get up. The older boy had exhausted himself searching back and forth along the edge of the water for his friend. Three times, Joel saw Mark's body floating in the water and swam out to rescue him. Each time the "body" turned out to be a log. The last time, Willawic swam out and dragged Joel back, half-drowned.

Billy felt trapped in the middle. He wished he could reason with Willawic, but didn't understand his language. He wanted to help Joel find their friend, but didn't know how.

"It's too hard having two leaders. I have to think for myself now. And the first thing I'm gonna do is get you moving—I'm not gonna lose you, too."

He reached down and tugged at Joel's arm, trying to pull him to his feet.

"No, lemme 'lone."

"Mark'll catch up with us. He just *has* to."

Billy looked back over his shoulder and saw Willawic picking up his belongings and walking into the trees.

"*Now,* Joel!"

"No—too tired."

Billy kicked the older boy right between the legs. Joel screamed and rolled on the ground, holding himself, tears spilling down his face.

"You little shit—I'm gonna kill you!"

"Well, you stupid dumbass, you fuckin' mama's boy, come and get me."

The ground trembled.

Unsteadily, Billy started in the direction Willawic had taken. He heard Joel getting to his feet and coming after him, but he resisted the urge to look back.

"You're dead!" Joel said, tackling him. Billy fell on his face and the older boy turned him over, sat on his chest and pummeled him. Joel stood, dragged Billy up by the shirt collar and slugged him in the gut.

Billy coughed, trying to look Joel in the eye. "I ain't gonna cry. You can beat me up all you want. I ain't gonna cry."

Joel relaxed his grip, glaring at the boy.

"I ain't gonna cry for Mark neither, 'cause he ain't dead. He'll catch up with us."

Joel fell to his knees, grabbed Billy and hugged him tight. He shook with terrible sobs and his tears dampened the little boy's shirt.

73

Since he wasn't very far ahead when they caught up with him, Billy realized the Indian had never intended to leave them behind.

Ever since the quake had stopped and the water had settled, the voices of the forest had been silent. The boys too were quiet as they hiked mile after mile, following Willawic. Billy's aching feet scuffed noisily as he dragged them along in the weeds. His muscles ached and he was hungry. He felt a tremor in the ground through his feet and his head began to throb.

Joel trudged along beside him, his unfocused eyes, slack features, and the language of his movements saying to Billy, "I know exactly how you feel."

They left the hills behind and moved into lower land where Billy could see the terrible effects of the flood up close. The wet ground they slogged over was crisscrossed by downed trees. In the crotches of the trees still standing, there were tangles of vegetation and dead animals. A residue of mud and detritus was smeared over everything.

Willawic seemed to have boundless energy. He moved at a consistent and constant pace, untroubled by the sloppy ground. It was all the boys could do to keep up with him.

"Goddam you, Mark," Joel muttered, "you didn't have the slightest fucking idea what that Indian was saying. He didn't understand your shitty-ass-failing-grade-French. And he doesn't know what Nikes are, neither—fucking dumbass."

Somehow, by saying these things, Billy thought, Joel was making his worst fears real, but he was unwilling to say anything about it.

"Hey, Willawic!" the older boy shouted.

The Indian glanced over his shoulder without slowing.

"You don't have any goddam idea where the fuck we are." Joel was trying to sound derisive, but there was a note of desperation in his voice. He seemed to be on the verge of tears and that scared Billy bad, down deep.

Willawic shrugged his shoulders and smiled as if to say, "Don't worry."

They walked on and on, until Billy was so tired his feet were stumps of pain. Evidence of the flood was diminishing. There was less debris in the trees and the muddy ground was firming up. The matted underbrush was spreading back out and drying in the late-afternoon sun.

The birds and insects had started speaking again, and there was an indefinable smell in the air, a tenuous odor that came and went. It brought back memories of Billy's home and his mother. His heart was suddenly tight in his chest and tears rolled down his face. He quickly wiped them away.

To their right, a stream cut a deep trough through the forest. The flood had eroded its steep banks, rounding off all sharp edges.

Willawic followed it for a mile or so. The sun was pinking in the distance when he turned and led the boys into the chilly waters and across the stream. He stopped on the other side and looked up and down the deeply cut banks, confusion spreading across his face.

"Ou'est-ce que c'est?" he said, pulling on his ear. "C'est tout mal. Le cours du fleuve a changé."

"Hunh? What'cha sayin', you stupid Injun. You lost? That it? Like I figured, you're not a real Injun after all."

"C'mon Joel, don't be so mean. He's doin' the best he can."

Joel spat in disgust, his face red with frustration. Billy thought he saw his own uneasiness, however, his own fear in the older boy's harried gaze.

Willawic jumped down into the water to closely examine the eroded walls of the steep bank. "La tombe—où est l'endroit d'enterrement?"

"What are you jabberin' about?"

"Où est l'homme qui a porté ces chaussures?"

"I think he's talking about the shoes, Joel."

"What do you mean? How do you figure that?"

"I just remember those words from when Mark talked to him."

Willawic was digging in the thick brown clay of the creek bank.

"Looks like he's lost it, to me." Joel kicked dirt into the water.

Billy's gaze locked on the bones half-buried in the gravel of the creek bed. He scrambled down the bank, splashed into the stream, and fetched them out of the water.

"Oui, oui!" Willawic snatched the bones away. He slipped off one of his buckskin-patched Nikes and held it out before him. He inserted one of the bones into the shoe and held it up for the boys to see, nodding his head enthusiastically.

"Oh shit," Joel said. "He's telling us that he got those damn Nikes off a dead man."

Billy plopped down on his butt in the water, his eyes unfocused. "We ain't never getting home."

"Wait a minute, Billy—those bones look like the roots I pulled out of the bank when I fell on my butt!" Joel jumped down into the creek and ran splashing through the shallow water.

Now, Joel was the one who sounded like he'd lost it. Billy got up slowly and followed, Willawic behind him. The older boy came to a stop before a rooty overhang where the stream had undercut the bank.

"And this is where. . . ." He poked around in the tangle of sycamore roots that hung down from above. "Aha!" he cried, pulling the skull out of the snarl and holding it out like a prize.

Willawic excitedly pointed to the skull, the leg bones and the Nikes and said, "Le voici!"

"We're home!" Joel shouted, dancing in the creek and splashing water all over the others. "This is The New Cut!"

Billy stood, dripping water. "I don't get it. I never saw that bone." He tried to see what was above the steep banks, but they were too tall and the golden afternoon light reflecting off the water was blinding for a moment.

Joel continued to dance, the shards of light bouncing off of him from too many angles. Billy stomped his feet and yelled at him, "Why are you saying we're home?"

"C'mon, I'll show you."

The boys scrambled up the left bank, while Willawic climbed up the other side. Billy heard a car horn in the distance and his heart leapt. He climbed to his feet, hearing the muted sounds of distant traffic.

"There's your house, Billy!"

"Mama!" He turned in the direction Joel pointed and there was his big white house with the green shutters, sitting on the broad three-acre lawn. Warm light shone out through the windows. Billy grabbed Joel and the two tumbled to the ground, laughing and rolling in each other's arms in the grass. When they had become still and Billy lay on his side, his giggles trailing away, he looked across the creek at Willawic. The Indian's image shimmered and flickered.

"Aren't you coming with us?"

The Indian smiled, waved, and began walking back the way they had come.

"He's not coming with us, Billy. C'mon, let's go!"

Joel stood up and tugged on him, but Billy wouldn't budge. Staring at Willawic's back, he realized he would never see him again. He wiped away a sudden tear, got up and walked along next to Joel, heading for home.

"How's he gonna get home, Joel?"

"Aw, don't worry about him." Joel was laughing again. "He's an Indian—they *never* get lost."

Billy glanced back for one last look at his friend. "Joel, Willawic's gone."

"It's okay," Joel said. "Let's get you home before dark."

Billy hadn't really noticed how dark it was until Joel said something about it. Now, he could see that the streetlights were coming on. He heard dogs barking, a siren in the distance and then a car whooshed by on the nearby road, its red taillights flashing briefly between the trees.

He could smell the exquisite aroma of car exhaust. It made him think of the stinky bus he rode to school. The summer was almost over and he was already looking forward to school, the second grade. With a lump of excitement in his chest, he knew that this year would be different—different with the kids at school and different with his mother. This year, he was going to matter.

"That's right, Billy," Joel said, if not reading his mind, then sensing his mood. "We've been through some terrible shit and we've come out of it stronger than we were."

Billy giggled. "That's the silliest thing I ever heard you say."

"Yeah, but you know it's true." Joel punched him playfully on the shoulder.

Reflecting the warm light of the sunset, a cicada shell hanging from a sapling maple caught Billy's eye. He plucked it from its twig as he passed. "I'd forgotten all about these guys."

"For a while, I thought we weren't going to get back without 'em."

"What're we gonna do about Mark?" Billy asked, dropping the husk.

Joel was silent for a moment. "Nothing we *can* do—can't even tell his mother what happened to him."

"What're you talking about—'happened to him.' He might wander down The New Cut anytime."

"I hope you're right."

" 'Til then, I guess you won't have anyone to hang out with in the tree house, hunh?"

As they walked up the concrete path to Billy's front door, Joel put an arm around his friend's shoulders. "Of course I will, Billy."

EXCERPT FROM *THE BLOOD OF FATHER TIME, BOOK 2: THE MYSTIC CLAN'S GRAND PLOT*

Late on the fourth day of Joel's trip back to Adairville, four heavily armed men stepped into the road and demanded that he stop. He recognized one of them as Job Hayes. The other three were unknown to him. Hayes went to his left, one remained in front of Joel, and the others boxed him in, one on his right, one behind.

Hayes gestured with his scattergun, and ordered Joel to dismount.

"I have a deal with Mort Puckett," Joel said.

"Don't know nothin' 'bout no deal," Hayes said.

Either Puckett had not kept his word or news traveled too slowly in this century for all the Mystic Clan to have been informed of Joel's deal with the outlaw.

"Couldn't you just shoot me right off my horse?" Joel said, tired and disgusted. Even so, he hoped the man wouldn't take him up on it.

Hayes didn't say anything for a moment, but all four of them drew closer. There was a deliberateness and determination in their expressions, but Joel also saw fear in their eyes. And that made him wonder what they had to be afraid of.

Perhaps, he thought, they think I'm one real tough bastard since Cotten took me under his wing. They may also know I was responsible for Sharpe being injured.

Joel had two pistols ready, one held in his right hand under his greatcoat. He wished he had Rachel's .45.

The man on Joel's right was within twenty feet and armed with a squirrel gun. The man in front was carrying a pair of horse pistols. Joel was unwilling to take his eyes off the three in front to get a look at the one behind him.

He was burning adrenaline. The reins were moist in his grasp. He was ready to whip Gailey and cause her to bolt, hoping she would pull him away faster than the outlaws could aim and fire their weapons, but he sat frozen, unable to act.

Hayes moved closer, within spitting distance, and again ordered Joel to dismount.

"If I have ta git ye down, boy, yer horse's liable ta git hurt." Then he leveled his piece at Joel.

Joel swung his pistol out from under his coat and pulled the trigger in Hayes' face. The outlaw's head snapped back and he was thrown off the road. His scattergun went off between Gailey's legs and struck the fellow on Joel's right in the knees. He sank to the ground, howling. The man in front, advancing on him, fired one of his pistols and missed. Joel heard the man behind pull the trigger of his firearm. There must've been just a flash in the pan as the firearm did not discharge. Then, the man in front was advancing on Joel, to make certain he didn't miss with his next shot. As he raised his other pistol, Joel threw his firearm. It struck the man full in the face, just above the eye, and he went down hard. Gailey reared in terror and came down on his skull with her hooves. As Joel struggled to stay mounted, he felt something strike the base of his skull. Later he would decide that the man behind him must have struck him with the butt of a rifle. It rattled Joel from head to toe, and he found himself lying across Gailey's neck. She had delivered him from the fight, and when he was fully conscious again, he found he was far from the highwaymen.

His dizziness and nausea might be attributed to an overdose

of adrenaline, but he suspected he had a concussion. There wasn't much he could do about it at the moment.

ABOUT THE AUTHORS

Alan M. Clark grew up in Tennessee near a creek. He is most known for his work in illustration, which appears in books of fiction, nonfiction, textbooks, young adult fiction and children's books. His awards in the illustration field include the World Fantasy Award and four Chesley Awards. His fiction has appeared in magazines, anthologies and a collection released by Scorpius Digital Publishing. *Siren Promised,* his Bram Stoker Award–nominated novel, written with Jeremy Robert Johnson, was released in 2005. Mr. Clark's publishing company, IFD Publishing, has released six books, the most recent of which is a full-color art book of his work, *The Paint in My Blood.* He and his wife, Melody, currently live in Oregon. Visit Alan on the Web at www.alanmclark.com.

Stephen C. Merritt has collaborated with his cousin, Alan M. Clark, on previously published short fiction. He is a native of Nashville, Tennessee, where he lives with his wife, Cynthia. *The Blood of Father Time* is his first novel.

Lorelei Shannon was born in the Arizona desert and learned to walk holding on to the tail of a coyote. She now lives in the woods outside Seattle with her husband and two small land pirates, also known as her sons. Lorelei has two previous books out: a horror novel called *Rags and Old Iron,* and a collection of short stories called *Vermifuge and Other Toxic Cocktails.* Her short fiction has appeared in numerous magazines and anthologies. Visit Lorelei on the Web at www.psychenoir.com.